A DIP AT THE SANGAM

REUBEN LACHMANSINGH

WestBow
PRESS
A DIVISION OF THOMAS NELSON
& ZONDERVAN

WestBow Press books may be ordered through booksellers or by contacting:

WestBow Press
A Division of Thomas Nelson & Zondervan
1663 Liberty Drive
Bloomington, IN 47403
www.westbowpress.com
1 (866) 928-1240

ISBN: 978-1-4908-3028-5 (sc)
ISBN: 978-1-4908-3029-2 (hc)
ISBN: 978-1-4908-3027-8 (e)

Library of Congress Control Number: 2014904804

Printed in the United States of America.

WestBow Press rev. date: 7/22/2014

DEDICATION

This book is dedicated to my eldest granddaughter, Jet Lachman, who will be touting it long after I'm gone.

The author is a graduate in Biology of the University of Toronto and an Honourary companion of the University of Guelph.

He's worked as a civil servant, science teacher, multi-award-winning motelier, entrepreneur. In his free time he travelled the world, practised Taekwondo and played League as well as Oldies International cricket tournaments for a Canadian and Australian team, earning two medals.

CHAPTER ONE

Calcutta, 1869

Raja would have made a fine soldier for the British. Instead, the much heralded year of 1869 had ended in infamy. Thugs had captured him to make up the quota for a shipload of indentured servants bound for Demerara, where they would be doing the work of former slaves.

One morning, with the desire to escape weighing on his mind, he pressed an eye against the barricade.

"Keep away from the fence!" a guard shrieked.

Staves that ended in pointed spikes would have been difficult to scale anyway, despite Raja's six-foot frame.

He retreated, but with the guard's back turned, he seized the branch of a lone magnolia tree that stood just inside the compound. Back and forth he worked it until it snapped. With his bare hands and feet, he tore off twigs, pared the limb down and planted the pointed end in a dug-up area.

The stick's shadow was at its shortest at noon when the sun was at its peak. At that time, one squad of guards replaced another. They clicked boots and presented arms. Just before the ceremonial change, Raja observed that they became sweaty and restless.

At noon, he retrieved the stick. Working a minute here, a minute there, he tried prying two laths apart. Tightly woven in and out of three horizontal strands of wire rope, they shifted just enough for a mouse to squeeze through. He replaced the stick in the soft dirt, where it would be available for him to dig his way out of the compound.

More than forty guards in blue turbans, armed to the hilt with shouldered muskets or bamboo rods, patrolled the quarantine depot—all under the command of British officers in khaki shorts and knee-high hose socks. Raja shook his head at what appeared to be an uphill task.

Days later, after he'd discovered the stick missing, he broke off two other limbs and pelted one hard against the fence, hardly disturbing it. With clenched jaws, he used the pointed end of the other to dig around the area, merely scratching the surface.

A guard tapped him on the shoulder. "You get buckshot in your buttocks if you try anything."

Raja sneered at the man. "Don't your masters need fit men to work as slaves on their overseas plantations?"

The guard delivered a glancing blow to Raja's thigh. He would have to be more careful about what he said. Massaging the sore spot, he scuttled away and found himself in the midst of a group of young men gawking at the women dressed in attractive saris.

News had filtered down that recruiters had bribed the manager of the Calcutta Temple Bazaar for his dancing girls. Those recruiters in turn had received triple commissions for the females, a scarcity in the compound.

Raja figured that the Indian women, eager to seek their fortunes in a foreign land, were needed to provide a continuous supply of labourers to work on the sugar plantations.

One beautiful dancing girl with hazel eyes had become the centre of attention. Slim and of medium height, she flitted about, chatting with one woman after another, flipping her green embroidered shawl over her shoulder. She smiled at Raja showing her even teeth.

At that moment, Raja truly believed that no one could replace his wife, Savitri, who lived with his parents back in Bihar.

The young men soon formed a circle around the women and clapped while they danced. Raja was in no mood for pleasure. As soon as the young men paired up with the dancers, a young officer in a rumpled suit and drenched in sweat shook his head. He beckoned a senior security guard and shouted, "Take those lechers over to the next compound!" He scribbled on a document. "Show this paper to the officer in charge."

"You're a disgrace!" the guard yelled. "Don't you have sisters?" He summoned help from four of his colleagues, and together they seized the men by their kurta shirts and dragged them toward the gate.

"Let them make up the quota for Mauritius!" the officer shouted. He pointed in the direction of a ship. "That schooner has been waiting two hours for a few more coolies. Demerara or Mauritius! It makes no difference to me."

Raja was appalled at the insult. *So I'm Demerara bound. I have no idea where it is, and that man doesn't care where the coolies end up.*

A seagull cried and hovered over the depot, an ill omen perhaps of what awaited him. The stench of the compound was overpowering. He knitted his brows and kicked up a cloud of dust toward the officer, who paid no heed. Curiosity led Raja to a young man who stood alone. "What brought you here?"

"I was walking along the road when a man asked if I wanted to make something of my life."

Some men standing nearby leaned forward to hear more of the conversation.

"What happened when you got here?"

"He told me that in a couple of weeks a ship would take me to a real paradise."

"Did he explain how such a journey would improve your lot?"

"He said that in five years, when my indentureship contract is over, I would return as a man of wealth." The young man's head pivoted from side to side as he spoke.

"That recruiter who brought you here feeds upon poor folk," Raja said.

To him, the depot was a large animal pen, nothing natural about it. The magnolia blossoms had long disappeared. No birds came to sing, certainly not the koel. Whatever grass had once grown on the clay soil had been trampled. Even a goat would have found nothing to nibble on.

The compound had two open, thatched buildings. The kitchen staff prepared food in one of them, and the doctors, nurses, and depot officials stored their equipment in the other.

Their job was to screen the recruits, checking them for infectious diseases that could put the entire trip in jeopardy. After they'd examined one batch of depot people, the medical staff separated some two dozen men and a few women and children. Whatever diseases they had, Raja could only guess.

Perhaps he didn't have to break out after all. *Why not pursue a novel way to avoid boarding that ship?*

He inched toward one of the men. Before he could say a word, the man turned aside, retched and vomited.

Raja approached after the man had taken a huge gulp of air. "Why did the doctor put you here, babu?"

The man gestured to the others. "We are all sick as you can see. They need healthy young men like you to cut sugarcane in Demerara."

That set Raja thinking. He sauntered over to the magnolia tree and gathered several of its leaves. He squeezed their juices, licked some and rubbed the rest over his body to create an unhealthy look.

Soon his turn came to be examined. The doctor placed a funnel-shaped device on Raja's chest and instructed him to inhale. He managed to throw up some of the magnolia juice and faked a coughing spell.

"You're healthy as a horse," the doctor said. "Get over there!"

Raja couldn't believe what he was hearing and headed for the group of sick people.

"Not there!" the doctor shouted. A few nurses fell over laughing.

The staff handed a document and a few coins to each of the sick adults and said, "Find your way home." They applauded their sudden change of fortune. Some who had been limping danced a jig.

Raja shook his head. His good health had worked against him.

Around noon, he wandered over to the cookshack, where a helper was chopping green chili peppers and onions. Though Raja's eyes watered from the onion fumes, he still had a good look at the knife and the storage cupboard above.

As he turned to leave, he bumped into a man who had been eyeing the food. He told Raja that he lived right there in Garden Reach at the Kidderpore Docks. In response to Raja's puzzled look, he said, "The sea was my home. If a captain ever came around and asked for a good sailor, I usually got hired on the spot."

"So you were a ready-to-go sailor."

"For most of my adult life."

Raja studied the ex-sailor, who introduced himself as Sen. "Why turn your back on the sea to work on a sugar plantation?"

Sen's voice quavered. "Better than handling opium."

"You transported opium?"

"From Calcutta to Canton. Chinese tea was draining silver from the British coffers, so they paid with Indian opium."

"Then why did you leave?"

"You would too if you'd seen how the opium addict in Canton would sell his possessions to support his habit." To further questions from Raja, Sen said, "A seaman's life is a burden when his ship becomes a prison." Sen looked away for a brief moment as if collecting his thoughts. "I have no wife, no family nor friends to come home to." His head stayed bowed as if to hide his loneliness.

Raja was grateful that he at least had a wife, parents, and a brother. Now this man needed his support. "I'll be your friend," Raja said, resting his hand on Sen's shoulder.

Sen's eyes glowed with warmth. "As a sailor, I've always answered the call of the sea. Now it beckons me no more."

Raja took a long, hard look at Sen. Was the man tired of living? "It puzzles me why you'd want to join a shipload of coolies."

"To get to a better place," the ex-sailor said, with a dreamy look in his eyes.

"Better place?"

I take pity on this man, but I could make use of his knowledge of the ocean and boats.

In the morning Raja sat on his haunches waiting for breakfast. The line of young men, a few women, some with babies, and older children stretched from one side of the bamboo fence to the other.

A server scooped a helping of rice from a large pot and dropped it onto a banana leaf in front of Raja. Another server following behind poured a cupful of yellow dal into the tiny pond Raja had created on his rice heap. This was Raja's first good meal since his kidnapping.

He ate hungrily and had just taken his last mouthful of food when Sen walked up saying the words he longed to hear, "Let's go look at the ships."

They chatted as they walked along the edge of the compound toward a sandy hill littered with dead seaweed and scum in full view of seagulls and cormorants that skimmed the surface of the Hooghly River.

"Those seagulls are a fisherman's curse," Sen said. "There are few fish left in the river because of them."

Echoes of their screeching cries filled Raja's ears, in sharp contrast to the monotonous lap-lap of waves against the mangrove shore.

A ship with square sails attached to four poles caught Raja's attention. Anchored in the water like a ghost, it stood out from the rest. He lifted a hand in its direction. "I wonder if that is the SS *Arcot*."

The man from the Calcutta docks raised his eyebrows. "Who mentioned that name to you?"

"A recruiter. He said the SS *Arcot* would be taking the depot people to Demer-ra-ra or some such place."

"I'll look for my man. Perhaps he knows how to read English lettering."

Sen led Raja to the top of the hill and shaded his eyes. "There he is." He pointed at a short, thin man dressed in kurta and tie. "Let's catch him before he disappears."

They ran over, and Sen, out of breath, jabbed a finger in the direction of the vessel in question. "Babu, can you read out the name of that four-masted schooner with the bold black letters?"

The recruiter spelled out, "There's an S and another S." He hit his forehead and made an about-turn. "I know someone who can help."

Raja tried his best to restrain a grin. "You treat that recruiter as though he's your peon."

"I earned him a commission," Sen faked a punch at Raja's chest, "now he'll do handstands and cartwheels for me." He wagged a finger at the crew of Indian sailors scrubbing the deck on their knees. "That's what I did before and throughout each voyage whenever the weather held up." He then gazed upwards at the sailors poised in the rigging. "I hated climbing masts like a monkey except in emergencies."

At that moment, the recruiter trotted up to Sen and pointed. "That is the SS *Arcot*."

"So I was right," Raja cupped his mouth, "and if those scoundrels ever drag me on board, you think you could find me a hiding place on deck?"

"What for?"

"So I can dive and swim ashore."

Sen raised his eyebrows and stared at Raja. "You'd never make it."

"I used to swim long distances back home."

Sen's brief laughter turned into a sneer. "That was down a quiet river. Here you'd have to contend with the Portuguese man-of-war and the powerful undercurrents of the Bay of Bengal."

"Bhai, I'd do anything to get back to my family."

"Are you out of your mind?" Sen's voice must have really carried, for it soon brought the crunch of a guard's boots.

"You two, break it up," the guard yelled.

Later, with the man nowhere in sight, Sen said, "Think before you act. Unlike me, you have a life ahead of you, a family, bhai."

That evening, as Raja lay on his jute bag on the beaten earth, sleep evaded him. A sprinkling of stars shone above while mosquitoes pestered him. Back in Belwasa, he would have smoked them away. He gritted his teeth and prepared himself for the task at hand.

He got up, inhaled the cool night air and looked around. In the dim light cast by a lantern, with guards sipping chai out of clay cups, the smell of spices from the kitchen rose to his nostrils.

He crouched and tiptoed to the shed. Sprawled out on a sheet, fast asleep, was a watchman. While he snored, Raja sidestepped him and passed his hands over the chopping table in search of the kitchen knife. Satisfied it wasn't there, he reached for the cupboard above. In his haste, he knocked the knife off a shelf onto the table. A loud crash and a sting on his finger made him wince. He held his breath.

The guard mumbled, "Darned rats," and Raja quickly dropped to the ground. *All praises, the man has resumed his snoring.* Raja tucked the knife in the folds of his dhoti and darted for his sack. Now, with a new moon just days away, he had a weapon that could come in handy, providing no one missed it.

At noon the following day, when the guards were about to change, Raja made a trip to the back of the latrine. With the sun directly overhead, he pulled out his knife and chipped away at a bamboo stave. In no time, he made a circular ring on the hard shell just below the joint. To camouflage his action he hugged the fence, but there was no need because the smell from the latrine seemed to have kept the guards at bay.

Around midnight, with the night guard occupied elsewhere and the others taking their usual chai break, Raja headed again for the latrine before swerving toward the bamboo piece he had been working on.

A man on a mission, he used all his strength and cut neatly through the bamboo's tough fibres. Pulled apart and jammed together, the cut portions fitted flush. No one could have detected the break in the joint without careful inspection. He collected the chips and scattered them.

After five nights his palm had developed blisters, but he didn't care a whit. He had cut through enough pieces that, when separated, would allow a man to pass through.

The time had almost come for Raja to flee the compound. If more than one person were involved, it would provide a distraction. All he had to do was choose trustworthy people bent on escape.

He had just returned from breakfast, when he witnessed an argument among a group of men, several of whom were in favour of a revolt. Raja's eyes widened as the guards attacked the rebels with their batons. They singled out three. A struggle ensued as the guards put them in leg irons and marched them over to a trapdoor that led to an underground holding cell. This was the punishment pit Raja had heard so much about.

Two days later, the guards removed the overhead planks. The poor wretches staggered to their feet and, with trembling hands, shielded their eyes from the sun. An odour of urine and excrement wafted in the air. Despite covering his nose against the stench, Raja couldn't hold down his earlier meal.

A plump man with a hangdog expression caught his attention.

"What's bothering you?" Raja asked.

"A recruiter lured me here with jalebis."

"Jalebis!" Raja could hardly suppress a smile.

"How he guessed my craving for those sweets, I couldn't tell."

Raja patted the fellow's waistline. "I think I know. What did he say once you got here?"

"He told me that after a short boat trip," the jalebi lover wagged his head in rhythm with his singsong accent, "I would arrive in a country called Demerara where, for only three to four hours of work a day, I would earn big money."

Raja broke out into a wide grin. He held the man's shoulder. "That's a pack of lies. We have to find some way to escape."

The man's eyes got all watery. "I think I've been fooled. I'm with you, babu."

"Stay close to me," Raja said.

Later, he ran into a group of people taking part in a discussion. He introduced himself and whispered, "How many of you came here willingly?"

"None," one of them replied. "Those who are happy to board ship keep to themselves." Like Raja, he came from Bihar and spoke Bhojpuri.

"Trust me, I too will not board," Raja said. "Bhai, are you with me?"

The Bihari conferred with the person next to him. "If you are thinking of a breakout, you can count on Muhammad and me."

Raja took those two men and the jalebi lover to a soft spot away from everyone. With a pebble, he drew a sketch in the dirt showing the barricade, the cane field, and the settlement. He outlined the escape plan and swore the men to secrecy. "Tomorrow at midnight," he said, "we'll meet at the fence, behind the latrine."

The Bihari replied, "Leave it to me. I will gather up the others."

"Sleep next to me," Raja said to him. "I'll nudge you and you can go get the men."

Around midnight, with the lanterns dimmed, a lowing wind whispered into a moonless night. The stars provided the only light, and Raja sensed that the conditions were right.

He placed his hands together in silent prayer. A rooster at some distant farmhouse shrieked "cocorico," although dawn was still hours away. Fortunately, the others did not pick up the chorus.

Inside the compound, several guards snored while others, their muskets slung over their shoulders, sipped chai brewed over an open fire. Just as they turned their backs to get refills, Raja gave the signal to the Bihari, who crawled away to find the others.

"What took you so long?" Raja whispered when the Bihari returned with the men.

"This Lunghiman kicked up a fuss."

The man's bare chest and bright red lunghi skirt tied at the waist did not find favour with Raja, whose preferred garment for this venture was the loose fitting dhoti. "You should have left Lunghiman," Raja mumbled. Rather than create problems at this stage, he said, "Chalo! Let's go!"

They made a dash for the fence and within seconds reached the break in the barricade. Fortunately, the sentry was nowhere in sight and the wind direction was favourable, wafting the stench away from them.

Raja sniffed the chilly night air before he raised each of the cut-off tops of bamboo, exposing the opening.

"Now hurry through, and don't leave a piece of your clothing behind." He discovered he had to cut through another bamboo stalk to allow Jalebiman to pass through. "You should have cut down on those jalebis," Raja scolded.

"I'll take this stave along," the Bihari said, placing his hand around the pointed end of one.

"No! It would cut down your speed and leave a gap," Raja said, as he dashed across the swamp where visibility was no more than a few feet. "First we'll aim for the cane field then regroup," he said over his shoulder.

The plunk-plunk of footsteps broke the silence of the night as Raja waded through the weed-clogged marsh, the soft muck massaging his bare feet.

If only he could reach that settlement!

CHAPTER TWO

Even the cane field now seemed far away for within minutes, buckshot pellets whizzed overhead as Raja ducked under the pondweed, shivering.

The rotten, swampy smell, combined with that of gunpowder was suffocating. The loud thuds of his heart raced and kept pace with his footsteps.

It puzzled him how a guard could have discovered the break in the fence so quickly. More likely, guards could have been posted outside of the barricade. Quite upset, he wondered if he'd done the right thing disclosing the plan of escape ahead of time.

The guards were advancing in droves, their boots crashing through the swamp.

"Get those coolies," the English commander shrieked, "dead or alive."

Raja withdrew the stolen kitchen knife from his dhoti. He was ready to grab a few guards by their beards and slit their throats.

Sounds like thunderclaps broke the eerie silence of the night.

"Ugh!" someone groaned, gasped and gurgled as another explosion sounded.

"That one was for you, Commander Sahib," a guard yelled.

As Raja crouched, the knife dropped and disappeared into the water. A desperate search brought up a body, causing him to fall over backwards.

His hands traced over the bulging belly and moved upwards. A bullet had blown apart most of Jalebiman's head, spilling gobs of slimy material where his brain used to be. The big man had fallen to the enemy, and that broke Raja's heart. He passed his hand along the lower jaw that was still intact. Shreds of soft tissue at the base of the skull made him retch. That he might never see his wife and family again had become real, akin to war.

Raw fear overcame him as more volleys flew overhead. Should he surrender or fight? He tried not to think as he let go of Jalebiman's body and watched it sink under the tangled weeds.

The plunk of a pellet forced him to move deep into a mass of pondweed. Out of nowhere, he bumped into Lunghiman, who was hiding among the water chestnuts. "I was dodging buckshot behind the big fellow," Lunghiman said. "Now that he is gone, I should turn myself in."

"Too late." Raja wished Jalebiman were alive instead of this coward.

Ripples formed round Lunghiman's feet as he cried out, "They'll pick us all off!"

A crackling sound from the cane field jolted Raja. Orange tongues of flame flickered and leapt high into the air while thick, yellow-white smoke billowed into the sky. The officer had ordered his men to set the dried cane leaves on fire.

Then came the voice of the commander, "Shoot if anyone tries to escape. Soon they won't be able to breathe, if they don't get burned alive."

With the wind blowing the smoke Raja's way, he feared the men would cough and give away their location.

"Breathe through your wet sleeves," he whispered.

The only escape route was across the swamp, through a meadow that led to a settlement of cottages. From there, they would be able to hide in a thicket of trees and shrubs that gave way to dense forest.

"Keep low and head for the settlement. We'll soon be in the clear," Raja said.

They took off like madmen. A volley of pellets hit Muhammad when Raja could almost make out dry land in the distance.

Raja dragged the dying man a few paces in the muddy swamp, along sedges and rushes.

"Leave without me," Muhammad moaned, and as blood gurgled out of his mouth, he formed the words, "Allahu Akbar!"

It broke Raja's heart to leave a brave man to the black vultures.

He bored through the muck, then zigzagged his way to stay alive.

Panting for breath was Lunghiman, all splattered in mud. "I'm going to die," he screamed. "I'm done for."

"Come on! We've almost reached the cluster of trees yonder," Raja said. Partially blinded by mud, he threw himself flat on the ground only to get up and make a desperate push for the settlement. One final rush sent him headlong into a guard who, with musket aimed, kicked Raja to the ground. "Got you!"

Without thinking Raja rose and, in one motion, knocked the musket from the guard's hands. It plunked into the water. He grabbed the guard's neck and in a tight grip submerged his head. At that moment, three other guards and their commander came upon Raja. One of them slammed his musket stock against Raja's temple, turning everything around him topsy-turvy.

Up on wobbly legs, he heard a distant voice calling out, "Hands up! Shoot the coolie for disobeying an order." His arms went numb and he could not lift them, though he could smell the muzzle just inches from his face. At any moment, the guard would fire.

Beside him stood Lunghiman, who whispered to Raja, "There was an order to shoot. You're lucky the guard's gun had failed to go off."

Raja figured that the guard's musket must have collected water.

The commander now glared at Raja. "March them over to the depot!" he barked.

Raja dreaded being manacled again. On his way to the compound, he mourned the death of two of his men. Yet in the process, the Bihari had escaped, though at a price—he had lost his good friend, Muhammad.

Now he was back at the depot, shivering and coughing, reeking of rotten pondweed.

Guards worked at making him presentable and dragged him to face the emigration agent, who with Lunghiman next to him, growled, "This man tells me you've incited the men and led them on a failed escape."

"Sir, I never forced anyone," Raja said, staring at Lunghiman.

Any hope Raja had for leniency was dashed when the emigration agent conferred with the commander. "Keep them manacled," he shouted to a guard, "and throw them in the pit for the full treatment."

CHAPTER THREE

The image of the three men Raja had seen being hauled up days earlier, smeared in excrement and urine, appeared before him, and he wished he'd been shot down in the swamp.

Inside the hole, when the first few whiffs hit him, he retched and soon became delirious.

As the hours rolled by, Raja had bouts of lucidity. He got to thinking about how the administrators had found ways to discourage recruits from trying to get out of their contracts. It had to be similar to the army experience his father had told him about: once you were in, getting out was difficult. He would not wish this form of punishment on his worst enemy.

What he perceived to be the second day was worse. Soaked as he was in the vomit, urine, and feces, giddy from the darkness, loneliness, and isolation, his entire body shook.

His head had cleared by the time guards opened the trapdoor and dragged him out. Buckets of water did nothing to wash away the lingering stench as he staggered around in irons.

A shaft of morning sun broke through black clouds, illuminating the full-rigged SS *Arcot,* docked in the harbour.

"They're scraping barnacles off the hull," Sen said. "Ship's getting ready to set sail, bhai."

Nearby, a woman screamed and yelled in a high-pitched lilt, "They are taking us across the kala pani—the dark waters, where we will become outcasts."

Why was she so worried when others were willing to leave their families and work for a pittance just to put food in their bellies?

The next morning, dark clouds scudded in from the north on a howling wind.

"That storm coming in would be bad for sailing," Sen said. He looked up. "It's not the best weather for the captain to start a voyage."

Raja raised his manacled hands as a protest. "Perhaps our lives mean nothing to him."

"Who cares?" asked Sen with a shrug.

What Raja saw in Sen's eyes made him sad. It was so hard to describe, he put it out of his mind.

The Indian stevedores, in threadbare blue coats, trotted to the boat carrying bags of rations on their heads.

"Provisions for the voyage?" Raja asked, trying his best to get Sen interested.

"Rice, lentils, potatoes, the usual stuff for a long trip," Sen replied.

As deckhands rolled a cask up the gangplank, Raja exclaimed, "Ganges River water!"

"Ha-ha! Grog—watered-down rum with lime juice for the crew."

The stevedores had all but left the gangplanks when a loud whistle rose above the chatter of the depot emigrants. Sikh guards, dressed in blue turbans and khaki shorts, moved briskly among the passengers.

"Onto the sailing ship! You don't have all day." They prodded a few men with their batons to urge them along.

The rain seemed to be letting up, but Raja's attention was on the poor souls, he being one of them, who were driven like cattle toward the gangplank. Few carried belongings except for the clothes on their backs. Two men, however, had brought along their musical instruments, one stringed with a gourd base and the other a bansuri flute made of bamboo.

A woman who'd fallen in line shouted at the bansuri musician, "Bhai, we are bidding farewell to our homeland." After she'd gotten his attention, she pleaded in a voice that could have melted a heart of ice, "Won't you play us a tune?"

He obliged with a sweet lament that floated in the air amid the quiet shuffle of feet and the occasional bawling of babies in arms.

To Raja, the melody told a story of love-cut-short for dear ones and country, and of good wishes and hopes that the day would come when they would reunite. There was that hint that he might never see his family again. Though he missed them much, he chose not to cry openly as others did, for he must be strong. A wild rush for freedom would have been futile. He had to stay alive at all costs.

After everyone had boarded, two guards led Raja to the ship. Head down, shoulders slumped, he shuffled across the gangplank and onto the deck.

Before he went down the narrow stairway, he peered at the Calcutta skyline. Whitewashed stucco buildings and elegant country houses stood among huts made of bamboo, straw, mud and palm thatch. Above the horizon, the sun peeped through the clouds, for the rain had stopped. Small fishing boats with single sails plied the river, while overhead, large flocks of seagulls squawked as though they hadn't eaten all day. One of them landed, hopped around on deck, flashed its eyes, bobbed its brownish head, and fluffed its wings at Raja.

Was the bird mocking him because it could fly away and leave him a prisoner like some bird in a cage? Freedom was not something he would ever take for granted again.

"Shoo, bird!" Raja yelled.

It took moments for him to get the gull to fly away—precious moments. Moments that gave Raja the chance to take one last look at his native land. Would it ever beckon him to its shores again? Would the wee things, like a bee humming, or the voices of children, ever be the same again?

The guard escorted him to the stairway that led to the tween deck above the cargo hold. A weight came off his shoulders when the man removed his handcuffs. Raja clenched and unclenched his fists to start the blood flowing and get rid of the numbness. Relief only came when he rubbed his hands together as he descended the ladder-like stairs.

The red-bearded boatswain in his blue cap shouted in Hindi as he worked to balance the boat. "Half of you men over there, move to the stern. The rest of you, join the single women and families in the bow and amidships."

A guard swung his baton at a few men. "Move, you coolies!"

Raja shook his head. *Here is an Indian calling his countrymen coolies. What wouldn't he do for a few rupees!* Under his breath, he said, "Give him a uniform and he thinks he is Governor Sahib."

Tempers flared. "Why do you hit us?" one man yelled. "First time we are on ship."

"Then follow instructions," the guard replied.

So far from home, Raja was quite happy to mix with the single women; if that is what the boatswain wanted, so be it. *Forget Indian customs! The safety of the ship is more important.* Come to think of it, he was curious to know why women, outside of the dancers, were going to this place called Demerara.

Minutes went by before he got used to the dim light that came from the few hatches that were laid open on hinges. He squinted and tried to focus on the ocean of faces. Everyone squatted on the floor, tightly packed, legs tucked in. How long would he be in that dark prison in such crowded conditions?

"Why did you sign up to go to Demerara?" Raja asked a woman with hollow eyes and sunken cheeks.

"Babu, once my husband passed away, my life was over."

"In what way?"

"My parents-in-law considered me a financial burden to the family and put me out of the house." Raja was sure his parents would never put Savitri out of their home. "I was forced to scavenge a garbage dump for food. That's when a recruiter came up to me and asked if I wanted to join a trainload of passengers going to Calcutta to find work."

Raja propped his head with his hand. "How can I blame you, Sister?"

Babies bawled, and mothers hushed them by letting them suckle their breasts, even when dry.

Things had just quietened down when the storm broke out again. It slammed the deck with curtains of rain that washed over the boat. Sailors rushed with tarpaulins to seal the hatch. Just as suddenly, the rain let up, and a blast from the ship's horn came through as the hatch was swung open once again. The voice of the captain followed: "Departure of the SS *Arcot* from Calcutta to British Guiana on this the first day of March, 1869. Three hundred and thirty-eight coolies on board."

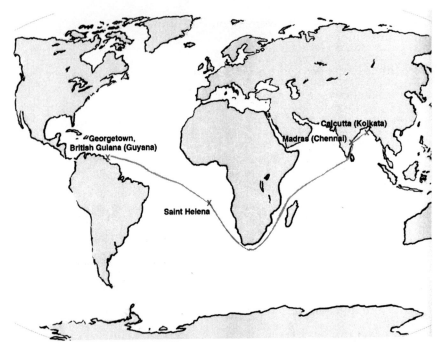

Route of SS *Arcot* from Calcutta, India, to Georgetown, British Guiana

Raja clenched his jaws and ground his teeth. *Ha! So Demerara is British Guiana.*

In his mind's eye, he pictured the Calcutta shoreline disappearing from view, perhaps taking with it all hope that he would ever see his wife, parents, and little brother again. He asked Lord Vishnu to give him strength. Here he was, bound for a foreign land, all because he'd gone to purchase egg plums for his little brother. Savitri would be going through similar agony. He could see her pulling at her hair, not knowing what had happened to him. What would become of her now that he was gone? That was enough to break any man.

He kept dwelling on what had gone wrong, going over the events that had placed him on this ship.

CHAPTER FOUR

Belwasa, Bihar, 1869

Three months earlier, Raja had lain on his rope-strung bed on the balcony of his parents' mud house without a care in the world. It was after a hard day's work harvesting mustard with his father. He'd stayed up until the bulbuls, parrots, and sparrows had long retired to their roosts on branches in the guava trees and mulberry shrubs. His days so far had been mostly humdrum, and he thought perhaps he should put some spark into his life.

One day at the village temple, Raja heard a priest sermonize about AUM signifying the Hindu Trinity, and being symbolic of the three main gods of Hinduism: A for Brahma, U for Vishnu and M for Mahadev—Shiva. Creation, according to the Hindu scriptures, began with the sound of A-U-M, three syllables uniting to form one. The tale of the Kumbh Mela and the significance of the meeting place of the three sacred rivers so inspired Raja, he wanted to learn more about his religion.

According to the holy texts, during a twelve-day battle between the gods and the demons for possession of the urn known as the kumbh, drops of nectar had fallen onto four places. Those locations from that time had taken turns sharing the Kumbh Mela, the Festival of the Urn. Prayag, or Allahabad, named the City of Allah by Emperor Akbar, was the site of the current year's Festival of the Urn, an occurrence that came about every twelve years.

Feeling that the time was right to learn more about this festival, Raja met with the priest and expressed his desire to go on a pilgrimage to Prayag.

"By all means, go," the priest said, "and while you're at the sacred Sangam, pray that the farmers of Belwasa would have a change of fortune in the coming years."

After Raja had been crowned wrestling champion at the local gymnasium, he recruited his best friend, Prem and his cousin Roy, a fellow wrestler—Puran, and his younger brother, Raj; they all shared Raja's enthusiasm for visiting the Kumbh.

Raja had been married to Savitri for more than a year. His parents had met this slim attractive girl, of medium height, at a wedding ceremony in Siwan. They had chosen her to be his partner and he couldn't have asked for better. A newborn to enrich their lives was on his mind. That evening, when he told Savitri about his desire to go on a pilgrimage, she said, "A dip at the Sangam would so please the gods, they might bless us with a child."

Raja's mother worried about his safety and could not stop crying. "Hundreds of pilgrims died during a stampede at the previous Kumbh Mela," she said.

"Ma, the chance of that happening again is low," Raja said. To please his mother, he joined her in prayers to Lord Vishnu, the preserver. Yet he never wavered from his desire to go on a journey that would unite his mind, body, and soul.

Early in the month of January, 1869, he prepared his first-string pair of bullocks for this leg of their journey—fifteen miles of dirt road from Belwasa to Siwan. Because of their willingness, Raja had chosen this pair for the start of his pilgrimage. On the morning of his departure he brushed their coats to a sheen and garlanded them with marigolds. To Raja's amazement, they left their mound of hay and water trough and took up their positions beside the whitewashed cart.

One last look at his house, the river, the thousand-year-old peepal tree, and the farm, and Raja was overwhelmed by worries. Fields remained unploughed, pulses needed to be harvested, and half-dozen cows needed to be milked daily. His father would have been too proud to ask for help. For a brief moment he closed his eyes and wondered if he should bow out.

At the doorway, he waited for Savitri to come and say goodbye. She appeared radiant in her blue gemstone sari and matching scarf. Her bedraggled hair betrayed their passionate lovemaking. She had burned incense sticks far into the night for that seductive aroma. After they had bathed, they had anointed each other with essential oils— jasmine and patchouli for Savitri and sandalwood for Raja.

A night to remember, the moon peering from behind clouds, they had gone to sleep to the sound of the koel's melodious calls of "kuhu-kuhu."

Finally, the moment of parting had arrived. He looked at Savitri long and hard, up and down, their eyes locked in an embrace. "You look beautiful, Savitri," he whispered. Minutes went by, and Raja just stood there, torn between his need to go and his desire to stay. Bulbuls and sparrows, perched on nearby mango trees, burst into frenzied chirping. The wind from the north, though biting, rustled the branches of trees, while behind the Daha River purred.

Savitri whispered in her husband's ear, "Raja, words cannot say how much I love you. Take care, my sweet."

"I will, my dearest. Within a fortnight, I'll be back."

Raja turned toward the front yard where Ma stood next to the bullocks. He stooped and touched her feet; she kissed his forehead and gave him her blessing.

"Watch the crowds, son."

Raja's father—Pitaji, gave his approval with a hesitance that Raja could sense. Was it because Allahabad was also the headquarters of the Eighth Division of the Eastern Army Corps where the old man had enlisted as a youth?

Raja hoped that Pitaji didn't think that after the pilgrimage he would scuttle off and sign up for the army. It was something that his father need not worry about. While Raja, true to his Rajput heritage, would have loved to serve, he now had a wife to look after.

Seven-year-old Baran walked to the cart with his brother. Raja threw him up in the air, then caught him on the way down. He was still laughing when he said, "Bring me back some ber, Bhaiya. Don't forget." Baran addressed Raja as "Big Brother" as was the custom.

Little boy buying egg plums at the market next to the Sangam

The saliva of children flow at the sight of yellow egg plums because of their distinctive honey flavour, and it was common knowledge that Allahabad's markets, home to the tastiest varieties, attracted buyers in droves. "Ha, ber! I will get you nothing but the sweetest," Raja said to the boy.

The early rays of morning and the aroma of jasmine blossoms hanging in the air promised a spectacular day as the companions set off in style from Belwasa.

Adorned in elaborate white turbans and cardigans over their starched, white dhotis and kurtas, they waved to the villagers who lined the narrow bullock lane. Women hanging clothes out on bramble bushes turned their faces away, perhaps too shy to watch the five young men as they went by.

High above, Raja spotted the crested serpent eagle soaring and gliding in the sky. To him, that bird represented freedom, strength, and grace. *Perhaps the eagle will give me protection on my first journey away from home.*

Soon the bullocks found their own rhythm. On the route, the pilgrims stopped beside the road and prepared rice and yellow lentils, using patties of dried cow dung for fuel. "Food always tastes better out in the open," Roy said, and everyone agreed.

At Siwan, Raja left the bullocks and cart with a market vendor for safekeeping and, along with the others, boarded a train headed for Allahabad. Farmers were up at the crack of dawn harvesting their crops or tending to their livestock, and Raja thought that he wouldn't want to trade such a simple, pastoral life for all the world.

The young men arrived in the midst of the celebration. Never had these village lads seen such a large crowd, so many tents and shacks—thousands of them packed together. Pilgrims who had arrived earlier seemed comfortable in their makeshift shelters supported by bamboo posts.

Prem scouted the area. "It's impossible to find a vacant site to build a tent within a mile of the Sangam," he reported back.

"We must stay close to the crowds," Raja advised.

And so they did that first night, camped under a teak tree where they slept to the singing of mantras and bhajans.

Early next morning, the pilgrims met an old man who offered them his open-air shack. Though the contraption could not have withstood a good wind, Raja was thankful for the gesture. After they had secured the joints with rope, everyone made a beeline for the Sangam. Raja sniffed the air tinged with the scent of burning incense. Joined by his companions, he threaded his way past holy men chanting, "Victory to thee, Mother Ganga," past dancers and naked ash-smeared sadhus, all trudging along to the thump of drums and Vedic mantras. Women carrying their belongings on their heads, trailed by the infirm on palanquins, old folk led by caregivers, trekked along as though in a trance.

Raja's heart thudded with excitement and gratitude, so sure he was of the blessings to come. Life for him could never be more blissful.

How then could a journey so full of promise and hope be foiled by the cold hand of fate?

CHAPTER FIVE

The Sangam, 1869

Raja shaded his eyes and peered at the sea of pilgrims adorned in colourful saris, turbans, and shawls. Two ruffians, armed with steel-tipped bamboo rods, jostled their way through the crowd. One talked to the other as they kept looking in Raja's direction. Of above average height, he always seemed to attract attention.

Despite his suspicions, he still tried to focus on the big attraction—the meeting point of the Ganges and Yamuna rivers, a thousand miles from their source in the mighty Himalayas. At the Sangam, the devout would take the holy dip and cleanse themselves of sins.

He wondered how many pilgrims would make it back safely. Stories of people trampled to death, robbed, and kidnapped were commonplace. However, why should he worry? After all, he'd arrived at the king of all pilgrimage centres.

He led the way down the ghats, jumping from one sandbag to another to join the mass of people who lined the riverbank. The fragrance of incense intermixed with jasmine and marigold garlands greeted him.

"This way!" he called to his friends.

At the edge of the river, Raja found himself caught up in the frenzy of the crowd that stretched for miles. A dozen years had passed since the last major Kumbh Mela had been held at Allahabad. A mere child then, he now looked forward to this visit.

"Over here!" a boatman in his saffron turban called, waving at the young men.

Raja strode toward him but slowed his pace when he approached the rowboat, which should have been long retired.

"We might take the holy dip while still sitting in your craft, Mr. Boatman," he teased. His friends broke out in loud chuckles.

The man muttered his resentment but in the next instant, with a broad smile, beckoned the group over. "Ah! You'll be safe."

"Row us to the Sangam, Mr. Boatman, and show us what this old wreck can do," Raja said.

With each drop and pull of the oars, the boat creaked and crept forward. Around them, swallows flew low to snatch insects from the water and in the air.

"Don't you worry," the boatman said. "I've been plying the Sangam for fifty years." With his right hand, its knotted veins seemingly ready to pop out, he pointed. "See the difference. Here the pale yellow Ganges, there the bluish-green Yamuna," he dipped his oars, "and now I will row you to the Triveni Sangam."

"Of course, the third river lies in our hearts," Raja added.

"Oh yes. How can we forget the Saraswati though it dried up long ago? Our holy books mention it as a once-great river."

"Will you let your boat drift awhile at the holy Sangam?"

"The time is yours," the boatman replied.

At the hallowed waters of the Sangam, Raja's body shook as though a spirit had entered him. Here at Prayag, Brahma had offered his first sacrifice after creating the universe.

Raja, so proud to be there with friends, truly believed that this dip at the Sangam would fulfil his wishes, cleanse his sins, and bring him salvation.

Stripped to his dhoti, he lowered himself into the chilly waters, joined by his companions, while above a lone seagull squawked. He inhaled deeply and felt like a new man. With eyes closed, he asked Lord Vishnu to bless him and his wife with a child. "May our crops be bountiful," he added. "Our destiny is in your hands."

He chanted "Aum" several times, setting off a vibration that forged a union of his body, mind, and spirit like that of the three great rivers.

The Ganges represented his mind, the Yamuna, his body, and the Saraswati, his soul. The symbol Om, carved on the ceiling at the entrance to his village temple in Belwasa, said it all. The word Om— made up of three sounds, aa-uu-mm—and its unifying sound of Aum, stood for the number three that together formed one: Brahma the Creator, Vishnu the Preserver, and Shiva the Destroyer. United, they become the One Omnipotent God.

Back on shore, chants of "Hare Krishna, Hare Rama" and the scent of burning incense trailed them as the pilgrims mingled with the crowds, past saffron-robed holy men, whose chants rose above the din of camels and oxen, and the tinkling of bells.

With each rumble of Raja's stomach his stride lengthened.

"Slow down," Prem begged. Far shorter, he had to take twice as many steps to keep up.

Without breaking stride, Raja urged him on with a wave. "Sorry, but my belly is complaining."

Raja led them straight to their shack where a man nearby had a wood fire going and was preparing chickpea dal and chapati.

Before they could pack up to leave, Raja snatched up a gunny sack. "Oh, I must get to the market to buy Baran his ber. I won't be long."

Prem rushed forward. "Why not take the boy some jalebis?"

Raja raised his hand in protest. "Sweets! He begged me to bring him egg plums."

"You're going off to buy fruit just when we're ready to leave?" Prem shook his head and grimaced. "A cartload of ber stood opposite the Sangam. Why didn't you get a bundle of those?"

"They were overripe and had brown spots."

"Then let me accompany you." Prem wrapped an arm around Raja's waist and walked a few steps with him.

Raja freed himself. "No need. You fellows can tour the Hanuman Temple while I'm away. I'll meet you at the stone pillar beside Akbar's fort."

"Try to return in an hour—"

Raja held up his hand, cutting Prem short. "Don't worry; I'll be back much sooner."

"Perhaps you'll change your mind and allow me to go with you," Puran pleaded.

Raja would have been happy to have this rugged young man by his side. He tilted his head and considered the offer, but he figured he'd make quicker progress alone. "Why bother, Puran?"

Roy, whose mouth looked like he had just sucked on a lemon, broke into a silly grin. "My wife will be missing me by now—"

Raja did not wait to hear the rest. He sprinted to a crossroad and dashed down the path that led to the market. Out of earshot from where his friends had remained, two men armed with short bamboo rods pounced on Raja. They were the two thugs Raja had seen before.

"Give us your money," one of them shrieked.

"Thieves!" Raja yelled, hoping someone would come to his rescue. His voice didn't seem to carry while the holy men continued their pious chanting:

Hare Krishna Hare Krishna
Krishna Krishna Hare Hare
Hare Rama Hare Rama
Rama Rama Hare Hare.

Blow after blow landed on Raja's arms and legs. Numb with pain, he dropped his sack, threw himself onto the ground and crouched into a ball, his head buzzing with the vibration of that ancient mantra that was meant to take its devotees to a higher state of consciousness.

Hare Krishna

"Let's get his money."

Hare Rama.

"It must be around his neck," one of them said.

The two attackers leaned over, giving Raja the opportunity to aim a kick that sent one of them crashing into a rubbish heap.

Raja rose and faced the other man, his training in the Indian martial art of wrestling taking hold. Side stance, knees slightly bent, feet planted firmly on the ground, shoulder-width apart, he ducked a blow, but when he made a grab for his opponent's club, his arms went numb. He retreated a few steps, ducked another blow, and in the same motion butted the man in the midsection. The victim uttered a loud grunt and collapsed to the ground.

Raja massaged his arms, dusted himself, grabbed his sack, and stumbled off to the sounds of *Rama Rama Hare Hare*. He looked back and saw the two struggling to their feet. *Perhaps I should have made sure they stayed down.* Fortunately, they were staggering about in the middle of the path and gave no sign they could give chase.

Despite the tingling in his limbs, the nearby smell of vegetables, mingled with the odour of spices, urged Raja forward. He was anxious to get back to his companions.

At the market, green, orange, yellow, purple, and dirt-brown vegetables and fruits lay spread out on the ground. Vendors sprinkled them with water. Women in colourful saris, men in white dhoti kurtas, walked barefoot or in flip-flops.

With so many plum vendors to choose from, Raja had his pick. Though he rejected several choices, one vendor grabbed his sack and filled it with fruit. Before he could come up with a price, Raja yelled, "Not the kind I want." He dumped the plums back onto the ground.

"You owe me for the ones you just bruised," the vendor screamed.

"I owe you nothing." Raja walked away and found an old, blind plum vendor at the edge of the market.

"Babu, how much for a bundle of your green plums?" he asked the old man. Raja paid him from the change in his cloth purse, put the fruits in his bag and slung it over his shoulder. "I have to get them to my little brother," he said in his native Bhojpuri dialect.

Before he could make any headway through the marketplace, four men, including the two thugs he'd beaten, jumped him. With lightning kicks and throws, he sent the men crashing to the ground. Vegetables and fruits flew everywhere. Spectators cheered him on, but the vendors' shouts and screams brought the local police, who rushed in with raised clubs.

"Who started the fight?" one of them asked.

"That one," said the vendor whose plums Raja had rejected.

"The police won't be able to protect you from your lies," Raja said. He glared at the vendor before gathering up his spilled fruits.

As he turned to leave, a policeman latched onto his arm, making him once again drop his sack of plums. "You're coming with us." The officers put one of Raja's wrists in a handcuff. As they tried to seize his other hand, he snatched the plums and bolted, the handcuff still dangling from his wrist.

They caught him, manacled his hands and shoved him along a narrow, winding lane flanked by a ditch choked with weeds and refuse. As if to cover up his captors' behaviour, the sun chose to hide behind a cloud.

A chilly wind made him shiver. Voices in his head advised him to resist with all his strength, but he reasoned that it would be better to wait for the right moment. Perhaps the gods would save him for after all, had he not taken the sacred dip at the Sangam during the Kumbh Mela, the holiest of festivals?

The policemen pushed him along the centre of the path toward an official-looking compound, forcing him to sidestep fresh cow dung. A born farmer, Raja did not mind its grassy smell. A cream-coloured two-storey building covered with ivy now came into view, its stone blocks polished to a smooth finish. The windows and arched entrance meant it could very well have been the headquarters of the Eighth Division of the Eastern Army Corps, where his father had signed up.

An uneasiness told him that something wasn't right. He shaded his eyes and squinted at the black letters of a sign attached to the building, wondering what the writing said.

"Move, you peasant," snarled one of the police officers. "You can no more read than my grandmother can."

A local armed guard at the gate saluted the officers and waved them in.

Around the compound, mangy goats nibbled on patches of winter grasses. The ribs of the poor beasts revealed that they barely had enough to eat. They had taken advantage of a break in the barbed wire fence to forage among the marigolds.

As soon as Raja entered the door to the building, his heart quickened. With so many British officers around, he truly believed he was going to be drafted into the army.

The policemen handed him over to an old English officer dressed in uniform with knee-length brown socks, pith helmet, and holstered pistol. Coins jingled as the policemen shook hands with a clerk.

Raja became wary. Why did the police accept silver rupees for his transfer? Were they in league with the old officer, as well as the thugs? Still, when a policeman removed his handcuffs, he became sanguine and expressed his thanks.

He rubbed his wrists, and greeted the old officer, whose eyes lit up. "Officer," Raja said in his best Hindi, "I do not wish to join the army."

The officer's mouth took on a twisted expression, giving Raja the impression that he did not understand Hindi. How could that be? In his native district of Siwan, he had heard the English give commands to the Sepoys in that language.

"My father served for twenty years and trained under one Colonel Sands. Would you set me free on his behalf?"

The officer mumbled a few words which made no sense to Raja.

"Sir, I do not know why I'm here. Some men tried to rob me, and I defended myself."

A faint smile crept over the officer's face.

Raja bellowed, "You understood what I said?"

The smile disappeared from the officer's face. He blew hard on his whistle and, in less than a minute, two khaki-clad local guards seized Raja by the arms and took him to a room to join some thirty other men around his age squatting on the floor.

Soon, several official-looking Indian men in dirty jackets and ties filed in and planted themselves among the group. Something about the sneaky look and behaviour of these "officials"—their shifty eyes perhaps—made Raja distrustful.

The old officer he had first met now entered the room. He spoke to the group in English. In the end, he asked a question. The snakes who had intermingled with the young men answered "yes" in unison.

What had they agreed to? Raja had no idea, but he was certain that the suspicious-looking men who had mouthed the word "yes" had collected their own handfuls of silver rupees.

Before the meeting ended, Raja rushed for the door only to be blocked by Indian guards under the command of a young officer. They aimed their muskets at his head. One of them jabbed a bayonet into his left elbow, drawing blood. He yelped, as much from the shock as the sting.

Why were they treating him like a criminal? No one had ever pointed a gun at him before. They dragged him by his kurta to rejoin the other victims, the old officer having long since disappeared. This turn of events left him shaking his head. Worst of all, the "officials" who had betrayed him were his own compatriots, who would do anything for a few paisa. Distraught, he addressed the guards, "If you won't allow me to notify my family, let me at least inform my friends about my whereabouts. They wait for me beside the pillar near the fort."

The guards spoke back and forth in Punjabi, not seeming to understand what Raja had said. This only made him wring his hands and scream like a lunatic.

Following orders from the young officer, the guards manacled Raja's hands behind his back and attached a chain to his feet. They took him and the other young men along a dirt road. He tripped on spiky grass and pebbles, and caught himself a few times, but that only caused the leg irons to bite further into his flesh.

"Why did you try to run away?" a young man said to him, covering his mouth. "Now they handle us like convicts."

"They treated me like one from the start," Raja whispered back. "I fought off robbers, and that's what got me here."

"It looks like we've been recruited into the army."

"Army?" Raja formed the words with his lips. "This is no way to recruit people for any army. Something darker awaits us."

Smoke eddying from mud stoves, the cling-clang of temple bells, and the smell of freshly-made chapatis, all reminded him that his own family would be sitting down to dinner at this very hour.

The guards took the men past a whitewashed building. A man in a white turban and dingy robe scrambled to his feet at the click-click of the young officer's boots. He blinked once, saluted the officer and, using his big toe, tugged several times at the rope attached to a ceiling fan. The punkah wallah muttered, "Darn convicts," and promptly went back to sleep after the officer had turned his back.

Half an hour into the march, fresh guards arrived and forced the men through the door of a one-room, stone-and-concrete building. The young officer removed Raja's handcuffs. However, when he slammed the solid wood door shut in Raja's face, that ended any hope he had of reuniting soon with his friends.

Like the others, he lay on the cold, dirty floor. His arms ached and his ankles had been rubbed raw where the leg irons had bitten into his skin.

As time passed, he forgot his pain and got interested in the antics of a stray cat that chased rats hunting geckoes. The tiny, barred window that allowed fresh air in might have provided entry for the vermin.

What am I doing here? What true wrestler would have allowed himself to be captured without a struggle to the end? Hadn't Prem warned me about going off alone? Why didn't I buy plums at the Sangam? It had been such a trivial matter.

Raja got up, struck his right fist against the hardwood door, and shouted, "Help! Prem! Puran! It is Raja! Come help me, bhai."

The sounds bounced off the walls of the small building. He beat his head against the door, but the pain only drove him into uncontrollable laughter and cries.

"This man is mad," an inmate remarked.

Raja worried the man might be right. That, together with the flow of blood, wet on his hand, shocked him into calming down.

"Lord Vishnu," he pleaded, "did I not bathe at the Sangam? Do not abandon me in my time of need."

CHAPTER SIX

Sleep finally overtook Raja after having lain on the cold, damp concrete floor for hours. Roosters were crowing their hearts out when a guard poked him with his bamboo rod. Freed of his leg irons, he shook his head and shuddered when he found himself still in the "prison."

By the time he joined the other men outside, dawn was breaking. A guard passed out clay cups and brought them a bucket of water to wash off the filth from the previous night. Another brought cold chapatis, which the men snatched right off his hands.

Raja bit into the flatbread. No sooner had he finished a few mouthfuls when the guard shouted, "Fall in line! You're not on holiday!"

Almost at the breaking point, Raja conformed as best he could to avoid being hit.

Guards, dressed in khaki uniforms, armed with muskets, some with bamboo rods, marched the men along a dirt track.

Before boarding a bullock cart, Raja looked up only to find a serpent eagle soaring overhead, a black speck against a clear blue sky. As always, the bird gave him inspiration and courage to live up to his Rajput heritage and his name, Singh.

"Stop your skylarking," the leader shouted, pointing his musket at Raja. "We have to get you scoundrels to the train on time."

Along a winding dusty track, the bullocks laboured over rocks and potholes, upsetting his stomach.

"They are treating us like murderers off to a prison camp," one of the men said.

"Shut up. You are all recruits," the guard waved his baton, "so treat this as a military operation."

Someone whispered, "It looks like we'll end up at a training barracks."

"A slave labour camp more likely," Raja exclaimed. He bent his head in shame. "What have I got myself into?" he muttered.

Through village after village, in pouring rain, his clothes would dry out and become soaked all over again. He shook like a wet dog, hoping for an early end to his punishment. Three days later, still on the road, with the bullocks snorting in rebellion, he wished they would drop dead.

In the city of Banaras he longed to get lost in the crowd of worshippers of the holy Ganges.

Along the way, stray dogs searched for food at roadside dumps, and cows nibbled at refuse, pausing momentarily to stare at the rumbling bullock carts and their human cargo.

Raja woke from a doze as his cart rolled across a bridge over the yellowish waters of the Damadar River.

Out of the crevices of grimy stonework grew banyan trees, whose wide trunks provided a safe haven for boys who pelted the carts with mango seeds.

What a relief it was to hear the cartwheels creak to a stop at a railway platform! There, additional recruits with their guards joined the group, and everyone boarded the train, convincing Raja that this operation was much bigger than he could have imagined.

The train with its ten carriages stopped while a crew switched it to the "right track" before it chugged into the Calcutta Railway Station. Never before had Raja seen such chaos. Families with their possessions in jute bags squatted or lay on the floor, covered up in dirty blankets.

That evening, in dense fog, guards drove the recruits toward the Hooghly River, then onto barges. At ebb tide, rowers took them upstream to Garden Reach on the southern bank, where they were discharged.

On the bare ground, Raja shivered from gale-force wintry winds and pondered his fate, which at that point looked extremely grim.

The next morning, an English officer hailed a few guards. "March the lot of them over to Camp Demerara." He pointed at the compound.

Ten-foot bamboo staves barricaded the square that was more than twice the size of Raja's parents' farm. Around fifty armed Indian guards, many of whom could have had military training, guarded the area. So few women and children among some three hundred men convinced Raja he'd been sold into a prison camp.

A man in dhoti, jacket, shirt and tie, strutted around, striving to look important. Raja tapped this "official" on the shoulder. "This is all a mistake, bhai; I don't belong here."

"See this certificate," the man removed from his shirt pocket a curry-stained document, "says right here I'm a licensed recruiter, who works according to set rules."

Recruiter for what? Raja looked up at the sky as if seeking help from above.

A light-skinned Indian man, dressed in a dark suit, his white collar held in place by two strips of linen, nudged aside the recruiter and faced Raja. He clasped his hands together and bowed. "Namaste! I'm an English returned advocate of the High Court of Calcutta," he said in cultured Hindi. He glanced over at the recruiter and back at Raja, and with a raised finger, emphasized each word. "If you have any questions," he now pointed at himself, "address them to a man of law."

Raja's eyes brightened. "The police sold me out for a few rupees. Can't you use your position to get me home to my family?"

"Not when you're under contract."

"Contract!" Raja shook his head in frustration. "If that is so, can you not help me get out of it? Someday . . . bit by bit, I shall repay you."

The lawyer wagged a finger while grinning. "I work for shipping agents, who act on behalf of British West Indian sugar planters. They pay me, shall I say, handsomely, not in annas, which would be all you could afford."

Raja was tempted to bite off the offending finger. Obviously, he could never compete against such powerful people. Far away on a treetop, a dove cooed a mournful tune. His mother's words rang in his ears. He must be respectful to his elders and those in authority, so he softened his tone. "The officer asked a question in English, sir. Others answered for us." Raja hoped that he had evoked some sympathy from the lawyer.

"I'm sorry. You've signed on to become an indentured servant for five years at a sugar plantation in Demerara. If you didn't understand the contract, you should have asked for a translator."

"To tell me that I will become a slave for five years?"

"No! A well-paid cane cutter."

Raja breathed heavily. He didn't believe that he'd be well paid. "Cane cutter!"

"Since you have no proper questions, I must leave."

"Hey! We're fellow Indians, leaves of the same tree!" Raja shouted, but his countryman had already melted into the crowd.

The recruiter jumped in, "Don't worry, babu."

"How far is this place?" Raja asked.

The recruiter waved his hand. "Demerara! A few weeks by sailing ship and, bam," he clapped his hands for effect, "you come to a real paradise."

Raja rolled his eyes. "Oh Lord, I will cross the dark waters and arrive at a paradise. How can I believe this?"

"Because you'll return with plenty gold and money for your family." The recruiter's head kept beat with his singsong accent.

"They may never bring me back!" Raja cried out.

The recruiter tapped the back of his brown hand. "Would a Rajput brother lie to you? It's all in the contract, which states that they must do so at company expense."

"Men like you sold me out for a handful of rupees. Why should I believe you?"

"Because I speak the truth. Listen to me! Three, four hours of light work each day will not kill a strong Rajput like you." The recruiter walked Raja over to a tall, freckle-faced official sporting a handlebar moustache. "Come hear it for yourself." Dressed in a long khaki jacket and brown leather belt, with matching long hose socks and pith helmet, the official carried a baton. "Sir, Babu Raja Singh wants to say a few words to you." The recruiter now turned to Raja. "This is the Protector of Emigrants."

Hmm! Protector! Raja presented his problem and was surprised at how bold he'd become.

The Englishman fingered his fiery moustache and assumed a stern expression. "Our lawyer, a minute ago, explained to you the terms of the contract."

How did he know? Did he have his eye on me? Raja's voice rose, "Recruiters used crooked means to sign up young men like me."

"Listen, Roger boy!" The Englishman signalled for Raja to be quiet. His face showed impatience, as though he'd already spent enough time with this coolie. "You've agreed to a five-year contract to work at a sugar plantation in Demerara, plain and simple."

Raja gritted his teeth. "Sir, I'd rather serve as a soldier, like my father."

"Tut-tut. You'll be working for British sugar planters and return a rich man. Didn't this recruiter tell you so?" The recruiter nodded.

"But I will lose caste and never again be accepted by my people."

The Protector of Emigrants shook his head. "You'll attend a Hindu temple, boy; speak your native tongue, and preserve your Indian customs and traditions in the colony."

"I doubt it," Raja said. "Besides, it is too long to stay away from a young wife."

"It will go just like that." The official snapped his fingers. "Let's look at it another way. She'll be counting the days when you'll rejoin her." With those final words, he left.

"Sir!" Raja cried out, but the Protector had already vanished into the crowd.

The recruiter again stepped forward. "The agents have a set quota for the SS *Arcot*. It is ready to sail in three weeks' time. You have no choice but to board, babu."

Raja's shoulders sagged, as did his spirits. *We'll see. The SS Arcot would never have me as a passenger.*

CHAPTER SEVEN

SS *Arcot, 1869*

On the high seas, Raja's eyes struggled to adjust to the feeble light that came in through the thick glass of the portholes and open hatch. He scanned the ship's hold but could not see his sailor friend. A man in a richly spun dhoti and kurta caught his attention.

He inched his way next to a dark, fine-featured man and introduced himself. "Babu, how did you end up in this ship?"

"I signed up to cut sugarcane," the man, whose name was Ramdas, answered. His head moved from side to side in time with his musical voice.

"But you're dressed like a man on vacation."

"These clothes are my own handiwork, so I might as well wear them," Ramdas said, tugging at his garment. "I was a master weaver, a family tradition."

"Your family must have special skills," Raja said.

"In the sense that we could weave muslin fine enough to pass through a woman's ring, yes."

"Why are you leaving the business?"

Ramdas swung his head from side to side. "It has become too dangerous. The best Bengali weavers of such fine cloth have ended up with their thumbs chopped off."

Raja winced. He shuddered to think that people could go to such extremes just to eliminate competition. "Perhaps you could have stuck it out with coarser fabrics."

"Cheap imported linen drove us out of business."

Raja took some time to digest what he'd just heard. "At our family farm in Belwasa," he countered, "I dropped my prices just to stay afloat. That's how I managed to retain my farm and stall at the market. Couldn't you have done the same?"

Ramdas made a noise with his tongue. "We might as well have given away both shop and goods."

At Raja's farm, little was left after taxes. "To survive," he said, "many Belwasa farmers grow indigo to make dye for those machine-made products."

Ramdas took a deep breath. "Indigo farmers in West Bengal are starving because of high taxes on the land and a shortage of wheat and rice."

Raja shifted his weight from one leg to the other. He got Ramdas's attention when he related the circumstances that had placed him in the boat. "If they had tricked me into serving in the army, I wouldn't have minded."

Someone nudged Raja from behind. Thinking it might be Sen, he quickly turned around only to face a thin, acne-faced man, who looked a bit older than most on the boat.

"Why would you want to serve in the British Army?" the man asked.

Raja lifted his eyebrows. "Because it's part of our Rajput tradition."

The thin man waved his hand in disgust. "It's mine also, but I would never take up arms against my own people."

"The British pay their soldiers well, besides feed and clothe them."

The strange passenger bared his stained teeth and said in a harsh voice, "You speak like a peasant."

"Are you any different?" Raja now raised his voice, "How come you're on a coolie ship?"

"That's my business." The man, looking quite embarrassed, turned to Ramdas, "Do you know the reason for high taxes on your lands?"

Ramdas, in a high-pitched voice, said, "I never asked."

The man laughed. He dug into a cloth pouch and brought out a betel leaf folded around a paste. He rolled the paan into a ball and placed it in a recess of his cheek, which bulged as if he'd tucked a marble inside. "Our rulers have appointed zamindars to be their tax collectors," he mumbled. "They are the true owners or lords of all the cultivable lands, and peasants are just serfs."

Raja glanced at Ramdas, who seemed just as suspicious about this passenger. "You speak like a rebel," Raja said. "Who told you such nonsense?"

The passenger moved his hands around. "At university I read a book by Marx and Engels. It spoke of European nations killing each other for the products of Asia."

"I'm a poor farmer who only care about feeding my family," Raja said. "Perhaps those messages at the university have poisoned your mind." The student merely shrugged off the latter comment. "Tell me, why do you wish to work on a British sugar plantation?" Raja asked.

The man stroked his chin as though he were looking for a way out. "Let's say I'm in search of the lost city of El Dorado—the City of Gold that Raleigh failed to find. And it happens to be located in the very country where we're going." He winked at Ramdas, who appeared just as perplexed as Raja.

Raja looked long and hard at this interesting man. "Something tells me you're on the run."

The pimple-faced man's jaw dropped. He covered his mouth and muttered, "I'm going to seek my fortune in the colony."

Raja did not wish to offend the ex-student further. "But you didn't tell us your name."

The man hesitated, looked around and whispered, "Shankar. Shankar Singh."

"You know, Shankar," Raja said, "since you are a student, I will tell you this. Something tells me that in the new land, they might try to change our customs and religion."

"As an unbeliever, I care nothing about religion. And as for customs, India has many ancient traditions. We are going to a youthful colony, where a new culture will be born."

Raja gave Shankar a confused look. "Culture!"

"It is the way people behave with each other," Shankar added.

"I will stay within my own culture." Raja patted his chest. "I'm a proud Rajput." He put a hand on Ramdas's shoulder. Together, they squeezed between passengers and distanced themselves from Shankar.

Raja examined Ramdas's hands. "Do you think you can cut sugarcane from dawn to dusk, bhai?"

"Hard work never kills, but starvation can." Ramdas's lips trembled and his mouth sagged. "That won't happen anymore to my wife and two children."

"Why is that so?"

"For one thing, they sleep at the Calcutta Railway Station."

Raja was so taken aback, he looked deep into Ramdas's eyes. "What about food?"

"I paid an unlicensed Bengali doctor twenty rupees to chop off my son's right hand and mangle the left one."

Raja's eyes formed slits and his face contorted. He covered his mouth to avoid vomiting. "You're crazy."

"I had no choice. Now from his beggar's income he is able to feed himself, his sister, and his mother."

Raja kept shaking his head at the utter desperation of Ramdas, who would resort to such cruelty to ensure his family's survival while he sought to improve his lot in a foreign land.

Ramdas looked from side to side. His lips quivered, and his voice cracked with emotion. "That is what starvation does to a man. I am only one of many. If you had walked the streets of Calcutta, instead of the country lanes of Belwasa, you would know what true poverty is."

Despite the high taxes, Raja's family always had food, shelter, and clothing. How could he condemn poor Ramdas? Indeed, Raja's education had just begun. He hugged Ramdas. "Now I understand," Raja whispered.

Another glance at the passengers showed desperation in the mothers' faces. Empty eyes darted from one face to another as though looking for support. They spoke in soft, trembling voices.

How many of them had experienced the hopelessness Ramdas spoke of? Who in fact knew the number of months they'd have to spend in such cramped quarters?

Raja turned his attention back to the former weaver. "So, after five years, you will return to your family a rich man."

Ramdas's jaw tightened. It brought a mocking chuckle. "How could I return to the life of a low caste and the daily humiliation that comes with it? Death is better."

Raja bowed and covered his face for quite some time; his Rajput Kshatriya heritage had been torn to shreds.

Ramdas whispered, "Back in India, my mother had upper-caste Kshatriya blood but lost her caste when she married my low-caste father. By acting as a low-caste woman, she'd saved both of their lives."

Raja rested a hand on Ramdas's shoulder. Raja's lips formed a circle, showing no trace of a smile. "From now on," he said, "I will call you Ramdas Singh and treat you like a full-fledged Kshatriya."

"So you've turned me into a ship-Kshatriya," Ramdas said, with a sheepish look. His lips barely formed the words. "Therefore I will ask you to be my ship brother, my jahaji bhai, if Shankar doesn't mind."

"I'd rather keep to myself," Shankar said. He moved away.

Raja embraced Ramdas. "Yes! Through happy and sad times, we are bonded and we'll be there for each other in the new land."

It was already the second day on the ship, and Raja still had not seen Sen. After a meal of rice and dal, Raja stood up to ease his leg cramps. A guard placed around his neck a circular piece of tin the size of a fist. "Keep this tag till you get to the plantation," he said.

Raja looked at the markings and turned the tag this way and that. With a smile on his face, he called out to Shankar, "They've given us necklaces, I see."

Shankar sidled up to Raja. He lifted Raja's tag so that it faced a beam of light coming from an open hatch. "It's your tin-ticket number; it says that you're Number 198."

"You mean from now on we'll just be numbers."

"In some ways, yes."

The guards handed each emigrant a clean gunny sack, a metal plate, a cup, and a bucket for emergencies. During good weather, they were expected to line up and go above deck to use any of the four latrines. Built over slots that hung over the bow of the ship, they were regularly flushed with seawater.

Guards issued the young women long, printed cotton skirts, fitted tight at their waists with strings. The married women snatched up the discarded saris and placed them in their own sacks.

Shankar touched Raja on the shoulder. He pointed at the women's skirts. "Those Manchester-made textiles are what drove our friend Ramdas out of business."

"I've never heard anyone speak like you," Raja said and turned away.

The tallest of the women donned a skirt that had a flounce at the bottom. "Make room for me," she said. "I miss my dancing." She slapped her feet on the floor setting up her own rhythm. Some women clapped their hands, lifting their shoulders to the beat. The dancer's facial gestures, graceful neck, hand, body, and foot movements turned all eyes her way.

A guard bawled out. "Stop this racket. This is not a temple courtyard."

One of the women shouted right back, "Leave Jasmine alone. If you've danced every night for the last couple of years," the woman swallowed to catch her breath, "it gets into your very bones."

"This is just the beginning," Raja whispered after the guard had disappeared. He moved closer to his companions. "That's Jasmine dancing. Next thing you know, her sort will be performing half-naked for the English."

"Let her be," Ramdas whispered.

Shankar added, "We're leaving India. Let's forget about old country customs and habits."

A few days of smooth sailing under gentle winds went by. One morning, Sen forced his way through the throng of people and announced to Raja. "The ship's docking at the Port of Madras, bhai."

Raja watched with interest as additional recruits came through the hatches. By twos and threes, in either white dhotis and kurtas or colourful lunghis, more and more new recruits poured into the crowded space below.

In a shrill voice, Sen blurted out, "The ship has too many passengers for her size. Now everyone is in danger." He wiggled his way between passengers. "I'll have a talk with the boatswain."

Additional guards dressed in khaki drill tunics and shorts supervised the newcomers. Several times Raja, now seated, had to make room for the darker-skinned people.

Some time later, Sen jumped over legs, a worried look on his face. "I warned the boatswain that the ship is too low in the water. He agreed and said the skipper accepted too many people from Madras."

Raja didn't want to be buried at sea. If that happened, his wife and parents would never know that he was gone from this world for good. "Why would he do that?" he asked.

With a smirk, Sen replied, "The more coolies that arrive in Demerara, the more paisa for the captain and his crew."

That night Raja curled up so as not to have his feet in someone else's face. He could hardly breathe. A smell like rotten vegetables and the odour of unwashed bodies hit his nostrils. What he needed most were a few hours of sunlight and some fresh air, well-nigh impossible in his shipboard dungeon.

One morning before daybreak the boat heaved from side to side as wave upon wave lashed against the hull. Raja stood up just as Sen came boring through.

Raja had to shout to be heard over the crashing waves. With arms outstretched, he asked, "Where are we, Sen?"

"We're rounding the Cape of Good Hope."

"It's more like bad hope to me." Amidst the children's cries, Raja's voice shook. "The storm is picking up, bhai."

"Every seventh or eighth wave covers the deck and threatens to wash the crew overboard. Everyone is up there working."

"Why don't you help out, Sen?"

"I'll see if the boatswain can bend the rules," Sen replied. "All those years at sea, and I never had an opportunity like this."

Sen would be fearless, Raja knew, since without a family, he had nothing to lose; life meant so little to him. Raja marvelled at the strange turn of events that had placed Sen in a position where he could save lives and, at the same time, add meaning to his own.

Ramdas, whose face had taken on the colour of pond scum, threw up in a bucket. "We are g-going to d-drown," he cried out.

Loud wails from women and children rose above the roar of an angry sea.

"The boat is sinking," Jasmine screamed.

"The ship will ride it out in no time," Raja shouted above the cries of the women. Though his words were empty, he wanted to give them hope.

Quietly, he said to the men, "Let us show courage and not panic, especially around the women and children."

At that very moment, Sen showed up quite out of breath. "New and old waves coming at an angle to each other are uniting," he said. "That spells trouble for the ship."

Raja had shown great courage facing bullets in the swamp. He tightened his fists and vowed to show the same mettle combating the sea.

The sound of the wind rose and Raja could sense its force on the sails and the waves. A high cross swell tossed the ship upwards, downwards, and side to side. It rocked his guts. *This voyage could very well go down as one of the great tragedies at sea.* "So what have they decided?" he asked Sen, trying to appear calm.

"The boatswain got approval from the captain to allow me to work the sails. I came to say goodbye."

As Raja embraced his sailor friend, he could sense a mix of fear and sadness in his demeanour. Raja hoped he hadn't put the man in any danger.

Buckets of human waste, plates, and cups slid around as the ship rocked and pitched. Raja skidded his way through the mess and joined the passengers who were on the windward side of the ship. Water splashed through a hatch and washed his feet. Jammed together with the other passengers, he shivered as thunder cracked.

Toughness was something he took pride in. Now he was no different from the other passengers. He studied them as they huddled together— fear written on their faces.

"Child, do not cry," a mother said to her son. She held him close to her chest. "Bad weather will soon be over."

"It's too far," the boy said. "When will we arrive?"

"Soon."

A slender young woman, whom Raja had first seen at the depot with her baby, tugged at her hair with both hands as her head swayed from side to side. Drenched eyes told the story of despair.

"I was going to Demerara to find work so I could feed her," the woman said. "Now there is no need. She is gone."

Raja said to her, "These women," he waved his hand about, "will support you in the new land, dear Sister. Everyone suffers loss. Try to be strong."

Whether through instinct or fear, the passengers' wailings soon turned to silence. Perhaps they did not wish to hinder the work of the crew. Indeed, so many passengers were dying every day from typhoid, cholera, and dysentery, the surgeon superintendent and his helpers could not cope. Raja wondered who would be next.

He came down with diarrhea. A man opened a pouch and passed a bottle of medicine to him. "This is from my Ayurvedic doctor. You must take it twice each day."

Raja squeezed his nostrils to avoid inhaling the strong smell of the yellowish mixture and sipped a few drops.

"Raja, why are you killing yourself?" Ramdas asked. "Don't you trust the ship's surgeon?"

"No! He uses the same medicine to treat every sickness."

"How do you know?"

"Sen and I watched the compounder mix up dried herbs, crushed bone, fat, and calomel in a mortar and pass the lot to the doctor. To our surprise, that is what made up the mixture he gave each sick person."

Shankar cut in on the conversation. "Lately, he has provided fresh water and soap. As a result, fewer people have been getting sick."

The next morning, Ramdas rushed and squeezed in between Raja and Shankar. His face said it all. "One passenger told me many bodies were thrown overboard after the storm," Ramdas said. "He lost count—over twenty so far." Ramdas put an arm around Raja's shoulder. His lips trembled and his voice cracked, "Prepare for some sad news. The crew has been talking."

"Speak up, bhai."

"It's about your sailor friend."

"What about?"

"Sen is gone."

Raja raised his voice. "What do you mean, 'gone'?"

"Sen lost his grip high in the riggings and got washed overboard."

Raja could not speak for quite some time. Many thoughts went through his head. "Did they try to rescue him?" he asked. Raja raised his voice again and stamped his feet twice in anger. "The man put his life at risk for the safety of the ship and its passengers; yet they did nothing to save him!"

Except for a few sips of dal, Raja did not eat for days.

When the ship no longer rolled, the boatswain bawled out, "Open the hatches!"

A sailor gagged after he had complied. Later, he brought a piece of red-hot iron and plunged it into a bucket of tar. Smoke and steam filled the passenger area and masked the foul smell but left another offensive odour that soon disappeared. Before long, the ship was under full sail again. Gentle waves lapped the hull.

At long last, the boatswain shouted, "Port Saint Helena! Guards, prepare the coolies to come on deck in batches."

Anxious for a breath of fresh, salty air and to see the sun, Raja was one of the first to stumble up the stairs. A deep breath cleared his airways. He blinked several times to adjust his eyes to the bright sunlight.

On deck, armed guards used their batons to control the crowd. Members of the crew supervised a dozen or so natives of the island, as they loaded the boat with fresh vegetables, bags of lentils and various other foodstuffs, and water.

Raja lingered on deck long after the others had been herded below. He was still mourning the loss of his sailor friend. For a few moments, he watched the storm petrels as they flew low over the waves, and the seagulls that seemed to mock him as they swooped in and veered off at the last moment. A strong breeze picked up from the west. It blew him about, but he managed to stay topside.

Before sunrise the next morning, the captain emerged through the hatch onto the tween deck and spoke with some crew members. Raja found himself no more than twenty feet from the master of the vessel.

He wore a black cap with a yellow cord around its brim. His black jacket and pants completed his outfit. Green eyes glared through narrow slits, and his grey beard shook as he bellowed, "No coolies on deck for the rest of the journey!"

Raja clicked his tongue. *What could have caused that reaction?* Later he learned that two passengers, in a daring attempt to escape, had plunged from the deck a mile from the island of Saint Helena, only to be swallowed up by strong currents. Sen had been right with his warning. It had saved Raja's life.

Several weeks went by and, when Raja's nerves had just about reached the breaking point, the boatswain announced that the ship was heading for Trinidad. The news brought relief to Raja, for the rocking of the ship and his guts had ceased.

Later that day, the boatswain returned below deck and got the attention of the few sailors settled in among the passengers. "Shore leave cancelled!" he shouted. "We have to repair the fore, main, and mizzen sails!"

"Come on, bose," a sailor yelled back, "three months at sea, our hips need some loosening up; so how about a night out for some Cuban motion merengue at Club Trinidad?" Loud cheers went up from the few sailors around.

"Why!" the boatswain bellowed, raising his hands in the air, "Under full sail and fine weather, in four days flat we'll be in Georgetown." After a pause, he said, "There you can dance the night away with all the leggy mulatto girls who frequent the night clubs along the Tiger Bay waterfront."

Dawn had just broken on the fourth day when the hatch cover tipped open. Raja stood at the foot of the stairs and soaked up the warmth of the sun's rays. A gush of sea breeze came through, and he took several gulps with the sun beating down on him. Never again would he take the sun and the wind for granted.

The captain's voice thundered, "Guards, start matching each passenger's number with a name. Remind them to hold on to their tags."

Some time later, he announced, "All numbers checked. Three hundred and eight coolies survived the voyage. Bravo to our able boatswain, the crew, and one fearless ex-sailor who is no longer with us."

Obviously in a jolly mood, since only thirty passengers had perished, the captain shouted instructions to the helmsman on the starboard side of the ship, "The tide's a bit low, so watch those wicked sandbars at the mouth of the Demerara. Use the lighthouse to navigate your way."

The passengers were all jabbering away, hardly able to contain their excitement, for their imprisonment at sea had come to an end.

Raja rolled up his dhoti, gathered up his sheet, stuffed it into his cotton sack, and jostled for a position just below the hatch. Hoping to be among the first passengers on deck, he signalled for Ramdas and Shankar to stay close.

As he climbed the first rung of the stairs, his knees buckled, and he fell backwards into the arms of Ramdas. On his second try, he succeeded and went all the way up.

He kept his eyes shut to avoid the full glare of the sun, but as he opened them, the Atlantic Ocean loomed large and majestic. On the port side, the city of Georgetown stood poised on the eastern bank of the muddy Demerara River, almost a mile wide. A sand and silt beach stretched from the low river mouth all along the coast as far as he could see. Inland from the beach, small whitewashed wooden houses stood on posts. In the distance, the sun's rays bounced off the corrugated zinc roofs of tiny shacks that lay amidst coconut and shade trees. Faced with such an unusual sight, so different from Calcutta, Raja shook his head and raised one corner of his upper lip as if to cry.

He turned to his two shipmates. "It looks as though I've given up my country for one of mud flats and swamps," he said. "And as to those buildings, a good monsoon flood would make rafts of all of them."

"Perhaps inland it gets better," Ramdas said with a shrug, his voice having lost much of its music.

A red and white lighthouse came into view. Seagulls screamed, and bluish-black cormorants dived into the shallow, silty water. They surfaced with fish held fast in their yellow beaks. Raja recalled that Sen had pointed out close relatives of those birds that had dotted the Calcutta shore. Violet balloon-like floats, like early tulip blossoms, danced on the waves. They must be the Portuguese man-of-wars Sen had warned him about.

A sharp blast from the ship's horn flushed a large flock of scarlet ibises. Even the captain took time to watch them in their brilliant hue as they rose from the seashore in unison and flew off to alight on clumps of black mangrove trees.

Still in his element at the bow, with his long telescope of polished wood and brass, the captain moved his arms around as though he were doing his morning exercises.

"A quarter mile from the river mouth is as close as we can get," he shouted. "We'll drop anchor here a safe distance from those two cargo ships."

The long-awaited announcement through the megaphone followed: "Arrival of the SS *Arcot* in Georgetown, British Guiana, this twentieth day of June, 1869."

That day would be etched forever in Raja's memory.

CHAPTER EIGHT

Demerara, 1869

At mid-morning, the sun shone bright through an indigo sky. Raja lifted his hand over his eyes and, with a sweeping glance, took in the vast panorama of the coastline of Demerara. The smell of the sea grew stronger. Wave after wave slammed against the ship's hull in staccato rhythm. On the horizon the glittering billows tumbled. If only he were a free man, he would have enjoyed what appeared to be a tropical paradise of swaying coconut palms and tall spreading trees.

Guards repeated the captain's instructions in Hindi, Tamil, and Telegu. "Prepare to leave ship!"

Crew members worked feverishly. By means of a simple lifting tackle from the main mast, they launched two dinghies and, with guards on board, paddled with quick strokes toward shore. In no time, the crew returned with ten boats, each manned by two shirtless men whose dark skin and short, curly hair captured Raja's attention.

Shankar stared wide-eyed at the men. "People from Africa!" he exclaimed.

"From wh-where?" Raja had never seen people, so different from his countrymen, except for the few Chinese in Calcutta, and the British who ruled his country. He focused his eyes on the men's muscles, rippling with each pull of the paddle, and marvelled at their sheer power.

Together with Ramdas and Shankar, he squeezed into one of the vessels. The boatmen greeted the party with huge grins, and one of them uttered a few words in a slow singsong accent. "Coolie babu! Massa goin' break your back. We finished with that long time, man."

Raja's head hung low. He frowned when Shankar translated for him. "It looks like we'll become slaves," he said with a groan.

Shankar's face tightened. He lifted his shoulders and extended his palms. "It was my choice. I only hope I can survive."

One look at Shankar's frail physique, and Raja couldn't agree more.

The two African men dropped the group off at a small, barnacle-infested wharf surrounded by floating red seaweed, crabs, and snails. Raja stumbled off the boat, and like an animal that had been freed from a cage, he hobbled around. Just the touch of the hot, gritty sand under his feet gave him comfort.

Under the watchful eyes of a guard, the young men sat on driftwood by the water's edge and waited for the others to reach shore.

Shankar, who had been busy chewing the last of his paan, spat a blob of red-stained residue onto the sand. It quickly got sucked up and formed ruby-like crystals.

Raja crossed his arms over his chest and looked toward the sea. He lowered his head onto his palms and took loud, deep breaths. Images of Savitri, his old parents, and Baran appeared before his eyes. *If only they were here with me, life would be bearable.*

A soft breeze caressed his face and rustled the limbs of a tamarind tree. Nearby, black vultures alighted in the crook of a coconut frond. Long-horned humpless cattle grazed in the company of white egrets in pastures drained by sluice gates. Boys with long sticks tended them giving Raja the impression that cows were not held with the same reverence as in his native land.

Barefoot stevedores in patched trousers pushed handcarts filled with sacks of potatoes, onions, flour, cloth, and iron tools—some sticking out—that had been offloaded from ships. White women and their top-hatted men in twirled moustaches travelled along in buggies driven by black men wearing what appeared to be shabby, hand-me-down clothes. As in Calcutta, white men in jodhpurs rode by at a canter.

Guards in shiny khaki uniforms herded the Indians to an enclosure barricaded by staves made from coconut fronds, interwoven in and out of barbed wire. The foul smell from pockets of water trapped with rotten seaweed made Raja pinch his nostrils. It reminded him of the Calcutta swamp that could have been his graveyard.

On firm land, he threw himself onto the ground and massaged his leg muscles. Free of leg cramps, he announced, "Let's shift these staves. We need to see what is going on outside." Despite a sharp pain in his back, he managed to create a gap. This gave him a view of Georgetown as it stretched away from the Atlantic Ocean.

Several canals choked with duckweed and giant water lilies intersected the city. Tiny stalls selling imported goods lined the street close to the river while, in the distance, two-storey houses with open verandas and louvered wooden shutters gave way to zinc shacks where dark-skinned children played.

"A guard is coming," Shankar whispered.

Quickly, Raja tried to replace the staves but the guard was upon him. Raja grabbed his stick before it landed. A whistle brought the clippity-clop of a horse.

A young gentleman with black moustache and white pith helmet arrived on the scene atop a grey mare, ahead of a couple of other guards, who backed off.

"I am James Crosby, Immigration Agent-General of the colony," he said to Raja in understandable Hindi. "What's the problem?"

Raja waved his hand and pointed at the guards. "These men treat us like bullocks to be whipped."

"I can see that," Crosby said.

"Mr. Crosby, they have taken me away from my family and brought me here against my will."

Crosby's eyes widened. "Do you want me to lodge a complaint on your behalf?"

"That will make me happy." Raja gritted his teeth. "You see, sir, my wife and parents wait for me, not knowing my whereabouts."

"I'm sorry." Mr. Crosby lifted Raja's tag and unfolded a few sheets of paper. "Ah, Roger, Number 198."

"My name is Raja, sir."

What Crosby scribbled into his notebook while he listened to the various stories, Raja could only guess.

As the day progressed, Raja looked on with curiosity at the brisk horse-trading between two rival companies for the Indians. Shankar's words were beginning to make sense.

An official rang a bell. "Guards, take note." He pointed to a spot under a palm tree.

"All coolies for Davis Sugar Estates, gather over there," he shouted.

"Coolies for Jones Brothers, next to this post," another yelled, clanging his bell.

The officials lined up the immigrants and mixed and matched them. Curious to know the role of a group of Indian officials and the guards working with the white men, Raja turned to Shankar, who befriended a messenger attached to one of the officials. Within minutes, Shankar made a beeline back to the group. "The Indian officials work for the Immigration Department. They're helping to choose each person's sugar plantation."

"How are they able to do that?" Raja asked.

"With our emigration passes." Shankar stopped to catch his breath. "You remember in Calcutta when an official entered each person's name, caste, and village on a document? They will use those to separate husband and wife, friends, and people from the same village."

Raja stared at his fellow Indians. "Tut-tut!"

"Like they did in India, like they did with the slaves—the old divide-and-rule policy," Shankar said. "Now we can never speak our dialect and unite against the ruler."

Raja lifted his palms in frustration, assuming there was some truth in Shankar's rantings. "There goes our language." *How wrong could the Protector of Emigrants be?*

A loud whistle blew forcing the three companions to listen to instructions.

"I'll take this brother, and you can have the other," a manager said.

Raja sidled up to Ramdas, who had been placed in the Davis group of sugar estates, hoping they would be able to work together.

A manager decided otherwise. He examined Raja's tag. "Roger!" he shouted, "you're with Jones Brothers. Move over there, boy!" He shoved Raja in the other direction.

He almost fell over and his face contorted. "My name is Raja, and I'm a grown man!" he shouted right back at the manager, proud that he had the gall to stand up to him.

The manager stared at him in shock. "Guard, let this coolie know his place."

The guard raised his baton, but Crosby extended his riding crop and stopped him from striking.

"He wants to be called by his correct name and be treated as a man."

Wagging his finger at Crosby, the manager said, "We didn't spend a fortune in sterling to bring the coolies here to show them respect."

"They're not slaves."

"Mr. Crosby, coolies are not much different. Whose side are you on, anyway?"

Crosby's eyes narrowed, and his forehead wrinkled. "I'm here to see that the Indians get fair treatment—and they're not coolies."

"Really?"

Crosby shook his head. "Sir, I hope you appreciate my position regarding the interests of the sugar planters as well my role as a representative of Her Majesty's Government. Unlike the former slaves, indentured labourers are contract workers."

"Very well, Mr. Crosby. I shall apprise Governor Hincks about your concerns. Good day, sir."

A guard yelled out, "Roger! Shankar! Come over here!"

Ramdas clasped his hands together and bowed to Shankar, then turned to Raja and hugged him. "Farewell, jahaji bhai."

"I hope we meet again," Raja said.

Guards with batons marched a batch of forty Indians, including Raja, Shankar, and Jasmine, to a shell beach. Among them were crying babies and a few children who had become quite restless. They ran to play with the shells and bottles that lay scattered on the sand. Before too long, the sentries hustled them back to be with their parents.

Raja and Shankar looked on with interest as the local guards passed out cold slices of a pale-yellow boiled vegetable they called breadfruit.

Raja bit into a slice. "The taste is like a cross between a roti and a potato," he exclaimed, laughing.

"Slaves in Jamaica refused to eat this food," Shankar said, "because they had never seen it in Africa."

To Raja's surprise, the Madras Indians ate the food with gusto and washed every scrap down with water.

Under a full moon and the watchful eyes of the guards, the Indians had just spread out their cotton sheets and prepared to bed down on the beach when Jasmine announced, "How many of you will join me in a dance?" She turned to whoever would listen and then locked eyes with Raja. "This is our first night in this country."

"I am in no mood to dance," Raja said.

Another man, with a wobble of the head, said, "Arrival in this strange land is a dark day for me to celebrate. Besides, I am still weak."

"Better to dance than cry," Jasmine said. "Life must go on."

"Yes," a number of men said half-heartedly. "Let this sad day be one to remember."

Most of the women took part in the classical Indian dance known as the kathak. In the end, Raja lent his support. He snapped his fingers and made a clicking noise with his tongue. He pictured Jasmine's slender hips swaying beneath her floral frock, while her bare feet created a rhythm on the sand. And what better place than under the moonlight, where her body movements and facial expressions of sorrow and anger told a story.

The solemn performance went on far into the night, as one dance led to another. In the end, Jasmine, joined by other women, closed the evening with a Bengali song and dance of longing and separation from one's country. Just before she slipped away, Raja caught her. "I don't understand why your parents let you become a dancer."

She regained her breath and whispered, "My mother died when I was a baby, and my father had no work." She smacked a mosquito that had lit on her forehead. "So he took me to the temple, where I worked my way up to be lead dancer at the bazaar." To Raja's shake of the head, she added, "Dancing kept us one step away from hunger. I was not one of those wild types, if that is what you think."

"Not at all," Raja said, attempting a smile. "I guess you might want to settle down in this country."

"If they give me work, and I find a kind and gentle man, sure! If you really want to know, I would prefer the life of a simple farmer's wife to that of a dancer."

Since Raja was married, he excluded himself as a suitable partner for Jasmine. That night in a dream he saw Savitri struggling behind the plough. Relief came only when the morning sun had hit his face.

He brushed away the cobwebs of sleep and looked around. Birdsong filled the air. Perched on a nearby tamarind tree, the bird pushed its yellow breast outwards, pulled in its white-banded head and sang, "Kiss-kiss-kiss-kiskadee." Its soothing and spirited melody was something the koel—the Indian nightingale—could never match. *Is this bird trying to charm me? Will I ever find true happiness in Demerara?*

Raja and Shankar trudged through a bushy shrub topped with clusters of yellow flowers, past cattail sedges and fragrant frangipanis toward the riverbank. They waded into the silty water, scrubbed their hands and faces, and gargled. That's when a guard pointed at a shrub with red berries.

"Break off a twig from that wild black sage over there," he said. "Chew the end of a piece and make a brush to scrub your teeth."

Raja relished the pleasant taste of the shrub and found it to be as good a neem.

The aroma from two huge pots of dal and rice caused his saliva to flow. Not at all satisfied with the small portion of food being served, he looked around and pointed. "Over there in the bushes," he said to

Shankar, "I see a green leafy vegetable, and if it's good for a caterpillar, it's good for me." He trotted over and gathered a handful of the leaves, passing some to Shankar and using the rest to garnish his dal.

Guards and armed overseers on mules hustled the Indians down a gravel path that led to a main road. Ahead, a train with ten red carriages hooked to a black locomotive was puffing smoke.

The Georgetown Railway Station, a narrow wooden structure with a steep gable roof and a central peak, stood out among cords of four-foot logs stacked beside the track. Outside the station, people carried on their heads flour or jute sacks filled with their wares. Inside, local African men and women in small groups gawked at the newcomers, as they lined up to board the train.

Comfortable in his seat by the window, Raja gazed at the wisps of grey-black smoke, which curled and drifted into the air. The locomotive chugged along its journey, stopping at the Plaisance and Belfield platforms to pick up and let off passengers. The trees and shrubs were so green and lush in the bright sunshine, Raja figured that no one should ever starve in this country.

As the train picked up speed again, plantain and banana plants, wattle-and-daub huts supported by posts with smoke floating above the thatched roofs flashed by. The clickety-clack of the train wheels caused Raja to doze.

However, it was not for long. The steam whistle blew to signal that the train had reached its destination. Raja jumped up. Memories of his first train ride came back to him. He couldn't help but wonder how a journey that had started out as a pilgrimage could have brought him to such a strange place.

The attendant announced, "Plantation Sugar Grove."

Raja's heart sank as he trailed behind the group headed for the sugar plantation. He gestured toward the two-storey, white wooden mansion, sheltered by tropical needle-leaf trees some fifty yards from the road.

"That most likely is the Big House, where the manager lives," Shankar said.

"How do you know?"

"From reading the *Narrative of the Life of Frederick Douglass*. The slave, Douglass, who wrote that book, worked in a similar house."

"If a slave can write a book, then shame on me," Raja said.

"Don't worry, I will teach you."

Across a bridge, the smokestack of the sugar mill stood tall, and beside it sat huge piles of golden sugarcane stalks ready to be crushed. Raja inhaled the fragrance of sugarcane juice. *So sweet, yet it comes from the sweat of slaves and coolies.*

He was taken aback at the vast area of barren land where narrow, straight lanes criss-crossed at every corner. Beside these lanes, blocks of rundown shacks interconnected in several long lines. They stood on hard, barren ground—no trees, shrubs, or grasses, no welcoming kiskadee. It was as though an army of insects had invaded the settlement and had chewed everything in its path.

Raja closed his eyes for a moment, finding it hard to accept. The "real paradise" had turned into a wasteland on a scale he could never have imagined, the song of the koel only a distant memory.

Despite the desolation, barefoot girls played hopscotch using a mango seed in the middle of a lane. Nearby, boys played a bat-and-ball type of game in which a long stick hit a shorter stick. As a boy, Raja had almost lost an eye in such a game.

Some boys shouted, "India babu!" when Raja walked by. He couldn't make out much more.

He turned to Shankar. "Those lines of joined-up shacks all look the same. How will you know one from another?"

"It suits me fine," Shankar said.

A lopsided grin spread across Raja's face. *So that's the reason why Shankar left India: to get lost away in a far-off country without having to pay for travel.* Raja exclaimed, "My mud house in Belwasa would look like a mansion next to one of these cow sheds."

"Early slave barracks, I'm sure."

"But now coolie shacks."

"They are called logies," a guard chimed in.

Raja counted ten openings for each range of units. Men, women, and families were in separate sections, Jasmine's unit poised at the edge of the female section. Raja was looking around for the men's set of units when he realized that he must answer nature's call. "Latrine!" he yelled.

"Over there. That row is for women!" a guard shouted. "The men's is the next one. Your friend will bring you a jug of water."

Raja barely made it to the string of latrines connected to one another like the huts. The side-by-side cubicles had no doors. He squatted over a long slit on the floor. His feces dropped into an irrigation canal where scavenger fish, raising their open mouths above the water, vied for the "treat." In India, his family preferred the fields next to the river.

In exchange for his tin ticket, Raja received a one-room logie. At the entrance, he made a grab for the door jamb but ended up with a fistful of wood dust and termites.

Like the other units, the outer walls of Raja's lean-to were made of boards and shingles, the roof thatched with palm leaves intermixed with zinc sheets.

He sniffed at the smooth cow dung under his bare feet and scoffed at the cracked clay plaster, covered by old newspapers, which lined the inner walls. Pictures of the Hindu god, Shiva, and his wife Parvati adorned one wall.

Raja's only furniture was a rope bed similar to the one he had in his mud house. An inner zinc sheet attached to the ceiling would keep most of the rain away while he slept. A jute bag on the glazed mud floor acted as a mat and stood ready to absorb any water that would make its way through the thatched roof.

"Make sure your provisions last you the entire month," the guard said.

Raja looked at his meagre allotment and shook his head. It consisted of crude sugar, rice, coconut oil, weevil-infested wheat flour, dal, and a mixture of ground spices.

Night was upon him when he went outside to gather scraps of firewood from the rear of his unit. No sooner had he stepped outside than it started to pour. He rushed back in and had the presence of mind to place his bucket on the jute mat to collect the water that dripped through the roof.

Thunder rumbled and flashes of lightning streaked the black sky. The wet wood made it impossible to start a fire for cooking. Fatigue had set in anyway and he collapsed on the rope bed. The sound of raindrops bearing down on the zinc sheets lulled him to sleep.

Before dawn the next morning, he woke to the sound of a bell. What was in store for him, he had no idea.

CHAPTER NINE

After his morning ablutions, Raja met the rest of workers at a clearing. A man, with a translator beside him, brandishing a cane knife addressed the workers, "From now on, you call dis machete a cutlass. Use it like a weapon to attack de sugarcane." He handed out a cutlass and file to each worker. "Watch how to keep your cutlass sharp." He demonstrated the way to hold the cutlass at the correct angle and proceeded to run a file back and forth along the blade until it gleamed. Each of the men picked up his cutlass and file and did the same. "Now go prepare a quick breakfast and meet me here," he said.

With the wood now dry, Raja managed to light a fire in the built-in mud stove at the rear of his unit. He prepared a meal of rice and dal, all spiced up for himself and Shankar who lived nearby.

"Now I will not starve," Shankar said as he licked his fingers clean.

"Your turn to cook for me will come," Raja said. "Let's hurry for we don't want to be late the first day."

They picked up their cutlasses and joined the group headed for the cane field.

High above the thick stands of sugarcane, the clouds floated like giant fluffs of cotton balls. Over the thump-thump of his heart, Raja listened to the slapping of bare feet on the narrow trail. A soft breeze caressed his face, reminding him of Belwasa, where at dawn he would have been treated to bird song.

Hardly had Raja arrived at the field when he found himself facing the man in charge of the gang of workers.

"Me, Driver Mathusamy," the man said, again with the aid of a translator. "Call me Driver Mathu."

Raja repeated the words and only realized later that Mathu was the man's name.

"Keep your eyes open. I will show you how to pull out weed. Use de cutlass to dig out de root, not just chop it." Mathu dug around the roots of weeds growing between the rows of cane. "Pull de weed out and pile dem up so we can burn dem later. And one ting, you must be on de move all de time."

The translator advised the men to start learning the local lingo if they wanted to avoid the lash. Raja made good progress and only turned to Shankar for help when he was in doubt.

After a long shift in the hot sun, Raja's legs became unsteady. He was about to collapse when a boy no more than ten brought him a gourd filled with water. Raja quenched his thirst and poured the rest over his head. The work was demanding, but he was grateful to be out in the sun and fresh air instead of in the dark hold of a ship.

Into his second week of work, Mathu tapped Raja on the back. "Don't you like to pull out weed?"

"Yes, babu," Raja answered, hoping that would get the driver to stop looking over his shoulder.

"Den use dat cutlass faster."

Four weeks into the punishing work of keeping on top of the fast-growing weeds, Raja understood why his father's back always hurt.

In the predawn darkness one day, Mathu, now brandishing a slender tamarind rod, met the workers at a crosswalk.

Raja took a deep breath; his body tensed. He bared his teeth and resisted the urge to make a grab for the rod. He was not an ox to be beaten.

Mathu relieved a worker of his cutlass. "Today I'm going to show you how we cut cane," he said to the men. He held the cane stalk with one hand and slashed at its base with a single chop. "Now, get started."

Raja's back ached, the result of the many months at sea and the constant bending during the previous weeks. As a result, he chopped a few stalks high above ground level.

"Not like dat, Roger."

Whack! The rod landed on Raja's back.

Stunned, he dropped his cutlass due to the pain that shot through him like a lightning bolt. He clenched his fists, shaking his head in a frenzy to withstand the sting. Irritated further by being called Roger, he head-butted Mathu and sent him crashing several yards into the cane field. That knocked the wind out of Mathu and he lay prostrate on the ground gasping for breath. After he'd recovered, Mathu dusted himself off and limped away without a word.

If Raja believed he could get away with such behaviour, he was in for a surprise, for Mathu returned with five sturdy-looking men carrying whips.

In an instant, they seized Raja, tied his hands behind his back with vine and took turns dropping lashes over his body. They laughed when he winced and groaned. By the time the whipping ended, he'd already collapsed among the cane stalks, his face buried in the dirt. More than anything else, he loved the smell of the earth after a rain, but on this occasion it stunk like rotten fruit.

Mathu walked up to Raja, who now rested on one knee and struggled to get up. Mathu put his face next to Raja's. "Next time, I will inform de overseer. He could add years to your term. You might be grey by de time you get out of your indentureship."

Back on his feet, Raja smelled his own blood as he spat out the dirt. Now he understood what the bullocks must endure and what the word "driver" meant. If he wanted to return to his homeland, he would have to control himself and not lay his hand on a driver again. He had no choice but to cut the cane the way the driver wanted.

What bothered Raja even more was that Mathu seemed to enjoy beating the men under his control. In conversation with a senior worker, Raja asked, "Why is Driver Mathu so brutal with the workers?"

"A person who has been abused will do the same to people under him."

"Was Mathu abused?"

"I heard he came with the first ship that brought Indians to the colony. They were treated like slaves."

"So the stick that was used to beat the slave is now used on the coolie."

"I couldn't agree more," the senior worker said.

Raja, with the words, "Massa goin' break your back," ringing in his ears, faced the senior worker. "Before that slave driver, Mathu, breaks my back, I will tear his limbs apart."

The man shook his head. "The stipendiary magistrate will lock you up. They are under the thumbs of the sugar planters."

Raja soon realized that the forces that had seized him in India were similar to the ones that drove him like an animal in this country. How could he blame Shankar for talking like a rebel?

Raja kept a close watch on his friend who, with his small frame, was constantly on the receiving end of Mathu's stick. Lash after lash sliced into Shankar's back.

"You are not cutting enough cane," Mathu said, punctuating his words with blows.

At times, the whipping got so bad the blood soaked through Shankar's shirt. That's when Raja would clench his jaws and resist the urge to go after Mathu. Under his breath, he said one day, "That's enough you musahar."

Raja's voice must have carried, for the driver scowled. "You refer to me as belonging to de rat-eating, landless community of India?"

With a flick of his whip, Mathu hit Raja. His arm swelled up and became purple.

"Driver," Raja said. "In India, lower castes like you would have been clearing lands of weeds and rats, not whipping a high-caste man like me."

"Oh yes! I will knock de Kshatriya out of you and your skinny friend. In dis country, de Singh name is not'ing. You hear? Not'ing. Don't forget what you upper castes have been doing to our people for thousands of years."

Raja reflected on what Mathu had just said. Ramdas had used more or less the same words. In his heart, Raja knew that a man should not be judged from birth for what he had no control over.

"You're right, Driver Mathu. I'm sorry about the name calling," Raja said. "But I lost my temper when I saw you whip my friend."

Mathu hesitated, and for a moment it seemed as if Raja had evoked some sympathy from the driver.

"We have a quota to fill," Mathu said. "Overseer expects me to whip anyone who falls behind, so don't tell me how to do de white man job."

On the two-mile journey home that evening, Raja asked Shankar, "Is slavery not over?"

"It never ended, my friend, and indentureship is slavery by another name."

"Hmm! But Mathu is one of us."

Shankar feigned laughter. "Can't you see through it? The planters are deliberately using Madrasi and African drivers to break both the caste system and our backs at the same time."

"Especially yours."

"It was my choice to come to this colony."

Puzzled by those words, Raja said, "I still can't understand why you spoke ill about our rulers in the old country but tolerate the cruelty of planters over here."

Shankar's forehead crinkled. He stroked his beard and turned to face Raja with a smug look on his face. "Would you join me in an armed struggle against an unjust system?" Shankar leaned closer to hear Raja's response.

"This is not India," Raja replied. "How can coolies armed with cutlasses rise up against their masters?"

"Therefore I cannot count on you."

"It would jeopardize my return trip." Shankar slowed his pace and appeared to consider what Raja had just said. "Violence breeds violence," Raja continued, "so we should try other ways to achieve our purpose."

"Like writing a book to show that slavery never ended."

"For a start, why don't you scribble a few lines to my wife? Tell her that I'll return in five years' time."

"Find me a quill pen, ink, paper, and an envelope, and I'll write your letter. Let me know when you've got everything together."

Raja knew Shankar would never accept money from him, so he advised, "You could make money writing and reading letters for other people, Shankar."

"How do you think I was able to pay my university fees?" Shankar looked at Raja. "I had a stall next to the post office in between classes. Even prostitutes posing as house cleaners sent letters home through me. I never charged them much."

"Why not?"

"It was difficult to take their money when I heard some of their stories."

Week after week went by, and Raja had little time to think of letter writing. A skilled cane cutter working by his side set a fast pace all day. He wouldn't want to be facing that man in a fencing match, so sharp was the edge of his cutlass.

It didn't take Raja long to find out why he was being pushed to the limit.

"Driver Mathu says you are a big man and must take up the slack for your scrawny friend," the worker said. "He wants you to cut and load up one punt per day."

Raja surveyed the row upon row of burnt sugarcane stalks. "It will take plenty of cane to fill that punt, babu."

The man rubbed his fingers on Raja's cutlass. He shook his head. "With a sharper blade, you will cut twice the amount of cane than you do presently."

So far, Raja had been a reluctant worker for the plantation masters. He had not found the time to sharpen his cutlass the way he was told to do on his first working day. At home that evening, he filed his cutlass so that it looked more like the "weapon" it was meant to be. He protected the edge of the blade with a cloth.

A born farmer, he understood why the cane had to be harvested quickly. Wet weather could bring mildew and ruin the crop. Now he would prevent that from happening and, at the same time, take pride in his work. It would make his five-year term so much shorter.

On Mathu's weekly inspection of Raja's work, he said, "For de next couple week, you get two-three extra ounce dal. For dat you mus cut an even bigger section of cane."

Raja swore under his breath. He had expected a pat on the back for his extra effort. "A few extra mouthfuls of dal would mean nothing to a dead man."

The driver either did not hear or chose to ignore those words.

Early one morning the following week, as Raja lay half-asleep, a bell sounded, followed by a voice announcing, "Wake up. We leave in one hour."

Raja jumped out of bed. The eastern sky was all tinged with red and gold. After a light breakfast of a chapati dipped in dal, he prepared a lunch of curried eggplant and rice. With his cutlass, and his lunch pail warm against his leg, he set out for the field.

At an intersection, he met his driver and a group of other workers. Just a couple of steps behind the leader, Raja walked along the narrow, winding path bordered by crabgrass. A snake with grey-brown diamond-shaped patterns prominent on its back sprang out from the grass. Twice the length of a cutlass, it pounced at the lead man, seizing his ankle with its long fangs. The man fell to the ground. Raja rushed forward and, using the blunt side of his cutlass, struck the snake with a swift blow to the head. Wounded, it slithered away through the bushes.

Everyone formed a circle around the man, who moaned in pain.

Mathu ripped his cloth belt down the middle and bandaged the leg above and below the wound. "Would anyone volunteer to suck de venom to save dis man's life?" He looked at Raja. "You can spit de poison out after."

Raja put little faith in what he'd just heard and was quite honest when he said, "I bite my lip from habit so I cannot do what you ask."

"Let's not waste time. I cannot afford to lose a worker." The driver took Raja's cutlass and lunch pail and handed them to Shankar. He turned to Raja and yelled, "Rush dis man to de clinic! Tell Doc he got bitten by a labaria."

Raja hoisted the man onto his shoulders and trundled along the path that led to the estate clinic, a whitewashed wooden hut, a mile away.

"Don't let me die!" the man cried out.

As his breathing became faster and shallower, Raja increased his pace. "Hold on! I will get you help."

Almost out of breath, Raja climbed the stairs of the clinic and laid the victim out on the table, all the while repeating, "labaria, labaria."

"I'll get Doc," an attendant shouted as he ran off to find Doc, the dispenser on duty.

A strong carbolic acid smell soon announced the presence of Doc, who rushed in wearing a white coat. Raja waved his hand about and jabbed the air several times to describe the snake, the name of which he had forgotten.

Doc showed Raja three stuffed specimens.

"This one!" Raja exclaimed.

Doc shouted, "Labaria!" and quickly went about trying to save the victim's life.

Raja trotted back to the cane field hoping for the best. He took the lead the following morning, the others too afraid to walk the same route, especially since the victim had died.

The next Saturday after work, Mathu said to Raja, "Go and line up at de payroll office for your first weekly payment."

"What about the other weeks?"

"During dat period, we gave you free provisions and taught you how to cut cane."

"But I've cut cane all my life."

Mathu looked hard at Raja. "Not our way. Look, if you want your pay, you better line up at de payroll office."

Raja walked past lush, green vegetation where swarms of butterflies flitted among the golden flowers, and iridescent green hummingbirds, their wings whirring in his ears, awaited their turn.

After he'd collected his shilling, twenty-four cents, for the six-day workweek, he asked, "Can you give me paper and whatever is needed for this letter-writing business?" The clerk nodded, and Raja continued, "Break up this shilling and take whatever it costs."

The clerk kept two cents and handed Raja paper, envelope, a one-cent stamp, pen and ink.

Raja rubbed his finger against the sharp point of the quill and held up the bottle of blue ink against the sun. He shook his head at the wonder of it all—how a simple pen dipped into a dark liquid could "talk" to someone far away. The mystery of that one-cent stamp baffled him, and he could hardly wait for Shankar to perform his magic.

Like a boy with a candy, Raja rushed over to Shankar and, panting for breath, said, "I have all you need to write my letter."

Shankar waved Raja away. "Keep it until we get home." He didn't appear very happy.

"So, how much have they paid you?" Raja asked.

"A few cents less than a shilling." Shankar pivoted his head from side to side. "Mathu should have given you extra for helping me."

Jasmine now joined them. "Maybe they want us to pluck money from the money bush over there," she said with a forced laugh. She had lined up behind Raja. "I received only half a shilling."

With a sly grin, Raja said, "Ha! All you did was throw ashes on cane roots and hand-pick insects from cane leaves."

Jasmine stared at Raja. "Don't I also need to eat?"

"Sure!" Raja patted the water-boy who was staring wide-eyed at his few pennies. "And so does this little fellow."

That evening, Raja invited Shankar over to his unit. He dictated a brief letter to Savitri. It included a love verse that Raja had composed with Shankar's help:

Each day I love you more
While here I pine on another shore.
Though a thousand miles between us lie,
My love for you will never die.

And while drowsy Nature slumbers still,
And morning dawns o'er yonder hill
Fare thee well my darling, until.

"While at university," Shankar said, trying to look serious, "I translated Kalidasa's *Sakuntala* into English, and I can tell you the greatest Sanskrit poet would have been proud of this poem."

On Saturday, when Raja handed over the letter, the mulatto payroll clerk said, "Your letter writer friend is the only coolie on the estate who reads the *Royal Gazette*." The clerk placed the letter in the mailbag. "It will go out by horse and buggy on Monday morning."

While Raja was at the payroll office, he took the opportunity to find out a driver's wage.

The clerk grinned. "You must serve out your five-year indentureship before you think of promotion," he said. "A well-built bloke like you should try his hand at cricket. Take Mathu's son, Sonnyboy, the cricketer—he gets the same pay as me, and like you he doesn't know A from B."

"I've watched him head for the cane field, cut across to the jamun tree, and all morning hurl his cutlass at the trunk like some knife thrower."

"That's to strengthen his wrist so he can flick the cricket ball and give it that nip off the pitch. On top of that, his father gives him the afternoons off to prepare the pitch and outfield."

"So he gets paid just to play cricket while I break my back cutting cane." Raja shook his head and walked away. *I'd like to see for myself how good this player is that everyone talks about.*

Sunday afternoon came around and he said to Shankar, "Mathu's son is playing cricket today. Let's go watch the game."

Raja was pleasantly surprised to see Jasmine and her female friends sitting in the shade of the half-thatched spectators' stand. In her ankle-length red floral skirt, white bodice, and matching head-and-shoulder scarf, she appeared to be out "to catch a man."

"Look at Jasmine," Raja whispered to Shankar, "all dressed up in Western clothes and exposing her legs."

In the same breath, Raja placed a hand at the side of his mouth and threw his voice in her direction. "What are you doing here, Jasmine?"

"I came to cheer for Sonnyboy and our home team." She turned her gaze to the field. "There he goes!" Her voice rose to almost a shriek.

With a white silk kerchief draped high around his neck like a scarf, Sonnyboy led his team onto the field to loud cheers. His shiny, dark complexion contrasted with his cricket whites. His graceful left-arm bowling of leg cutters flicked over the wrist, and a change ball that turned the other way, were almost unplayable. He got the crowd fired up whenever he took a wicket, and he did so five times against a strong Plantation Providence team. The winning runs came with his lofted drive that sailed the ball over the long-on boundary for a huge six, which Jasmine greeted with hands high in the air.

"That's our Sonnyboy," she screamed.

I wish I had won the match for the home team instead of that show-off.

After the game, Sonnyboy, towering over his admirers, mingled with the other cricketers. The man looked over and flashed a toothy grin at Jasmine, who said, "What a shot!"

He walked up and whispered in her ear. Whatever it was he said, she burst out laughing.

"He's just a showman who performs for the women," Raja said to Shankar. "Be a star player, and you can have the most beautiful girl on the estate."

Shankar patted Raja on the back. "Don't be jealous. Let Sonnyboy have his day."

Several weeks went by until one evening, Raja and Jasmine happened to dip their pails into the creek at the same time. Jasmine lifted her pail onto her padded head while Raja carried his in his hand. An image of Savitri going to the river and carrying a bucket of water on her head came to him.

On the way home, Jasmine said, "Carrying the bucket by hand causes much of the water to spill. Let me help you."

She headed for his logie with her pail of water and by the time the barrel was filled, it had gotten dark.

Not knowing how to show his appreciation, Raja said, "Please take a chapati with you."

She looked at the bread. "It smells good. However, I only entered your hut to give you a hand."

Raja decided that it was a good opportunity to warn Jasmine about Sonnyboy. Raja's breathing got faster, and he blurted out, "What do you think of Sonnyboy?"

"Well, he won the game for our team."

"Just be careful, Jasmine."

"Other than his cricket performances, he is of no interest to me."

She bade Raja goodnight. Her words gave him the comfort he needed, but they did not calm his thudding heart nor curb his distrust of the man.

That night the rains came down. They fell for days on end and continued into the New Year. The dikes around the living quarters broke. The creeks overflowed. Floodwaters, mixed with the spillover from the latrines, seeped into the logies. There was rain, rain, and more rain. The water kept rising. It was no different from monsoon season in Bihar.

Another evening Raja found an alligator lurking outside his logie. That sent him scurrying in ankle-deep water to the estate clinic, which was on higher ground. There he found many of the workers occupying all the beds and suffering from vomiting and diarrhea. In a panic, he looked around and saw Shankar beside the office looking up from a newspaper. Paper in hand, he walked over to Raja. "I brought my neighbour to the dispensary," he said. "The *Royal Gazette* headline says there's a typhoid epidemic at several sugar plantations in the colony, including ours."

Shankar had become privy to private information and Raja was happy to have him as a friend. "What should we do to stay healthy?" Raja asked.

"Same as we did on our ship, when proper hygiene made a difference."

Eight people at the estate died of typhoid, and many were isolated at the sick house. Doc and the nurse worked overtime.

Many days later the rain stopped, leaving a trail of fear approaching hysteria. Through the turmoil, Overseer Van Sluytman called for a meeting of his few healthy workers. Raja and Shankar were among those who showed up.

The overseer addressed a man who stood beside him. "Kwame, everything is in your hands, boy."

Driver Kwame, a man of medium height, balding, and of dark complexion, had a stone-like facial expression. His weather-beaten felt hat covered most of his matted, curly hair. A khaki drill shirt and shorts showed off his muscular build. Like the labourers, he was barefoot.

"Kwame is going to be your driver," Van Sluytman said to the group. He turned to Kwame. "I expect you to get the same amount of work done with these men. Do whatever you have to do to get the cane to the factory before mildew sets in."

Kwame shook his head as his eyes went over the few men and two women still standing. "Not enough workers, sir."

"That's all we have," Van Sluytman said. "Drive them hard. I told you to carry a tamarind whip like Mathu."

Early next morning, Raja and the remaining workers walked along the earth-filled dike that bordered the canal. Despite the torrential rains, it kept the floodwaters away from the sugarcane crops. Obviously, the management had made that a priority.

Raja, who had prepared himself for the worst, couldn't believe his eyes when he saw that Kwame still carried no rod. After he had set the men their tasks, he borrowed Shankar's cutlass and worked alongside Raja. Between them, they did the work of the missing men.

One day as Raja and Kwame headed for a log to sit on and take a much-needed rest, Raja saw a labaria snake come within striking distance of Kwame. Raja swung his cutlass at its head. The wounded snake darted away.

Kwame, who was still shaking, turned to Raja and said, "I should have been more wary. Floods always bring the snakes out. They're on the hunt for rats."

"Rat-catchers and mongooses take care of this problem for us in India," Raja said, rubbing the bloodstain off his cutlass with a leaf.

Kwame grasped Raja's shoulders. "You saved my life. I'm forever in your debt."

"You owe me nothing," Raja said.

"It's the African way to never forget."

Raja embraced Kwame, believing that this moment would be the start of a long and deep relationship with someone so different. For Raja, this friendship took on added importance because of the loss of his family and friends back home.

At the end of the workday, after Raja had picked up his lunch pail, Kwame said, "You and Shankar come over to my bush house tomorrow before it gets dark."

Upon hearing that Raja would be visiting Kwame, a worker asked, "Why do you go to the house of an African? He believes in massacouraman, that half-human creature, said to live in water and on land."

Surprised that one of his countrymen would judge Kwame by his beliefs and the fact that he was not Indian, Raja became annoyed. "He is a much better friend to me than any of you."

In the twilight hours, Raja and Shankar set out for Kwame's bush house. Raja's muscles still ached from the hard day's work, and the good half-hour walk to get to Kwame's house did not help. Upon arrival, the rich aroma of Kwame's cooking, and the sounds of chirping crickets, croaking frogs, and sparrows greeted him.

Kwame's house blended with the trees and plants. The solitude, despite the strange animal sounds, so enchanted and charmed Raja, he could only gasp. To live so close to nature, far away from his fellow man, made Kwame very special to Raja.

"Kwame!" he called out. "Kwame!"

At the second shout, Kwame ambled out to greet his guests. He led them to his hut in a roundabout way.

One particular tree caught Raja's attention. He dipped his finger into a blob of the milky, rubbery gum that oozed from its trunk. It had no taste.

"This is the balata tree," Kwame said. "All those chops you see are spots where Sonnyboy bled balata to make cricket balls."

"So that's another reason for his good bowling."

Kwame shook his head. "He used to practise for hours bowling all sizes of balls, which he made from the gum of this very tree."

"I just don't take to the man."

"He is the son of a driver, so I'd stay clear of that one."

Raja reached up to examine the roof. "I could use this type of weave on my roof."

"An Arawak worker thatched it for me using branches of the ite palm."

Shankar, who had been quiet up to that point, asked, "And what is the name of that large, spreading tree?"

"I'm glad you asked," Kwame said. "It's the silk cotton but many people call it jumbie tree. Avoid it after dark if you want to stay clear of jumbies."

Raja smiled since he'd been forewarned about Kwame's strange beliefs in ghosts and other strange creatures.

Kwame led Raja and Shankar through a swinging door that opened onto a living space. Like Raja's hut, it combined with the kitchen and sleeping area. In one corner sat a wooden bench.

"Living by yourself must be lonely, Kwame," Raja said as he and Shankar sat down.

"Not when you have your friends to keep you company. Watch out! Olu is coming."

Kwame's pet monkey leapt onto Raja's shoulder. He looked like a boy with a mask around his eyes.

Shankar made faces at the monkey. He laughed when the monkey did the same. "Our monkeys are larger, Kwame," he said.

"That's a sakiwinki. White people call it a spider monkey," Kwame said. "See how friendly he is."

Shankar told Kwame that Hindus worship Hanuman, the monkey god. "Monkeys, like cows," he continued, "occupy a special place in our country. They roam freely in some towns and villages."

"Olu is very special, too, and acts like a son," Kwame said.

Kwame was in the cooking area when Raja heard, "Olu, you hungry?"

"Were you speaking to Olu?" Raja asked.

"That was my macaw imitating my voice and talking to the monkey," Kwame said, laughing. "To avoid loneliness, I sometimes speak to both of them."

Kwame added a piece of firewood to his mud stove. "There he comes. He's quite rough."

A large parrot, which Kwame called a macaw, with bright plumage of red, green, and blue, landed on Raja's forearm and chased the monkey away. "I love all birds," Raja said, "but this one is special; I have never set eyes on one so beautiful."

"There is one ugly bird you must stay away from," Kwame said. "Listen!"

In the distance came the cry, "Ooo-eeek, ooo-eeek."

"That is the jumbie bird. Don't ever let that black bird come near you. It will bring you bad luck."

If Kwame was right, Raja wouldn't want to be near any jumbie bird on a jumbie tree at night. "Who is this massacouraman you told the men about?" he asked.

Kwame told the story about Kofi, the great Ashanti warrior in the colony, who led an uprising of slaves against their former Dutch plantation owners. "In order to keep the slaves in line, a French manager for the Dutch told the slaves, 'If you escape, massacouraman will get you.'"

"Have you seen such a beast?" Shankar asked.

"No, but my father did," Kwame said, as he attended to his mud stove. In no time, he prepared bush tea for his guests. "My tea is a special blend of sweet-broom bush and lemon grass that I grow myself," Kwame said, as he placed white enamel cups in front of his guests.

Shankar turned the cups this way and that. "These cups belong in a home of the rich, Kwame."

"That is so. I used to serve Massa's guests in the Big House afternoon tea with these cups," Kwame said. "When Missus replaced the set, she gave these to me as a gift."

"Why did you leave an easy job to work in the hot sun?"

"My father was a house slave with privileges. As soon as I became a free man, I gave up that life to become a driver," Kwame said.

From a steaming pot, Kwame brought out eddoes, yams, and plantains boiled in coconut milk. He served the meal in calabash bowls. As if that were not enough, he handed them each a thin flatbread. "The Arawak man who became my friend made me a stack of these cassava breads. You can store them a long time."

Raja broke off a piece of the hard, white bread and dipped it into the soup. He wished for some hot spices to flavour the food. So as not to offend his host, he pretended to enjoy the meal. In between munching and sipping from a wooden spoon, Raja asked, "What is your friend's name?"

"I called him Ar'wak because I couldn't say his Arawak name. And much of what I know about the medicinal plants and trees growing in the bush I learned from Ar'wak."

"In my country, such plant remedies come from the sages who treat the mind, body, and soul as one," Raja said. He looked at Shankar, whose eyes seemed to light up. "If any of the three is unwell, the person will be sick," Raja continued.

"Our healers use ancient obeah," Kwame added, "a sort of folk magic, to invoke the powers of the spiritual world."

"You could make a living by practising bush medicine, Kwame," Raja said.

Kwame waved his hand. "I'll never do it for money." He looked serious when he continued, "Who knows, I may come begging one of you for a job some day."

"You won't get a job from me," Raja said, looking at Shankar. "I expect to serve out my indentureship and return to my country, unlike my good friend here."

Kwame arched his eyebrows at Raja. "Oh!" He now pointed at Raja's leg wound. "Then you must watch those cane leaves that can lacerate your skin."

Kwame went to work. He crushed up some bellyache leaves, warmed them over the fire and spread the green paste on a clean rag, which he tied over Raja's leg.

The soothing effect was instant, and Raja smiled. "Kwame, in many ways you are better than Doc."

During a lunch break, the following day, Kwame came over to meet with Raja. He walked Raja over to a plot that had previously been cleared of weeds. Raja rubbed his beard stubble in disbelief. The rains had undone his previous hard work, and the few women available for weeding couldn't cope with such an abundance of unwanted plants.

"After you complete your task, can you help the women?" Kwame said, giving Raja a sly look. "They tell me you're the best weed puller on the estate."

Raja smiled, for he could see through the flattery.

Later, Raja found himself in the company of several women, including Jasmine. He could not resist teasing her, "Now I should be paid more for helping you."

"No," she said. "You should be paid less for doing a woman's job."

They shared a laugh and stared at each other for a moment.

Raja joined the women in singing folk songs. No one seemed eager to quit when the factory whistle blew.

On the way home Kwame hailed Raja. "Better watch out. One woman in particular seems to have an eye for you."

"My wife waits for me. I must not start anything I can't finish."

"Why not? Many Indians find a woman here in the colony and settle down."

Raja remembered telling both Ramdas and Shankar on the ship that he would stay within his own culture and in the end return to his native land. Though Raja had a lot of respect for Kwame, his Indian customs kept him miles apart from his African friend. So Raja said, "Marriages are arranged in India and we are paired for life, Kwame."

"Five years is a long-long time to wait, man."

CHAPTER TEN

Plantation Sugar Grove, 1871

Well into his second year at the plantation, Raja had built up a reputation as their best cane cutter, always managing to cut enough cane and load up his punt before everyone else.

On completion of his task one day, he spotted Van Sluytman riding by on his mule.

"Get those mules to make more trips," Van Sluytman yelled to a mule-boy.

"Overseer, they cannot take more punishment," the mule-boy pleaded, "they will rebel."

The overseer swished his riding crop in the air. "Show them who's boss."

A chain of cane-filled, flat-bottomed wooden punts lay waiting in the canal. The mule-boy turned to the whip when one of the mules refused to be harnessed. It leaned back on its hind legs, raised its forelegs, snorted, and sped across the pasture straight for the woods.

"Go after that mule!" Van Sluytman shouted to Raja. "Don't return without it."

Raja raced after the mule but was no match for an animal that was a lot more surefooted on a surface dotted with hoof holes.

A grass cutter gazed at Raja sprinting through the open savannah, his white kurta flapping in the breeze. He asked, "Are you running from lashes, babu?"

"No. I'm after a mule. Did you see which way it went?"

The man gestured with his sickle. "It bolted into the bush over there."

Raja dashed headlong into the forest, jumping over rotten logs and landing once on a giant turtle. Snakes and wild animals were far from his mind, for he must find that mule before the sun disappeared from view.

It didn't take Raja long to realize that his search would be fruitless. So he chose a route that he hoped would get him out of the bush. He fumbled his way between the buttressed roots of mora trees whose foliage blocked the sun. The harder he tried, the more he found himself surrounded by mixed stands of trees. Darkness threatened to swallow him.

The sounds of "Ooo-eek, ooo-eeek" and "Who you?" startled him. A black bird with a mismatched parrot-like beak, perched on the limb of a silk cotton tree, was causing a racket. Its head feathers stuck straight out making it the ugliest bird he'd ever seen. *Could this be Kwame's jumbie bird?*

Raja shouted, "Go away!" but the bird only laughed at him before melting away into the forest, causing Raja's hair to stand on end as he wandered around in circles.

In times of difficulty, his mother had taught him the words of the "Gayatri Mantra."

"It will give you wisdom and courage," his mother had said. To rid himself of fear, he must address the lyrics to the Sun god, the Life Giver on Earth, if only the Hindu god would hear him in this far-away, unforgiving tropical jungle.

With nothing to lose, he recited the mantra, "Om bhur bhuva swaha, tat savitur varenyam," and intoned the proper incantation, AUM in its three sounds, which like the three sacred rivers, united as one and vibrated through the forest. Lo and behold! The vibrations created had entered his soul, his mind and his body right down to the earth.

His mother's image appeared before him. "God's protection is not on trust," she told him. "You must pray daily for all of His blessings."

Raja had accumulated God's graces on credit ever since he'd arrived in Demerara. Now he had a lot of catching up to do. A strong believer in the power of Brahma, he could sense a spirit watching over him as he lay stretched out on a bed of moss. And in the golden moonlight came a haunting "garr-cluck-cluck-cluck" call like that of a chicken that had just laid an egg. In the pale light, he made out its source, a screech owl at the edge of the forest. Its call kept sleep at bay.

"Shut up, owl!" he cried out. "Let me sleep. I've got a job to do on the morrow."

Worried that Mr. Van Sluytman might think that he had run away, he fell into fitful slumber and had the following dream:

Kwame covered for him that first day. After dinner, he rushed off to meet with Mr. Van Sluytman at his residence.

Kwame addressed the overseer with the demeanour of a child reporting to his father that he had lost a precious toy. He stated that his best worker, Raja, had gone missing.

The lanky overseer brought out his tobacco pouch, packed his pipe and lit up. He took several puffs and blew rings of smoke into his driver's face. The sweet scent of tobacco smothered Kwame, who broke out in a coughing spell.

Van Sluytman pointed his pipe stem straight at his driver. He told Kwame that he sent Raja into the woods to look for a mule and that Raja might have used the opportunity to escape. Gurgling noises, but no words, came from deep within Kwame's throat.

Van Sluytman's eyes shone like hot coals. He hailed three mule-boys, and together they rode toward the edge of the jungle until nightfall, when strange jungle sounds spooked the animals.

After a quick look around on foot, Van Sluytman abandoned the search.

When the sun finally woke Raja up, he was much relieved it was all a dream. However, he still had to confront the jungle and find water? Far off, several palm trees beckoned. He trudged headlong through tall grasses to a grove, where he discovered one particular tree shorter than the others and laden with what looked like plum-sized coconuts.

He clambered up the tree as best he could, but as he reached for the nuts, a monkey-sized animal, with a long, pink snout and pointed teeth, uttered a shriek. With several babies clinging to her pouch, she pounced. Startled, Raja lost his grip and fell on a blanket of wild daisies, and razor grass that ripped his dhoti in several places.

Undaunted, he climbed the tree a second time, only to discover that the mother, in its rush, had left one baby at the edge of a crown of fronds. Without disturbing the tiny animal, he picked a bunch of the tiny nuts. Their white succulent jelly provided barely a mouthful.

He skipped over sedges that sprouted from sloughs and headed in the direction of a distant roar of falling water. Seeds with burrs stuck to his clothing and left green splotches. Tracks from an odd-toed, hoofed animal contained water. With the aid of a hollow piece of grass, he sucked every drop out of the holes.

A crackling sound brought him back to reality. Vaguely, he made out the outlines of a dark, bearded figure. Piercing eyes stared at him from behind a balata tree. A long, hairy hand reached for the grey sap that oozed from its trunk. Before Raja could get out of the way, a ball of gum landed smack on his chest. It was like being struck by a cricket ball. Raja let out a sigh as the creature dashed away through a clump of swamp sedge. Was this the massacouraman Kwame had talked about?

A rainbow shimmered above the thunderous roar, causing him to quicken his pace. If only he could reach the source of the sound, he might get water. Surrounded by trees that dwarfed him, he had no choice but to spend his second night in the jungle on a bed of crabgrass.

The next morning, a deafening roar tugged him toward clouds of vapour that rose like smoke. Before long, he faced a fifteen-foot cataract, its water the colour of tea.

He could not take his eyes away from the falling water, and when he did, he walked headlong into trees that seemed to mock him. The wind spoke to him in garbled Bhojpuri and he responded in kind:

"Raja, you abandoned your wife and young brother, dishonoured your parents."

"No, no!"

"You deserted your friends. And you call yourself a Rajput? You've lost caste!"

He dragged himself below the falls and, with cupped hands, drank the cool, sweetish water. It eased his stomach pain, while all around the trees danced to a frightening tune.

"I'm a good man," he shouted. His empty words echoed through the trees.

"Ha-ha!" the river taunted as it cascaded over mossy rocks and tumbled into a foamy chasm.

On and on, he struggled to free himself from an invisible chokehold. Exhausted, he fell asleep only to be wakened up by two bare-chested men, who with faces like masks, mumbled words that he could not understand.

One carried a long bamboo tube and a conical bark quiver of bamboo-splinter darts that dangled at his side. The other held a bow over his shoulder and arrows in a quiver made of the same hide as the clothing they wore around their hips. One on each side, they led him away.

Slate-coloured clouds hovered over the forest, while the soothing sound of the rapids ebbed into oblivion.

Raja asked in Creole, "Where do you take me?"

The man with the bow and arrows waved his hand along the course of the river above the falls and said, "We take you to Arawak Village." After Raja had introduced himself, the one who spoke Creole English said, "Call me Ar'wak," and pointing to his companion, he mumbled, "Me friend, Mani."

Since Kwame had mentioned the name Ar'wak, Raja suspected that this Creole-speaking man could be Kwame's friend. Left on his own, Raja believed that he could easily perish in the jungle in a matter of days. Devoid of energy, he had no choice but to place his trust in Ar'wak and Mani.

They took him to a dugout on a sheltered riverbank. "Canoa," Ar'wak said as he invited Raja to board the craft, its length three times Raja's height.

They were both short, stocky men of bronze complexion. Compared to the black men who had paddled him to shore in Georgetown with so much power, these men dipped their paddles with style in a rhythmic fashion. Raised lines across Ar'wak's back and a cutlass at his feet confirmed Raja's suspicion.

Later, Ar'wak reached into the pouch around his waist, brought out a few leaves, and passed them to Raja.

"Chew," he said.

Raja accepted, but as he chewed he became sleepy and soon curled up on his side at the bottom of the canoe. After a long sleep, he found that he had arrived at a settlement of some fifteen houses deep in the rainforest. The walls and roofs of the huts were thatched with branches from the ite palm, the same material used on the roof of Kwame's bush house. The reddish-brown clay soil was so well beaten down, Raja assumed people had been living there for more generations than he could count.

Naked children gathered around him watching his every move.

Hunger pangs gnawed at him. Just when he had become somewhat unsteady on his feet, Ar'wak passed him cassava bread. Though he hadn't cared for it at Kwame's place, he now devoured every scrap. He wondered why Ar'wak did not sense his need for more. In the end, Ar'wak did reach up and give him a couple after he'd pointed at the bread spread out on the roof to dry.

As the evening progressed, the women stopped what they were doing and set about preparing a meal. On an open fire, they heated cassareep, a liquid that resembled molasses. To the pot they added brown beans, green peas, squash, and red peppers.

Ar'wak offered Raja a calabash of pepperpot with some more cassava bread. As he would with chapati and curry, Raja broke off small pieces and dipped them into the pepperpot. He chewed slowly. The cassareep had transformed familiar vegetables and cassava bread into a meal with a strange taste that Raja did not quite relish.

While he ate, a few village men chewed a batch of cassava, which they spat into a large hollowed-out tree trunk. Ar'wak scooped the frothy liquid from an older batch and served it to Raja.

"Parakari," he said.

Raja sniffed the fermented brew. A gurgling noise from deep down his throat made him wave the drink away. The look on Ar'wak's face told Raja that he should have accepted the man's hospitality.

Ar'wak slung a large piece of ite cloth between a pair of balata trees. He called it a hamaca and invited Raja to test it for comfort.

As Raja did so, his kurta lifted and exposed his bare back. Ar'wak ran a finger along the whip marks, so similar to his.

"I, too, have been beaten," Ar'wak said. "I went on a hunt too close to the coast. Bad men captured me. They turned me over to the overseer, who forced me to join a gang of workers."

"How did you escape?"

"An African driver hid me in his bush house. He took care of my wounds and helped me escape."

"He's also my friend."

"Good man, Kwame," Ar'wak said, his eyes opening widely. He added, "Now my turn to help. You stay with us?"

Those were the words Raja wanted to hear. Now he had a choice. "In a couple of days, I'll give you my answer."

Before dawn, Raja's newfound friends took him on a hunt. The air was crisp. Ar'wak carried his cutlass tied at the waist, along with a bow and a few arrows, while Mani held in position his six-foot bamboo tube, its quiver of small darts close to his side.

Along the forest floor, beside the river, the men followed some tracks. All of a sudden, Ar'wak signalled for Raja to stoop.

Woof!

At a flash, Mani blew into the blowpipe and let fly a dart. It caused a slight rustle among the ferns and crabgrass.

"Labba," Ar'wak whispered to Raja.

Raja exclaimed in panic, "Labaria!"

Ar'wak grasped Raja on the shoulder. "No! No! It is a labba—an agouti."

Raja retrieved a reddish-brown, spotted animal that resembled a large rat with a pig-like face. Upon examination of the tips of the darts, he discovered that a black paste, which Mani called ourari, had caused the labba's distress.

Next, it was Ar'wak's turn to show off his skill. He signalled for Raja to be quiet and lie low in the damp undergrowth, thick with the fronds of salt ferns. As soon as a spider monkey, similar to Kwame's Olu, landed on a splintered, deep purple branch, Ar'wak fired an arrow. Thump! The monkey landed hard on the forest floor.

Raja covered his eyes and looked away. It bothered him to see the animal suffer. To him, it was like seeing Kwame's Olu dying before his eyes.

A troop of monkeys sat on a trunk of the mora tree, unaware of the hunters' presence. Before too long, they shrieked and darted from limb to limb.

Raja searched the sky to find out the source of the commotion. Above, a magnificent eagle glided, started its descent and circled the monkeys. Its crest of head feathers looked like a crown, the expanse of wings wider than any bird Raja had ever seen. It swooped down on the monkeys but at the last moment swerved and dived straight down. Raja watched in awe and regret as the bird's huge talons locked onto its prey. Had he not become so attached to Kwame's pet, he would not have pitied the macaw.

As if in protest, a few macaws circled the sky in colourful patterns to bid farewell to a lost member of the group.

While the shadows cast by the forest trees lengthened, Raja accompanied his friends toward a stand of wallaba trees that formed a canopy high above. They collected bundles of the vines that draped the tree trunks. Raja helped them beat the vines against logs until they became pulp.

While Mani positioned himself with a basket downstream, Ar'wak and Raja threw handfuls of the mash into the river. Mani scooped up the fish that had been stunned by the mash and had turned belly-up: haimara, patwah, houri, piranha, and a couple of lukanani, local names Raja had picked up from Ar'wak.

Back at the family compound, bathed in the orange light of a fire the women had already lit, Ar'wak and Mani got busy. They built a wooden framework that Mani called a barbacoa, under which he lit a fire. He impaled the labba and monkey with pieces of wood and burned off the hair over the barbacoa.

With the aid of his plantation cutlass, Ar'wak removed the guts and slowly roasted the labba. He sliced off a piece of flesh and offered it to Raja.

For Raja, this would be a life-changing moment. Like other members of his family, he had never eaten meat. They considered it a sin to kill an animal for food. Raja would have to make a decision that would ensure his survival in the forest. He chewed and swallowed the meat. It stayed down after several sips of water.

Just when he thought he'd let his family and himself down by eating animal flesh, Ar'wak patted him on the back. "Now that you've eaten labba and drunk creek water, you're forever tied to this land."

Raja did not put much faith in what he'd just heard. The attachment for his motherland was unshakeable.

However, he found himself at a crossroads. Should he join these forest dwellers where he could listen everyday to an orchestra of birds singing ancient ragas, where he could follow the antics of dancing monkeys that would make life so much easier? Or should he return to his wife and family?

Among the Arawaks, he'd be a stranger. Living out his life in the jungle was not what he'd planned. Gone would be his present friendships with Ramdas, Shankar, Jasmine, and of course, Kwame. Granted, Ar'wak and Mani could teach him to survive in the forest, where he'd be closer to nature and its creatures.

However, though plantation life is hard, it comes with a huge benefit—the promise of a free return passage to India at the end of my indentureship.

Far into the night he weighed the different possibilities, for tomorrow he must decide. Never before did his fate rest on an act that appeared so simple—to stay or not to stay.

Early next morning, he approached his hosts and said, "While I would like to live among you as a free man, I prefer to return to the plantation and, in the end, to my family."

Ar'wak spoke briefly to Mani. "How can you trust those plantation people? We will never work for them because shillings, gold, and stones mean nothing to us."

Raja almost fell over backwards. "Stones! What stones?"

"Our rivers have plenty gold and stones," Ar'wak said.

Raja tried to hide his excitement. The sound of gold bangles jingling on Savitri's arms came rushing back to him. "Your women will look prettier with gold earrings and bangles," he said to Ar'wak.

Ar'wak moved his head up and down. "Our women used to wear necklaces of gold nuggets and stones. No more."

"Why not?"

"It attracted invaders who forced some of the men to act as guides."

With time, after some prodding by Raja, Ar'wak filled in some of the details. The newcomers had ordered the guides to take them to the rivers rich in gold and diamonds.

To Raja, the drive for riches, whether it be sugar or gold, was all the same. "So what happened?"

"They handed us wooden bowls and forced us to pan the gold for them. One night, we got them drunk on parakari," Ar'wak broke into a strange giggle, "threw the gold back into the river and escaped."

"Your people did the right thing," Raja said.

"Later, with our weapons, we forced them to flee."

"Before I leave, could you and Mani take me to a river that is rich in gold and diamonds?"

With an expressionless face, Ar'wak consulted with Mani. "We can take you there, but you bring nothing back."

Raja tried to hide his disappointment at what he heard. *Perhaps Ar'wak might make an exception and allow me to keep a gem or two.*

Days and nights went by without incident until Raja said to Ar'wak, "You promised to take me to a river rich in gold and diamonds."

"We have not forgotten," Ar'wak said. "Mani and I will take you to such a river tomorrow, but remember what I told you."

Raja knew that Ar'wak had meant what he said. All he wanted was to set eyes on that river, and the rest would take care of itself. For the rest of the day, he whistled as he chopped a good week's supply of firewood for the women.

CHAPTER ELEVEN

Dawn had just broken the next morning when they set off, Raja trailing a few paces behind his new friends. Ar'wak brought along his cutlass, while Mani carried a bow and a quiver full of arrows. Raja wore a skirt made from ite palm, his torn dhoti left behind. Except for his height, he was beginning to look like an Arawak.

He lost count of the number of days they'd been travelling. One afternoon they shot and roasted a watrush, an animal that resembled both a rat and a pig.

The next morning, the sound of rushing water grew in intensity and before too long Raja came face-to-face with a fast-flowing stream.

Ar'wak soon went to work; he whittled away a section of limb from a fallen simarupa tree and carved out a circular bowl, sanding it smooth with a stone. The pan he created had a diameter of almost two hand spans. He selected a spot where the water was clear and the current not too fast. With deft hands, he dipped his pan into the streambed and scooped some mud and gravel. He lowered the pan into the water and shook it from side to side and in a circular manner, all the time keeping the rim just under the water. The lighter materials rose to the top and these he poured out. Again he submerged the pan and continued to shake and wash. He repeated this action several times. Finally, only the heaviest particles from all that swirling remained in the residue.

Raja, who had kept a close watch on this simple process, stared wide-eyed at the flakes of gold and placed them on a leaf to dry in the sun. All the while, Mani sat on the riverbank and looked as though he'd rather be somewhere else.

Several times, Raja tried his hand at panning and though he added only a few gold flakes to his own leaf, his heart still pounded inside his chest.

Ar'wak moved on to a spot where there was a bend in the stream. Here the current slowed and picked up again. At the outer curve, he dipped his pan into the clear streambed. Not only did he end up with tiny gold nuggets, on his last dip, he brought up a stone that stood out from the washed material because of its colour.

"Diamond—king of all stones!" Ar'wak cried out, passing it to Raja.

Much bigger than a sugar crystal, he could only guess the value of the find due to its size. A real beauty, it was very hard with sharp edges. *If I could keep this diamond, my family would be set for life, and I would never have to work again.* For a brief moment, everything around him went blank. By the time his head cleared, Ar'wak had snatched the stone and thrown it back into the creek.

Speechless, Raja quickly seized the pan and jumped into the water. He scooped up debris at the spot that seemed rich in diamonds. Ar'wak's loud grunt caused him to abandon the search.

Ar'wak mumbled a few words to Mani and turned to Raja. "Plantation people would kill just to get their hands on such a beautiful diamond, which to us is only a white pebble."

"I would have . . . ." Raja did not complete what he wanted to say and tried his best to hide his disappointment. *Was this Shankar's El Dorado?*

Ar'wak, in studied silence, looked at Raja. "You can always change your mind and stay with us."

Didn't Ar'wak see the longing in Raja's face at the sight of the diamond? "I can never live as you do," Raja said. He would return to the plantation, at least, with the gold flakes.

Raja stumbled forward when Ar'wak reached for Raja's own parcel and spilled its contents into the stream. "We must not upset the spirits of the rivers," Ar'wak said. "They can become very angry with us." He beckoned Mani, and they both turned around, anxious to head back to the village.

Ar'wak had acted so fast, all Raja could do was raise both of his hands in protest. *Upset the spirits of the rivers?* "Wait!" Ar'wak's fierce look reminded Raja that Ar'wak had meant what he said. There was no way he could contradict Ar'wak and Mani, for he relied on them to show him the way out of the jungle.

His hopes of returning to his country as a man of means had been dashed. One or two nuggets would have made life so much easier. Now he was back to being a lowly coolie, bound for the plantation to serve out his indentureship. To hide his disappointment, he borrowed Mani's bow and aimed an arrow at a fish. He missed by a long shot. His anger spent, he rubbed his eyes, but there were no tears.

Back at the Arawak settlement, he would stay for a while and see if he could adjust to jungle life. He had not gotten over the loss of treasures that could have changed his life forever.

Day after day, the women gathered corn, cassava, pumpkins, and other vegetables they grew for home use. When food was short, Ar'wak and Mani went hunting or fishing before Raja had woken up.

Life should have a bigger purpose. This slow, easy way of living is not for me. My world is the other world out there, full of challenges and day to day struggles.

No matter how hard he tried, he just could not be an Arawak. Again, he reminded his friend that he must get back to the plantation.

"We would miss your company," Ar'wak blurted out. "Perhaps you'll reconsider."

Right up to the end, Raja was of two minds, especially since Ar'wak and Mani had opened their hearts to him. If he lived with the Arawaks, there would be no need for gold or diamonds. At last, his mind was made up, and he never wavered. "I will miss you too," Raja said, his voice cracking with emotion.

Long before the sun had risen, dressed once more in his torn dhoti, Raja boarded the dugout where Ar'wak and Mani waited. The canoe cut through the water as silent as the night. A huge jaguar, resting on the slanted limb of a balata tree on the bank of the river, barely opened its eyes as the canoe went by. A pheasant-like bird stood guard in the crook of a tree branch next to a nest made of a criss-cross of sticks and dried twigs.

"This is as far as we'll take you. Keep walking on this bush path along the riverbank," Ar'wak said as he pointed out the direction to the plantation. "Give Kwame my regards." They left him with a gourd of water and a few days' supply of cassava bread, wrapped in paper-thin bark.

Raja tried to embrace Ar'wak and Mani, but their reactions told him it was not their way of saying goodbye. Expressionless, they simply nodded, jumped into their canoe, and, like jungle cats, glided away into the rainforest. Raja kept looking back at them until they were just tiny specks.

He walked and walked until the sun was low on the horizon. To keep on course, he used the river as a guide as his friends had suggested.

Oftentimes he struggled through sloughs choked with pond scum. No birds chirped, no insects buzzed, no wind rustled through the leaves— all adding to the silence and loneliness of the forest, which made him now all the more desperate to get out.

As evening approached, it came to life with frogs croaking and crickets chirping. Raja picked a few bunches of jamuns. The bird-pecked fruits tasted sweeter than the untouched ones. He ate his fill and folded the rest in a water lily leaf for Kwame's pets, providing he had luck on his side.

An old wallaba tree limb snapped, missing him just as he stepped onto the riverbank. Within minutes, a jaguar sprang from a tree, a stone's throw from Raja, startling him. Its shoulder muscles rippled under its black-spotted orange coat. Raja had no fear, so transfixed were his eyes on the stealth and grace of the animal as it sneaked up closer to its prey.

The cat, the size of a big dog, pounced on a watrush, which happened to be much larger than a labba. The cat locked its jaws around the animal's skull, crushing it. Raja's stomach churned.

Days later, evening was upon him when a soft breeze wafted the sickly-sweet smell of boiling sugarcane juice over the savannah. On the western horizon, smoke belched from the smoke stack at Sugar Grove Estate.

"Yippee!" Raja screamed, as the chimney stack loomed ahead. He skipped through tall "busy-busy" grass at a fast clip.

Night caught up with him when he turned left onto a dirt road toward a whitewashed building, illuminated by gaslights. Much to his surprise, he came upon several stalls where the mules were housed. He would not have minded living there.

Save for the owls, nothing stirred at the plantation. The stars were nowhere in sight as he wended his way in the chilly air across hoof holes to get to Kwame's hut. "Kwame!" he shouted. He banged at the door and yelled, "It's me."

Kwame's voice came through. "What in . . . ." After a pause, he continued, "Is that you, Raja?" He opened the door a crack and peeped, holding his lantern. Quickly, he flung the door open. "I took you for a thiefman," Kwame said with a toothy grin. "Let me look at you. Ju-ju man brought you back. Ha-ha. What did I tell Overseer? I told him you'd come back, em . . . some good day."

"I just couldn't stay away."

Kwame grabbed Raja and shook him. "Coolie boy, you did just that. Overseer is annoyed with you. Oh my! Privates all exposed?"

Raja looked down at his torn, mud-splattered dhoti, aware that he presented a sorry sight.

"What happened?" Kwame asked.

"I fell from a palm tree and landed on razor grass."

"Tut, tut! What caused the fall?"

"A furry animal with babies fell on me, causing me to lose my grip."

"Those yawaris make nests up in the fronds." Kwame handed Raja a white sheet.

"Make yourself a dhoti. You must look decent when you appear before the manager."

Raja, with trembling hands, wrapped the cloth around his waist and pulled it between his legs.

"Jasmine and Shankar visited only yesterday," Kwame said. "They were worried they might never see you again."

"Jasmine!"

"Yes, she was weeping." Kwame continued, "Overseer said you used the mule incident to run away from the estate."

"No. I got lost."

"You have some explaining to do when you meet with him."

Raja sighed, lowered his head before facing Kwame. "Can you not put in a word for me?"

"You should know that Bakkra man never listens to Black man," Kwame's eyes glowed in the soft light. "I tried my best to convince Mr. Van Sluytman that you did not run away."

"I'll clear that up when I see him tomorrow," Raja said. "Now can you help me get rid of these leeches stuck to my legs?"

Kwame lit the wick of candle grease. "I'll set fire to their tails." He held the wick on each of the worms until they fell off. "Take some soft grease to your logie. It is very useful for rusty nail punctures and cuts on feet," Kwame said, as he put a piece of the soft candle in his friend's hand.

"In return, your pets will get a treat." Raja opened his leaf parcel and passed out jamuns to Olu and Polly.

Kwame lit a fire and heated up some food for his guest. "How about some fu-fu?" Kwame asked. "It goes well with lemon grass tea."

"Fu-fu?" Raja exclaimed, quite puzzled.

"Yesterday I pounded boiled plantains and cassava in the mortar over there. Now I will make a good West African breakfast for you."

Raja ate the fu-fu from a calabash. While he sipped his bush tea, he described how he had gotten lost and had been rescued by Ar'wak and his companion.

Kwame's jaws hung open in amazement. "Ar'wak! Did he help you?"

"Yes, Kwame, and he sends you his greetings. Oh, I also ran into massacouraman, but that's for another time."

Kwame's eyes almost popped out of their sockets. "I can hardly wait to hear."

Raja thanked Kwame and promised him he would see the overseer first thing in the morning. Worried about his meeting with Mr. Van Sluytman, he disappeared into the night.

CHAPTER TWELVE

The following morning, Raja stuck his head out of his logie. A cloudless sky with no suggestion of a wind greeted him. He put on a tattered kurta and dhoti. At his own home, his wife would have taken better care of his clothes. Since he was now a lowly worker, he was satisfied with what he had.

Upon arrival at Mr. Van Sluytman's compound, a gateman walked him over to the rear entrance of a whitewashed bungalow, its green louvered jalousies similar to those he had seen on houses in Georgetown.

"Go tell Mr. Van Sluytman that a coolie by the name of Raja is here to see him," the gateman shouted.

A black butler clip-clopped on his wooden clogs into the residence to get the overseer.

Raja steadied himself against a house post as Van Sluytman, in slippers and robe, came to a dead stop. "Well, well! Look who's here. Do you have the ague, Roger?"

"My name is Raja, sir."

Van Sluytman gave Raja a sharp look. "Very well, Raja. Where were you the last six weeks?"

"You sent me into the bush to go after a mule, sir. I got lost."

"And how come you're here?"

"Two Arawak men showed me the way out, sir."

Van Sluytman's smile turned into a sneer. "Not after six weeks. You give me no choice but to inform the manager."

The manager called for an afternoon court at his bottom house.

**A typical bottom house upriver in the interior
of British Guiana, now Guyana.**

Those present at the hearing, over which the manager presided, were the defendant, three overseers including Van Sluytman, Doc, houseboys, Mathu, and another driver.

Shankar and Kwame joined a handful of spectators just before the hearings began.

Prosecutor Van Sluytman opened the proceedings with Mathu acting as translator. "I ordered Raja to go after a mule, and he went missing for six weeks."

The manager stomped his boot. Through clenched jaws, he said, "Aha! You're the one who sent him off." He pulled Van Sluytman aside and gave him a real dressing down, causing the overseer to reappear fiddling with his cork helmet.

At this point in the hearings, Mathu switched to Creole. "Raja, Manager wants to know how come de mule was smart enough to come home de same day but not you."

Raja took a deep breath looking for a way to ease the insult. "I couldn't find my way out."

"Did you see any of the runaway slaves?" the manager asked.

"No, but I caught a glimpse of a strange creature."

The manager chuckled. "So you did see a Bush Negro."

Before Raja could make sense of those words, the manager turned to Van Sluytman.

"There's no doubt as to guilt. However, we must take into account that you are the one who sent the defendant into the woods."

"Still, for such a long absence from the plantation," the overseer said, "we must decide on an appropriate penalty."

After a short discussion with the overseers, the manager addressed the court, "The defendant has completed two years of his indentureship without any previous mishap. True, he carried out an order from my trusted man here and left in search of a mule." The manager's finger now stabbed the air as he shouted. "Nevertheless," he lowered his voice, emphasizing each word with a side-to-side movement of his index finger, "he returned because no one except the Arawaks and the Bush Negroes could survive in that jungle for long."

Van Sluytman cleared his throat and asked, "What punishment do you have in mind for this runaway coolie, sir?"

"Fifteen lashes on the back with the cat o' nine tails," the manager said, "plus a fine of one guilder, to be paid over eight months. Add the six weeks he went missing to his indentureship term." After a pause, he turned and looked at the crowd of onlookers. "Let this be a lesson to all of you coolies."

Raja hardly had time to absorb the full impact of the sentence when the manager continued, "Raja, I shall make a journal entry of this incident which I hope will never again be repeated by any coolie."

Raja bit deep into his upper lip. *I wonder what the full punishment would have been had I no excuse.*

Van Sluytman beckoned Mathu over with his finger. "Come here, boy. I want you to wield the cat."

"No! Raja screamed, as he looked at Kwame and Shankar for support.

"Start the bloody whipping. What are we waiting for?" the manager yelled.

As Mathu pranced around, Raja hoped the man would find some old nagging pain in his arm.

But it was not to be. As though savouring the opportunity, the driver pawed at the greyish stubble sprinkled over his shrivelled face. Next, he removed Raja's kurta with a flourish and proceeded to rotate his right arm like a fast bowler in cricket winding up before his first delivery. After a quick look around at the spectators, he shouted at the houseboys gathered on the sidelines. "Bring de man out to de yard and tie him up to de whipping pos'."

Mathu strutted around like a rooster. He flicked the cat at two houseboys. "You deaf or what?" he asked.

They scrambled forward, hooked Raja under the armpits, and dragged him to the backyard. The men tied his hands to the post in a way that he could still survey the crowd that had gathered.

Raja had learned that to withstand pain he must tense his muscles and so he did.

The first blow made him wince. The pain was intense, but he shook his head from side to side and managed it well. Whether he could handle fourteen more was a different matter. It seemed such a long way off.

After several blows, Mathu's breathing became heavy on Raja's back. "Sir," he called out to Van Sluytman, "I need a break." The driver dashed for the area overgrown with weeds, but before he reached it, he threw up.

The stinging pain in Raja's shoulders and back travelled to the rest of his body. He chanted under his breath "A-U-M," spreading out each of the three sounds. He did so for the rest of the beating while gritting his teeth, so severe was the pain. This most sacred of sounds, the greatest of all mantras, penetrated the centre of his being, to his very soul.

Mobilizing his immense powers of concentration, Raja willed himself into a semiconscious state just as Van Sluytman yelled, "Your turn," and beckoned the second driver.

At each whack of the whip, Raja tightened his muscles and continued to chant until Van Sluytman said to the driver, "Take a rest."

Minutes later, the overseer said, "Give it your all, boy."

The driver raised the whip high in the air and delivered a lash, the force of which seemed to have dislocated his shoulder. He cried out, "Ow, Ow!"

A huge gash, like a knife to the heart, spurted blood onto Raja's dhoti, some of which found its way to his bare feet.

When it was over, the overseer yelled, "Rub pickling salt into the wounds, and let the culprit dry out in the sun."

"Sir, let Mathu take over. I need treatment myself." The driver clutched his shoulder and moaned as he headed off in the direction of the clinic.

Raja scanned the sea of blurred faces but he recognized no one.

The sting from the salt was worse than the pain from the actual beating. He shook his head like a wet dog. All his ideals about caste had fallen apart. No more would he think of himself as a high-class Kshatriya.

All around, bullfrogs croaked while a mongrel licked at the scarlet puddle at his feet. The sun had long set on the crimson horizon, and shadows had encroached upon the land when Van Sluytman signalled for the men to untie Raja.

He clutched the post with both hands and slid to the ground. Minutes passed before he eased himself up. Several times he stumbled, got up and staggered toward the cane fields, frothing at the mouth and bleeding from the nose.

The ceaseless hum of mosquitoes disturbed the air. They sucked his blood but he did not feel their bites.

As if from nowhere, Shankar appeared; he gripped his friend around the armpits, turned him around, and guided him home.

Raja gritted his teeth and stopped groaning when Jasmine joined them. "Shankar, take my shawl and place it on Raja's back," she said in tears. "Please keep the mosquitoes off his wounds. Only time will heal such pain. I will check on him later," she whispered.

While Raja lay face down, groaning on his rope bed, Shankar heated a pot of water. With the skill of a nurse, he washed the deep gashes on his friend's back.

Before it went pitch black, Jasmine returned to Raja's logie with a clean rag caked with green paste.

"What's this?" Shankar asked.

"It is Kwame's poultice made from crushed leaves of the bellyache plant." She sat on the rope bed. "Kwame said to warm it first before wrapping—to promote healing and prevent infection of the wound."

As she applied the warm paste, its soothing effect was instantaneous.

"Thanks," Raja said.

Shankar prepared lentils, greens, and rice for all. "My turn to prepare you a meal has finally arrived," he said to Raja.

"Sorry! Just a sip of tea will do," Raja managed to say.

"You recall our first morning at the plantation when you cooked for me?"

Raja suspected that Shankar was trying to get his mind away from the pain. "Oh yes," replied Raja, gritting his teeth. And with the voice of a child, he continued, "And I remember the sound of raindrops on the zinc sheets that first evening."

The next morning, an African driver, a stranger to Raja, got him out of bed and prodded him along to join a gang of men. The deep gashes on his back compounded with the pain caused him to stagger. What made it worse, this man was a real slave driver. Raja believed this was to discourage him from running away again.

Because of his recent whipping and humiliation, he lost his appetite. For weeks, he ate only one meal a day until he was nothing but skin and bones. As time went on, he added a second meal with tiny portions of rice, dal, and okra or string beans, which he ate alone.

Still, on Saturday afternoons he went to the payroll office to collect his pay. With his earnings tucked away safely in his drawstring purse, he hung around a bridge with Shankar. Along with the other men, he would perch high up on the bridge's railing over the irrigation canal that drained water from the estate to the sea. This impromptu gathering place had become so crowded that if Raja did not get there early he would be hard-pressed to find a seat.

As the months went by, he discovered that time had healed the mental and physical scars caused by the beating. Strangely, there was now more room on the timber railing. After he had collected his pay one day, he asked Shankar. "What's keeping the men away from the bridge?"

"Chan-a-Sue serves up a mix of lime juice and rum," Shankar said. "It draws the men in like bees to honey."

Raja didn't like what he heard. He grabbed Shankar and guided him to the bridge. "Come keep me company," he said. "I'm worried about my wife. Since I have not heard from her, I asked Doc to write a follow-up letter for me."

Shankar freed himself from Raja's grasp but continued walking toward the bridge with him. "You wasted your money. Mail delivery in a remote village such as Bihar would be unreliable. Thankfully, I have no letters to write."

Those last words stunned Raja. "What sort of a man are you? You care nothing about loved ones," Raja said, shaking his head from side to side, "while hardly a day goes by when I don't think about family." Raja's voice had reached a crescendo. He hoped Shankar had taken the hint and realized the folly of his ways.

Shankar shrugged and led the way toward Chan-a Sue's Salt-Goods Shop. "There's Chan-a-Sue's indentureship certificate pinned to the wall," he said. He gestured with a nod of his head. "Ask him if he drops a line to any family."

"Never mind," Raja said with a wave of his hand. He faced the grocer to place his order. "Two pounds of flour."

"You wang two pung falawung," Chan-a-sue repeated to make sure he got it right, as he proceeded to weigh the item.

After they'd taken home their groceries, Shankar moved on to the rum shop, while Raja headed back for the bridge. He remained there until the frogs had become quite noisy and the sand flies a real nuisance.

As he got up to leave, Van Sluytman approached astride his mule. With him was a riding partner, dressed like an overseer, yet far from being one. The two men were deep in conversation but kept quiet as they rode past Raja, who immediately became suspicious. Much about the stranger was bothersome. Was it the mean look, the buttoned-up jacket, or the way the man looked at him?

That evening, Raja walked over to Shankar's logie. "There's a stranger riding around with Mr. Van Sluytman," Raja said, as Shankar's breathing quickened, "and I have a creepy feeling about him."

"Did he ca-carry a gun?"

"Who knows what's behind that buttoned-up jacket?" Raja got up to leave.

"Take a closer look at him, Raja. Please!"

Perched high above the slow moving-water the next Saturday, Raja sat and waited until it had got dark. This time only the overseer rode by.

A few weeks later, around evening, his wage safely tucked away in his cloth purse, Raja headed for the cane fields to be alone. He had just lain down on a bed of dried sugarcane leaves when the rustle of leaves and the crackle of twigs disturbed him. The footsteps came closer, the sugarcane stalks shifted. Raja rose and turned around. It was Jasmine.

"Are you sure you want to be alone with me?" he asked.

"Oh Raja, let's just talk."

"What about?"

"Well, I met Shankar at the payroll office . . . he was shaking like a leaf when I mentioned that I had seen a stranger around the plantation."

Raja's heart pounded hard against his chest. "Where and when did you see the stranger?"

Jasmine rearranged her shawl across her shoulders. "The first time when he was riding a mule alongside Mr. Van Sluytman as he made his rounds. Another time as he hung around a short distance from the payroll office, watching the workers as they lined up."

"Jasmine, something tells me that stranger is after Shankar. Who knows? I might be in trouble, too."

"That's why I wanted to see you."

Words just seemed to flow as Raja chatted away until Jasmine added, "Night is upon us."

Raja pretended he did not hear a word. He pulled his sleeves over his arms to protect himself from mosquitoes. "Let's sit down and give the mosquitoes fewer places to bite." He moved over to make room for Jasmine. "Life in Demerara has not been very kind to me," he said in a raspy voice. "My ship brother works in a different estate, and now a stranger might be after Shankar and me."

He tried to make conversation, but as it got darker, his breathing became heavier. A crescent moon showered the cane field with a soft light.

Jasmine placed a hand over her knees. "Poor Shankar." She shook her head from side to side. "He's just skin and bones."

Raja looked at her skirt stretched out. Here he was, alone with a woman. He could feel the blood rushing through his body, to his head. He could hear his heart pounding, for in his native India, he would never have found himself this way.

The moment, however, was too precious to lose, and it had arrived when he'd least expected it. Why should he not seize the moment? Though his heart always quickened whenever he saw her, he now became powerless in her presence. It could all have been so simple.

Jasmine continued, "And so much a loner he is. You're his only friend."

After a bit more small talk, she said, "Raja, let me dance for you. It will cheer you up."

Without waiting for an answer, she got up and sang a song of love. Her soft, haunting voice touched his very soul. Her hips swayed, her hands and arms picked up the rhythm as she darted in and out of the sugarcane stalks. In the pale moonlight, she gave such a performance, he forgot about loneliness.

He raised a hand. "Stop!"

"Why?" she asked. "Raja, you are a special friend and this is the only way I can express my feelings for you."

"It's more than I can take."

"Then I shall quit." She led the way out of the cane field.

Raja caught up with her and whispered, "Shh! We have company. Someone has been watching us."

The tramping of feet came closer.

From the corner of his eye, Raja saw Sonnyboy dart out of the cane field. This was strange. Had he followed Jasmine? *Perhaps he looks upon me as a rival for Jasmine's affection.*

Another weekend, Raja hung around the area between the payroll office and the big attraction, Chan-a-Sue's Rum Shop. As Shankar was about to enter the premises, Raja called out to him.

Instead of walking up to meet with Raja, Shankar beckoned him with a crook of his finger. "Come inside," he whispered, "I want to talk to you."

Exactly as Jasmine had said, Shankar had become extremely nervous and worried.

"In there?" Raja asked.

"You don't have to drink."

A quick peek through the door convinced Raja that the rum shop was indeed the new watering hole for youths. Everyone was in an ecstatic mood and shouting. The place was as crowded as the canal bridge had been in its heyday, a bench much more comfortable than any railing. Raja squeezed in behind Shankar. The strong smell of rum made his head spin, forcing him to lean against Shankar.

Raja's eyebrows lifted when he ran into Sonnyboy and his teammates, who occupied two tables. "No practice today?" Raja asked, wagging an accusing finger back and forth at Sonnyboy.

"We're celebrating our victory in the finals for the Jones Cup. Would you like to play a friendly game to wrap up the season—married men against single men?"

"The last match I played was for our village team back in India some seven years ago."

"We can play some of our second-string players. Are you single or married, Raja?"

Raja thought before answering, "Married."

Sonnyboy smirked. "Well, I would never have believed . . . ."

"What do you mean?"

"A married man should not meet secretly with a woman."

Raja ignored the comment and went to sit with Shankar, who ordered a shot for himself and wasted no time in getting down to the topic of the stranger.

"That man watches my every move," Shankar said.

"Come clean, Shankar. What are you hiding?"

Shankar seemed deep in thought. "If you can keep a secret, I'll tell you over a drink some day."

"You can trust me."

Another evening, Shankar broke lustily into a song of the pain of separation at the entrance to Raja's unit. Had Shankar been able to carry the notes and add some melody to embellish the lyrics, it might have touched Raja's soul.

As Shankar tried to lean against a door jamb that wasn't there, Raja caught him and eased him onto the daubed floor. With saliva dribbling all over his kurta, Shankar hiccoughed and slurred his words, "Raja,

I believe that stranger is a British agent. With help from the estate management, he is going to arrest me."

"Are you sure?"

"My drinking buddy is going to check that out for me. You know," he raised his voice half a notch, "the man I meet with every second Saturday for a drink."

"Who is he?"

"The Director of the Rum Marketing Board."

"What? Be careful. Such a big shot would be on management's side."

"Not quite. He's mulatto, so he can clink glasses with Van Sluytman as well as me."

"Why would a director sit at a table with a coolie?"

"Because I'm intelligent, Raja." Shankar flashed a toothy smile. "After a few shots, he loosens up."

"And says what?"

"That it's a competitive business. You see Davis Holdings also makes high-quality rum. To come up with a better product and push Davis out of the rum business, our company imported a chemist from England."

"You mean a professional like Doc?"

"Good heavens, no. We're talking about an Oxford University Fellow, a scientist."

"Ha-ha! To make a drink for the barefoot coolie?"

"Don't be a fool, Raja." Shankar covered his mouth with his hands, hiccoughed and babbled on, "We locals get the cheap stuff made by dispensers. I'm referring to the blended and aged Demerara Special, and the 80 proof rum schnapps."

As soon as Raja collected his next week's pay, he ventured out onto the path that led to his bridge-railing hangout. Shankar caught up with him, spun him around, and guided him through the entrance of Chan-a Sue's Rum Shop.

Raja was struck by the loud noise and foul language. "But I've never had a drink in my life," he pleaded.

"It's liquid gold, bhai. Good for the ticking heart." Shankar tapped Raja's shoulder. "Come inside."

At the counter, Shankar ordered a half-bottle of rum and picked up a jug of water and two glasses he held between his fingers. Raja chose a vacant table. As Shankar poured himself a drink, Raja took the opportunity to look around. This time he was more relaxed. He'd never seen such a setting in his native Belwasa. The walls of the rum shop were made of rough-hewn, unevenly spaced planks. Most of the light came from two wooden windows, held open by jute twine tied to nails. Iron bars, leaning against the wall, would secure the door and windows after hours.

Men sat on crude benches sipping from thick, cone-shaped shot glasses. Some sat in groups of four at square tables. A few tables had full bottles, large and small.

A single whiff of rum intermixed with sweat, urine, and vomit was enough to make Raja place his hand over his mouth.

"Pour Raja a shot," someone yelled.

"Baptize the man, Shankar," another shouted.

"No. Don't." Raja raised his palms outward. "My family would disown me if I drink spirits."

The men burst out in raucous laughter. Had the way been clear, Raja would have escaped such an embarrassing moment. It made him feel very small.

Shankar acted as though he'd heard nothing. His mouth formed a misshaped circle. "Family!" He poured himself more rum, downed it in one gulp, chased it with a glass of water and smacked his lips. "Ah. Good stuff."

Raja rolled his eyes as his mouth took on a twisted expression. "Yes, family. My wife, parents, brother."

Shankar waved his hand in Raja's face. "You are a dead man to them now, my good friend. It's been years, years since-since they set eyes on you or heard-heard from you. Savitri nev-never replied to your letters. Right?"

Raja stood up to leave. "Listen to what the drink makes you say."

Shankar rose and threw his arm around Raja's shoulders, but Raja freed himself. "The drink makes me say the truth," Shankar said. He poked Raja in the ribs with his fist and pulled him back into his seat. "Oh, don't be so angry with me, bhai." Shankar grunted and rolled his head as he sat down. "You know what I mean. We're all dead men, forgotten, mourned for perhaps, now and then, but gone forever as far as our loved ones are concerned."

What Shankar said could very well have been the truth, but Raja would not stand for it. His anger was ready to boil over. He shook his head and wagged his finger at his friend. "They will not forget me. You hear." He looked like he wanted to cry when he pounded his fist on the table. It made Shankar spill his drink. "I will return to them—to Savitri," Raja shouted.

"That's wonderful," Shankar said. He placed a glass gleaming with the golden stuff in front of Raja. "Let us drink to their health, my go-good man." Raja stared at the drink causing Shankar to shout, "Rum will make you a real man."

"Shankar, I have a lot of respect for you. Why don't you tell me why you left the university?"

"I will soon enough. Right now, bottoms up."

Raja liked being around Shankar especially at a time when he missed his family and his native land. Perhaps a drink would make him forget. He picked up the glass of rum, sipped, and downed the rest in one gulp. He winced and almost choked as the liquor exploded in his head like a musket ball. He mimicked his friend, slamming the glass onto the table and chasing the drink with water. *Could it be that simple?*

This time the men broke out in loud cheers, making Raja big once again. He pretended to listen to his friend talk about his university days, but all he heard was a droning hum and a voice that sounded distant. His loneliness all gone, he became a man without a care in the world.

CHAPTER THIRTEEN

Two weeks later, Shankar once again lured Raja into the rum shop. Shankar picked up a full bottle and signalled to Raja with his chin. "Let's move to the corner table."

Raja let his friend pour for him. He downed his drink and chased it with water; the rum slid down his throat like a hand running over silk.

Shankar's eyes darted around the room before he whispered, his voice shaking, "Raja, I've got all the information I wanted. That stranger is a British secret agent. In fact, there are two of them, but the other chap stays mostly indoors in Mr. Van Sluytman's house."

Raja tried to focus on what Shankar was saying, but faces became blurry, voices became distant. "What would secret agents be doing in this colony?" he asked.

"They've come to capture me. I heard that the stranger carries a revolver concealed under his jacket."

"Why would agents go after a coolie?"

Shankar leaned closer and spoke in Raja's ear, "In the eyes of the British, I'm a big fish. The last straw for me was when the British sent Mangal Pandey to the gallows back in 1857."

"My father told me about him. Many soldiers in his regiment looked upon Pandey as a martyr."

"Mangal and I are from the same village of Nagwa, United Provinces. While still a young man, he joined the army of the British East India Company." Shankar downed another shot. "After he was hanged by the British for treason, I became a student leader." Shankar was now sobbing openly. He did not even try to wipe away the tears; the rum must have loosened his tongue as he leaned back, seemingly unafraid. "The sepoys wanted to overthrow the British," he said, "and many students supported them." Shankar's eyes became distant.

Raja wondered if Shankar now regretted leaving the university. "But you were a raw recruit with no knowledge of guns."

Shankar poured himself another drink, downed it and placed one hand against his mouth so his voice would not carry. "You're wrong. I joined others in a secret training camp—a vacant warehouse outside our university dormitories. Sepoys drilled us in loading and firing Enfield rifle-muskets and revolvers until it became second nature, even taught us techniques to extract information."

Raja's eyes widened. "You must have tortured prisoners."

"We were at war against a powerful enemy."

Raja stared long and hard at his friend, too drunk to take it all in. His head swayed as he pried into the dark secrets of Shankar's world. "But those were British army weapons."

"We stole them together with ammunition from the army barracks in Meerut."

"It is amazing how you avoided capture."

"The British officers . . . ." Shankar's words got swallowed up and he could not continue.

Raja allowed Shankar time to regain his composure. "Well, what happened?"

Shankar took a deep breath as though he wanted to spill it all out. "Not so loud," he looked around, "I wanted to die beside my friends whom they strapped across the mouths of cannons. They, however, had me clean up the bits of brains and body parts after." Shankar leaned over the window and retched. After a few moments, he continued, "That was the most difficult thing I ever had to do; talk about nightmares; some say I scream in my sleep."

Raja tried to visualize the scene as described but the gruesomeness of it overwhelmed him. "What was your punishment?"

"They locked me up in a dark cell in the Andaman Islands, supposedly for twenty years."

"So how did you escape?"

"A prison warden took pity on me. He snapped me out of my illness and disguised me as one of the Sikh guards who left for the mainland. Back in Calcutta, I gave up the turban, cut my hair and chewed paan to stave off hunger. That's when a recruiter signed me up."

"Aha! So Shankar is not your real name."

"Shh!" Saliva trickled down to Shankar's beard. "My real name is," Shankar cupped his mouth, "Sagar. Sagar Singh."

"But why did you come to a British territory?"

Shankar became silent for quite some time as though deep in thought. He uttered a sound like the whistling of wind through the trees. The expression on his face reflected the harsh reality that no country within his reach would be safe from the British. "I never believed I would be found here; that's why I endured so much punishment."

"I wonder how management suspected you in the first place."

"I made a mistake letting them know that a coolie can read and write."

"Hmm! I never thought about that. Even so, you know how to defend yourself."

Shankar laughed. "If you and I can raid the overseer quarters, where they keep a stockpile of guns, we could take care of those spies and their supporters."

Raja chewed the inside of his cheek. The Bhagavad Gita speaks of another way to combat injustice. *But would Shankar listen?* "Keep me out of that one. However, of one thing I am sure: I'll never betray you, my friend." Raja stood up, holding on to the table for support while he cried drunken tears.

Shankar managed to steady himself. "Time to go," he said. He held Raja's arm and they both stumbled out onto the dirt road.

Raja broke loose from Shankar's grip. With rubbery legs, he wandered from one side of the path to the other. Shankar caught up with him, grabbed his arm and steered him through the entrance of his logie.

After they both had sobered up with some of Raja's food, Shankar said, "I will need your help to protect me from those scums."

"Ask your drinking pal to tip you off before they close the net."

Shankar hiccoughed, took a sip of water. "I have to be careful for his sake."

"But we must act fast to free you from their clutches."

Shankar squatted on the floor propping his head with his hands. "Wait until you hear from me."

"Are you sure you can trust your friend?"

"Completely; all over a bottle."

Far away, someone was playing a bansuri flute. It took Raja back to the time when he'd boarded the SS *Arcot* that had taken him away from his country.

"So you have a good man working for you."

Shankar shook his head. "He told me that if all else fails, the agents are prepared to secretly ship me out of the colony to face trial in India, where most likely I'll be hanged."

Two weeks had gone by when Shankar dropped in at Raja's logie and announced, "My pal said he cannot meet with me anymore."

"Why not?"

"He said that he is being watched. Further, he said that the agents have moved away to give me a false sense of security but will return at the end of my contract."

"To keep you away from their reach is not going to be easy." Raja scratched his head. "During the time I went missing, an Arawak man invited me to stay with them. Perhaps I can take you to their village, if I can find a canoe."

Tears came to Shankar's eyes, but he wiped them dry. His voice cracked with emotion. "You mean for me to link up with either the Arawaks or the Bush Negroes! Oh my! It would mean the end of our friendship, Raja; I will become a stranger in a forgotten world."

Raja wondered how a man trained to kill could become so emotional. In some ways, Shankar reminded him of Sen, the man without a family. Raja, too, would find it difficult to survive in the colony without his friend. After a period of silence, he said, "It is the sacrifice you must make if you want to be safe from the agents."

"That's one way to look at it." Shankar was obviously trying his best to present a strong front. Finally, he said, "Raja, you find me the canoe; the rest will be up to me."

Raja looked upon those words as empty talk. His friend was all skin and bones and he seemed incapable of withstanding the rigours of canoeing for days upriver to where the Arawaks lived. Raja would worry about that another day. "Let's wait for the final year of our indentureship," he said. "I must complete mine if I want to return to my family."

"My contract should end a little after yours for failure to complete my daily tasks."

"That's when I'll paddle you to the Arawak village."

"In exchange for your help, I'll give you lessons in English and Sanskrit." Shankar sounded as though he meant it.

The fourth year of Raja's indentureship arrived and with it came the April rains. For the first few days, there was no let-up. Because of widespread flooding, the management team shifted the workers away from cutting cane to draining the land. Labourers manned the sluice gates and opened them at low tide to get rid of the floodwaters. However, as the flooding intensified, the water no longer drained, and Plantation Sugar Grove was in trouble. The entire crop was threatened.

Many workers came down with alternating bouts of shivering and fever. To avoid being fined or whipped for missed days of work, men staggered along the footpath that led to the cane field. However, as the situation got worse, the estate management realized that they had an epidemic on their hands. Doc and his assistants could not cope with the malaria, which they said was caused by "mal" or bad air from the swamps. The swamp fever had been taking its toll, necessitating a steady replacement by recently arrived workers.

Payday arrived and Shankar took Raja along for a weekend drink. Since it was Raja's turn to treat, he went for half a bottle.

They chose a window seat for the soft sea breeze that blew onto their faces. Shankar's sunken cheeks caused Raja to ask, "What's the matter? You look like a ghost."

"Every third night I have short spells of chills followed by longer periods of fever and sweating."

"You might have the ague. Better inform Mr. Van Sluytman."

"He would only refer me to Doc who, if he doesn't place me in the sick house, would send me home with the usual brown mixture. That man should practise obeah; it might save some of the workers." Shankar poured himself a shot and downed it in one gulp.

Unable to match his companion, Raja went for a tiny drink. "No time to joke, Shankar. Doc may have some new pill to keep workers alive."

"The sick house is probably full anyway." Shankar's head swayed like the branch of a coconut palm, and his red and swollen eyes remained half shut. "Tell me, bhai, how do you stay healthy?"

"I always wear white clothing, so I perspire less. Mosquitoes are attracted to sweat and body heat."

Shankar downed another shot. "What do mosquitoes have to do with my illness?"

"You were supposed to be the smart one. Ancient Ayurvedic writings say ague—what Doc calls swamp fever or malaria—has some connection with mosquitoes after heavy rains."

"That's all folklore."

Raja downed his drink and chased it with water. "No! I heard it myself from the elders. Back in my village, during mosquito season, all members of our family rubbed themselves with juice from neem leaves; at night, we burned the leaves to make smoke. It chased away the bloodsuckers, and perhaps that was why we stayed healthy."

Shankar uttered a strange sound. "Too late for me, bhai."

"If the overseer puts you on the sick list and you give up drinking, you might stand a chance." Raja led his friend out of the shop.

That very night, despite the effect of the drinks, he pondered the situation. Why were so many workers falling ill? Doc had told everyone that poisonous swamp air from stagnant water was the culprit, but Raja was not convinced. He knew that the swamps provided the perfect breeding ground for mosquitoes, which had something to do with the ague. Perhaps Doc had it only half-right.

Here on the estate, no one seemed to care about mosquitoes much less smoking them out. Raja, however, decided he would keep on doing what he'd done in the past to avoid this swamp sickness. He'd use his white scarf to cover most of his face and ears. His long-sleeved kurta would do the rest.

A week later when he met up with his friend in the rum shop, Shankar left his drink untouched, so Raja drank alone. The stiff shot of rum he took gurgled down his throat like a hand rubbed over calico. He made a face as though in pain and at that very moment vowed to make that his last drink.

One look at his friend and it dawned on Raja that there might be no lessons forthcoming, neither in English nor Sanskrit nor anything else for that matter. Shankar was dying before Raja's very eyes, and any information Raja needed had to be gleaned in a hurry. "You told me that a new culture would spring up in this country, Shankar. I wonder what you think now."

A sober Shankar always made a lot of sense, like the scholar he was. His eyes narrowed for an instant as the words flowed. "This country is still growing and its position in the world is what the people here make of it. If they aim high, the change will be noble, even for a small country. People like Kwame and you will mould a new culture, set new standards by example. Even Ramdas will make a contribution."

"The devils sent us to different estates," Raja said.

"But they haven't broken your spirit."

Raja pushed the schnapps glass away. "This country has changed me in many ways; I drank too much rum for my own good, hardly practised my religion, and now I speak Creole."

On the way home, Shankar placed his arm on Raja's shoulder. "Whether you like it or not, the country changes the people and the people change the country."

Raja decided to cherish those words from his friend. How fortunate he was to have crossed paths with Shankar.

Monday morning, on the way to work, Raja went over to Shankar's logie to pick him up. The man's legs were buckling so Raja had to carry him on his back, all the way to the cane field. With the driver out of sight, Raja helped his friend complete his task. In the afternoon, Shankar had regained some of his strength, and Raja guided him home.

The following day, Raja was relieved when Van Sluytman shouted, "Shankar, I want you to work under Kwame."

"Thank you, sir," Shankar said. He clasped his hands together, bowed to the overseer and left to join Kwame's gang.

Raja bore no animosity toward Van Sluytman, nor did he wish Mathu ill. According to his way of thinking, no human or beast should be beaten to get more work out of them. If only the drivers could be like Kwame, life on the plantation would be bearable! However, with Van Sluytman's one apparent act of kindness toward Shankar, Raja's previous perceptions of the man had unravelled, or so it seemed.

One afternoon, Kwame escorted Raja to the manure gang where Shankar was working. "Your friend is doing fine," Kwame said, "but if he wants to win the battle, he must stay away from the bottle."

Shankar smiled. "My last drink was left untouched. Isn't that so, Raja?"

Without waiting for an answer, Kwame reached forward and shook Shankar's hand.

During the half-hour lunch break, Jasmine joined Raja. They chatted throughout the meal, hardly able to take their eyes off each other.

"My conscience is killing me," Raja said. "It is not right that we meet like this. People will gossip."

"I don't care what people say."

A dry coconut came straight at Raja's head. He ducked. "Who did that?" he shouted, looking around. "That could be the work of only a coward like Sonnyboy, using the coconut as a ball and my head as the wicket," he exclaimed.

"He is jealous because of my feelings for you," Jasmine said in a soft, soulful voice that made her so irresistible.

Raja resumed his seat. "Jasmine, I care for you and would marry you if only to keep you away from that prowler. However, this could never be since I have a wife."

"Do you hear from her?"

"According to Shankar, one cannot count on mail service in a remote village."

Jasmine appeared to consider those words. "I'm sure she loves you, Raja, and thinks often of you, so I must not get in the way." A single teardrop rolled down her cheek.

Raja plucked a blade of grass and chewed it. "What about Sonnyboy? Is he interested in you?"

Jasmine appeared quite serious when she said, "He wants to meet with me in the cane field after work on Tuesday. He said he would skip cricket practice on that day."

"Stay away from him," Raja said. "He acts like a sneaky mongoose." Those words brought a smile to Jasmine's face.

A redbreast uttered a long shrill note and alighted on a near-by clammy cherry tree. Its song signalled the end of the lunch break. "Time to get back to work," Raja said.

For the next few days, he made sure he always ate with the men. That kept Jasmine away for weeks until the day when Raja had a visit from her before lunch.

"Oh! I'm so lucky to find you all by yourself," she said.

Her eyes flickered in the sun's rays, and Raja was entranced all over again. They shared lunch after which he accompanied her to her work area. They held hands as they jumped over several drains, choked with weeds. Whenever they missed a drain, they would laugh. Young and carefree, they both seemed to realize the pleasure they were missing.

Before they parted, she said, "When can we meet again?"

"I don't know," Raja said, yet all the while he wanted to see and talk to her.

For weeks, his life was misery as he did his chores like a man in a daze.

One day a driver ordered Jasmine to weed the drain bordering the field where Raja worked. At the end of the day they met, and soon he was embracing and smothering her with kisses. She pulled away to catch her breath for she seemed to be choking. Obviously, kissing was not her way of showing love. Raja, who'd experimented with Savitri in this regard, understood and would be patient. Again, he had to be careful since he did not wish to create a scandal on the estate.

Despite their mutual attraction, he trusted that one or the other would have the willpower to keep their romance to just kissing. At the back of his mind, he was sure that Sonnyboy would like to damage his reputation and at the same time win over Jasmine.

Raja's old country beliefs still lurked in the background. He was not accustomed to seeing women in Western clothing. The way he was brought up, he considered Jasmine's dresses revealing and suggestive. However, because of his affection for her, his Indian code of behaviour was being chipped away bit by bit.

In the colony, a single girl like Jasmine could dress as she wished. Her floral frocks showed off her slim, shapely figure. While most of the South Indian women tied a Madras-patterned kerchief on their heads to keep the sun out, the youthful Jasmine chose a red scarf. Like those women, she wrapped the fabric on her head in the style of the black estate nannies who worked in the homes of their former masters. A matching silk shawl around her neck gave her a sexual charm and mystique.

Over time, Raja's resolve to stay away from Jasmine went to pieces. He shook his head and covered his face with his hands. How could this be happening to him? Now he was looking forward to Saturdays when they would meet. The young wife he had left back in the village was far from his mind.

As Raja was about to leave for home one afternoon, a gentle breeze kissed the cane field, bathed golden from the rays of the sun. He found himself in an embrace with Jasmine—an interval like no other when for a moment the world stood still.

Electricity flowed to his lips, to his tongue, to every part of his body. The rustle of wind swayed the sugarcane leaves. A head-banded kiskadee, high up on a tamarind tree, sang its melody, "kiss-kiss-kiss-kiskadee." Jasmine's hair was filled with the smell of cane leaves. She fell to the ground, taking Raja with her. A bed of sugarcane leaves cushioned their bodies, setting up a vibration that shook the air. She acted as though she might settle for that particular moment. Raja's wraparound clothing parted as they touched. Nothing separated them as they melted into one. He had no feelings of guilt for meeting this way with Jasmine, and according to his way of thinking, he had done nothing wrong.

Crunch! Crunch! The sound of bare feet on sugarcane leaves startled them. Raja held her hand and brought her to her feet. Hurriedly, they dusted themselves off just before Driver Kwame walked by on his way home.

"I saw nothing, Raja," Kwame said, as Raja tried to block Jasmine from Kwame's view. He, however, rubbed his chin and, with open mouth, winked at Raja. "Payroll office will soon be closed. Not interested in pay this week?"

Raja smiled, looking quite embarrassed.

Another driver would have reported them, resulting in both he and Jasmine being punished.

Later, Kwame said to Raja, "Watch yourself, man. You can't suck cane and blow whistle at the same time." That brought a smile from Raja.

His romance with Jasmine went on for months. In some ways, he was happy his love affair had ended Sonnyboy's advances toward her. However, doubts about his relationship with such a beautiful woman soon started to plague him. He was getting upset with himself for not having the willpower, the inner strength she seemed to lack.

After they had made love in the cane field one afternoon, he wondered if Jasmine was really a loose woman. He'd told her he was married, yet she threw herself into the affair with reckless abandon, not caring about the consequences. "Jasmine, what we're doing is wrong," he said to her one day.

She pulled herself away. "I don't understand."

"This is not right since I have a wife."

She broke out in tears, smoothed out the creases in her frock, gathered up her lunch pail and left in a huff.

Ashamed, he bit his lip until it bled. By the time he left for home, a heavy mist and darkness had fallen upon the land. Had Raja stayed away from Jasmine from the beginning, he would not have created the situation he found himself in. He had brought it upon himself and now he had become entangled in a love affair that was more complex than he had bargained for.

Sunday's arrival saw Raja visiting Shankar, who had been admitted to the infirmary. The combination of smells from Jeyes fluid disinfectant liberally sprinkled on the floor, and gangrenous pus, upset Raja's stomach.

As he walked toward his friend, Raja heard the familiar voice of someone who was already there. His heart pounded hard, but Jasmine's distant manner seemed cold. "I'm sorry for what I said the other day," he said, pulling her aside.

Her silence gave Raja the impression that she was not ready to forgive. Minutes went by before she pointed toward Shankar and whispered, "Your friend is very weak."

Those words gave Raja the opening he craved. "That's why I'm here," he said in a low voice, "but first I want to speak to you."

It was some time before Jasmine again found her voice. "Why must our lives be such misery, Raja? Why can't we have something warm and wonderful, something to look forward to?" Raja seemed tongue-tied, and so Jasmine continued, "Why don't you marry me and settle down in this country? Marriages back home are not recognized here."

Raja was taken aback. He realized that Jasmine was pleading with him and he wished he could have given her the happiness she longed for. He held Jasmine's hand. "My duty is to my family in Belwasa," he said. "I must return to them. I wish you'd understand."

Jasmine's eyes narrowed. "My heart is a shattered glass. But if you change your mind, I'll pick up those pieces one by one."

She pulled herself away and slowly walked past the door into a light drizzle. Raja watched her until her red headscarf had faded into a haze of nothingness.

He stood there a long time wishing that life could have been simpler without its many challenges. The difficult choice he had to make of duty over love had caused him to hurt Jasmine more than he would have wanted and he regretted it.

Raja hid his shock when he took a good look at his friend. The once thin, pimpled, but healthy face had become misshapen, the cheeks sunken and sallow.

"How are you, Raja?" Shankar asked, after he had woken up.

"Forget about me," Raja said. "You look very pale," Raja rubbed his hand across Shankar's face, "I'm so glad you've come to the sick house after all."

"Mr. Van Sluytman told Kwame to bring me here," Shankar whispered. "Though I don't get those bouts of shivering anymore, I have no energy."

Raja now placed the back of his hand on Shankar's neck. "While you don't have the fever, yet this disease lies in wait and might strike at any time."

"Just like those two agents."

"That's why they want you to stay alive."

Shankar, with palms outstretched and shaking, said, "Each day could be my last."

"I wish you wouldn't say it that way." For Shankar's sake, Raja fought back tears.

"Don't be sorry for me. If I had to relive my life, I'd do the same thing."

"For now, I must save you. Remember that canoe trip that you . . . we have to make," Raja said, his voice cracking.

Shankar looked away. "Is that trip still on?" he asked in a faint voice.

"Sure, it is. I will ask Kwame to find us a canoe. But we must be secretive in case those agents get wind of our plan."

Shankar expanded his chest and made a fist. "Raja, I will make myself strong for such a journey."

Raja hugged his friend, believing in his heart that the time to part was near. *Would it be for all time?*

CHAPTER FOURTEEN

As the fifth year of Raja's contract rolled in, he continued distancing himself from Jasmine.

To Raja's surprise, she joined him once again for lunch one day. While he ate, she left her food untouched.

"Will you change your mind and marry me, Raja?" she pleaded. "It is important you tell me now." Jasmine was shaking all over; there seemed to be a lot on her mind.

Raja wished he were free to marry a girl who was beautiful in so many ways. His feelings were strong, but the relationship was a complex one. So, without responding, he got up and walked toward his work area.

A few days later, on his way for a drink of water, he spotted Jasmine's red headscarf floating in the canal beside the sandkoker tree. In a flash, he jumped into the water and dragged his hands back and forth, searching. Before too long, he pulled up a body among foamy bubbles and floating duckweed. "Help! Help!" he cried. In a panic, he dragged Jasmine to dry land and rocked her body back and forth.

Water gurgled out of her mouth just as Overseer Van Sluytman came galloping on his mule. He dismounted, checked for a pulse, and worked on Jasmine like a man who had been trained for that very purpose.

Jasmine's chest rose as she groaned causing Raja to take a deep breath, much relieved that she had started to breathe on her own.

"Jasmine," Van Sluytman called out, "did Raja try to drown you?"

Stunned, Raja waited to hear Jasmine's answer. Moments went by before she found her voice. "No sir. I lost my balance and fell into the canal."

After Jasmine had straightened her soaked frock that had crept up over her knees, Van Sluytman said to Raja, "I'll take Jasmine to her hut. She needs a good rest."

Van Sluytman placed Jasmine sidesaddle on his mule, one hand firmly around her waist, and rode toward the line of logies where she lived.

Raja wondered if Jasmine had tried to drown herself. Still confused, he visited her logie the next evening.

"Why did you do it, Jasmine?" Raja asked.

"What do you mean?"

"You should know."

"What I told the overseer was true."

Raja took the liberty to embrace Jasmine. "I'm so happy I reached you in time."

Whether Jasmine's near drowning was accidental or not, he'd find out later.

Everyone on the estate was talking about Sonnyboy's cricket performance in Georgetown. The *Royal Gazette's* headline in the sports section read: Sonnyboy bags six wickets at Parade Ground for the Governor's XI against a strong team from the Georgetown Cricket Club.

That made Sonnyboy the pre-eminent bowler in the colony since one of his victims had scored a century against a strong Barbados Eleven.

At the start of the long-awaited friendly match against the single men, basically the Sugar Grove First Eleven, Raja went up and congratulated Sonnyboy on his recent achievement.

Sonnyboy brushed it off as though it was all in a day's work. "Your bowlers can bowl underarm if they choose." He smiled but it was more of a sneer. "It's hard to hit sixes off ground balls, you know."

"Underarm! Do you take us for sissies?" Raja asked.

He'd tried his best to keep his voice low, but his teammates, many recruited from neighbouring sugar estates, chanted, "Rah! Rah! We'll trounce the bachelors."

Sonnyboy took a few steps toward the group and gritting his teeth, said, "Very well. We'll show you no mercy."

The bachelors batted first and made 148 runs, Sonnyboy contributing forty-five. Raja surprised himself by capturing four wickets for forty-six runs. He credited his father with having shown him to use his other arm in a high action to propel the bowling arm for a pitch right up to the batsman. In addition, he varied his trajectory somewhere between a high and an almost side-arm delivery.

"Good bowling, sir," Sonnyboy said to Raja. "Now let's see what you can do with the bat."

In a game where each side would bat once, Raja expected his team to be bowled out early since, as the saying went, if you never played on a Georgetown pitch you were most likely a cross-bat slugger with no forward defensive shot.

Sonnyboy opened the bowling. He banged the ball from the centre of the pitch, hitting both opening batsmen on the arms. After he'd softened them up, he turned to left-arm outswingers and leg cutters, which the batsmen edged to the safe hands of slip fieldsmen.

Raja blocked each delivery in his first over but hit twenty-five runs off the next thirty balls. In the end, he was clean bowled, neck and crop, by one of Sonnyboy's yorkers that dipped under his bat.

"Just stay there and try to reach fifty," Raja yelled to the last pair of batsmen. He was pleased that his team had mustered seventy runs, thus avoiding humiliation.

"After you finish your indentureship, you should become a cricketer," Sonnyboy said to Raja. "You'll make a two-bit all-rounder." He smiled, displaying a full set of white teeth, polished from years of chewing sugarcane.

"It won't happen, since I'm anxious to return home."

"Everyone knows about you and Jasmine. Are you going to marry her and settle down here?"

Was Sonnyboy testing him? Raja sensed that Sonnyboy would like to replace him as Jasmine's boyfriend. "She knows my feelings toward my family," he said.

"Well, in that case I'm free to move in."

Raja wagged a finger at Sonnyboy. "Jasmine is a nice girl."

Sonnyboy grinned and walked away.

Later that evening, in Chan-a-Sue's Grocery, Jasmine sported a sterling silver bracelet.

"Who gave you such a beautiful gift?" Raja asked.

"Sonnyboy. He said that it was the governor's prize for best bowler."

"You should not have accepted it."

"Why? He's been my boyfriend ever since you lost interest in me."

As Jasmine walked to work one morning, she was vomiting all along the footpath.

"What's the matter, Jasmine?" Raja asked when he found her alone.

"I think I'm pregnant."

Raja had no doubt as to who the prospective father was. Later, during the lunch break, he called Jasmine aside. "I will have a talk with Sonnyboy."

"Raja, let me give him the news first."

On Monday morning, Jasmine appeared rather sad. "Was Sonnyboy excited?" Raja asked.

"No. He said that the baby might even be yours and that he is not ready to be a family man."

"Don't worry. I'll deal with him."

Before the lunch break, Raja went up to the jamun tree where Sonnyboy had just completed the last of a series of knife throws. Raja said, "You got Jasmine pregnant. Now you must do the honourable thing and marry her."

"Why?"

"Because Jasmine's child will need a father." Raja never expected to find his eyes level with Sonnyboy's. "Well, tell me what you intend to do."

"You know who my father is?"

"One who drives the coolies like bullocks."

Sonnyboy clenched his jaws giving the impression that he was going to go for a throw. Instead, he said, "You and your skin-and-bones friend are a couple of useless drunks."

Stung by those words, Raja walked up to Sonnyboy and eyeballed him. At that very moment, the hissing sound of a snake from deep inside a bramble bush caused Raja to glance to the right whereupon Sonnyboy took the opportunity to drop his cutlass and land a right-cross flush on Raja's jaw.

His world went topsy-turvy and only through instinct he grabbed Sonnyboy in a bear hug until his head cleared.

The men wrapped one another's legs, waist, and arms like two boas. With one final trick up his sleeve, Raja applied a body scissors coupled with a headlock that seemed to sap Sonnyboy's strength.

"I surrender," Sonnyboy said, panting. He rubbed his neck as if it were on fire.

Wrestling for half an hour had drained Raja's stamina due to his past indulgence in rum. He relaxed, but as he let his guard down, Sonnyboy reached for his cutlass. Like a jungle cat, he advanced upon Raja with his weapon poised, ready for a throw.

Raja trembled at the sight of the sharp-edged pointed blade of the cutlass in Sonnyboy's throwing hand. A quick look around reminded Raja that he was in a battle, not for the championship, but for his life. Escape was out of the question for the dense cane field stood on one side and the canal on the other.

Raja took a deep breath and screamed when he realized that Sonnyboy intended to wield the cutlass instead of going for a single throw and would apply his cricketing skills in a fight in which he now had the upper hand.

Quickly, Raja moved clockwise away from the striking hand. Like a magician, Sonnyboy switched the cutlass to his other hand. With his back to the canal, Raja dashed to the other side before faking a move toward the cutlass.

Sonnyboy did not fall for that trap; instead he struck out at Raja's right biceps, missed, but connected on the second try. Raja was bleeding from a deep gash and fell to the ground. As he lay there ready to aim a kick at Sonnyboy if he ever came close, the man slipped away.

As news spread about the fight, a crowd gathered around Raja. Jasmine was among them yelling like a crazy woman.

Kwame came rushing to the scene, panting for breath. "Who did this?"

"Accident," Raja said, knowing full well he had no business leaving his work area to confront Sonnyboy. Had he not acted as Jasmine's guardian, he would have been fine. "My fault," he mumbled and fell in a pool of blood.

Kwame rolled up Raja's sleeve to expose the cut that was bleeding so fast it had soaked his kurta. "That's a bad chop." He placed a clean rag over the wound.

"Take him to the dispensary, Kwame," Jasmine pleaded. "Don't let him die."

Broad-shouldered with a rock-solid physique, Kwame raised Raja to his feet and, with fingers wrapped around the wound, helped his friend along the path that led to the emergency clinic.

"Just stay alive," Kwame said as Raja moaned. "We're almost there."

Doc, who performed a double function as both a nurse and a dispenser, stopped the bleeding with cobwebs and sterilized the cut with carbolic acid.

"You owe your life to Kwame. You could have bled to death," Doc said to Raja as he wrapped a bandage around a soap-and-sugar poultice over the wound.

"Thank you, Doc," Raja said as he sat up in the cot.

"To keep my job, I must make a report, Mr. Singh."

Three weeks had gone by when Van Sluytman said to Raja, "The manager made an entry about the fight in his log book. It might come back to haunt you."

Meanwhile, the manager met with Sonnyboy, his father, and Jasmine. With father and son's careers on the line, it didn't take much prodding for Sonnyboy to agree to marry Jasmine.

Raja and Shankar attended the Madras ceremony, which was held under a tent and presided over by a priest. The night was dark with no wind. Mathu and Van Sluytman sat up front—the only ones on chairs. Jasmine and Sonnyboy wore yellow chrysanthemum necklaces.

Raja grew restless. He couldn't bear seeing Jasmine wedded to Sonnyboy. *Did I make a mistake?* Part way into the ceremony Raja made a move and was about to get to his feet. "I will end this right now," he whispered.

Shankar placed an arm on Raja's shoulder. "It's too late."

"It can still be done," Raja said. In his heart, he wept. "She must not belong to any other but me."

"Marriage is serious business. You cannot act on the spur of the moment."

Raja nodded, trying his best to dispel his confusion. Something told him this man was not the right person for Jasmine. Had he obeyed his natural impulses, he would have cried out in protest. Instead, he tried to be stoic and not reveal his inner torment. *Oh, Jasmine, that should have been me next to you.*

As Jasmine's pregnancy came closer to term, Raja was happy that Van Sluytman had decided to shift her to the children's gang.

"Mr. Van Sluytman held you by the hand as you crossed the ditch," Raja said, sneaking up to Jasmine on the way home. "He talks to you often."

"He is only trying to be helpful."

"I'm worried about what Sonnyboy might think."

"And you also should not be walking next to his wife. He is jealous of both of you."

"He shouldn't be. And as to Van Sluytman, the man turned out to be a fine fellow after all."

"You're right. He will give me leave when the time draws near. But you see, Sonnyboy thinks that the overseer wants to win favours from me."

From the goings-on around the plantation with so few women workers, Raja knew that jealousy could drive a man to drink and make him crazy. Now Sonnyboy seemed to be following that pattern.

Though the rum shop was closed on Sunday, Sonnyboy gained entry through the back entrance. With shoulders slumped, he looked like he had not slept for many nights.

On the way to work, Raja asked Jasmine, "What's bothering Sonnyboy?"

"He lurks in the background whenever Mr. Van Sluytman talks to me. Please stay away. He's acting strange, filling himself with rum."

On Saturday, Raja came face to face with a haggard-looking Sonnyboy as he headed for the rum shop—this time through the front door. "Wait," Raja said. "I'd like to have a man-to-man talk with you."

"Leave me alone," Sonnyboy shouted, as he elbowed Raja aside and entered the premises.

That night flashes of lightning, claps of thunder, and heavy bouts of rain bombarded Raja in his shelter. His body shook from the explosions. While raindrops pounded his roof, he lay in bed and listened for any sign of a row taking place in the family quarters. With all that noise, he couldn't possibly hear screams coming from anywhere.

He thought he should have sought out Sonnyboy in the rum shop, and there he could have told him he had nothing to fear. As a man, Raja could understand why Sonnyboy, married to the most attractive woman on the estate, would be jealous. However, when it came right down to it, there was no reason for Sonnyboy to look upon Raja as a rival.

When Raja could not stay another moment in bed, he got dressed in the dark. He headed toward Sonnyboy and Jasmine's hut and listened at the door. Sonnyboy's drunken sobs told him something was wrong.

As soon as he pressed his weight against the door, it gave way. The light from the kerosene lamp revealed Jasmine's lifeless body lying face down in a river of blood. Raja's knees buckled. He swayed and collapsed onto the floor.

On wobbly legs, he moaned out like that of the night wind, realizing that if there were some way he could sacrifice his life so she could live, he would do it. Only now he knew how much he had cared, how much he had loved. *The lamp of my life has been snuffed out leaving only darkness. My reason for living has been taken from me.*

He fell silent for a long time, trying hard to believe that what he saw was not real. *Let it be just a dream.*

After his head cleared, he became aware of several deep gashes on Jasmine's arms and the cutlass, next to her body, with blood dripping from its blade. The very cutlass used to chop his arm in the fight with Sonnyboy. He could only imagine how she must have suffered, and he hoped that she had died quickly. If only he'd come sooner, he would have saved both mother and the child, who was soon to be born. Now there was nothing he could do. He mouthed the words, "please forgive me."

The sound of a male crying and sniffling made him turn. Sonnyboy, his body and clothes dripping with blood, sat on a bench in a corner weeping, his head in his hands. He smelled of rum. "Why! Why!" Raja screamed, but amidst the sound of falling rain, his voice was drowned out.

He grabbed Sonnyboy by the collar and tightened his grip. Sonnyboy's body went limp. Raja lifted him off the bench, rocked him back and forth, dropped him, slapped his face, backhanded and repeated the action again and again.

Raja was losing his mind, and he forced himself to stop. He realized that he was out of control and did not want to commit his own act of murder.

Sonnyboy blubbered like a baby. He had found his voice. "I went crazy. I accused her of meeting in secret with Van Sluytman." He could not continue for some time. Finally, through sobs he said, "Her last words were, 'Oh Sonnyboy, I still love you . . . I'm sorry for you.'" He cried louder. "Now I can never bring my darling back. What am I going to do, Raja?"

"Nothing! Just plain nothing!"

"Can you not help me clean up? We can say that we discovered her body after a night of drinking and talking cricket."

"Yeh. You no-good scum."

Raja peered outside. There was a lull in the storm, and the night was cloaked in an eerie silence. All of a sudden, the storm again erupted. A bolt of lightning accompanied by a crack of thunder made him fearful to go outside, but he had to act.

Dogs howled as he grabbed Sonnyboy, who offered no resistance, and hustled him along the path toward the manager's compound. Raja's teeth chattered and he was shivering uncontrollably by the time he reached the shed.

He addressed the half-asleep gateman. "I've come to turn Sonnyboy in," Raja said, his voice cracking, "for murder."

The gateman rubbed the sleep from his eyes, shook his head a few times as if to clear it, and called for help. Two houseboys came forward, exchanged words with the gateman, seized Sonnyboy and took him to the manager's compound.

On Sunday morning, when Sonnyboy would normally have been playing cricket, three police officers from the district rode in on horseback. After a statement from Raja, they tied Sonnyboy's hands, attached a rope to his waist and led him away like a dog.

Some children and Sonnyboy's teammates, all teary-eyed, came to give him support. Sonnyboy, however, kept his eyes on the ground.

"They are taking from us the sweetest bowler in the world," a boy cried out. He sobbed uncontrollably.

A few scraggly young men tried to block the policemen from taking their hero, but they were shoved aside.

Raja ran into Kwame later that day. "Sonnyboy deserves what's coming to him," Raja said, "but I am partly to blame for what has happened to Jasmine." Raja continued to spill it all out, "The culprit has taken a part of me, the only person who could have tied me to this country. Now I must live with that loss." Raja clutched his chest as though that would ease the pain.

"You had a weakness for Jasmine and she for you," Kwame said. "I told you a long time ago that you should have married the girl and settled down in this country. She really loved you."

"Kwame, if only I could relive my life."

Kwame embraced Raja. "You made a big mistake, Raja. As the old Fante proverb says, 'When wind passes, you can never bring it back.'" The narrow slits of Kwame's eyes shone through with warmth and kindness. "Come visit when you have time."

CHAPTER FIFTEEN

Raja visited Kwame one evening, under the cover of darkness. "When my five years are up," he whispered, "and that should be any time now, I will take Shankar to Ar'wak. But I'll need to borrow a canoe."

"I'll arrange for you to pick one up from an old friend," Kwame said. "He lives in a hut beside the old silk cotton tree over yonder." He indicated the direction of the jumbie tree with a tilt of his head.

The following week late on a Saturday afternoon, Overseer Van Sluytman summoned Raja and handed him a document.

Raja beckoned the black butler and passed over the paper. "What does it say?"

The butler, sporting a pair of spectacles perched jauntily at the tip of his nose, leaned his head back, pored over the sheet as though performing a noble service and read aloud, "Passenger No. 198 ex SS *Arcot*, having completed his term of five years, is hereby released from his indentureship and contractual obligations . . . ."

Van Sluytman cleared his throat and said to Raja, "Collect your pay. You have one day to leave the plantation."

In no time, Raja grabbed a few things and headed for the cane field where he found Kwame pacing back and forth. "What's the matter?" Raja enquired.

"Follow me," Kwame said. He took Raja to where Shankar was stumbling and picking himself up, trying his utmost to complete his task of spreading manure on a patch of young cane shoots.

"They brought me a sick man with a week to go before his contract ends," Kwame whispered.

Shankar looked up from what he was doing. He took short, rapid breaths and was shivering from head to toe. "The cold and hot spells and the sweating have returned," he said to Raja in a weak voice. "But don't worry; I can still make that trip."

Raja held his friend by the shoulders and spoke in his ear, "My contract is over, and I'm free to take you upriver."

"It worked out just right, Raja."

"Just you hold on."

"Raja," Kwame whispered, pulling Raja aside, "that canoe is ready. It is stocked with salted cod and cassava bread."

"Now I'm the one who's indebted to you," Raja said, but Kwame waved him off.

The hot season had not yet set in, and the air was rich with the aroma of burned sugarcane. Kwame held Shankar's hands and hugged him for a moment before dashing off to the gang he supervised.

Raja hoisted Shankar piggyback style and tore across the open savannah. A gentle Atlantic breeze caressed Raja's face. He could hear the crunch of grass under his bare feet as he headed straight for the huge silk cotton tree whose buttressed roots gleamed in the slanting light of the sun. There was no need to avoid that tree, for the last haze of daylight still hung over the river valley.

The thatched hut where Kwame's friend lived came into view. Several canoes were tied to a sandkoker tree on the bank of the river. Raja let out a sigh of relief when he saw two paddles and a basket of food in one of them.

If only Shankar could find the inner strength to stay alive till they reach that settlement, Ar'wak might know of some bush medicine to cure Shankar of his illness.

Raja was leaning over and attempting to seat Shankar in the canoe when a hard kick on his bottom made him let go of his friend and shout, "Who the devil . . . ." He turned and faced two men in khaki outfits, their revolvers drawn. They had sneaked up on foot. Raja recognized the leader and realized they were the British agents who were after Shankar.

"Hands up, both of you," the Agent-in-Charge, the taller of the two, said. "You Sagar Singh?" He waved the gun at Shankar, took aim and shouted, "Isn't that your correct name? Answer before the count of three. One, two."

"Ye-yes, sir."

"We arrest you as a fugitive from British justice. And you, Roger Singh, for being an accessory."

Before Raja could get his hands up, Shankar grabbed the second agent's weapon just as Raja head-butted the leader, knocking him to the ground and causing his weapon to fly through the air.

Shankar cocked the hammer of the revolver with his left hand and pulled the trigger with his right. Each action flowed into the other with blinding speed. Raja blinked from the white muzzle flash and the loud bang, and when he opened his eyes, the second agent lay prostrate, bleeding at the chest. Shankar repeated the same action with the Agent-in-Charge, who was trying to get up.

Raja shook his head to clear it from the fog of the world of secret agents and dangerous missions involving gunfire. He could not believe that Shankar's legs had held up. The man's skill and speed with the revolver showed that he must have rehearsed such an event hundreds of times at his secret training camp back at the university.

He fired again at the agents' heads. Raja turned aside and threw up at the sight of what was left of the two bodies lying on the ground.

Speechless, he could only stare at his friend who, in a moment of danger had called upon some inner strength that was nowhere evident before his illness.

Shankar left the bodies lying in a tangled mess on a bed of crabgrass and fallen leaves. He turned and looked at Raja, giving no hint as to what was going through his mind. "I'll take these revolvers and try to make it alone," he said, as he staggered toward the canoe, looking a sordid mess with blood and brain tissue splattered all over his face, hands, and clothes.

"You'll never make it. You're too weak for such a journey," Raja said, as he caught up with Shankar.

"Better this way. I do not want you to be charged with helping me to escape."

Raja walked back and forth and rubbed his hands together. Sweat poured from his forehead. Such cold-blooded murder by Shankar seemed like a dream. The agents were already disarmed, and Raja might have considered another way. *But did Shankar have a choice?*

Not sure of what to do, Raja turned him around, but Shankar, with some hitherto unforeseen strength, broke away.

"I'll paddle and rest and take my time until I get to that village," Shankar said. "Ar'wak, you said his name was?" he asked before stumbling off and lowering himself in the canoe. "Raja," he continued, his voice shaking, "you must return to Savitri. Forget what I told you before. She'd be waiting . . . ."

Raja screwed up his face. "Wait!" he shouted. He rushed forward, but Shankar had already paddled out of reach.

He must have heard Raja's call for he waved his paddle and dipped it with rapid strokes, which Raja knew was only for show.

As twilight descended on the plantation, Shankar became a tiny speck of a man looking for that home where he would no longer be hunted down. Raja hoped that he'd find it. That haunted look in Shankar's eyes and the image of him paddling away toward freedom would remain with Raja for a long, long time.

With watery eyes, he took one last look at the bodies of the agents swarmed with large blowflies, before rushing off to his logie.

Later that evening, a worried Raja paid Kwame a visit. The wooded lot around Kwame's home beckoned Raja, perhaps for the last time. A full moon had started its ascent when he approached the hut. The balata tree, with its soft gum and the chattering house wrens flitting about calmed his thudding heart; it helped him understand why Kwame found peace there.

At the doorway, Olu and Polly competed for attention. The smell of fu-fu, well seasoned with homegrown shallots, filled the air, but Raja had no desire for food. "I came to say goodbye, Kwame," he shouted.

Kwame walked around as though looking for prowlers. "I hope your friend can find some hidden strength to reach that Arawak settlement." He gestured for Raja to come inside.

Raja made himself comfortable, sitting cross-legged on the bench. "When it comes down to it, Kwame, it does not matter as long as those men failed to get him." Raja's mind went over the gruesome scene. "Too bad it was his life or theirs."

"It must have been tough on him knowing that illness was lying in wait," Kwame said.

Raja wiped his eyes. "That's why the question would always remain. 'What happened to Shankar?'" *Would anyone ever know?*

"I hope no one knows," Kwame said, "because I am involved in this same as you. Despite all, I never expected Shankar to do what he did."

"That sickly man was trained to be a fighter, Kwame." The expression on Raja's face said it all. "It broke my heart to allow poor Shankar to set out all by himself on such a long journey. It's a burden I must bear."

"You did the right thing," Kwame said. "I will report that Shankar asked for a latrine break and escaped from my manure gang."

Remembering that Kwame was in many ways a bush doctor, Raja took the opportunity to show him the red itchy spots on the soles of his bare feet.

"You've got chigoes," Kwame said. "Open the wounds when you get home and dab them with lighted soft grease." Kwame continued, "Now the time has come for me to lose my best friend and worker. It seems like only yesterday you came to the estate."

"For me, it was a long time, Kwame."

Kwame's eyes grew distant. "I will surely miss you." He gave Raja a tight hug and with his usual gentle voice said, "Walk good, man! Walk good!"

If there was one thing Raja learned from his relationship with Kwame, it was that the real worth of a person lay deep inside. To Raja, this African was a true friend, a man who would gladly lay down his life for him, a man whose word was as good as gold.

At the logie, Raja opened the swollen spots with a needle, heated over the flame of the candle grease. The glow from the kerosene lamp showed him where the sand fleas had burrowed and laid their eggs.

The next morning, as he was about to leave the estate, a group of men were heading off with shovels.

"Where are you going so early?" he asked.

"Didn't you hear? Shankar shot a couple Englishmen and escaped with their guns. Mr. Van Sluytman invited us for a drink and asked us to bury them."

Raja hitched a ride on a donkey cart heading for Georgetown. It moved at a snail's pace on the powdered brick road, yielding the right-of-way to horse-drawn buggies, transporting plantation owners or overseers.

For the first time, as a free man, Raja had an opportunity to exchange a few words, mostly in Creole, with some of the villagers who lived in that part of the country. Unlike India, posts or columns supported the wooden houses. This created at each home an open-air bottom house, used as a living area for work such as chopping firewood, husking coconuts or for lazing in a hammock and enjoying the cool tropical breezes.

Upon arrival in the city, Raja was more relaxed than the first time. Now he could admire the many flowering trees that bordered the few paved streets.

Fortunately, he arrived in time to purchase a pair of long riding boots, a white shirt, and tight leggings at a clothing store.

"Rush me to Crosby's office," he said to his driver, who was just coming out of Uncle Sam's Rum Shop.

Mr. Crosby, with only a fringe of grey hair around the sides of his head, ambled over to the public counter.

"This is my certificate of completion of indentureship, Mr. Crosby," Raja said proudly.

"Ah, Raja Singh. Do you know they'd threatened to retire me if I'd taken your complaint further?"

"That's over with." Raja cleared his throat while he chose his words. "Now I want the Immigration Department and the Jones Sugar Estates to return me to my country."

Mr. Crosby stuttered, "Mr. Singh, to claim a free return passage, an indentured servant needs ten years residence in the colony."

"Who said so?"

"It's in the contract," Crosby said. Just when Raja's temper was ready to boil over, Crosby asked, "Did no one explain the written terms to you?"

"No. The Protector of Emigrants and his lawyer—all they said was that after five years I'd return a rich man." Palms outstretched, Raja now asked, "Mr. Crosby, How long can my wife wait?" For a moment, an image of his parents standing beside the bullock cart and seeing him off on his pilgrimage appeared before him. "I also want to see my parents before they pass away."

After a long silence Crosby said, "Pay for your ticket from your savings."

Raja hit his fist on the counter. It attracted the attention of a clerk who left his seat to stand beside Crosby. "What savings? From the few cents we are able to set aside each week? Five years have now become ten." *Perhaps I should become a freedom fighter like Shankar.*

Crosby waited for Raja to calm down. "Why don't you consider setting your roots in the colony? You can forsake that return passage to India and five years from now accept free land."

Raja waved his hand at Crosby. "Is this another lie?" He was sure that the government's intention all along was to avoid their obligation to return people like himself to their country and at the same time provide a steady stream of cheap labour. As matters now stood, another five years of solitude in a country he still could not call home was enough to kill the soul of any man.

Dressed again in his dhoti and kurta—he had used the back of some bushes as a dressing room—Raja said to the waiting driver, "Do you know where I can find work?"

"I can take you to meet my Auntie. She and her husband have a good-sized farm a short way back on the East Coast Road we just travelled. They could use a strong fellow like you."

"To do what?"

"Work in the rice field, tend cows, pick coconuts. That sort of thing."

Raja shrugged. "I'll do anything but cut cane," he said under his breath.

It was a much slower ride to get to the farm. The donkey did not seem happy going back so quickly on the same road. Despite the bit in his mouth, he stopped often to nibble on grass by the roadside or drink from a puddle beside the village well.

At the farmhouse, where chickens were wandering around the yard, the driver addressed his uncle who had walked up to the cart. "Mamoo, this is Raja. He is looking for a job with room and board."

Mamoo's eyes moved from Raja's head to his feet. He turned to his nephew and asked, "Has he ever worked on a farm?"

"All his life. You can never find a better worker." The driver winked at Raja.

"Let's hear what your mamee has to say."

Mamee chimed in, "He's a big man with a hearty appetite, most likely."

The driver called his aunt aside and whispered in her ear. Raja managed to lip-read what was said: "This man is desperate. Work him to the bone and just rake in the money. You want your sons to be doctors and lawyers, don't you?"

The exchange left a sour taste in Raja's mouth, especially when the woman nodded in agreement. He was further taken aback when Mamee said, "If you want to work here, babu, you must get rid of your dhoti." She quickly added, "My husband has some old shirts and trousers I can patch for you."

Raja's grin turned into a scowl. "Why do you want to change my clothes?"

"Because you're not in India."

Raja knitted his brows, showing his displeasure at what he'd just heard. "Shirt, yes, but I'll insist on wearing my cotton leggings, which I have in this jute sack." Raja proceeded to sift through his belongings, holding each one up for inspection.

Before Mamee could say another word, Mamoo jumped in, "Babu, if you can work as well as you talk, you have a job." He looked at his wife as though seeking approval.

"Where do I sleep?" Raja asked.

"In the paddy room beside the cow pen," Mamee answered.

Whether in the burning hot sun or in the pouring rain, Raja rode bareback on the couple's golden white-faced chestnut mare. He rounded up cattle on the open savannah and never allowed them to get close to plantation property where they could be impounded. He loved tending cows, since it made him free as the white herons and cattle egrets that kept him company all day. Furthermore, a mongrel dog followed him around and kept up with the horse as much as she could. He developed a special bond with the mare that had so much character. He'd whistle his favourite Bihari folk songs as he chased after strays in gale-force winds and pouring rain. On cattle drives, he and his horse devoured the endless miles over the trails and savannahs.

His other jobs included harvesting several acres of rice with a sickle, picking hundreds of coconuts and dehusking them, not to mention bathing the family's two young sons.

Life went on like this for weeks until the arrival of a scar-faced man and his herd of twelve mature steers. He was driving them to the Georgetown slaughterhouse when darkness fell. He stopped at Mamoo and Mamee's place for shelter.

"Looks like a storm's coming," he said to Mamee, who was at her bottom house instructing Raja about his chores for the following day.

Mamee had her eyes on the animals that looked eager to settle down. "No man or beast should be on the road in weather like this," she said.

After she had exchanged a few words with her husband, she said, "Mister, you can spend the night with us."

"You're a blessing," the herdsman said. "How much will you charge me for lodging?"

"Pay us whatever you can afford," Mamee replied. The man gave her one bit from a purse filled with other coins. He replaced the purse inside a flour sack that held his belongings. After he had washed his hands and feet from a bucket of water, he joined the family in the living room.

That night the winds howled and rattled the zinc sheets on the roof. The mare whinnied and the family dog whined far into the night.

Raja had dozed off for quite some time but woke up in a cold sweat, startled by what sounded like a man's scream followed by silence. His hair stood on end. The "Ooo-eeek" of the jumbie bird made him shake with fear, too afraid to check the source of the piercing cry. He tossed and turned until sleep overpowered him.

In the morning, the scar-faced man was gone, but the steers were still penned. Puzzled, Raja recalled the sounds of the previous night. After he'd prowled around prior to going about his chores, he discovered a big patch of freshly dug earth in a vacant cow pen.

That day, he completed his tasks as though nothing bothered him. He even whistled several tunes like a man without a care. After an early breakfast the following morning, he picked up his lunch pail and on his way to work made an about turn and walked up to Mamee. "I'm leaving," he said. "Keep my wages for the last two days."

"Why? We're happy with your work."

"What you want is a slave," Raja said, keeping to himself his suspicions of the incident two nights before.

Again in his kurta and dhoti and now wearing a moustache and beard, he walked the mile-long road to Plantation Green Grove. He swallowed his pride and asked to see the head overseer.

"I would like a job cutting cane at your plantation," Raja said to him, biting his lip.

"Do you have work experience?"

"Five years at Sugar Grove."

The overseer looked him over. "How long a contract do you wish?"

Surprised at the mention of contract, Raja answered, "Week-by-week."

"Very well. Start tomorrow."

A family living beside the public road provided room and board. This time Raja slept in the kitchen above the chicken coop.

That first morning he joined a gang of young men who'd arrived earlier from Madras.

Two weeks later, on his way back from collecting his fortnightly wage, he met the overseer, who said, "Raja, I have some good news for you. My head driver told me you're the best cane cutter that ever worked for him."

"Well, thank you, sir. I hope that will be taken into account when I get my next pay."

"For now you'll get a regular wage; after three months you can work your way up to our maximum for a cane cutter. It is way above the Crosby-minimum."

By the fourth month, Raja's pay had risen to two shillings per week, the highest for any labourer on the estate.

A real asset in meeting quotas, Raja soon made a name for himself. Now he could make certain monetary demands, which he could not have done when he worked as a bound coolie at Sugar Grove Estate.

At the end of the year, he tested the waters and got the gatekeeper to give him special permission to visit the manager's office.

"Sir," he said to the manager, "since I'm your best cane cutter, could you consider me for the position of driver?" The position paid two eight-cent bits more per week.

"Raja, you just can't walk into my office like this without an appointment. Speak to your overseer first," the manager said.

Accordingly, Raja appeared at the administrative office the day of his appointment. His heart sank when a junior overseer came out to meet him.

"Raja," he said. "Regarding your request to be a driver, we found out that you have quite a record at your previous estate."

"That's nice to hear, sir."

"Not so fast. They stated that you were involved in a fight that turned violent and that you'd also deserted for six weeks."

"I-I can explain."

"You don't have to. From what I can see, you're only cut out to be a cane cutter."

Raja waved a finger at him. "And what are you cut out for Mr. junior overseer?"

"Get out!" he bellowed. "My opinion of you hasn't changed."

Raja left the office with the overseer's words ringing in his ears.

As the ensuing years passed, labouring at Green Grove Estate became an ongoing monotony, rarely broken by anything unusual, until one day a driver announced at a gathering, "For the next few weeks, the overseer wants everyone to work two hours extra every day."

Raja raised his hand. "Everyone?"

"Yes, even the women and children in the moulding gang."

For four weeks, the labourers put in extra time, for which they received no payment. On the last payday of that period, about fifty men milled around and griped noisily outside the rum shop.

"Join us," a worker shouted to Raja. "Support our request for overtime pay."

"Go home," Raja said, loud enough for everyone to hear. "We must lodge a protest and work things out peacefully. Too many of you are drunk."

Raja was pleased when the men began to drift home, some in groups and others one by one.

At around 7:00 a.m. Monday, however, about the same number of workers sat in a vacant lot in front of the sugar mill, without their cutlasses. They were sober and had the benefit of Sunday to think things over.

A worker came forward to meet with Raja. "On Saturday, you told the men to go home when they were ready to make a stand and demand their overtime pay." The man gesticulated. "Is this not a peaceful gathering?"

The fellow was correct, and Raja had to think fast, since his reputation was at stake. "It will be better if a handful of us ask for a meeting with the manager and his top overseers," he replied.

The men discussed this among themselves and decided that Raja was right. They went about selecting a smaller group to represent them.

Raja was about to lead the way to the manager's compound when he heard the sound of marching feet in the distance and turned to look in that direction.

A contingent of some thirty black policemen—some armed with truncheons, some with muskets—approached in two columns, under the command of a white police superintendent. Raja could tell his rank from the number of stripes on his shoulder and his neat khaki uniform with brass buttons.

The officer spoke to the assembled workers through a megaphone.

"I'm reading from a wee book, but this proclamation carries a big stick. Listen carefully. On behalf of Her Majesty the Queen, I order the dispersal, within one hour, of this group of twelve or more people unlawfully assembled. Anyone remaining is guilty of a felony and subject to removal by deadly force."

Raja understood the consequences of any refusal to leave: workers could be shot. He walked up to the police superintendent. "I was about to take a few men with me and request a meeting with the manager."

"You coolie!" the superintendent shouted. "You have the nerve to stand up to an officer of the Crown."

Raja shuddered at the insult but ignored it. "All we want is our overtime pay."

"You and all these men here gathered, return to work. You can negotiate later."

Raja had the support of the workers. "We will do no such thing. The men will leave when management can guarantee their back pay."

At a hand signal from the officer, several policemen waded into the crowd of workers and rained blows all over their bodies. As blood flowed freely, a few workers fled.

Raja took a head blow that sent him reeling. A worker grabbed the policeman's club and hit him exactly as he had hit Raja.

Blood poured from the policeman's head as he cried out for support from his fellow officers. They took turns kicking the worker and clubbed him to the ground.

Finally the superintendent shouted, "Enough!" He gave private instructions to the policemen who carried guns. Events seemed to be taking a turn for the worse. After the police had taken up their positions, the superintendent shouted, "Prime and Load! Make ready! Present! Fire!" Each of the policemen loaded his musket, knelt on one knee, pointed his gun, and fired.

Workers ran helter-skelter toward their logies except for a handful, including Raja. Fortunately, no one was injured—the police had fired into the air as instructed.

Quite unexpectedly, the manager came galloping in on horseback, note in hand. "Sorry about all this blood-spilling, Mr. Singh," he said as he walked up to Raja. "Let the dispenser take care of that wound. Everyone will be paid their overtime wage."

Loud cheers broke out from the few men left standing. *What could have caused the sudden change of events?*

On Monday morning, as Raja was on his way to work, a messenger told him to drop in at the estate office. When he got there, the junior overseer approached waving an official-looking document. "Put your X on the dotted line."

A sinking feeling came over Raja. "What's this?" he asked, holding the document with both hands and looking at it suspiciously.

"We are terminating your contract forthwith for good cause."

Raja frowned but deep inside, he was not surprised. Still, he asked, "Why?"

"Management has labelled you a troublemaker."

"That's fine if it wins us our rights." He recalled how many of his fellow Indians had been tricked into indentureship because they could not read their contracts. "I want Doc to be my translator," he said.

Raja beckoned the mulatto dispenser with a wave. "Doc, what does this paper say?"

The dispenser read aloud, "Raja Singh and The Plantation viz. Green Grove and its directors." He moved his eyes back and forth over the pages before continuing, "The sum and substance of this legal rigmarole is simply this—that both parties agree to part ways and owe each other nothing."

Raja placed his X, and Doc and the clerk signed as witnesses. A few of Raja's fellow workers lined up and shook his hand. Thus ended his stint at Plantation Green Grove.

CHAPTER SIXTEEN

With cutlass dangling in one hand and lunch pail in the other, Raja walked the mile-long dirt road.

His turbaned head had been sagging against his chest when someone called out, "Seems like they gave you the sack."

Raja took a few more steps before he turned around. "Yes," he replied, startled. "The estate doesn't need me anymore." He raised his head and as he looked at the speaker, a smile spread across his face. "Goodness, Kwame, it's you."

"Who else?" Kwame lifted his felt hat that almost covered his eyes.

"How did you know where to find me?"

"Crosby gave me the name of the plantation where you worked. In our discussion, he mentioned that he'd sent a strong message to your manager to make the overpayment owing to the workers."

"That man does not miss a thing," Raja said, before continuing, "There must be a reason for your being here."

"Ever since you left the plantation, they couldn't meet quotas. Naturally, they wanted me to whip the workers."

"So your refusal has cost you your job."

"That's why I went to see Crosby."

"My estate also let me go," Raja said, "so let's link up and help each other." Raja patted his friend on the shoulder. "Come with me."

On the way to his lodgings, Raja said, "Tell me about Sonnyboy's case."

"His white cricket captain in Georgetown raised enough money to hire a lawyer-cricketer who at trial argued that Sonnyboy was too drunk to know what he was doing."

"I bet he got off lightly."

"Seven years plus an extra two because Jasmine was soon to become a mother. But this beats all. Three years later, the governor commuted his sentence. I tell you, it's the kind of law we have in this country."

Raja shook his head, clicking his tongue at the same time. "Jasmine will never again walk the face of this earth, but that swine will continue to bowl for the Governor's XI."

"No, he won't. An upcoming star has since replaced him."

Raja swung his head to face Kwame. "Good. Now tell me what you did with Olu and Polly."

"I set them free." Kwame appeared uncomfortable when he added, "I left plenty of food and water in their troughs."

"But you never taught them to survive in the wild, Kwame."

Kwame shrugged and spread his palms out. He obviously wanted to change the subject.

While he waited on the front porch, Raja went to his room and unstitched the seam of his mattress. One gold sovereign and several shillings, not counting the shiny bits and coppers, fell out. He placed his money in a string purse around his neck and, with his friend in tow, walked in silence mile after mile toward the city to find work.

As evening approached, heavy rain forced them to take shelter under a silk cotton tree. Darkness cloaked the countryside while the rain continued to pour. To ease their discomfort—they were soaked to the skin—they reminisced about their days at Sugar Grove Estate.

From out of the bushes, with its eyes glowing in the dark, a black cat rushed forward and yowled at Raja. He stifled a scream and breathing rapidly, turned to Kwame. "Remember you told me once to stay away from the silk cotton tree, especially at night."

"I sure did," Kwame said. "But now jumbie has to deal with a big coolie man and one tough black man. Ha-ha."

After the downpour had subsided, they continued to walk until they spotted a shop with a covered front porch. They passed the rest of the night sitting on one of its benches.

Strangely, they seemed to have no desire for food. The following morning found them stopping several times to quench their thirst at the wells. Around noon, they arrived in Georgetown and wasted no time in their search for accommodation.

The majestic Guest Inn, with its high pointed arches and elaborate windows proved to be out of bounds. It was where people of European origin stayed. On the other hand, the London Hotel, located on Lombard Street, presented itself as a well-appointed rooming house that catered to transient guests. The owners referred to it as a boarding house, to dissociate it from the disreputable City Hotel nearby.

Operated by an Englishman and his mulatto wife, the London had a reputation for serving up the best local cuisine and tea with biscuits every Friday afternoon. Raja inhaled the aroma of food that floated into the lobby, and his stomach growled, as he had not eaten a meal since he'd left the estate. Nonetheless, he realized that he must first book a room.

"How much do you charge for room and board for two?" Raja asked the manager.

"For how long?"

Without missing a beat, Raja said, "Two, maybe three months if you treat us well."

Upon hearing the price, he decided to bargain for a better rate. "What if we clean rooms for our keep?"

"If you fellows can do as good a job as my wife, the room is free. Just pay for food."

They agreed on a price for meals, and Kwame ordered a mouth-watering fante-fante bangamary fish stew served up with boiled pigeon peas and rice.

During the following days, Raja considered his options. With two months remaining on his ten-year residency, what better way to put in the time than to find a job. He decided to seek the help of the hotel manager. "Do you know where we could find work?" Raja asked after tea on Friday.

The manager hesitated as if weighing the possibility of losing his room cleaners, but relented. "My Scottish friend owns Plantation Vlissingen, and a wharf called American Stelling on America Street. Mr. McDavid can do with a couple of strong men."

"To do what?" Raja asked.

"Discharge tobacco, clothing, and iron goods from ships and reload them with greenheart timber, sugar, and molasses, all headed for the port of Boston."

The next morning, Raja and Kwame cleaned their allotted rooms in record time and set out for America Street along the waterfront, past Uncle Sam's Rum Shop, past several trading posts selling items salvaged from ships, until they reached the wharf. While Raja stayed a few paces back, Kwame approached the overweight black foreman. "My friend and I would like to sign on as stevedores."

The man rubbed his ample belly and said, "I like the positive way you ask for work, Mister." He looked Kwame over. "You're a bit on the old side but will do. As for your coolie friend, he ain't going to pass for any Bajan. You see all of us here are from Barbados."

"Ow man," Kwame pleaded, slipping the man a tarnished guilder. "You'll never find a better worker."

"Shut up, African. Consider yourself lucky; it will cost you this beat up guilder anyway."

The big Bajan foreman pocketed the coin, leaving Kwame standing with his mouth wide open.

In the city, where so few Indians lived, Raja foresaw great difficulty in finding work. He accompanied Kwame to the nearby Bajan Quarters, where Kwame rented a room and in no time mingled with the islanders, one of whom said to him, "One British Guianese among us will make everything look nice and dandy."

A few days later, Raja tried for employment at Werk-en-rust Saw Mill. It was no secret that the African descendants held down all the jobs there, even the woodcutting ones up river.

"Give me a chance," Raja pleaded with the supervisor.

"Go back to cutting cane, coolie boy," he said. As Raja squirmed and turned to leave, he added, "You won't know how to wheel and deal with we black carpenters and joiners, anyway."

Raja did not blame the boss man. He remembered one of his discussions with Shankar and Kwame and got to thinking.

Those whose foreparents had been brought to the colony in chains still associated cane cutting with slavery and wanted no part of it. No wonder they became artisans. Further, while the coolie could look forward to free land or a passage back to his homeland, what did they get?

Back at the hotel, Raja bumped into a crowd of Indians in the lobby. It looked like "country come to town." One Indian man, darker than the others and dressed in Western clothes, was wobbling his head and speaking to the desk clerk. As Raja moved within earshot, the voice became unmistakable.

"Jahaji bhai!" he yelled.

"Raja!" Ramdas sang out.

The shipboard friends embraced. They pumped hands, slapped each other on the back and exchanged broad grins.

"What's the big attraction for all these people?" Raja asked as he and Ramdas made themselves comfortable on the windowsill.

"Like me, they've come to watch horse racing."

"It's not my sport, but I can join you just to have some fun."

After they had freshened up, off to the races they went.

"Right off the ship, they took me to Plantation Ruimveldt, where I served out my five-year indentureship," Ramdas said. "I'm now manager at the Ruimveldt Cattle Ranch, owned by a Scotsman. We have a couple hundred head of cattle—Brahman bulls crossed with Herefords for beef, and Jerseys and Holsteins for milk."

"Your employer must be a nice fellow to allow you time off for sport."

"Shh! My cowgirl wife fills in for me."

Puzzled, Raja said, "I thought your wife was in India."

Ramdas thrust out his lower lip and was quiet for some time. "I hooked up with a mulatto woman." He looked at Raja as though seeking approval.

Raja shouted above the noise of the crowd, "Not me. I'll return to my wife in Belwasa," but Ramdas's focus was on the race.

Finally, the last and biggest race of the day was about to begin on a well-trodden, muddy track. Ramdas placed a fistful of coins on two horses—to win—just as the trumpeter played the "Call to the Post."

A mare caught Raja's eye. "I'll place a shilling on number eight, the dirty, black one with the limp and her bones sticking out." He placed his wager—to win—on the counter.

Ramdas burst into hysterical laughter. "You must be joking. That's Seabreeze, a hundred-to-one long shot." He continued to giggle and only stopped when he squeezed his nostrils and covered his mouth.

Everyone became quiet as the jockeys urged their respective mounts to form a circle around the starting position. At the same time, people jostled for positions close to the finish line.

A roar from the spectators coincided with the start of the race. Seabreeze faced the wrong way when the horses broke into a gallop. She stumbled and gathered herself. It did not prevent her from being left some thirty lengths behind.

This time Ramdas was too much involved to laugh. "Eh-eh! Like she broke down already. Too much ground to cover."

"There goes my shilling," Raja cried out. He closed his eyes and made a face.

While everyone screamed for the favourites, one horse covered ground like few had ever seen. It moved like a shadow, racing neck-and-neck with the favourite. Down the homestretch, it appeared to tire and fade a touch behind the white face of the champion.

The race over, the crowd watched dumbstruck as though they didn't want to believe what they'd just witnessed.

"The greatest last-to-first dash in the history of the sport," someone cried out. A man with a child on his shoulders had blocked Raja's view just as the two lead horses passed the finish line, so he didn't yet know the outcome.

"Which horse won?" Raja asked.

"Seabreeze!" Ramdas was jumping up and down, no longer giggling. "Only in the last stride or two did the black face nose ahead."

"Don't joke with me, bhai."

"I'm not. A miracle has just taken place!" Ramdas slapped Raja on the back, causing him to trip.

"How could this be?"

"The soft track—your horse just ate it up. Go and collect!" Ramdas shrieked. "You might be the only winner."

Minutes passed before Raja could gather himself together. Meanwhile, Ramdas swiped the stub from Raja's hand and dashed for the pay booth. Raja followed and stood wide-eyed as Ramdas collected three gold sovereigns, several crowns, and some florins and shillings. At the bar, he ordered a shot for himself and a rum-free lime rickey for Raja. Ramdas downed his drink in one gulp.

Just when Raja was beginning to worry about his winning, Ramdas came forward. "Here," he said, "the money is yours. I'll keep a shilling to bet next time." He turned the rest of the coins over.

Still in a daze, Raja said, "Here's an extra crown."

"Well, thank you. And what will you do with all that cash?"

"I'll take it to India, of course. These gold sovereigns will make a fine necklace for Savitri."

Christmas Eve was spectacular in Georgetown that year. A lamplighter lit all the kerosene lamps on Water Street making the waterfront a fairyland.

Raja and Ramdas went window-shopping downtown, admiring the displays at the Jones Jewellery and Clothing Stores. On the way back, in front of Pereira's Grocery and Cook Shop, an old man wearing a conical blue cloth cap said to them, "You boys must be staying at the London."

"Yes," Raja replied, puzzled as to how the shop owner had figured them out.

The man showed the friends a dish made of Newfoundland salted cod with onion and garlic. "Bacalhau, cooked with cebola and alho," he said. "It's very tasty. And for Christmas breakfast, we serve up garlic pork and pepper pot. You're welcome to come over to Pereira's for a treat on the house. Yeh man!"

Raja suspected the manager of Pereira's would expect them to have the rest of their meals at his cook shop if they accepted his free meal. So, before Ramdas could answer, Raja said, "My friend will be helping me clean rooms at the London tomorrow."

Ramdas nudged Raja. "Will you be quiet?"

"In that case have a bit of Vinho da Roda—round-trip wine, straight from Madeira." The old man opened the spout of a wooden cask and poured the red wine into two small glasses.

Ramdas elbowed Raja aside, inhaled and took a sip. "Mmm. It's got that certain taste." He drained his glass and licked his lips.

Somewhat slighted by his mate, Raja sniffed the wine, its aroma much more pleasing than rum. He allowed the true flavour of the wine some time to dance around his palate, the experience more delightful than his first drink of rum.

The day after Christmas, the guests at the London were caught up in a masquerade parade. The sound of trampling feet on the street brought the two friends out onto the pavement. Barefoot black men performed the queh-queh dance, symbolic of fertility, to music played on the bamboo flute. Some wore imitation cow heads as they masqueraded along the city streets. Raja and Ramdas fell in with the crowd, caught up in the moment with the rhythm of the West African music.

The friends embraced and parted company the next morning. "Goodbye and take care," Raja said, believing in his heart that he would be leaving soon for India and might never see his ship mate again.

CHAPTER SEVENTEEN

Hardly a day had gone by since Raja's sad farewell with Ramdas when he presented himself at Crosby's office.

"I've completed my ten years of residence to the day," Raja said, as Crosby, now with a pronounced stoop, limped his way to meet him at the counter. "I wish to claim my free passage back to India."

The moment Crosby's smile disappeared, Raja's heart sank. Crosby could only stutter and when he managed to put his words together, he said, "Mr. Singh, we cannot requisition a ship until we have a full quota of passengers to make that journey. I know this is bad news for you."

"Just a minute. The last time I met you in your office, you told me to return at the end of another five years." Tears welled up in Raja's eyes. "That's a long time, Mr. Crosby."

After Raja had regained his composure, he reached for the cloth purse that hung around his neck, counted ten crowns and handed them to Crosby. "This is to help with my passage."

Crosby's pen dropped from his hand, his mouth hung open. "You're not expected to pay. However, if more people do the same, we can have a boat earlier than you think."

Raja didn't know whether he should believe the man. Either he or the administrators could very well be playing games with Indians such as himself. He banged his fist on the counter. The other employees stopped what they were doing and looked on. "In three months' time, I'll return." Raja glared at the old man. He marched out of the office, breathing heavily.

In need of something to boost his spirits, he ambled over to Jones's Clothing Store. Bolts of cloth in bright hues of green, yellow, and red lay stacked on shelves that seemed to extend to the ceiling. Several tweed suits draped over wooden hangers caught Raja's attention.

He walked up to a Portuguese sales clerk and said, "I would like a complete set of English clothing."

The fellow made several suggestions. In the end, Raja chose a bottle-green blazer, several shirts, cream flannel pants and regular ones, a pair of brown leather shoes, and white yachting ones.

Unsure of how and where to try them on, he was pleased when the clerk said, "Use the change room at the back."

Dressed in his new finery, Raja presented himself before the clerk. His confidence soared when the clerk said, "You're ready to light up the town."

That was exactly Raja's intent. As soon as the opportunity rose, he'd wear his smart outfit. He changed back into his regular clothes, paid for the items and returned to his hotel room.

If he wasn't looking for work, he'd hang around Bourda Green and play cricket. Six years had passed since he'd held a bat. His previous performances had been based on raw talent. Here, gangly young black men, far more skilled in the game, took him under their wings. What particularly impressed him was their fielding—covering ground like nothing he'd ever seen. To narrow the gap for Raja, an old Bajan cricketer showed him how to slope the bat at the time of contact to send the ball flying all along the ground. Because he had the natural ability to time his shots, he found that when he swung the bat with great speed and power during the drives, the balls flew like bullets off the sweet spot of his bat.

A few weeks later, the *Guiana Chronicle* reported in the front page of its sports section that Raja Singh, a new member of the Bourda Green Cricket Club, had given a match-winning performance in both batting and bowling against Vlissingen Park Cricket Club. Both teams selected him Man of the Match.

Around that time, a Jones talent scout paid him a visit. "Our company would like to make you an offer—employment as player/coach for our sugar estates team," the scout said. "The wage is three times that of a driver's."

"Your company owes me a return ticket to my country," Raja countered.

"You're mixing sports with politics." The scout's face contorted. "You'll be hearing from the boss."

It was not long before a messenger delivered a letter from the director of Jones Sports Club addressed to Roger Singh. It banned him from playing on their pitches.

The black cricketers wanted to lead a protest march, but Raja talked them out of it. In the end, they invited him to a house party to lift his spirits.

He contributed a bit-and-a-half to buy a bottle of rum for the mandolinist, bamboo flautist, and spoon-and-bottle percussionist, who performed at the party that evening.

Decked out in his bottle-green blazer and flannels, he became the star attraction. To make sure he had a good time, his Bourda friends taught him some fancy footwork and dance steps.

"Come show me your motion," a dougla woman said. Her curvaceous figure, a product of her mixed East Indian-African heritage, captivated him.

She led him along the dance floor and soon he was twirling with his partner to the waltz with slow turns and long gliding movements.

As he lay in bed that evening, his conscience got the better of him. Ma would never have approved of foreign clothing and dancing with women. And as for Savitri, she would have been upset to see him holding another woman that close.

In his village back in India, men always danced separately. Indeed, despite his personal vows, a transformation had begun. On the dance floor he tried to convince himself that he was doing no wrong as he danced the night away with the "yalla gyals."

Three months had gone by since Raja had left Crosby's office with the promise to cause some disturbance if he heard any more lies. A final effort to find his way home would be worth it.

When he showed up at the counter of the Immigration Department, Crosby shook his head. "We still have no shipload and no ship, Mr. Singh."

It took two messengers to block Raja as he tried to barge his way toward Crosby's desk with fists clenched. An earthen jug fell off a table, shattering into tiny pieces and splashing water across the floor. "To heck with Jones Brothers and Davis Holdings," Raja shouted.

Crosby, his entire body shaking, retreated a few steps. "Put him out!" he yelled.

A couple of clerks and a messenger grabbed Raja and hustled him through the door. "Don't worry! I'll be back!" he shouted.

After breakfast, he took a walk along the narrow Atlantic Seashore to clear his head after the confrontation with Crosby. He concluded that he should pay his own way back to his native land. Since he didn't have the full fare, the quickest way would be for him to pan for gold and diamonds. Ever since he'd brought up shiny flakes of gold with Ar'wak, he'd wanted to try his luck at panning on his own. So he made inquiries.

With his clothes tucked away in a jute sack slung over his shoulders and his savings deposited at Barclays Bank, he hired a boatman to take him forty miles up the Essequibo River. The boatman rowed for four days, sleeping at night, until they arrived at the settlement of Bartica. There, Raja checked in at a boarding house run by an East Indian couple.

The constant slamming of doors as couples went in and out of rooms disturbed Raja. "This is nothing but a brothel," he complained to the owners.

"Things are bad," the husband said. "We have to make a living."

Raja had no choice but to stay put, since it was the only rooming house in this frontier town. Except for a few Arawaks, East Indians, and Chinese cooks, the few African settlers and gold seekers were the only ones walking the unpaved streets.

"Why do you come here, babu?" a man with matted hair asked Raja, flexing his muscles.

"The same reason you came—to do some panning."

"For your own good, stay out of the prospecting business," he said. "Your kind of people get their heads busted up."

Raja looked the man over and was confident that he could easily handle him. "I only came to try my luck," he said.

"Leave him alone," a dougla man piped in.

The man with the matted hair jumped on the dougla, who sidestepped and threw punches from all directions. But as the dougla helped his opponent to his feet, Raja couldn't help but smile.

"Look at this coolie," the dougla said. "The two of us alone can take care of you and your gang."

Raja was glad that he'd stayed out of the fray and that someone else had stood up for him.

Most of the African men panned for gold and diamonds up river. Before the journey, they always sought out Arawak hunters of wild hogs. The prospectors would buy their wild pork, cut the flesh into small, thin strips and beat them on the rocks with tree limbs. With the liquid all driven out, the men hung the pork on washing lines in the sun. That jerky, supplemented with cassava bread and farine, sustained them while upriver.

Raja found it difficult to link up with those pork-knockers, as they came to be called. They always worked in close-knit groups and never shared information with others. "We have our own staked-out stream," one of them said. "You must find your own."

To get around this barrier, Raja sought assistance from his dougla friend, who introduced him to Chi-chi, an Arawak guide.

"I own my own dugout," Chi-chi said. "I can take you to a special stream that lies up the Mazaruni River." They threw some figures around and finally agreed on a price.

"Will we find gold and diamonds at your site?" Raja asked.

"Enough for a 50-50 split."

Unlike Ar'wak, Chi-chi seemed to share Raja's love for gold and diamonds. If his special spot had half the gold as Ar'wak's, Raja would be satisfied. And so with the dougla's blessing, he decided to trust the guide.

Although the weather was very hot, Chi-chi insisted that Raja wear a white long-sleeved cotton shirt and full-length trousers to avoid the mosquito bites.

A week had gone by when they arrived at the mouth of a river that branched from the Mazaruni. Chi-chi selected a tributary that required two mini portages and one big one, which, according to him, avoided several rapids and waterfalls. In that final stretch, they carried their canoe for some two miles through a mora forest with sparse undergrowth.

Then to Raja's amazement, a bright orange-coloured male cock-of-the-rock landed in a clearing and danced for the female before mating. It was a pleasant escape from an otherwise hard day's work.

After Chi-chi had selected a sandy clearing to bed down for the night, he climbed the palm trees that grew around the camp. He picked bunches of awarras, and cocorites—miniature coconuts—fruits that Raja had first eaten when he was lost in the bush. Their meagre flesh provided some variety to the usual pork and farine.

Around midnight, with the full moon shining, Chi-chi scrambled out of his bed of mosses and ferns and groped his way into a thicket. Soon after, he uttered a loud scream. Raja grabbed his cutlass and rushed out only to find Chi-chi lying on the ground and a huge snake, with diamond-pattern skin that blended with the forest floor, slithering away into the bushes.

"A bushmaster snake grabbed my ankle," Chi-chi cried out. "I should have been more careful. It emptied its venom into me."

"Can I help in any way?"

Chi-chi shook his head. "I'll be lucky to see morning."

Filled with sadness and despair, Raja paced back and forth. After he had helped Chi-chi to his soft bedding, Chi-chi, despite his agony, said, "Don't give up. Keep walking with the sun on your back until you come to a clear stream. That is where you pan. Good luck, partner." Chi-chi's voice became weaker. "Same way in, same way out."

"Anything I can do for your family?"

"Give my share to my wife and son. Tell them I . . . ." Chi-chi's mouth formed the words but his voice faded.

Raja nodded, struggling to hold back the tears but failing. He had come to look upon Chi-chi as a brother. "I will," Raja said. He stayed up with Chi-chi through the night. Raja held him until he took his very last breath just as the sun rose above the horizon. Not knowing the ways of the Arawaks when a loved one dies, he covered Chi-chi's body with the ferns that were his bedding, bowed and recited a brief mantra.

Once again, Raja found himself all alone in the jungle. His heart pounded against his chest, and his body shook. *Is God angry with me or am I just a victim of fate? What good are gold and diamonds if you are lost in the jungle?*

He was tempted to return to Bartica and save his life. From where he was, he had a good chance of finding his way back, but travelling another three hours to find that stream could disorient him.

At that moment, a warm blanket of rain enveloped him. An image of Chi-chi appeared through the veil of raindrops, and a muffled voice said, *"I will guide you."*

Perhaps that image would take him to that stream but may not show him the way out. However, Raja was prepared to take that chance to become rich and so placed his faith in Chi-chi's spirit.

Before long, he arrived at what had to be the clear stream, but self-doubt crept in. Now that he had lost his companion and guide, he again wavered. What if he died in the jungle with his purse filled with gold? His loved ones would never know his fate. For two days, he stared at the stream and listened to the calming sound of water moving over rocks. His stomach growled. The jerky, cassava bread, and farine he had brought along remained untouched.

On the third day, he took a few mouthfuls. Acting on instinct, he carved out a pan from a fallen log, sanded it with gravel, and went through the process he'd learned from Ar'wak. Panning was painstaking and laborious work, and he kept at it for several days, or was it weeks? He realized he'd lost track of time. His food was now running low, so he ate a handful of wood-eating grubs and a few awarras.

Success came in spurts. At first, he got flakes and tiny nuggets of gold at a curve in the creek. Where the water slowed on the inside of a bend, he got larger nuggets and placed these in his drawstring purse. Now that Ar'wak was not there to throw his gold away, his heart was in it; he worked like a man with a purpose.

One hundred feet from the water's edge, he tried his luck at panning all sizes of rounded pebbles but got nothing. In desperation, he dug around gravel from the old riverbed. Lo and behold! A large gold nugget, almost half the size of his fist, came into view. A few days later, while digging at this very spot, his eyes bulged at the sight of small, round crystals that were whitish and almost as clear as glass. He had found small diamonds.

His persistence having paid off, the drive for riches grew stronger.

He wished Chi-chi could have been there to share in the excitement. *Nothing could be more satisfying than panning and retrieving your own gold and gemstones.* Shankar might have been joking, but this indeed was his El Dorado, and it was real.

Raja sang Bihari folk songs and danced on the riverbank until he'd attracted the attention of a squirrel monkey. There in the jungle, he could easily have gone crazy, and he reminded himself to be strong of mind. Besides, he must not be greedy for he still faced the problem of getting out of the jungle.

Carrying the canoe through a tangled growth of vines that draped the tree trunks proved more difficult than when he'd shared the load with Chi-chi. Disoriented and afraid, the thought came to him that he should throw out his gold and diamonds as Ar'wak had done; perhaps the gods would be pleased and save his life. At last, remembering Chi-chi's words, he tried to convince himself that Chi-chi was talking to him, showing him the way out. Between portages, he walked for days without a glimpse of the sun, cut off by the rainforest canopy. With

Chi-chi's cutlass, he dug up grubs and edible roots that he devoured just to stay alive. Culture and old-country traditions were far from his mind. He imitated the monkeys and drank water from the leaf bases of plants.

His energy almost sapped, he staggered onto the Mazaruni River junction that would lead him to Bartica, dropped to his knees and kissed the ground.

Back at the boarding house, some of Chi-chi's friends pestered him with questions about the trip. One of them expressed doubt that Chi-chi, an outdoorsman, who had guided countless surveyors, could have lost his life to a snake that rarely attacked humans.

"If you don't believe him, that makes him a murderer," the dougla said to them. "Does he look like one? Leave the man alone."

For the dougla's support, Raja passed him a nugget, which he refused at first.

The most difficult part for Raja was to be the bearer of sad news to Chi-chi's wife.

"Your husband accepted his fate with grace and courage," Raja said to her. "His last words were that he loves you and the boy very much." He placed on the kitchen table Chi-chi's one-half share of large nuggets and small diamonds. He threw in a few small grains because he wanted to keep the fist-sized gold nugget for himself.

At first, she did not seem eager to collect her dead husband's share of gold and precious stones. Her distant, almost vacant look made conversation difficult, so Raja left to give her the peace she needed.

On the Saturday night after his return, he wanted to celebrate. He bought a ticket for the dance on the first floor of the boarding house. Sporting his wrinkled green blazer, he asked a dougla woman in a long, red dress for a dance. She accepted, and they waltzed to the most beautiful music from the banjo, mandolin, and guitar. It was as though the floor belonged to them.

At the bar afterwards, a mulatto man offered Raja a drink of rum, but he told him he'd given up the habit. The man continued his harangue and would not leave Raja alone until "Just a taste, man!" became a shot.

Strangely, the drink made him quite dizzy. A more-than-friendly woman, also in red, helped him up the stairs. Though she had not entered his room and he had locked his door, he woke up next morning to the scent of perfume. He had no idea how it had gotten there. A search to find the cloth purse that had been tied to his neck turned up nothing.

Quickly he began to dress. In a panic, he rushed down to the first floor and looked around for his purse. His report to the owners and the hotel staff that someone had gotten into his room and stolen his purse only brought condemnation. They said it was his fault.

His heart sank for he had lost a second time. His journey into the jungle had been in vain. Had he refused the drink, he would have guarded his stash. Now it was too late. Far into the second night, he sat up in bed, his head lowered in his hands.

Ar'wak could have been right. Someone desperate for his gold and diamonds could have busted his head. He wished the thief had left him some. He remembered that he had placed one gold nugget in a piece of cloth, tied around his waist with string. Though he would have gotten more for the nugget in Georgetown, he exchanged it at the Bartica General Store for a safe journey back to the city.

CHAPTER EIGHTEEN

De Droom, 1879

Once again, Raja found himself in Georgetown. After he'd withdrawn his savings from Barclay's Bank, he took a long walk along the Atlantic Seashore. If he accepted the free land Crosby offered, it would mean that he was choosing to settle down in the colony.

He wrung his hands as he tried to come up with a decision that he could live with. Setting out from the dock was a sloop that bobbed with the waves. He watched the fishermen raising the mainsail. *If only that ship could take me back to my homeland!*

In the end, realism dictated he change course. His decision would be a life-changing one. With that in mind, he walked over to Crosby's office. "I will accept the free land."

Instead of flinching, a grin spread across Crosby's creviced face. In the presence of another employee, he opened a vault and retrieved a box, acting as though he were not at all surprised. "This is your deposit of ten crowns," he said, counting the coins as he handed them over. "Now put your mark that you agree to sacrifice your return passage." Crosby read from a document and pointed to a blank space.

Under different circumstances, Raja would have fumed or even laughed. All he could do was sneer. "How can I give up what never existed in the first place?" He shook his head as two clerks signed as witnesses to his mark.

Crosby handed Raja some papers. "Ask someone to help you with these."

Fed up with the entire situation, Raja took the forms and marched out of the office. Later, the manager at the hotel filled in the blanks for him.

After Crosby had processed the application, he said, "You have a choice between ten acres of acidic wetlands or three acres of abandoned farm land in the village of De Droom, two miles up the Aciah River." He waited for Raja to make a decision.

Raja always believed that less was more, so he asked, "What do you know about the smaller plot of land?"

Crosby shouted for his messenger, who climbed up a ladder and brought down an oversized ledger from the top rack. Crosby thumbed through a few pages. "It used to be part of a Dutchman's coffee and cotton plantation called De Droom, which means, 'The Dream.' The village took its name from the plantation."

Raja chuckled without smiling. "I hope the land satisfies my dreams after all I've been through."

Crosby rolled his eyes. "You might have to go through a lot more."

Raja shrugged. "Why?"

"Flooding, my good fellow. The owner had built a windmill on his plantation patterned after the one in De Droom, Holland. He adapted it to drain his land as well as to grind coffee." Crosby looked Raja in the eye. "You're not going to cultivate coffee or sugarcane, are you?"

"Mr. Crosby, luxuries such as sugar and coffee, worked in the past by slave, and now coolie labour, fill the coffers of the wealthy plantation owners. Rice is our people's staple food, which ensures our survival, so that's what I'll plant."

Crosby's raised eyebrows said it all. "Mr. Singh, you have certainly grown the last ten years. I admired the way you represented the workers at Plantation Green Grove." He extended a frail, shaking hand and Raja accepted it.

Raja concluded that it was just a matter of time before Crosby passed on. The man with such tireless energy would wish to die on the job, improving the lot of the poor Indian peasant. Raja had some empathy for Mr. Crosby, a servant of the Crown, who faced a difficult balancing act.

After publication of the transfer of the three acres of land in the *Official Gazette*, Raja visited the Deeds Registry Office.

"Take good care of your transport deed," the registrar said.

Raja looked at the neat lettering in black ink. He understood that the document gave him title to his land under Roman-Dutch law. What was significant was that he had chosen to make British Guiana his home. However, deep inside he planned to work the free land, sell out, and pay his own way back to India.

His parents might be dead, but not his brother; he could only hope that his wife was still waiting for him.

For now, he would preserve his religious beliefs and his Indian heritage. That he had danced close with the local women and had drunk alcohol, not to mention his affair with Jasmine—well, those days were behind him.

He returned to the London Hotel, discarded his English clothing and reverted to his white kurta and leggings, vowing to be his own man, free from the clutches of Massa.

It was drizzling when he trekked over to the Georgetown Railway Station to board a train that would take him to De Droom. Ten years earlier, at this very building, he had boarded the same train, bound for a sugar plantation. Now, much wiser, he would pick up the pieces of his life and put them together in his own way.

He disembarked at the coastal village of Aciah, where he rented a room from a shopkeeper who scraped by, thanks to a series of odd jobs on the side.

Early the next morning, the landlord said, "Jump into my canoe. I'll paddle you up river to an Arawak settlement, where you can purchase your own dugout."

The landlord's canoe, a true work of art, sliced through the water with barely a ripple. The view was breathtaking—a wide expanse of savannah lands interspersed with trees, and close by long-legged herons and spoonbills searching the water for a meal. At the Arawak village Raja picked out a craft and a matching double-ended paddle.

The following week, he took a mulatto surveyor with him to stake out his property. They paddled their way up the creek. Long strips of farmlands ran back from the river, each drained by a dike. Settlers of Indian origin reared cattle and cultivated rice there.

Situated a mile from the river, east of the De Droom Side Road, Raja's three acres became his pride and joy. Puffing out his chest, lifting a hand to shade his eyes, and squinting into the glare of the sun, he took it all in, his own piece of the earth.

His father, who had worked a lifetime to acquire four acres of land in India, would have been proud of him. Here he was, a start-up farmer, and already he owned three acres. For the time, Belwasa was far from his mind. He was going to make a name for himself right here in De Droom, in his adopted country.

"You must construct a dike regulated by a sluice gate," the surveyor said.

"What happened to the old ones?" Raja asked.

"Some of my Dutch ancestors, before they vacated their lands to the victorious English, broke the dikes," the surveyor gesticulated with his hand, "because the English planters failed to compensate our people for their pioneering sea-defence of this colony."

"But why did the English not rebuild the dikes?"

"They wanted to discourage the slaves and early indentured servants from getting into the farming business."

Raja reflected on those words. *Aha! So that they would be available to cut sugarcane.* "A dike and a sluice gate would be too much of an investment for just three acres," he ventured.

"Not if you buy the forty-acre portion surrounding your land," the surveyor said. "It would then make more sense to construct dikes north and south of your property."

"Right now I can't afford forty acres."

"Take a loan, man. Because of a change in policy and recent land reforms, lands are selling at bargain prices. With new indentured servants settling down in the colony and taking up more and more land, prices will go up."

Raja found himself wobbling his head, something he hardly ever did. "There's no harm in finding out the price of land per acre that's next to mine."

"I can introduce you to the higher-ups at the Deeds Registry Office."

"Will that help?"

"In this country! Well, you are a newcomer."

After a quick meal of curried fish, dal, rice, and okra, the two men set off in a donkey cart for Georgetown. The driver parked next to the Deeds Registry building, where the donkey began nibbling on roadside grass.

The registrar was on sick leave that day, so the surveyor introduced Raja to his deputy who said, "That forty-acre subsection is Crown land available with approval from the government."

"I already own three acres of it," Raja said.

The officer scrutinized a new entry on the plan. "You must be Roger Singh," he said, "and already you wish to make such a huge land purchase?" He stated the price which made Raja whistle.

"Don't be discouraged," the surveyor said, moving Raja away. "You can make a down payment and take out a mortgage for the balance."

To please the surveyor, Raja said, "I'll be back in the morning."

At the London Hotel, where he booked a room, he emptied the purse he carried around his neck. Of the coins that fell out, he separated three gold sovereigns for Savitri and counted the rest of his money. It consisted of another gold sovereign and several crowns and shillings, including those he'd won at the racetrack.

Though he had enough to make a down payment on the subsection of land, providing it was approved, the next morning he thanked the assistant registrar for his help, and said he'd forego the purchase of any more land for the time being.

Back in De Droom, Raja worked along with the surveyor to stake out the highest portion of his land to build a house. The De Droom Side Road, which was actually nothing more than the top of an embankment, provided easy access to his property. The surveyor also pointed out where he should construct a slough to drain excess runoff water.

From the village shopkeeper, he bought a shovel, cutlass, axe, saw, twine, hammer, and nails. A boy on school vacation became his helper. Raja took to calling him Beta because he looked upon him as a son.

"I suppose you prefer to assist me rather than your father," Raja said.

The boy grinned. "He doesn't need my help. He says I get in his way."

Under a hot sun, Raja planted bamboo posts on his lot to support the walls for a one-room house and a kitchen. Hewn mora and silverbally logs, supplemented with split bamboo strips, formed the laths to frame his shack.

Hardly had he completed his house when the rains came crashing down. Huge drops lashed against his face, and winds threatened to blow

Beta away. Raja tried to save some of the structure, but high winds tore away the bamboo and wooden laths that had been secured with twine. Worse yet, water washed away the frame of the shack, leaving only the foundation standing.

He pulled at his hair, then he remembered that Crosby had cautioned him that he'd have to go through much more like the Dutch owner, who could only dream but never did achieve much. *Next time, everything will be nailed down.*

After the rains had let up, Raja and Beta, together with hired hands, built an embankment all around his property. The sides sloped away from a flat top. They planted Bahama grass to prevent erosion.

In time, Raja rebuilt his house and plunged headlong into the dairy business.

For a start, he purchased ten heifers and a bull to make up his first herd. He let the animals roam freely in an adjacent pasture. So that no problems would arise, he paid a small grazing fee to the owner for that privilege. To vary his operation, he made a special paddy nursery, banked on all four sides with dirt. Beta insisted on sowing the rice seeds and did so with care.

"Uncle, these plants are like babies," he said to Raja. "They need to be nursed all the time." Beta was using that as an excuse to skip school.

"Taking care of rice brings pleasure, but you must complete your schooling," Raja advised. He wanted to teach Beta the value of education, a privilege he'd never had. He literally had to drag the boy away from the rice nursery, take him to the one-room school of twenty students, and plunk him down in his seat. "After school, you can work for me," Raja said as he waved goodbye.

As the plants got greener and taller, they became crowded and needed to be transplanted. Raja flooded his three acres of land and with one hand holding a bunch of rice plants, used the other to insert each plant into the soil. He did that repeatedly. There was something hypnotic about cultivating rice, the smell of the young plants so intoxicating, and Raja sensed that he'd get a bumper crop.

That afternoon Beta arrived to see the plants already in their new location. He rubbed his eyes as though he didn't want to believe what he was seeing. "Uncle, why didn't you wait for me? I wanted to plant the rice myself."

Raja patted him on the head. "Don't worry. Those baby plants are yours as well as mine."

Only twelve, Beta acted like a grown man. He had taken Baran's place.

CHAPTER NINETEEN

Raja decided to use the flooded rice paddy as a fishpond. He reared patwa and the local delicacy, hassar—the armoured catfish that feed on rice stalks and tiny water animals. Just to watch the fish chasing one another and hear frogs croaking gave him pleasure.

As he drained the field, he caught several pails of fish, which he transported in his canoe to the Aciah Market and sold to a wholesaler. To meet the growing demand, Raja turned to the more efficient cast net which he used in the surrounding canals. The learning process of casting the net was slow, but before too long, he swelled his catch to include hoori and yarrow. From a rice and dairy farmer-cum-fisherman, he progressed to become the most enterprising farmer in the district.

While he was busy with the fishery business, his paddy ripened. A new sickle made harvesting so much easier. He stacked the sheaves in stooks and later transported them to a threshing area. There, he tied six oxen in double rows to a central pole and marched them round and round over the rice straw. The hooves of the animals separated the sheaves from the grains resulting in a huge pile of paddy.

Eager to get the job done, he hardly looked up at the fluffy, greyish clouds that hovered above. Drops of rain fell hard against his skin. With no cover for the grain, he yelled in frustration but the thunderstorm drowned his voice. He stamped his feet, lifted his arms and looked skywards. "My first harvest is ruined. Oh Lord Vishnu!"

For four full days, the rains kept up. In the end, the paddy was too wet to salvage.

He had learned a lesson and decided to build himself a shed to protect his grain in the future.

In the second year, five of Raja's heifers gave birth. During the following years, heifers and cows would calve, resulting in a sizable dairy herd. It provided enough milk for him to become a contract supplier for a dairy company in Georgetown.

Every morning he loaded several cans of milk onto the train for prompt delivery to the city. In the evening, he picked up the empty milk cans from the last train.

On an open range, Raja's herd mixed freely with cattle belonging to the Madeiran businessman, Mr. Pereira, whom Raja had never met. He was happy that the man's cow-minder rarely checked on the cattle in his care. Raja's breeding stock, therefore, benefited from Pereira's superior bulls. In return, Raja watched over all the cattle, irrespective of ownership. Beta, who'd graduated with a Primary School Leaving Certificate, now became a paid worker. Besides his regular job as a farmhand, he now had an office where, for an hour every Friday, he did the bookkeeping, or so he said.

Early one morning, Beta rushed to Raja. "Mr. Pereira's pregnant heifer is in distress, Uncle. Its tail is up and it appears to be straining."

Mucus had fallen onto the cow's hind hooves when Raja got there. In Belwasa, he'd helped his father deliver a water buffalo calf, so he did not panic. In preparation for the delivery, he and Beta washed their hands and flushed the rear-end of the animal.

The water bag was taking ages to descend, and Raja continued to coax the animal. When at last the bag burst, and the hind legs of the calf came out first, he realized that it was going to be a difficult birth.

While Beta held on to the calf's tail, Raja used all his strength to pull the legs in line with the calf's body.

Sweat poured from Raja's forehead and stung his eyes. He was exhausted by the time a beautiful calf appeared. He did not shout for joy the way Beta did. However, at that instant, Raja felt a special attachment for the calf that he had brought into the world, a calf that was part of the mystery of life.

He cleared the calf's mouth and nostrils of fluid and let the mother lick the animal clean. The bonding between the cow and its calf was beautiful to see. Like a proud father, Raja watched his "baby" struggle to stand up and eventually suckle its first milk.

Before the year was up, he placed his own brand on the calf. He did not consider that stealing. According to his reasoning, the calf belonged to him because he had saved its life.

Like many others in the colony, he looked upon cattle and, to a lesser extent, rice lands, as an indicator of power and wealth. To own Pereira's plantation house would cement his wealth and make him a respected man within the community. He decided that if the opportunity ever arose, he would buy that mansion. His ultimate goal was to accumulate as many assets as possible and spend the rest of his life luxuriating in his native Belwasa. *No one should envy me, for I have sacrificed ten years of my life as an indentured servant, something that was akin to slavery.*

One morning, after he'd loaded the cans of milk onto the train's last carriage but one, it started to move with him still on board. He rushed for the door and jumped. The wheels of the train mangled his big toe and left two others hanging loose. So intense was the pain, he screamed.

Some bystanders dragged him away and placed him in front of the platform. Besides the injury to his left foot, his upper right arm appeared dislocated and broken.

Two men from the village placed him in a donkey cart and took him to a bonesetter, who practised African folk medicine. The man's biceps popped out of the short sleeves of his khaki shirt. Raja wondered whether the man set bones or broke them.

After the man had reset the fracture, he said, "I'll bandage two sticks against your arm and support it with a sling. But your toes are mashed up really bad." He bathed the injured part with iodine and added, "I suggest you go to the Georgetown Public Hospital right away." He stretched out his palm, "That will be a shilling, babu. Now for an extra bit, I will invoke African juju spirit so you'll never have to worry about accidents again."

"Lord Vishnu can do the same for me without charge," Raja said, still wincing in pain. "I'll just pay the shilling."

He sent a message to Beta and his other workers to run the farm in his absence while he rushed off to the Georgetown Public Hospital in a horse-drawn carriage.

The surgeon amputated the injured toes to prevent gangrene. Raja was going to be holed up in the old Seaman's Ward for weeks.

One morning as he hobbled around, he heard a familiar voice at the end of the hall, which prompted him to shout, "Jahaji bhai!"

"Raja, I'm surprised that you're still in the colony," Ramdas yelled back, limping toward his friend.

"I decided to accept free land instead."

Ramdas stared at Raja. "Aha! So like me, you've abandoned the old country."

Those words really hit home so Raja said, "I will return when I can do so as a man of means. But tell me, why is your leg in a cast?"

"Leg fracture. My horse threw me as I tried to lasso a wild steer." Ramdas made a click-click sound with his tongue as he pointed at Raja's foot. "It looks like your toes got busted up."

Raja told Ramdas the details of his accident.

"My new position is director of operations, Ramdas said. "My wife is manager and we live in a farmhouse on the premises. We supervise the farm hands in a mixed operation."

"He must have a large herd," Raja said.

"Three hundred head to be exact."

"That's a good size—"

Ramdas signalled for Raja to sit with him on a bench. "We have a contract with the slaughterhouse to supply them with most of their beef animals."

"Though I don't butcher my own cows, I have become more tolerant of the practice," Raja said with a wry smile.

Ramdas tapped his friend on the shoulder. "That's life, my friend. We all change."

"Here in Demerara, our old values are forever put to the test."

"I couldn't agree more," Ramdas said. "What did Shankar call it?"

"Culture. Right up to the end, he continued to spit out some noble words to me."

"What happened to him?"

"That's a long story." Raja swallowed before continuing, "As for Jasmine . . . ."

Ramdas lifted his eyebrows. "The beautiful one! Mmm! What about her?"

"She had a tragic end. I'd also leave her story for later."

"As you wish." Ramdas reflected on those words. "Man, I'm dying to hear what you do for a living."

"Like your employer, I'm into mixed farming."

Ramdas shifted his leg cast. "I won't dig into how many head of cattle you own," he said with a sly wink. "Too many farmers rustle animals. Over the years, we've lost a few. Now, everyone knows I carry a gun."

Raja stared at Ramdas. "I'm not a cattle thief. However, if all farmers watched over their animals and branded them on time, there would be no problem."

Ramdas chuckled. "Sounds like you've been fast with the brand."

A sheepish Raja spread his palms out. "Only once when I delivered a calf that would have surely died."

"That still makes you a thief."

Raja massaged his chin. "I've let myself and my family down." His voice cracked with emotion. "It comes down to greed. I wanted to get rich contrary to my beliefs."

"You struck me as a man I could trust with my life. Now I must change my opinion of you," Ramdas said with a wink.

"When I return," Raja said, "I will transfer one of my calves to Mr. Pereira's herd and ask forgiveness during a puja service."

Outside the gate, Raja had to settle for a donkey cart as he could not locate a horse and carriage. "They're all booked up for Sahib Crosby's funeral," the driver said.

Looking back, Raja had foreseen that Crosby's end was near. Despite his run-ins with the official, he had a high regard and an affection for the man. "Let's join the procession," he said to the driver.

Behind top-hatted Governor Cornelius Kortright, along with hundreds of Indians, Raja paid his respects while sitting in a donkey cart. He was sure Crosby, a man who had stood up for the downtrodden Indians, wouldn't have minded.

Upon Raja's return, he was greeted with some sad news.

"Half a dozen steers missing and the farmhands are all gone, Uncle," Beta said.

Raja took a deep breath and tried to cope with the news he'd just heard. "We can always replace the men, but those cattle are family."

"Uncle, I think it's the work of thieves and God will punish them."

The boy's words jolted Raja. "Beta, I branded a calf that didn't belong to me; so I'm the one being punished."

"Everyone knows you watched over Mr. Pereira's cattle."

"It doesn't matter. We must make it up somehow."

Beta nodded and left. In no time, he was back and placed before Raja a bowl of Creole soup and a leaf parcel of fried plantains. "My mother said this will get you back on your feet."

Raja, who had so far not experienced real home cooking in the colony, enjoyed the local dish.

Beta fashioned crude crutches out of mora wood, and for weeks Raja hobbled around. However, he discovered that he could not use his injured arm. He kicked himself for not having it checked at the hospital in Georgetown. Now he had no choice but to return to the African shaman.

"What kind of a bonesetter are you?" Raja asked. "My arm doesn't seem right."

The man looked at the crooked arm. "Open your mouth." He placed a piece of bellyache stem between Raja's teeth and said, "Bite into this."

Before Raja could do so, the man snapped the arm as if it were a dry twig. Raja bit the stem in two and uttered a scream that caused a large crowd to gather. The bush doctor reset the bones and placed two fresh splints against the arm. He caked it over with soft clay mixed with the juice of bellyache leaves. "You shouldn't have any more problems." Without looking at Raja, he stretched out his hand. "One shilling."

Raja shook his head. "Another shilling? I already paid you the first time. Now you owe me for all my suffering and the work I couldn't do."

"Had you paid one measly bit for juju, there would have been no cause for you to return."

"Here's your darn bit. This pain is too much."

Slowly, Raja regained the use of his limbs, though he still walked with a limp because of the missing toes. In truth, his accident had turned out to be a blessing. It showed him how much he had strayed from his principles and beliefs. Honesty and fairness in all his business dealings would now be his creed. That shouldn't stop him from still becoming the most progressive farmer in the district.

He got in touch with Ramdas, who sold him a golden-brown mare. In the village of Buxton, he located a black barefoot cowboy he nicknamed Cowboy.

"Cowboy," Raja said, "your first job is to search the neighbouring pastures for my missing steers." Raja pointed at the brand on one of his cows. "This is what you look for."

After several days of searching, Cowboy reported, "No trace of your brand, boss—not even at the pound. Someone must have driven your cattle straight to the slaughterhouse."

"Never mind," Raja said, "Just take good care of my present herd."

Soon after, Raja visited the Portuguese gentleman who owned the more built-up subsection of land that abutted the river west of his property. Rumour had it that Mr. Pereira's interests lay in his many grocery stores that dotted the length of the East Coast public road. Each month the man would leave his home in Georgetown to check on those businesses. Once every year, the family spent a couple of weeks at their plantation house in De Droom, beside the Aciah River.

Early that morning, Raja limped up the stairs to the mansion. He used the brass door knocker and addressed the gentleman, "Will you sell me your forty acre portion of Plantation De Droom?"

The man's eyes focused on Raja's poplin leggings and kurta. Though Raja always wore shoes except when working in the field, he could tell from the man's expression that he was being taken for a brown-skin peasant.

"I don't think you can afford it," Mr. Pereira said in a heavy, halting accent. "Besides, this is my country estate where I come to relax with a Scotch, fish for lukanani, and hunt labba."

"Well, could I see the inside of your house?"

From the entrance, just a glimpse of the interior made Raja's eyes light up. Inside, the coloured glass windows filtered the morning sunlight into shafts of green, blue, yellow, and red. More than anything else, he wanted this house by the river.

"It's not for sale," Mr. Pereira said, "and there's no point." He closed the door in Raja's face.

Head bent, Raja limped away.

He waited two years before making another house call. On that June day, the royal poinciana tree was in bloom in the front yard, its red flowers ablaze in the tropical sun. No wonder local folk called it the flamboyant tree.

This time Raja banged the door knocker three times in quick succession. He heard a shuffle behind the door before it opened.

The owner greeted Raja with a smile. "Hello, Mr. Singh, come sit down."

What a difference time had made! The man had developed a paunch. "Why employ a cowboy to tend your cattle?" Raja asked. "My own man can do the job for free."

Mr. Pereira rubbed the stubble under his chin. "Mr. Singh, if your man tends my cows like he does yours, I'll owe you a favour."

"I just want to be a good neighbour," Raja said.

As he left the mansion, he whistled a popular Bihari folksong he'd learned as a child and did his version of a jig, despite his limp. His goal was to please Mr. Pereira in every possible way so that on the next visit that favour would fall in his lap.

"Cowboy," Raja said the following day, "you're in charge of Mr. Pereira's herd. Treat all cattle the same, but for him do an extra special job. For that I will give you a raise."

In celebration, Cowboy donned a Stetson hat, black shirt sequined with red beads, a matching bandana, and new pants, all bought on credit from William Fogarty's store in Georgetown. He had lodged with the manager a statement of his wages signed by Beta, P.S.L.C., Accountant.

Beta had added letters after his name in reference to his Primary School Leaving Certificate, which he had framed and hung in his office. In the whole history of De Droom Primary School, he was its first student to have passed the examination. Further, rumour had it that he had topped the country in sums.

Though somewhat on the bulky side, Cowboy was popular with the villagers—especially the schoolmaster who referred to Cowboy Jack at a council meeting as "the darnedest best cowpoke who ever roamed the savannahs of Demerara."

"Much appreciated. Thank you!" Cowboy said to the learned gentleman as he pushed out his chest and tipped his "Boss of the Plains" cowboy hat.

"You heard what the schoolmaster said about me," he told one and all. "I am like them black cowpunchers who roamed the Plains of the Wild American West."

In De Droom, this grandson of a slave always sang as he rounded up cattle on the open savannah with his prized mount, whose back sagged under his weight. Whether he sang hymns to rid himself of loneliness mattered little. It certainly touched Raja whenever Cowboy belted out his version of a cowboy song and accompanied himself on a homemade banjo.

No mo bakkra wok fo' me
No mo, no mo.
No mo hundred lash fo' me
Cause ah free as a bird.
No mo picklin' salt 'pon me ass
No mo, no mo.
Cause ah ridin' me hass
fo' all to see.
Ay-Ee-Ooo.

One year later to the day, Raja again visited the Pereira mansion. On this occasion, the man was cradling a drink.

"Before we get down to business, Mr. Singh, can my butler get you a Scotch with a dash o' lime juice?" Mr. Pereira raised his glass that reflected the sun's rays.

Raja could tell that Mr. Pereira would rather conduct business over a drink. Raja, who had given up the habit, was tempted to go through the motions of drinking, but he wanted things his way with a clear head.

He knew that Mr. Pereira cultivated his own coffee shrubs, a carry-over from the De Droom plantation of the glory days. And that his kitchen staff still dried and roasted their own beans.

So Raja said, "Coffee would be fine." Pereira seemed disappointed, but Raja stuck to his principles. "After coffee, could you give me a quick tour of your beautiful country house?" he asked.

"Certainly, Mr. Singh. But first let me thank you and your fellow for taking such good care of my cattle."

The aroma of roasted coffee freshly brewed in an old coffee pot was simply breathtaking. The black butler, in white jacket and gloves, rolled up a service tray with a sterling silver coffee pot and bone china demitasse cups.

"Best coffee I ever tasted," Raja said to the butler. "Some day I must find out your secret to making this."

"I hire only the best," Pereira said. "Now let me start the grand tour."

Raja was so taken aback, all he could do was bow as an expression of thanks.

Pereira pointed to the floor of the family room. "Nova Scotia pitch pine all the way from Canada. Tongue and groove, perfect seal—never creaks."

Raja trailed behind as Pereira acted as the consummate salesman in describing the features that showed off his home in the best possible light.

Sturdy greenheart columns supported the Tudor style building. The steeply pitched gable roof gave it that majestic look. Framed inside with greenheart scantlings, the north and south walls enclosed five bedrooms, living, and dining rooms. They all sported louvered Demerara shutters. Fretwork decorated the overhanging eaves.

What better way for Pereira to end the tour than at the pantry, well stocked with old Madeira wines!

Politely refusing a glass of wine, Raja said, "Mr. Pereira, in the past few years, you've hardly visited De Droom. Besides, your family no longer comes along. Why not make some money and move on?"

"I've been too busy and have slowed down somewhat, but what are you getting at, Mr. Singh?"

Raja stuttered and couldn't quite come up with the words.

"If it's the house you're after, it is beyond your means."

Raja screwed up his face as he thought fast. "That's not my purpose for being here, I can assure you. How about you pay me the equivalent of one hundred dollars a year for Cowboy to continue tending your cattle?"

"I didn't expect your man to work for free all the time."

A few days later, Mr. Pereira approached Raja. "Why don't you accompany me tomorrow in my coach to Georgetown? If I can buy half of Henriette Estate, I will sell you my portion of Plantation De Droom."

"Of course, I'll come along." This was Raja's opportunity to learn how Mr. Pereira conducted business.

The man had no trouble meeting the top brass in the Deeds Registry. At Pereira's request, a clerk searched out the title to an abandoned coffee and cotton plantation, comprising also forty acres on each side of the De Droom Side Road.

Mr. Pereira wrote the name and land description down. "Who is the owner of the Henriette plantation?" he asked the registrar.

"It is reserved Crown land," the registrar replied.

"I don't know what you're talking about," Mr. Pereira said, looking utterly confused.

"A memorandum of understanding states that the land is reserved for a certain class o' people, and you don't qualify."

What Raja was hearing might have been addressed to him since Mr. Pereira was white.

"Why? My money is good," Mr. Pereira said, looking uncomfortable in Raja's presence. He demanded a piece of paper and scribbled something on it. "This is my offer for one part."

"There's no harm in presenting it to the Chief Secretary." The registrar leaned back in his chair. "Assuming, Mr. Pereira, that you're only interested in forty acres, which part are you after?"

"The western part that abuts the Aciah River of course, as stated in the offer."

"Just wanted to be sure," the registrar replied. "I'll let you know on the morrow."

Raja looked on in awe at the effortless way in which Mr. Pereira negotiated the purchase of a valuable piece of land. There was more to come.

"I'm inviting both you and the Chief Secretary for rum swizzles at Jones Sports Club after work this evening," Mr. Pereira said. "We can discuss the matter further there."

With a smile that turned into a wide, toothy grin, the registrar replied, "That's his usual hangout." Then with a sly wink aimed at Raja, the registrar said, "We'll see you at five, Mr. Pereira, providing they let you in."

The next morning, Raja again accompanied Mr. Pereira to the registrar's office to continue his education.

Without looking at Mr. Pereira, the registrar said, "We had a problem, sir."

"But there was none last evening," Mr. Pereira said.

The registrar tapped a cigarette on the packet and lit up.

"Chesterfield," Mr. Pereira whispered to Raja covering his mouth, "American brand."

"The Chief Secretary is on your side," the registrar said, inhaling deeply, "but he had a difficult time convincing the governor that you're a bona fide European."

Mr. Pereira yelled, "What in dickens is this? You can't be serious."

The registrar got up and, blowing smoke rings into Mr. Pereira's face, placed a hand on his shoulder. "Relax, man." He enunciated each word. "As a former indentured labourer from Funchal, Madeira, who came into new money—that's a stone around your neck."

"Wh-what do you mean?"

"While you're king among the coolies, you're considered lower in class than even an English peasant."

"Well, I never thought—" Mr. Pereira stopped in mid-sentence, cut off by the registrar, who raised his hand.

"Well, I understand how you feel. However, we must be realistic. I am Dutch and don't have the same privileges as the rulers." The registrar acted as though he was studying the offer once more. "Who cares how they categorize you? The main point is your offer is within range."

"So?"

"I'll take the liberty to accept the offer."

Before the registrar could venture to suggest that Pereira should again treat him to drinks at Jones Sports Club, Mr. Pereira shook his hand. He clapped Raja on the back, almost knocking him over, and said, "Let's get out of here." Out of the registrar's hearing, he added, "Look what free drinks can do to a reserve clause."

Raja now changed his mind about buying Mr. Pereira's half of Plantation De Droom. *If it isn't good for Pereira, why should it be good for me?* He would wait for bigger fish. However, there was one deal he still wanted to make.

"I can cut the trees in your West Henriette property and have the land prepared as a pasture for your cattle, Mr. Pereira," Raja said.

"What do you wish in return?" Mr. Pereira asked.

This was the moment Raja was waiting for. He tried to remain calm. "You owe me a favour. Remember? Sell me your mansion."

"Aha. The nerve. Can you afford one thousand dollars?"

Without batting an eye, Raja said, "I can give you a down payment of five hundred dollars, which should cover all the interest, and one hundred dollars principal at the start of each year for ten years."

When Mr. Pereira shook his head and muttered, "No, not enough," Raja could smell victory. He promised to meet with him soon.

Mr. Pereira agreed to an extra two hundred dollars down payment and Raja couldn't control his excitement. He even kissed Mr. Pereira on both cheeks. It would take weeks for his good fortune to sink in.

A week after he'd moved into the mansion, he extended an invitation to Mr. Pereira and the entire village to come to his new home for a feast. Before the meal, a Hindu priest offered blessings and reminded Raja that the more successful he became, the closer he needed to get to God.

True to his word, Raja had the land prepared for Mr. Pereira. A group of men worked eight-hour shifts, six days a week, and within four months, Mr. Pereira's land was cleared. Raja's workmen ploughed the field, on which they planted Bahama grass. The wallaba, simarupa, and mora logs from the clear-cut, Raja sold to a sawmill for a small fortune.

CHAPTER TWENTY

Raja stood on the front porch of the mansion, dazzled by the sun as he inhaled the bracing morning air. He was congratulating himself on his grand fortune in acquiring such a choice piece of property when a heavy-set man stepped out of a canoe and, in a shuffling gait, ambled his way to the house. In his worn-out pair of khaki trousers held up with braces, he looked familiar. Moments later, Raja recognized him.

Battered hat in hand, revealing a rich growth of grey hair at the sides and back of his head, Kwame bowed in greeting.

"Good morning, sir," he said, as though addressing the hat.

"What a surprise!" Raja exclaimed. After the usual greetings, he invited his friend in.

"You're doing well," Kwame made a sweeping gesture with his hand that ended with an aim at the mansion, "for a man who had his share of troubles at Sugar Grove Estate."

Raja winced at the mere mention of the plantation he'd rather now forget, but he managed a smile. "Those days are behind me, Kwame."

"Despite all the clashes you and Shankar had with the estate administrators, I always believed that you both would rise to the top some day."

Raja did not wish to dwell on such matters. The sight of Shankar paddling away appeared before him and he shuddered. Now, another friend of Raja's past had re-entered his life and he was happy. "Put your hat on," he said to Kwame. "How on earth did you know where to find me?"

"The clerk at Crosby's office described the exact location of your settlement."

Raja raised his brows, wondering if they were checking up on him. He now focused on Kwame. "So the Big Bajan has finally sacked you."

"He said I'm too old to work as a stevedore."

Raja led Kwame to the front landing of his house. "Don't worry. You've come at just the right time since I need a livestock manager."

"With the help of a good cowboy, I can take care of your cattle."

"I have such a man."

Kwame took his hat off again. He pointed to his bald head and grey hair around the fringes. "I hope my age doesn't get in the way."

Raja waved him off. "You can manage my cattle until we find someone permanent."

Kwame couldn't thank Raja enough. He said, "Boss, could you let me use a plot of land for a shack and garden?"

"Boss? Come inside and rest your legs. I'll get the fire going."

In no time, Raja served a blend of sweet broom and lemongrass tea, Kwame's favourite.

Though Kwame showed signs of fatigue, having just arrived, Raja used the opportunity to question him about his father. He was curious to know about the African's journey to the colony. Was it similar in any way to his?

"He was one of the last slaves out of Africa to this country," Kwame said.

"And how did they capture him?"

"The slave traders helped one tribe defeat the other," Kwame took a sip of tea, "my father, who was of the Fante tribe, became a prisoner of the Ashanti chief, who sold him along with others to a ship's captain. But Raja, you didn't answer my question about building the shack."

"I will, after I hear the rest."

"The Ashanti chief, for guns, rum, beads, and other trinkets, had his men take the prisoners to a slave castle by the beach. There, in the dungeon, my father was branded on the chest and chained to another. Along with hundreds of others, he and his shipmate were led through a one-way door leading to a dark tunnel. What about the plot of land, Raja?"

Raja pushed out his palm, signalling for Kwame to wait. He thought about how his own countrymen, just like the tribal chief, had "sold" him for a few silver rupees.

He pictured Kwame's father, branded and chained, stacked in close quarters. He imagined himself being chained to Ramdas, and his heart went out to Kwame's father and so many like him who had suffered much more than he had.

"Regarding the shack—build it at the southern edge of my property, next to the bottom side portion, close to the river. You can fence off a portion at the back for your garden."

"How much would I owe you, Raja?"

"What are friends for?"

Kwame peered out the front door. "Is it beside the wooded area over yonder?"

"Yes. The clump of balata trees will give you privacy. And Kwame, you're far from any silk cotton tree and jumbie bird." Raja burst into a fit of laughter and clapped his friend on the shoulder.

Kwame grinned and, on his way out to have a closer look at the property, asked, "Why do you treat me so well?"

Raja looked into Kwame's eyes. He remembered how Kwame had welcomed him and Shankar to his bush house. It had made those five years of servitude so much shorter. However, knowing that Kwame would not like that to be mentioned, Raja said, "Because your people got no contract to claim land. That makes me feel guilty and sad."

"Let's forget the past."

In no time, Kwame set himself to work. Cowboy and Beta were there whenever he needed a hand. The shack was framed with silverbally scantlings and supported by wallaba posts, all materials supplied by Raja. The mora flooring was three feet above ground to combat floods and to avoid the alligators. As soon as Kwame's hut was completed and his garden fenced with coconut branch staves, he got himself another macaw and a squirrel monkey.

CHAPTER TWENTY-ONE

One evening, Raja visited Kwame to find out how he was getting along at the farm. Kwame served up a cup of bush tea. "Raja," he said, as he got down to business, "seeing I'm your manager, shouldn't I run things as I see fit?"

"Of course, Kwame. What do you have in mind?" Though Raja had reassured Kwame that he was the boss, he still wanted to keep on top of things.

"A good-sized dairy herd is only half the programme," Kwame said. "We must also have beef animals."

Raja's eyes almost popped out of their sockets. So far, it was only his neighbours' cattle that got slaughtered. "What!" He found himself pulled by two forces—the cow as a sacred animal as well as a symbol of wealth.

For the first time in his life, Raja admitted to himself that the latter took precedence. *This country has really changed me.* "Do as you wish," he said.

"Where can I buy good stock cattle?" Kwame asked.

"At the Ruimveldt Cattle Ranch. Go see my ship brother, Ramdas."

Two weeks later, Kwame came back with five well-bred beef cattle and one dairy cow. He also brought some sad news from Ramdas that his wife had recently passed away and he wanted to know if Raja had a job with accommodation for him.

Raja replied in a letter: "Ramdas, come make yourself useful. Enough room in the servant's quarters."

Always well dressed and tidy, Ramdas got along well with the other workers. Though the music in his voice had left him, he was good company for Raja. Far into the night, they reminisced on that momentous journey to Demerara in the dark hole of a ship.

In exchange for room and board, Ramdas assisted in managing the cattle ranch. He was careful to stay away from the decision-making process, though he would have known more of modern ranching techniques than Kwame.

Before retiring one evening, Ramdas said, "You must make the move before time runs out on you, Raja. You need a woman in the house."

Had those words come from a stranger, Raja might have thought that Ramdas simply did not like his home cooking and preferred a woman's touch.

During the night, Raja reflected on what his friend had said. Kwame had suggested more or less the same thing. The past few years, he had rarely thought of Savitri. Twelve years in the colony had dimmed the chance of their ever reuniting on the beautiful bank of the Daha River. Poor woman! It was not something that he would brag about. It was cruel to abandon a wife. However, he had to be realistic.

In September of 1881, Beta's father suffered a fatal heart attack. Some months later, his widow, Sheela, took to wandering the riverbank on late afternoons. On one occasion, Raja sat with her under the poinciana tree. As they chatted, the fruity fragrance of flowers filled the air and swept Raja into a mood he had not experienced for many years. The two of them indulged in pleasant conversation until Sheela said that it was too late for a woman to walk alone and that he should escort her home.

Another time, accompanied by her two young daughters, Sheela stopped to speak to Raja. "You need flowers around your house," she said to him. "What's a yard without oleanders?"

She gathered potted oleander cuttings that she had started weeks ago at her own home. She planted them at the back of Raja's house to make a hedge facing the river. In the front yard, she added red hibiscus and bougainvillea shrubs to complement the flaming flamboyant tree.

Afterwards, Raja treated Sheela to tea and biscuits. He reminded her of the Creole soup that she had sent him while he was recovering from his train accident. "You must show me your secret for making that soup," he said.

Sheela covered her mouth and giggled. "I'll come to your house and make it from scratch. I promise you."

On one of their frequent walks, a man hailed Raja from across the road. "Raja, are you going to marry Sheela?"

Raja pointed a finger at the man and shouted back, "If you don't mind your mouth, you'll end up in the trench."

Despite Raja's attempts to quell the gossip, people made snide remarks about his regular rendezvous with Sheela. Even Kwame got in on the act. "You better marry the woman. Everybody's talking."

"Well, I'll give them even more to talk about," Raja replied.

The next week he hired a Hindu priest to conduct a religious service at his home and invited Sheela. She hung around after everyone had left. Once again, Raja became aware of her physical presence. Was it because he needed company? True, a house, especially a big one, could be a friendless place without a partner, but Raja, whether he liked it or not, had fallen in love with a widow.

A clumsy attempt at embracing Sheela ended with her brushing him off. For weeks she stayed away, and the few times she went for walks by the riverside, her two daughters trudged along.

One afternoon when she came alone to check on the plants around the house, Raja took the opportunity to invite her in.

After tea, they chatted for a long time. Just before she left, Raja kissed her on the cheek, and they parted on friendly terms.

As the months went by, he became more intimate with Sheela. To ease the guilt that built up within him, he contacted the local schoolmaster to write a letter to his wife. It read:

> Dear Savitri,
>
> Hope this letter finds you in good health. It would be nice to hear from you and "little" Baran.
>
> I am making a new life in British Guiana, a colony in South America, which I've come to love.
>
> Would give you more details in my next letter.
>
> Please write soon.
>
> Sincerely,
>
> Raja

He held on to the letter for a week and in the end burned it. What purpose would it serve he asked himself? Too many years had dimmed any hope of a reunion. And as for Baran, he would have been too small to remember much of his elder brother, anyway.

Meanwhile, Sheela lightened her complexion with turmeric and traipsed around the riverbank in her prettiest ankle-length frocks. They met often, sitting on a log beside the Aciah River. Romance was in the air, this second spring, filled with passion and excitement.

Sheela visited Raja's home one afternoon and made him the soup as promised. When they lingered in each other's arms, it seemed like the natural thing to do. They'd kiss every evening before she left until it came to a point where Raja had to admit that he did find her handsome features quite alluring.

Now came the long-awaited moment: the proposal that they unite as a couple. It ended with Sheela moving into Raja's house with her two daughters, aged thirteen and ten. Her teenage son, Beta, chose to remain in their old home.

Because Raja's Hindu marriage in India was not recognized in the colony, he could have married Sheela legally, but he chose not to do so. Moreover, at this stage, he was not prepared to tell Sheela that he had left a wife in India. And why should he mention his affair with Jasmine?

After several months of living together, Sheela announced to Raja that she was pregnant. This was a pleasant surprise, since Raja believed she had reached the end of her childbearing years.

Months later, at the onset of her labour pains, Raja sent for the lay nurse who delivered babies at Plantation Sugar Grove. Besides excelling in midwifery, she rivalled the local dispenser in her blend of bush tea and honey for ulcers, poultices of bellyache leaves for abdominal pains, and bitter aloe preparations for skin infections and constipation.

"What's taking the nurse so long?" Sheela screamed. "Oh my! The baby is here!"

Raja dashed around the yard like a headless chicken until he found what he wanted. "Bite into this bellyache stem," he said to her.

He dabbed her forehead with a wet towel as she bit down. Anyone would have concluded that he needed the same treatment, as sweat from his brows fell on her face.

A boisterous, "Ho, ho, jackass! Tie me donkey down theh, man," announced the nurse's arrival. She soon marched into the kitchen and yelled to Sheela's daughters, "Boil a large pot of water. What in dickens are you doing? Hurry up, man!"

Even Raja did not escape the nurse's rage. "Get out of here!" she shouted.

He'd wanted to witness the baby's arrival, so he ignored her. In the next instant, she eased the baby's head—all covered in a white creamy coating—out of the womb.

After a slap on the buttocks, she held up a bawling, bronze baby girl. In her singsong accent she announced, "She brings good luck to you, Raja—an extra toe on each foot. My-my. Now go bury the darn navel string."

He obliged by doing so under the sandkoker tree.

Later, the nurse ordered Raja to make Creole soup with plantains and ground provisions—cassava and yams—steeped in coconut milk. "It will bring her strength back, good," she said.

"You learned well, Raja," Sheela said when he served her.

The year 1883 had brought him good luck. Becoming a first-time father had put a spring in his step. He held his head high as he walked the De Droom Side Road and told passersby of his good fortune. Blessed with a seed, his offspring could now flourish and reconnect with his mother country.

He doted upon the baby and cooed at her whenever she cried. Far into the night, while the fragrance of frangipanis wafted through the windows and the yellow light from the turned-down wick of the kerosene lamp glimmered in the darkness, Raja rocked his baby daughter, Rena. Sometimes he sang his version of "Rock-a-bye Baby," which put her to sleep.

Two years went by rather fast and as the second rainy season approached in December, the rains came down with a vengeance. The Aciah River overflowed its banks. For days, the downpour forced Beta and Cowboy to drive the cattle to higher ground around the house. That alone could not accommodate the entire herd and many perished. Despite their vigilance, a prized calf got swept away by a flash flood.

Never the one to accept such a loss, Raja pointed at the river and screamed at Cowboy, "Get the canoe and go after her!"

Cowboy rushed to pick up a paddle, for every second counted, the river's current so unpredictable.

Beta screamed, "It will be too late Cowboy!" Then he plunged headlong into the water.

Raja could not believe his eyes. "No, Beta! Don't!" He remembered the two Indians who'd succumbed to currents off the island of Saint Helena, exactly as Sen had said.

"Wait for me, Beta! I'm coming!" Cowboy shouted.

Beta ignored the warnings and swam after the calf with powerful front crawl strokes. His right arm was around the animal as Cowboy paddled toward him. Then, before everyone's eyes, Beta and the calf disappeared, pulled under by a possible undertow.

Raja yelled like a man gone crazy. "Beta is gone!" He took over the canoe from Cowboy and paddled with all his strength but the current soon forced him to turn back. Dazed, he sat on the porch and stared out at the river, his eyes flooded with tears.

Later that day, news came that a fisherman had found Beta barely alive at the mouth of the river facing the Atlantic Ocean, his shirt caught on an overhanging branch of a black mangrove tree.

Upon arrival at the fisherman's home, Raja found Beta in a delirious state. Water had entered his airways, and it took him another day to speak in a coherent manner.

After he'd regained his speech, he said, "I would have drowned had I not surfaced next to the floating limb of a wallaba tree."

Almost cut down in his prime, Beta's life had been spared.

Raja's world around him fluttered like a butterfly's wings. He looked upon the Aciah as another Daha River—a tributary of the Ganges, the River of Salvation— sacred from its source in the highlands of Guiana to the vast Atlantic Ocean.

Beta's rescue became a cause for celebration when Raja held a puja thanking God for sparing Beta's life. The priest compared the young man to a shepherd who was willing to sacrifice his life to save one member of the flock.

Half of Raja's stock perished in the flood and he became a poor man once more. His farm could not meet its daily milk quota. He looked on with despair as the pair of oxen that normally transported milk to the train sat idly chewing their cuds.

Weeks later, when the excess water had made its way to the sea and the hardiest animals had returned to their pastures, Kwame approached Raja. "At my age, I can't handle crises anymore. Let Ramdas be your livestock manager. He's got the experience to get you back on your feet."

"How will you keep busy, Kwame?"

In his usual silken voice, though much weaker, Kwame said, "In the last few months, I've been stealing time and growing ground provisions, greens, and plantains in my back garden. You'll still allow me to live there, won't you, Raja?" Kwame's voice, so sweet and almost childlike, trailed off to no more than a whisper that floated away with the breeze.

"As long as you wish, Kwame." Raja's voice shook. Right then, from deep within the woods came an ooo-eek sound. "I was wrong about those jumbie birds," Raja said, "but don't worry, you'll be safe."

Months had gone by until one Saturday morning, Raja got the surprise of his life—Kwame was selling greens and plantains at the Aciah Market. "I never looked upon you as a businessman, Kwame. Why the change?" Raja asked.

"I had more vegetables than I could handle from all the kitchen scraps and animal dung I put back into the ground," Kwame replied.

"Do you use night soil?"

"Not at the present, although I do sprinkle urine. Mixed with the right amount of water, there is no better fertilizer." Kwame filled Raja's sack with garden produce. "As a trade-off, how about you supply me with milk."

Raja shook Kwame's hand to seal the deal. He was especially happy that Kwame had eased himself into an occupation he enjoyed, while at the same time paving the way for Ramdas to take over the livestock management.

And so he did. Now that Kwame was out of the way, Ramdas said, "During severe floods and droughts, Creole cows seem to do better than the mixed foreign breeds that my former boss favours."

"Yet he did well."

"Unlike you, he had emergency measures for drainage and irrigation."

With Ramdas's expertise and Beta's industry, Raja's herd bounced back such that in a few years he was able to push Pereira out of the cattle business.

About this time, Beta rushed up to Raja, the real estate section of the *Royal Gazette* in his hand. Out of breath, he said, "Uncle, Mr. Pereira has listed West Henriette for sale."

"Keep me posted if you hear of any offers," Raja said. "I don't expect any because of some reserve clause."

As soon as Rena had turned five, Raja registered her at the public school. Because of a great influx of Afro-Guianese students whose parents had come from neighbouring villages to settle in De Droom, the 1888 enrolment was the highest in the history of the school.

So that she would preserve her Indian heritage, Raja sent her in the early evening to the Hindu school at the temple, where she'd fill her slate with the Hindi alphabet. In time, Raja also found himself learning to read and write in both languages. With his daughter's help, he progressed to the stage where he could read the *Royal Gazette* newspaper and the Bible.

A new world had opened up. Shankar would have been proud of his erstwhile friend, who had had no formal education.

Though Rena's schooling had ended at age twelve, Sheela ensured that her daughter learned cooking and sewing to be an independent woman. Rena, however, took that a stage further. She became an expert canoeist. Later, she took it upon herself to round up the cattle in the evening, where she would ride her own dappled grey filly at a marvellous canter. By the age of fourteen, she had relieved Cowboy of most of his duties. Almost single-handedly, she tended the entire herd.

Meanwhile, Raja helped Sheela sell her family farm, except for the house, and find suitable partners for her two grown daughters. Beta continued to be in charge of rice production.

Night and day, Raja dreamed of owning Pereira's portion of Henriette, which was well above the flood plain and not susceptible to flooding. If he could get that land, it would fulfil his dreams. The government, however, would rather not have a coolie own the former reserve Crown land. He had heard words to that effect from the registrar. To get around this predicament, he devised a plan.

During the Christmas holidays, he bought a sheep. He hired the maitre d' and top chef from the Guest House in Georgetown to supervise the preparation of lamb curry, cooked in coconut milk with apples and raisins. It was the chef's specialty. Raja sent out special invitations to the deputy registrar and his boss, Mr. Konenburg—whom everyone called Kony—and their wives. Mr. and Mrs. Pereira were also invited. A butler, hired for the day, served up his own Johnnie Walker Scotch whisky garnished with lime wedges, while a brass band complete with trumpet and trombone played music for dancing until the early hours of the morning.

The guests were so pleased that the very next week the event hit the newspaper's social column.

Some weeks later, Pereira said to Raja, "In a spirited bit of conversation, after he'd downed a few stiff shots of scotch at your Christmas party, the registrar told his deputy that I could sell the Henriette Estate to anyone as long as the purchaser was respectable."

"And what did the deputy say?" Raja perked up his ears to hear the answer.

"'Kony, that should be Pereira's business, shouldn't it?' were his exact words."

The outcome of it all was that Raja, the now respectable man, soon found himself the owner of West Henriette facing the Aciah River.

After the rains, the floodwaters had left a lot of silt that replenished the soil around the Henriette estate. Raja concluded that this was the main reason why people of British Guiana lived mainly on the coastal areas. The pasture around his property looked lush and green and that meant it could support a lot more cattle or be converted into rice paddies.

Any seasoned cattleman might have known that Raja would never dismiss his faithful cowboy. However, the plump fellow solved the problem himself. "Time to bow out," he said to his employer one day. He took a long, deep breath, as one does when struggling to control his emotions. "The reflexes are just not there, boss. Rena does most of the roundup, anyway."

Raja dropped the pail he was carrying. "I'm sorry to see you go." He turned and faced Cowboy.

Cowboy assumed a serious air. "When I stopped singing my cowboy songs, I knew it was time to quit."

"You know best." Raja put an arm around Cowboy's neck, the man's paunch preventing any sort of an embrace. "I'm losing the best cowboy in the land."

"My happiest moments were the days when I rode my mare on the open savannah. It was fun working for you, boss." After a pause, Cowboy continued, "You paid and treated your workers well, but the time has come for me to move on. Because I can never again be Demerara's baddest and best cowboy. No mo, no mo." He dried a tear.

Never in Raja's wildest dreams did he think that Cowboy could become so emotional. "Well said, Mr. Cowboy, but do you have another job?" Raja asked.

"I'll get into the transportation business. I already lined up a donkey and cart to take fruits and vegetables to retailers at Big Market. On the way back, I'll load up with groceries and peddle them to the villagers."

"You'll be into big money, Cowboy." Raja clapped his worker on the back.

"I'm going to put Pereira's Groceries out of business. Heh-heh."

"Your jackass can always feed by the roadside and drink from the public well. Free food and water."

"But the output won't be free. I'll sell it as manure."

"Green gold galore. You better take good care of that donkey, Cowboy."

Like equals, not master and servant, they shared a good laugh, locked hands, ending an employer-employee relationship that had lasted some eighteen years.

For Rena's fifteenth birthday, three years after she had completed her formal schooling, Raja bought her a chain-driven safety bicycle with wheels of equal size and inflatable rubber tires. This new bike had created history in that women for the first time could ride without "taking a header."

To learn to ride, Rena wore baggy knee-length bloomers with stockings. This outfit caused the village overseer to ask, "What have you done to your daughter, Raja? She's scandalizing our village with such vulgar clothing—and riding a bicycle of all things."

"Worse is happening in the village right now." Raja gritted his teeth. "You should know about the couple of incidents recently where the police were called."

Not at all discouraged by what people said, Raja beamed while he helped to steady the bicycle and hobbled along as best he could behind his daughter.

Once she had mastered the art of riding a bike, she rode to nearby villages on business trips for her father. Besides tending to the cattle, she worked closely with her half-brother, Beta, who had converted most of the lands to rice cultivation.

"With the profits from rice, you should buy East Henriette, Pa," Rena said to her father one day.

That got Raja thinking. "Let's hear what Mr. Ramdas and Beta have to say."

"Mr. Pereira said the government people will block you next time," Beta said when asked his opinion on the matter.

"Why?"

"Mr. Pereira told me that while the Portuguese are not treated the same as the English, the coolies are lower down the ladder and must know their—"

Raja winced and cut his stepson short. "Beta, if you want to move ahead you must overcome barriers. We live in an evolving world, as my friend Shankar used to say."

"The pace is much too slow, Uncle. Moreover, your name is not Ewing—the planter's son—but Raja Singh. A big, big difference."

Raja wrinkled his eyebrows in disgust. "I'll prove you wrong. The whole of Henriette will fall into my lap."

He sent for Jack. "Cowboy," he said, calling him by his old name, "Can you take Rena and me to the Deeds Registry Office in Georgetown tomorrow? We'll leave when the rooster crows."

Just a slight breeze rippled through the early morning mist as Raja and his daughter left for the city. The rhythmic, jerky motion of Cowboy's cart and the odour of donkey sweat made Raja drowsy. He became wide awake as the donkey cart pulled into the dirt lot of the High Street office building.

As soon as Raja told the registrar the purpose of his visit, the man's expression changed. He was not the same Kony who had slugged down shots of Johnnie Walker at Raja's house last Christmas. He seemed to have forgotten his discussion with his deputy.

With a grin, Mr. Konenburg said, "Mr. Ewing has already filed with us an intent to purchase the land in question. You got away with Pereira's portion."

Raja was about to let out a sigh but instead chose not to be outmanoeuvred. Without allowing those words to sink in, he said, "Mr. Konenburg, since I already own half of the estate, isn't it natural that I should get the rest?"

Mr. Konenburg cleared his throat and grimaced. "There were some knuckles rapped when the chief secretary found out that you, a ship-coolie, owned West Henriette."

Hearing that kind of insult so often had inured Raja to any type of hurt, so he remained silent and let Mr. Konenburg rattle on.

"Let me give you a bit of background about that land. During French rule, prior to the French Revolution and the Napoleonic Wars, a planter from Provence grew coffee there. Before too long, Brazil captured the market, forcing him to switch to cotton. After the invention of the cotton gin, he could no longer compete, so he donated the Henriette land to the government, packed up and left."

Raja decided to give the deputy some leeway regarding the reserve clause. "So, Mr. Konenburg, it must have been of sentimental value to the owner."

"Yes, indeed. He had named the plantation after his daughter, Henriette, who fell to blackwater fever while they lived on the estate. She's buried there."

"Her tombstone is among some ruins near the mansion," Raja said.

"So you understand. To make a long story short, the bones of my Dutch ancestors also lie there. European bones, Raja."

Stunned by the last remark, Raja wondered if the burial site also had a reserve clause prohibiting coolie bones. Not to be dissuaded, he stepped aside and introduced his daughter to Mr. Konenburg. "If I get the land, my daughter, Rena, will inherit it and pass it on to her offspring who will do the same."

Mr. Konenburg turned to the clerk, cupped his hand over his mouth, and whispered, "Here's a man who thinks he already owns the whole of the Henriette estate." They both chuckled.

Raja overheard the comment, but all he could do was smile.

After some time, Mr. Konenburg said, "What a pretty young lady! Fathers will line up to get her for their sons."

Rena giggled, covering her mouth and clinking her gold bangles at the same time.

"Rena will take the place of Henriette," Raja said.

Mr. Konenburg's narrowed eyes and twisted mouth made it difficult for Raja to read what went on in his head.

"What you say rings true," the registrar said through his tobacco-stained teeth. "The French planter lived in a different time. It makes no sense sticking to that reserve clause. And as to Mr. Ewing's statement of intent, it's exactly that."

Raja's heart raced with excitement for he could hardly believe what he was hearing. He patted himself on the back for bringing Rena into the picture.

Mr. Konenburg lit up a Chesterfield, inhaled deeply and blew smoke rings into the air around Raja. "Anything you would like to add in support of your desire to purchase?"

Raja realized he must say something in support of what was already a foregone conclusion. "Henriette is a beautiful piece of land and I would cherish—"

"You and your daughter return in two weeks. I will have to convince the chief secretary, who in turn may have to speak to the governor, that you're a good Hindu." He winked at Raja. "You don't knock down rum swizzles, do you?"

Without waiting for an answer, the registrar continued, "Always helps, Roger." He scratched his chin and added, "I almost forgot, there's a colour bar. Hmm! I don't think you'd get past the door at Jones Sports Club."

"Not when they've banned me years ago from their cricket ground," Raja said, to save himself further embarrassment.

"I will give you our decision on your next visit," the registrar said. "By the way, we loved the lamb curry you served up last Christmas. It went well with the nutmeg-flavoured Scotch. And such good music. Man, in your old age, you should take up ballroom dancing. Swing the old girl around."

"Bad foot due to an accident, Mr. Konenburg."

Because the registrar had become so talkative, Raja became optimistic. Yet he could be wrong. Two weeks to the day, on Monday morning, dark clouds had gathered in the sky as he prepared to leave for the city. The train was not running because of a displaced track.

"Not the best day to travel," Rena said to her father.

"When you want something really bad, never let weather or anything else get in the way," Raja said just as the rain came down in sheets.

Even the donkey appeared hesitant to walk in the rain, and Cowboy had to prod him several times. It slipped and slid over the Aciah Bridge and stepped into potholes every so often along the winding road.

By the time they arrived at Plaisance, the rain had abated while a diffident sun peeped out from behind the rain clouds giving Raja some hope that things would go his way. After a snack of buns and a cool mauby-bark drink, consumed while standing inside a Georgetown cake shop, they arrived still wet and shivering at the entrance of the registrar's building.

Cowboy tied his donkey to a post with a half-hitch, while Rena held her father's hand and helped him into the building. They made it just as giant rain drops came pelting down.

In the office, Portuguese and mulatto clerks were sipping cool water poured through the spout of a clay vessel while they chatted about Saturday night's rum party. Raja walked past a clerk who appeared to be the biggest slacker of them all. He was trying to lean back in a chair that did not allow it and would have toppled over from the effort if Raja had not caught him in time.

As soon as father and daughter approached, Mr. Konenburg swung around his swivel chair, his eyes wide with surprise.

"In this weather! Man, you want that property really bad." Mr. Konenburg held up his hand as Raja tried to say something. "Save your energy. Mr Ewing's offer to purchase East Henriette has lapsed, so we ruled in your favour."

Raja didn't know if he should jump up for joy or cry. He hugged his daughter and could not thank the man enough. Like Pereira, he got out of there in a hurry before Kony changed his mind.

Cowboy gave Raja a big slap on the back, almost knocking him over, when he got the news. "Time to celebrate, boss."

"What are we waiting for?" asked Rena.

"Let's all go to Yong Hing's Cook Shop," Cowboy suggested. The sun had already shown its face when they arrived. At Raja's insistence, Cowboy ordered large helpings of shrimp lo-mein and dumplings to feed his hulk. They clinked handle-less cups of Chinese green tea, all the while laughing at their good luck. "Boss, you must be really happy to spend money like this," Cowboy said, his mouth so stuffed with soft noodles, they spilled out.

Later at home, Ramdas and Beta expressed disbelief at the news.

"Raja Singh Sahib of De Droom," Ramdas teased.

CHAPTER TWENTY-TWO

De Droom, 1898

Raja sat hunched next to Rena at the foot of the outdoor staircase of the mansion. Velvet clouds drifted overhead on a warm afternoon. She had been on her way out to do her chores when Raja invited her to sit down.

"Rena, there is something I must tell you," Raja said in his most pleasing voice. "Your mother and I have picked out your husband."

Rena jerked her head. "I'm only fifteen and not ready for marriage, Pa."

Though Raja agreed, he had decided to abide by the Indian tradition and see her settled. "Why not?" he asked. "Your mother has searched the entire East Coast and found a good match for you—a nice Kshatriya boy."

"I'm too young, Pa." Rena let out a long, deep sigh like an animal in distress. "This is not India, with their child marriages."

Her pleading broke Raja's heart. Still, he felt his intentions were for her own good. He would coax her. "In this country, as long as parents give their consent, you can marry," he said. "You're quite matured for your age."

"Enough to know that I cannot agree to spend my life with someone I haven't even met."

Raja clicked his tongue. "You will see him at the wedding ceremony."

Rena balled her fists, tilted her head, throwing her long plaits to one side. "If I don't take to him, can I end the marriage right there?"

"It takes time to like someone."

"My former classmates said their parents do not pick their partners."

"Child, we are Hindus and our culture is different."

She buried her face in her sleeve. "You're too concerned with culture, Pa." She stomped her feet and headed in the direction of the back dam.

Raja found her sitting on a buttressed root of the silk cotton tree.

"Pa, I know you love me, but I'm not ready to settle down," she said. "Besides, I don't know anything about the boy's ways or what he looks like."

In an attempt to ease Rena's worries, Raja smiled broadly. "All right. I will tell you all you should know. I've heard he's dark but not bad-looking."

"I have to help Mr. Ramdas with the roundup," Rena said as she got up and walked away.

Raja tripped on a piece of rope lying on the ground as he tried to catch up with her. He raised his voice. "People say that it is a man's job you're doing when you round up cattle, that you are too much like the English."

Rena turned and faced her father. "Such people are old-fashioned."

"Those so-called modern traits will not catch a good husband, my dear."

"I'll discuss this marriage business with Ma."

Raja extended his arms as if to embrace his daughter. "It's just about finalized, my dear," he said.

"Finalized!"

"Except for a few loose ends, yes." Despite her look of shock, Raja persisted. "The groom's parents are respectable and by no means poor."

"How much money they have is of no concern to me," Rena mumbled.

Raja stroked one of the braids that hung over her shoulder. "We want you to enjoy a comfortable life, Rena. You can't do that with a man who does not know where his next meal is coming from."

"So how old is he, anyway?"

"Nineteen, and his father is coming any day now to discuss the marriage arrangements."

Tears formed in Rena's eyes as she turned and walked away, her head bowed in resignation. She was not a rebellious girl and had always been obedient to her parents, but now she was being pushed into a marriage that she was not ready for. Further, she had no say in the partner chosen for her.

Raja paced back and forth, distressed to see his daughter that way.

True to his word, Nandi's father, accompanied by a male relative, arrived before the week was up. Just as they were about to enter the house, Beta rushed up to Raja. "Uncle, the calf we both brought into this world has got herself stuck in soft mud. She is sinking fast."

Raja had a difficult choice to make. In the end, saving the heifer's life took precedence, and he left the preliminary discussion about the marriage to Sheela.

Late in the afternoon, when he came home, Sheela was quite out of breath when she greeted him. "You should have seen his eyes, Raja. They were like hot coals, taking in everything we have in the house."

"Calm down, Sheela. Who are you talking about?"

"Nandi's father. He kept saying, 'Beautiful! Beautiful!'"

Raja burst out laughing. "You'd think the old fellow was the one marrying Rena."

"Ah, just sweet talking. He wanted to know how much land and livestock we own. For a moment I thought he was going to ask to see the books."

"I hope you didn't tell him much."

"I said nothing of Henriette. None of his business. But I mentioned that we lost a lot of cattle in the flood."

Raja motioned for Sheela to take a seat at the kitchen table. After she had regained her composure, he said, "I hope you found out how many cattle he owns."

"I didn't get that far."

Raja rolled his eyes. "For heaven's sake, Sheela, don't you know that financial background is the most important part of a wedding arrangement?"

"But you left."

"I trusted you. It was your chance to find out more about these people. You want Rena stuck to a pauper's son?"

"Don't worry. They are coming back next week to discuss the dowry, so please make sure you're around this time."

At that meeting, Nandi's father pressed for a dowry of fifty dollars together with a heifer. Raja thought he was not hearing right when the man demanded only one cow. Was Nandi not worth more? It seemed a very good deal for Raja, and before he consented, he winked at his wife, who responded in kind.

Sheela asked the guests to stay for a late morning meal. She served up a large helping of ripe plantains, curried eggplant, and fried bake. As they sat down to eat, Sheela said, "I imagine that heifer will join a herd of about a hundred."

"Oh, no!" Nandi's father shouted. "We have only fifty head of cattle."

Raja's heart sank. He wished Sheela had done her prying on the previous visit.

"We know you're not millionaires," Sheela said. "But your last name is also Singh, a good Kshatriya name." When he nodded, Sheela said, "That means a lot to us."

Soon Rena's future wedding became the talk of the village. As customary, friends passed out invitations in the form of a few rice grains dyed with turmeric. Invitees were told the date and time of the wedding ceremony.

In keeping with Raja's stature, the wedding reception would be hosted at the mansion.

Weeks in advance, women prepared mango chutney and other condiments. For the banquet hall, they built a bamboo tent, thatched with coconut branches, next to the house.

On the Friday night preceding the ceremony, women dug some soil and prayed to Mother Earth for a blessed marriage. Others anointed Rena with turmeric and coconut oil to make her skin more seductive to the groom. Men prepared huge pots of yellow dal, vegetables, rice, and barrels of puri for the guests.

On the big day, the sun was already up over the horizon when tassa drummers greeted the wedding party led by the groom, who looked dazzling in his elaborate tinsel crown, cream dhoti and kurta. Soon after, the bride's welcoming group escorted the groom's party to a reception for relaxation and refreshments.

As the ceremony began under a huge tent, Rena, who sat on a mat next to the groom, kept her eyes lowered. She sported an 18-karat gold tiara perched below the hairline on her forehead and looked sad yet demure in her red silk sari.

To Raja's surprise, she briefly lifted her veil and stared at the groom. The guests gasped. This was something not usually done.

For a brief moment, Raja worried that she might end the marriage as she had hinted. Whether she approved or not, he could not tell. It mattered little. According to the Indian custom, sons or daughters must place trust in their elders' choices. This was the norm since young men and women had little or no chance of meeting and getting to know their marriage partners.

Raja remembered his own marriage ceremony back in India, conducted in Sanskrit. So much had changed for him. Here the British Guianese pandit explained the vows to the couple in Creole and Hindi.

As soon as Raja had formally presented the groom's parents with the dowry, the wedding feast took place in two sessions.

After spending a week at the groom's home, the couple returned to take up temporary residence at the mansion. Within months, Raja built the couple a comfortable family home facing the road on West Henriette.

Before too long, Rena and her young husband settled down to married life. A year later, she had her first child, a boy named John.

Hardly had she recovered from the delivery when she could often be seen riding her bicycle to go shopping for groceries. In the afternoons, she'd mount her filly to do the roundup, riding bareback. As she rode toward home one day, Raja hailed her. "No decent married woman should ride a horse, much less a bicycle."

"Am I hearing right, Pa? You are the one who taught me to ride a bicycle."

"But you were single then."

Rena, always the respectful daughter, dried the tears welling up in her eyes knowing she must now keep herself busy at home.

Two years later, she and Nandi had another child, a son they named Paul.

One day Beta said to Raja, "Uncle, Nandi is the rum shop's biggest customer."

"How do you know?"

"I accompanied Mr. Ramdas there the other day for a drink. Demerara white rum mixed with lime juice and a squirt of cane syrup is Nandi's favourite drink." Beta looked at Raja. "From what I've seen with my own eyes, it's game over for your son-in-law."

Raja remembered his youth. "A man must have some fun in life. It won't last long."

Beta shook his head. "You can't say I didn't warn you."

Raja expected Nandi to straighten out after his third child—a daughter. Instead, Nandi added Wednesdays to his Saturdays at the rum shop. As his reputation for drinking sprees grew, so did his father-in law's shame. Villagers now called the young man "Coolie Nandi" in reference to his low esteem within the community.

Now Raja realized that he had made a big mistake forcing Rena into a marriage she did not approve of. He wondered if he had ruined his daughter's life, for here, as in India, a marriage was for all time.

Other than Nandi's binge drinking, which Raja mostly ignored, life for him was doing the same mundane tasks around the farm. After much consideration, unlike its western half, he had ordered the workers to turn East Henriette into rice paddies. From a fellow Bihari who operated an import/export seed business Raja obtained Patna rice seeds, which he planted in a nursery.

The Patna rice did well on the flood plains of the Aciah River. Raja harvested a bumper crop. Women and children took turns pounding the paddy in wooden mortars. Raja's brand of long-grain brown rice, with its fragrance, taste, and nutritional value, became the local favourite.

Around this time, Raja placed a lot more responsibility on Beta. If Raja puttered about the farm at all, it was to escape boredom.

Meanwhile, Ramdas had lost all interest in managing the cattle and spent more time at the track. So he could get to the races, Ramdas, in his dingy cream jacket and floral tie, would sit amidst all the produce in

Cowboy's cart. Once or twice he hugged a bundle of money, but most days he came home empty-handed.

Matters came to a head when Beta reported to Raja that Mr. Ramdas had sold one of their steers for money to gamble on the horses. Raja's cattle represented his wealth and the loss of a single animal really hurt him.

"This is not the Ramdas I knew," Raja said, his eyes staring into the distance. He remembered that Ramdas had once upbraided him for branding his neighbour's calf.

What should I do? Did I not also place a bet at the racetrack? Because of Ramdas, Raja had won the price of many cows.

"You must put him out," Sheela advised. "Raja, forget about friendship. You must make a decision."

"Ma is right," Beta chimed in.

Raja knew something had to be done. In the Bhagavad Gita, Krishna advised that one should act without being attached to the fruits of one's actions. What was important was that one's act should be selfless. If Raja asked Ramdas to leave his estate, it would be to prevent any further loss of money, which would be self-interest. Therefore, he chose not to take direct action in that regard except work around the problem. He would never evict his old ship brother, because Ramdas had never before coveted what did not belong to him. Instead, Raja would find a way to cure Ramdas of his gambling habit.

Later, when Raja learned that Beta had chastised Ramdas, causing him to leave the estate, Raja kicked a bucket that was in the way and screamed at Beta, "You should never have put him out."

"Calm down, Uncle. I did not throw the man out. I just explained that what he did was wrong. Next thing I knew, he asked Cowboy to drop him off in the city at some street corner."

Raja looked out into the sunset and hoped that Ramdas would soon return. "Hire Cowboy," he advised Beta, "and scour the racetrack."

Beta reported later that he'd looked around the racetrack but found no trace of Ramdas.

For days, Raja would just lie in bed thinking about the loss of his friend.

One hot, sunny day in the midst of all the usual activity at Plantation Henriette, a young Presbyterian minister paid Raja a visit.

"Mr. Raja, am I addressing you correctly?" he asked. "I understand you detest the name Roger." The sandy-haired minister continued in a husky voice. "I'm Reverend John Cropper. Do you have a few minutes to spare?" His huge frame cut an imposing presence, which seemed to impress Raja.

"Have a seat," Raja said, as Sheela served milky-sweet tea in a glass. "You speak good Hindi," Raja continued, "better than most Indians in this country. You should be proud of yourself."

Cropper, with his reddish features, stood out in stark contrast to the dark-haired Crosby. Were their likeable personalities a coincidence? Finally, it all became clear to Raja. While Crosby facilitated the transition of the former indentured servants into the colony with incentives of free land, Cropper did the same through his ministry. Each in his own way ensured a ready supply of producers and consumers for the entire sugar industry.

"I learned Hindi when I assisted my father with the settlement of indentured servants in Trinidad," Cropper said.

When he switched to Creole, Raja lifted his eyebrows. Now he was more than convinced that Cropper had been specially chosen to win over the hearts and minds of East Indians in the colony. Raja figured that his fellow Indians, having been transplanted to a distant colony, would be receptive to Christianity from a man such as Cropper.

Hinduism would be under threat, for here was a white man who could speak Hindi and Creole like any local.

The preacher continued. "My father's a Nova Scotian. My mother's mulatto from Antigua."

"You'll do well among the locals, Reverend. They'll warm up to someone in an elevated position who can speak at their level. But I'm eager to learn how you ended up among Indians in this part of the country."

"Mr. Ewing of Plantation Friends wanted a suitable preacher to minister to the Indians of East Coast, Demerara. He turned to the Canadian Presbyterian Mission who recruited me because I speak Hindi and Creole."

"So you can tell them in Hindi and Creole that there's a better place waiting for them in heaven?"

Cropper smiled. "Mr. Singh, I'm here to bring the word of God to a well-respected member of the community."

Raja chuckled. "You flatter me, Reverend. As a Hindu, I get the same message from my own religious books."

"I don't quite agree," Cropper said. "However, let me get to the point. Mr. Ewing said you bought Henriette right from under his nose. He said the owner, who retired to France, had stipulated that the purchaser must be a Christian with Christian values."

Raja grimaced. Now that the land was his, he did not care about any reserve clause. "Tell Mr. Ewing I bought the land fair and square. Good day, sir."

Though Raja had been frank in his rejection of the preacher, he had a secret admiration for the man. Perhaps he'd soften his tone if Cropper ever came back.

Sooner than expected, the preacher knocked on Raja's door once again, just after the following Sunday morning service.

Raja beamed with joy as he rushed to open the door. "Come in, Reverend," he said. "The rain is coming down in sheets. You better stay overnight."

"I'll check with my donkey cart driver. I'm sure he'll agree."

"Stay in the guest room," Sheela said. "Your driver can sleep in the paddy room."

After a meal of flatbread and eggplant curry, Cropper and Raja conversed far into the night.

Before he left next morning, Raja said to him, "You are welcome to spend the night here whenever you preach in De Droom."

"Why the change, Mr. Singh?"

"You might be able to help my son-in-law, Nandi. Rum is his ruin."

"Mr. Singh, like a ship with a broken rudder, he is adrift in the ocean."

Raja looked at Cropper with pleading eyes. "Can you put him on the right course?"

"Let me sound him out," Cropper said. "It is a gradual process, but he must meet me halfway before I can help. In a fortnight, I'll be back."

"I'll be indebted to you."

True to his word, Cropper held lengthy conversations, together and separately, with both Nandi and Rena. The clergyman prayed for them and asked Jesus to enter their hearts.

"Rena appears receptive, but Nandi is tough as nails," Cropper said to Raja when they met.

"What do you mean?"

"He said he cannot accept Jesus as his Lord and Saviour because he is a Hindu."

Raja broke out in laughter. For him, there was good in every religion. To set a good example to their son-in-law, he and Sheela attended Sunday services whenever Rev. Cropper preached in the village. On occasion, Raja would bring Nandi along if he could rouse the young man from his hangover. Raja liked the set of three parables in Matthew's Gospel, especially that of the Good Samaritan.

One Sunday, Cropper approached Raja. "You will soon be ready to become a Christian, Mr. Singh."

Raja looked skywards. "What makes you think so?"

"You're a regular at my church services."

"Not so fast. I believe a person can be a good Hindu and still follow the teachings of Jesus Christ."

"There is no place for Hinduism in God's house."

Raja's stomach churned. He knitted his brows. Still, he must choose his words carefully. "Mr. Cropper, you welcomed me into your church, what you call God's house," Raja said. "Nevertheless, you should not get into the business of trying to convert all Hindus. We must be allowed to retain our religion and identity, if that is our choice."

"Mr. Singh, Jesus said, 'No man comes to the Father except through me.' Not through Krishna."

"But he also says, 'In my father's house are many mansions.' I believe Jesus' life in many ways mirrors Krishna's."

"Mr. Singh, you seem to be as well versed in the Bible as you are with the Bhagavad Gita."

"Those verses in the Bible inspired me. That's why I consider Christ and Krishna the greatest teachers the world has ever known."

"Well said, Mr. Singh. I have studied comparative religions and truly believe Aum, Amen, and Amin unite the three great religions. When those three can meet and become one, however long it takes, there will be greater peace on earth."

Raja couldn't agree more. Because of such a brilliant statement, his admiration for the preacher soared. "Like the meeting of the three sacred rivers at the Sangam, this will be a union like no other. It will indeed be special," Raja added, and he really meant it.

"Do you think it can be achieved?" Cropper asked.

"I have no doubt." And with those words, Raja shook hands with the minister. From that time onward they remained close friends.

CHAPTER TWENTY-THREE

The Great War broke out in all its fury in 1914, and British Guiana, to help the cause started mobilizing soldiers to serve in Palestine.

At age sixty-four, Raja realized that time had run out on him. If only he were young again! Now he couldn't possibly be on Rena's side when she asked him to stop Nandi from going to war.

"My dear daughter," Raja replied, "it is Nandi's choice to serve his king and country."

"Even though the man is drunk half the time, I still have a husband and the children a father."

"I'm here if they need me."

"You're their grandfather," added Sheela, who had been listening in on the conversation.

But no matter how the women pleaded, Raja made no objection as Nandi set out for Georgetown to sign up.

He enlisted and wrote home from the Eve Leary barracks stating that he had received a uniform and had started training.

In some respects, Raja looked upon Nandi's move as a blessing. Without him, life on the farm was bliss. Raja's good fortune ended when Nandi showed up a month later in his army uniform, a sheepish look on his face.

"What happened?" Raja asked.

"I failed the physical because I couldn't run up a slope with a fifty-pound bag of rice on my back."

"Too much drinking?" Raja asked.

"Nah. Enlarged heart the doctor said, which is rubbish to me."

Despite his medical condition and the birth of a fourth child, a baby daughter, Nandi's drinking worsened to the extent that he became a complete liability to the family.

News reached Raja one night that his elder grandson, John, now a strapping young man, had locked his drunken father out of the house.

Through a tip from a neighbour, Raja found Nandi in Aziz's chicken coop, fast asleep on the bare ground. Without informing the homeowner, Raja, with a neighbour's help, washed the chicken droppings from Nandi's body at a nearby pond and took him home. The empty rum bottles at his house said it all.

One August night, no land breeze blew in to counter the sweltering night air. Raja tossed and turned in his bed as sleep evaded him.

"Bow-wow-wow! Those darn dogs," Raja said to Sheela. "Mark my words. Something grave is going to happen tonight."

Dawn had just broken when there was a knock at the door. At the second knock, Raja jumped out of bed and rushed to answer it. A police constable in black uniform, and a detective in plain clothes, faced Raja.

"Mr. Singh," the detective said, "we have a warrant for the arrest of your son-in-law, Nandi Singh, also known as Coolie Nandi. Based on the eyewitness account of one Gopal, he is charged with the murder of one Kuldip."

Sheela now joined Raja at the door. "My son-in-law is a drunkard but not a murderer," she said. She turned to her husband. "Put them out. They want to pin a murder on poor Nandi." She tugged at her hair and started to cry.

Raja's gut feelings that something bad was going to happen had been right. Nonetheless, the news seemed to suck his breath away. "You're after the wrong man. Please leave my house," he said, with a wave of his hand.

Sheela shouted, "Good! Close the door!"

"Mr. Singh, we came first to your house out of respect for you. We're simply acting on a report," the detective said.

"Report? If you two officers would follow me, I can clear this up." Raja and Sheela led the way to their daughter's house.

After several knocks and shouts, Rena, trailed by her children, opened the front door. As soon as the two officers stepped in, she screamed, "Oh Lord, what has Nandi done?"

"Mrs. Singh, we have a warrant for the arrest of your husband," the constable said.

They found Nandi in a bloodstained shirt and pants, drunk and sprawled on the floor of a spare bedroom. Enveloped by a miasma of stale rum that hung over the room like swamp gas, Raja emitted a sound like an animal in distress.

The constable slapped Nandi a couple of times and shouted, "Wake up!"

Nandi's body shook as if he had the ague. He blinked but seemed to have difficulty focusing his eyes.

Rena's daughters screamed when the constable seized their father's shirt collar, pulled him into a sitting position, rocked him back and forth, and manacled his wrists.

In apparent shock, Nandi yelled, "I didn't do anything."

"Agh!" The policeman pinched his nose and turned his face away. After he'd inhaled, he said, "Nandi Singh, you are hereby charged with the crime of murder."

Nandi blinked a couple of times as if to let the words sink in. "What? Are you crazy?"

Rena yelled. "Murder? Oh Nandi! What are we going to do?" She fell into the open arms of her mother.

"I didn't murder anyone," Nandi said after he had been forced to stand.

"We're taking you to the station for questioning," the detective said.

Raja and John followed the two police officers to the station. They were not allowed to speak with Nandi, who was locked up in a holding cell.

At a preliminary hearing the next morning, the magistrate deemed that there was enough evidence to put the accused on trial. He denied bail and signed an order for Nandi to be transferred to the Camp Street Jail in Georgetown.

John broke down weeping at the sight of his father being dragged away in manacles. Raja turned to him and said. "Crying won't help your Pa. We must hurry. Let's go see Reverend Cropper. He's the only who could help in this dark hour."

They found Cropper at the Archbishop's home in Georgetown. He had come to the front porch to meet them.

"We need your help, Reverend," Raja said. "Nandi has been charged with murder."

Cropper rubbed his fiery red moustache. If he was stunned by what he heard, he didn't show it. "I didn't see that coming. However, I will do anything for a friend in his time of need."

"My son-in-law has dragged me into the gutter," Raja cried out.

Cropper patted Raja on the shoulder. "You need a good lawyer."

"Whom do you suggest?"

"E.R., most definitely."

"Why him?"

"By all accounts, he's the best. He has never lost a murder trial."

Raja's jaw tightened. He was not about to hire any celebrity lawyer known only by his initials. "E.R. is the most expensive lawyer in the country. How can I raise enough money to pay his type?"

Cropper took a deep breath. "Do you want Nandi hanged? Sell Henriette and some cattle."

"I'd rather die than sell Henriette," Raja said, as he looked into Cropper's eyes.

"Very well, but do you have any other concern, old man?"

"Most of the older Indians know that E.R.'s father changed his Indian first name from Mohan to Morton. I, too, could have settled for Roger, but I didn't." Raja allowed some time for his words to sink in before continuing. "Mohan travelled on the same boat with me, dressed in a fashionable kurta pajama. Soon after arrival, he converted to Christianity and gave up his Indian clothing for Western-style shirts and pants."

The minister smiled. "So! You've retained your Indian clothing, I must admit, but you've also attended church, and no one complained."

"Because they know I remained a Hindu."

"But do you attend cocktail parties and rub shoulders with the governor and his Chief Secretary? Because of that family's complete acceptance of Christianity, doors opened."

"But there's always a price to pay. However, I admire the family, and I need their help right now."

Cropper turned to John. "Assist your grandfather. We'll walk over to E.R.'s office."

The lawyer agreed to defend Nandi Singh. The huge retainer made Raja whistle.

To raise the necessary funds, John sold several steers. He spared his father the ordeal of witnessing his prized animals' departure to the slaughterhouse by personally driving them along the public road in the dead of night.

On Raja's second visit to E.R., he again took the lad with him. E.R. wasted no time in presenting the witness's statement, which John read aloud to his grandpa.

All the while, Nandi languished in jail, waiting for the final outcome of his plight.

Two months after the murder in De Droom, the Great War came to an end. Raja went to the city jail to visit with his son-in-law. It so happened that it was also the occasion of the march of demobbed servicemen through the city streets.

From the pavement outside the London Hotel, among a standing-room-only crowd, Raja watched the victory parade.

"Here, soldier boy!" the women shouted as they threw flowers and blew kisses at the fighting men in their khaki uniforms.

Welcome parties had been arranged in private city homes that evening for the war heroes. Signs with the addresses for the soirees abounded at street corners. Pretty mulatto girls paraded the streets in ruffled tulle dresses. They would add spice to the revelry. Raja closed his eyes, and a picture of all the hoopla and hot dancing with the yalla gyals appeared before him. *Oh, to be single again.*

He recalled how Nandi, the patriot, had wanted to liberate Palestine from the Ottoman Turks. This was after an evening at the rum shop throwing back shot after shot of rum and ginger. Never mind his overhanging belly. In his drunken state, he'd give the hand salute dressed in his tattered army uniform and tilted beret. To anyone who'd listen, Nandi would often play the part of the commander and, in a moment of make-believe, recite his own commendations: "As commander of the British West Indian Regiment, I have the honour to present Major Nandi Singh with the DSO medal for bravery in the midst of enemy fire."

In the same vein, he'd act the mayor's part: "In my role as mayor, I hereby present the much-decorated ex-soldier with a key to the city of Georgetown."

Finally, Nandi would act the scene whereby a hero's welcome awaited him in his home village of De Droom: Nandi accepted a military salute in a walk past by the Home Guard. The school children welcomed their hero, Major Nandi Singh, as they marched to the bamboo flute, cymbals, tassa and bass drum—their own version of a fife and drum band.

Raja wiped away a tear. For a moment, the scene became fused with his own fantasy of bygone days: Raja became a member of the Light Dragoons, marching past Market Street in his native Siwan.

His own daydreaming ended with seeing Nandi in prison garb lying in urine on the bare prison floor. Now poor Nandi had a long prison term ahead of him or even the hangman's noose to think about.

As he'd done in an earlier time, Raja, his shoulders slumped, limped his way along Water Street, past Pereira's Grocery with their barrels of smelly bacalhau on the pavement. He spent a few coins on a curved, clay chillum pipe at a Chinese store that sold everything from Brazilian tobacco to salted butter. As a bonus, the owner packed Raja's chillum just right with tobacco and a tiny leaf of the ganja plant. With his sparse hair, and beard matching the white of his clothing, he looked a decade older as he headed for the hotel. No one could have guessed the burden on his shoulders as he took slow and steady puffs from his pipe.

As listed in the docket, the case was set for trial in the Supreme Court. L.R. would be assisting his brother, E.R. They were the first Indian solicitor and barrister respectively in the colony, and they made a formidable team.

On the trial date, many villagers from the East Coast of Demerara booked discounted rooms at the London. Some behaved as though they were going to the races.

A grey-haired, bearded man shouted in a broken voice, "Raja Singh! Now it is your son-in-law's turn to face the music."

Raja didn't like what he heard. He looked the man over—stooped posture, breadfruit face, nutmeg-textured skin—but did not recognize him. "Do I know you?"

"Yes. Sonnyboy, man."

Raja stepped aside to avoid vomiting. "They never should have let you out. You murdered Jasmine, you rotten—"

"Rum was my ruin. It played tricks on my mind like it used to do yours."

"You killed a very nice girl."

"I served my time; some of it, anyway. If you had married her, I would have been clear of trouble."

A lump rose in Raja's throat as he shrugged. More than fifty years had passed since that dark event. "It looks like you live on the street."

"The owner of the London lets me sleep in the lobby; I'm like a watchman. How about a small piece—an eight-cent bit, Raja?"

Raja squirmed, realizing that the once talented cricketer had now become a beggar without a home.

He reached for his purse. "Here," he said, throwing Sonnyboy a shilling.

Far from being the former fieldsman with quick reflexes, Sonnyboy fumbled the coin.

"You just dropped a slip catch," Raja shouted over his shoulder. "I have to get to the trial on time."

He lit up his chillum and recited a silent prayer to invoke the divine blessings of Lord Shiva. His head somewhat light from inhaling the sweet smoke, he shuffled off to join his family at the courts, thankful that the Chinese shop owner had guessed his need for relaxation.

The packed public gallery, where people spoke in whispers, reeked of sweat.

Raja, in his signature white leggings and boots laced to the ankles, sat next to Rena and her two sons in the front row. He clenched his jaws at the shame he and his family must endure. If only the earth could open up and swallow him. He could easily have stayed home and avoided the public disgrace to his family. All he could do now was sigh and wipe his forehead with a handkerchief as he settled down into his seat.

Gopal took the stand as the prosecutor's main witness. The prosecutor asked, "Would you describe for the court the events that took place on the night of the murder?"

"I asked my friend Kuldip over for some duck curry and drinks at my bottom house. Nandi invited himself. As I was about to uncork the second bottle, Kuldip asked Nandi for the dollar he'd lent him to buy rum. An argument started followed by a fight."

During the final arguments, E.R. in his closing address, said: "You have likely drawn the conclusion that Nandi is a flawed human being, as no doubt we all are. He admitted to drinking issues and is obviously not the perfect citizen. However, your task is not to judge Nandi's character. Your task is to determine guilt based on the evidence presented to you. And I put to you that the evidence falls far, far short of proving guilt beyond a reasonable doubt. If anything, Nandi is guilty of love for the bottle. Gentlemen, examine your consciences and be merciful; find this kindly, fun-loving man not guilty."

It all came down to the decision of the jury of twelve men. Friends of the family had suggested bribing some members of the jury, but Raja wanted no part of it. They deliberated for four hours, at the end of which they sent word to the judge that they had reached a verdict.

Raja scanned the faces of the jury, trying to read them. Quite expressionless, not one of them looked at Nandi. Raja took rapid breaths and his body shook in rhythm with the rattling of wooden jalousie slats.

The judge turned to the jury foreman. "Would you please give your verdict to the bailiff?"

The judge unfolded the paper. Except for the low humming sound of a bee, there was silence throughout the courtroom.

Raja's mind went numb. Darkness surrounded him and he smelled the sickening, sweet smell of flowers like those at Jasmine's funeral.

The pew-style bench on which he sat vibrated from his trembling. As much as one could in such a situation, he tried to be stoic and prepare himself for whatever outcome awaited the family.

The judge arranged his pince-nez and looked at the paper, then with a blank face, requested that it be handed back to the foreman. "Would you read the verdict, please?"

Raja closed his eyes; his body stiffened while his fists stayed clenched.

"We, the jury, find the defendant, Nandi Singh," the foreman took a deep breath before continuing, "guilty of murder."

Rena let out a scream that bounced off the walls of the courtroom. Raja let John console his mother. He himself fainted briefly and only came to after a woman fanned him with a folded newspaper. When he saw how badly Rena was taking it, his face creased with worry. All he could do was shake his head in disbelief.

The spectators gasped. For a few seconds, Nandi, who had been stone-faced all along, lost control of his jaws as his teeth rattled. He closed his eyes and swayed.

"They took advantage of my husband," Rena cried out.

The judge placed a black cap on top of his judicial wig. He announced, "Nandi Singh, I hereby sentence you to death by hanging. Because of the nature of your crime, the Georgetown jail is not the place for you. You shall be held at the colony's most secure institution—the Mazaruni Penal Settlement—where your sentence shall be carried out without delay. May God have mercy on your soul."

CHAPTER TWENTY-FOUR

Men and women in the gallery appeared stunned as they filed out of the courtroom.

As Raja let Paul help him toward a waiting E.R., Sonnyboy's words kept ringing in his ears, hitting him like a punch in the stomach. After all, he was the one who had turned Sonnyboy in.

"I know you're disappointed in the verdict," E.R. said to Raja. "What surprises me is that though the evidence was insufficient to convict my client, the jury still found him guilty."

Weeks later, Raja and Rev. Cropper went to meet with E.R.

"Try to work extra hard to save souls in De Droom. Invite the Gopals to your next church service," E.R. said to Rev. Cropper. "Better still, baptize them."

"What a strange request, coming from you," Cropper exclaimed.

Not the one to question E.R.'s judgment, Raja added, "That won't be difficult for you, Reverend." Though he didn't see the point, Raja continued, "Invite the Gopals to your church like you did me. They've stopped going to the Hindu temple, anyway."

With no response from the minister, E.R. continued, "If you don't come through, I'll get my own Anglican priest to visit the couple."

"Don't be so desperate, Mr. Lawyer. Have patience," Cropper said.

He visited the Gopals at their home every Sunday with an elder of his congregation. Well into the second month, the Gopals let it be known in the close-knit community that the following Sunday they would attend the De Droom Presbyterian Church.

After the sermon, Cropper announced, "Next month I will conduct a baptismal service for new converts. Anyone wishing to accept Jesus as his Saviour and repent his sins, please see me at the end of the service."

True, Raja was always moved by Rev. Cropper's sermons, yet he vowed to remain a Hindu. As long as he lived a good life, he saw no need to be converted, as he had pledged before Ramdas and Shankar. Privately, while retaining his Hindu beliefs, he would continue to study the Bible, take the best of both religions and apply them to the way he conducted himself in life.

As everyone filed out, Raja was standing by the church door where he couldn't help but overhear Gopal's conversation with Rev. Cropper.

"Could you baptize me and my wife?" Gopal asked the minister. "Our lives have been turned upside down."

"First you'll have to attend our regular services," Cropper replied. "And why not send your children to Sunday school! They'll learn to read Bible stories."

"I'll make sure they attend. It will provide a nice change from the Royal Readers."

Several months after the murder, Raja overheard Mrs. Gopal complaining to Cropper that her husband talked every night in his sleep and often woke up drenched in sweat, breathing heavily.

"Why?" Cropper asked her.

"For the same reason that I get nightmares."

Mrs. Gopal hesitated and cast a glance at Raja, who retreated and hid behind some bushes.

Mrs. Gopal's voice shook as she struggled to elaborate. "That night, I witnessed the murder. Please, don't let my husband know what I'm telling you. He'll kill me."

"I won't tell him anything, Mrs. Gopal," Cropper assured her.

"Kuldip cooked the duck curry in my kitchen. All the while, he had me laughing at his jokes, something my husband would never do. My husband came into the kitchen a few times, looking upset."

"I can understand."

"After they'd eaten, the drinking continued. In between drinks, I heard my husband say, 'You're always cozying up to my missus.' Kuldip laughed it off and said, 'It's because she has an eye for me.' That's Kuldip."

"Go on."

"My husband shouted, 'You know I can knock your teeth in for saying that.' I was surprised to hear Kuldip say, 'That will be the day.' At that point, I crept downstairs and watched the whole fight." Mrs. Gopal ended with, "I saw my husband stab Kuldip in the belly. He twisted the blade before pulling it out."

"Did Nandi see all of this?"

"He was too drunk. Kuldip's scream must have sobered him up. With Kuldip on the ground and his guts sticking out, Nandi struggled to his feet and staggered down the public road."

"You should have reported what you saw to the police, Mrs. Gopal," Cropper said.

"I wanted to protect my husband."

A few days later, Raja went to meet with E.R. at his office. He reported to him what he'd overheard and ended with, "Nandi is innocent."

"My brother and I suspected that all along," E.R. said. "Do you see now why I asked Rev. Cropper to bring the Gopals into the church?"

Raja nodded but checked himself, for he did not want to let on that the brothers were worth every penny of their fees.

"The judge has since stated that the execution will take place in three weeks' time," E.R. said. "We must, therefore, file a motion today for a retrial based on newly discovered evidence." E.R. continued, "It will cost you extra. Meanwhile, we'll subpoena Mrs. Gopal." He stated the amount required to commence proceedings, and the balance to be paid at the start of the hearing.

Raja almost fainted. He had not exaggerated when he'd told Rev. Cropper that E.R had the reputation of being the highest-priced lawyer in the country. He opened his purse, counted the coins and paid E.R. the initial fee. To help raise the rest, Raja instructed his grandsons to sell off more cattle.

At the next church service, Rev. Cropper preached a stirring sermon. He quoted from Matthew 7:14, "The gate is narrow, and the way is hard that leads to life, and those who find it are few."

After everyone had filed out of the building, Mr. and Mrs. Gopal walked up to Rev. Cropper. Raja hung around in the background.

Rev. Cropper exchanged words with them. "You must ask the Lord for forgiveness. This is the only way you and your husband will be saved."

"My wife and I will tell the court the truth," Gopal said. "To live with a lie and to let another man hang for a murder he didn't commit is not right."

"I hope you realize what this will do to your life."

"Our lives will be in God's hands."

Raja was breathing heavily. He now had a greater respect for the Christian religion, a religion that had encouraged a woman to come forward and tell the truth even if it meant the execution of her husband.

Mrs. Gopal never once faltered in her testimony against her spouse, whose confession resulted in a reduction of sentence from murder to manslaughter with the additional charge of perjury. Further, because of Gopal's remorse and Cropper's influence, the sentencing judge reduced Gopal's jail term from fifteen years to seven. He gave the order for Gopal to replace Nandi at the Mazaruni Penal Settlement.

Nandi's supporters picked him up at the train station and brought him home on their shoulders. Those who had grabbed front row seats at the trials now declared that they knew Nandi was innocent all along.

As though he himself might end up in jail some day, one of them enquired, "Did you pick up a trade, Nandi?"

This went on and on until Rena screamed, "Stop your silly questions. He has suffered enough."

At Raja's home, the village musical band set up a tent. Members took turns and sang ghazals and classical ragas accompanied by harmonium, drums, and a steel rod, struck by a horseshoe device to keep the beat. The most beautiful and haunting melody, however, came from the bowed sarangi, which imitates someone humming. Nandi had fallen in love with its sound on the day of his wedding.

Indeed, the prodigal son had returned, and that was a cause for celebration.

The entertainers passed the rum bottle around. Each member poured the golden liquid into his schnapps glass.

The lead singer said, "Let's drink to Nandi, who by God's grace has been given another lease on life."

Nandi filled his glass with water and that pleased Raja no end; a miracle had taken place.

Later, in the midst of the festivities, Raja rushed to his daughter. "Rena, I just received some sad news from a prison warden on vacation that Gopal had been placed in Nandi's old cell and—" Rena waited for her father to regain his composure. "Not long after, a group of inmates swarmed and beat Gopal to death with their bare fists."

"That's too bad," Rena said.

"It was not the ending I would have wanted for a man, who with great courage undid a lie."

"Pa, those chaps deliver their own punishment," Nandi said after he'd heard the news.

In private, Rena said to her father, "Nandi wakes up in the night, screaming and trembling."

"What could be the cause?"

"He complains that he can still hear the laughter of screech owls, the screams of the jumbie birds, and the howling winds over the Mazaruni River at midnight."

"Spending time in close quarters with murderers is bound to change any man."

"He sits and stares with vacant eyes."

"I'll have a talk with him."

Over a cup of bush tea at the mansion, Nandi, wiping away tears, related to Raja how some of the men had planned a breakout from prison: "They believed my story that I was wrongfully accused like some of them. It was the trigger for a grand escape. Two weeks before the date set for my execution, around thirty men assembled bombs with powdered matchstick heads and cloth. Though it was dangerous work, they said it would be worth it. With the aid of cold chisels and hammers, and working secretly in the workshop, they fashioned nails into rivets and made hoes, pitchforks, and cutlasses, hiding them under shrubs in the garden."

Raja shook his head and made a strange sound with his tongue. "Did they know about the dreaded Mazaruni? Eh Nandi? That it is one of the most secure prisons on earth?"

"They knew that they had to scale a concrete wall with broken bottles, climb a ten-foot-high barbed wire fence and swim in a river swarming with electric eels and man-eating black caimans. Yes!"

"Then it would have been impossible to break out of there."

"They solved that problem by assembling ladders from scantlings, later to be strapped with vines to floating logs for rafts."

After a pause, Nandi continued, "As the midnight hour struck for my death by hanging, the wardens led me to the gallows, placed a noose—well lathered with soap—around my neck along with a black hood over my head." Nandi took a slow, deep breath; his voice cracked with emotion. "Though I was never the praying kind, I said my prayers, believing it was all over—"

"Go on."

"With a noose around your neck, you lose all feeling. You go numb. It's not as if your whole life appears in front of you. Whoever said that is a liar."

"What happened next?"

"There was a sound like a thunderbolt. A bomb went off. It created a distraction. I heard clanks, whacks, and screams. Several shots rang out. The thumps of falling bodies brought me to my senses. Inmates removed the hood and the noose around my neck.

"There were bodies with their heads bashed in by greenheart timber and hoes." Nandi closed his eyes as if reliving that scene. "Despite my shackles and manacles, several inmates lifted me off the ground and dragged me away. As they helped me scale the ladder up the concrete wall, I thought I heard a garbled sound from a bull horn and the words, 'Nandi Singh, you're a free man.' I dropped to the ground and considered heading back.

"An inmate shouted, 'Don't be a fool, Nandi. They'll hang you.'

"Two inmates grabbed me but I was dead weight, so they left me and continued with their escape.

"Because of the prison breakout and the number of deaths and injuries, my execution was not carried out that night. How could it, just after the most violent prison riot in the history of the colony? Also, there had been no announcement. It was only in my imagination. Two days later, when things had quietened down, the warden-in-charge told me that they had just received an order for a stay of execution in my death penalty from the highest court of the land."

Raja hugged his son-in-law. "I'm sorry about Gopal's brutal murder, but your story has a good ending and I am proud of you, especially since you have quit the drink and come home to your family a new man."

CHAPTER TWENTY-FIVE

One year after Nandi's release from prison, Raja had been lolling back in his Berbice chair, puffing on his clay pipe and staring out the open front door toward the lazy Aciah River. It was late in the afternoon, and the sun had spread its hazy light across the landscape. Raja could almost swear that he'd heard a voice telling him to make a pilgrimage, a spiritual odyssey back to his homeland.

Later that evening at the dining table, Paul read aloud the opening sentence from a book, "Whether I shall turn out to be the hero of my own life . . ." when a streak of lightning, accompanied by a clap of thunder, brightened the night sky.

Raja held a match again to his pipe and sucked hard. He exhaled, and the sweet aroma of Brazilian tobacco filled the room. The smoke eddied through the soft, yellow rays cast by the table lamp. "I like that sentence you just read, son. Read it again for me," Raja said.

Past events in Raja's life unfolded before him. Looking back, he summed it up as a life unfulfilled unless he reunited with his Indian family. Otherwise, they would never know what had happened to him after he went missing. Even at his age, he would like to write that final page, that final chapter of his life.

The rain came down in torrents, pounding the roof, causing Raja to exclaim, "Were it not for this sound of rain drops on zinc sheets, I would have said, 'Monsoon season in Belwasa.'"

"Belwasa!" Sheela faced him with a quizzical look. "You must be losing your mind in your old age."

Raja gave her a sharp look. A whoosh-whoosh pull on his pipe got it going and gave him a few moments to choose his words. "Yes, Belwasa! The time has come for me to visit my native village in Bihar," he said.

Sheela shook her head. "All these years, and never once did I hear you speak of visiting such a place," she blurted out.

"Time's different. Now that my grandchildren run the farm, I'm free to carry out one final wish before I die." A cloud of smoke surrounded Raja's face; through it, he peered into Sheela's eyes. "In my latter years, I've learned to read, but that alone does not give peace of mind."

Sheela let out a deep sigh. "How can a village you left so long ago mean so much to you?"

"It's where I spent my boyhood days."

Sheela raised her voice. "You cannot leave us at a time when Nandi has returned to the bottle."

"I've given up on him." Raja covered the bowl of his pipe with a hand, sucked and extinguished it. "You see, I must make that journey while I still can."

"It might not be worth it."

Raja's wrinkled forehead betrayed his worry knowing that he had some convincing to do. "I had never wanted to settle in this country. However, with time, I became attached to the people and everything around me. I even got caught up with trying to become rich. Now I yearn for something different."

"It seems you've been using me all along." Sheela glanced at Paul who was squirming. "You should never have brought me into your life."

Raja was so taken aback by those words he decided to set her straight. "Don't ever think so, Sheela. Out of our relationship came a beautiful daughter and grandchildren."

A gust of wind howled through the front door, fluttering the page Paul was reading from. "Grandpa, it's just that we'd rather have you here with us," he said.

Raja looked hard at Paul and blinked back a tear. "It grieves me much. But don't worry, I'll be back."

"You are old." Paul's voice shook with emotion. "We may never see you again."

In his heart, Raja felt his grandson might be right, but he had to answer a call that had become relentless, like that of the salmon to its birth stream. *Dear Belwasa, I never really left you, and I won't rest until I see you again.*

His only regret was that it had taken him a lifetime to reach his decision. Now he had to tug himself away from a place where he had left his seed. Besides, the journey he wished to make would be difficult.

With his head bent low, he got up and shuffled toward his grandson. He hugged him, tapped his pipe in his palm, emptied the ashes into a brass bowl and turned in for the night.

The next morning, Sheela sent for Rena and the two lads. Nandi invited himself. Everyone sat on the floor in the living room except for John, who curled up in a corner, his head propped up by his hands, and Raja, who took to the Berbice chair. He sought comfort in his pipe, which he tapped once but did not light.

Sheela fixed her gaze at her husband. "I called this meeting with grown members of the family," she waited for her words sink in, "and now the head of this house wants to return to the old country."

Raja bit hard on the stem of his pipe. "Before I leave this world," he whispered, "I must fulfil a desire to visit my Indian folk."

Rena smirked. "Aha! Where a former wife would be waiting."

Raja's face flushed with embarrassment; he took a long time to reply. Everyone became quiet. "I'm too old for that and most likely she'd be dead."

The tick-tock of the clock broke the silence in the living room until Sheela stood up and, with hands on hips, spoke in a high-pitched voice. "You never mentioned you'd left a woman in India."

Rena clicked her tongue.

Raja cleared his throat. "That's a long time ago. And it won't be because of her I'm returning," he stuttered.

Sheela paced up and down between the kitchen and the living room. "A fine man you are," she shouted. "You're not going any place."

Raja shook his head. "My mind is made up, my dear."

"I wish I had never moved in with you," Sheela continued. "You're nothing but a rogue."

"Is that what you think of me?" Raja's voice was lower than usual. He tightened his hand into a fist and the muscles in his jaw rippled. He was boiling over inside.

"Forgive me," Sheela said. "But how can you walk away from us?"

"And into the arms of a former wife?" Rena asked. "That doesn't look good for me and my children."

Nandi spoke up, "Calm down, Rena. That first marriage may not be recognized here."

"So you're supporting him," Rena chimed in.

"When I wanted to go to war, Pa stood by me and was the one who saved me from the gallows. Now I'm with him all the way."

In frustration, Sheela raised her hands. "Nandi, you stay out of this. I brought the others here to put some sense into this old man's head. Instead, you—"

"Father is a member of our family," John cut in. "I join him in supporting Grandpa."

Sheela shook her head. "Not when he has a wife who will use any means to prevent him from abandoning his family."

"Can you stop him?" John asked.

"Ha! Ha! His age will do that."

"I can make it if Ramdas accompanies me," Raja said.

Paul, who was so far quiet, cut in, "I can ask Uncle Beta to look for him at the racetrack."

Rena got up, walked to her father and tousled a few strands of his grey hair. "Pa, I always wondered how a few juicy dunks, what you call ber, could have brought you to this country."

Sheela suppressed a laugh with her hand. "It wasn't just plums, dear. His own people sold him out, and now he wants to return to them."

Raja related the events of the pilgrimage, the trip to the market to buy egg plums for his brother, and the strange circumstances that had brought him here.

Rena, who appeared carried away by what she heard, rubbed her father's cheek. "Your brother might be alive, but not your wife, Pa."

"That's true. She might have seen hard times," Raja said.

Sheela sucked her teeth and marched out of the room.

One afternoon some days later, when Raja was relaxing on the Berbice chair, Beta barged through the door, shouting, "Cowboy and I located Mr. Ramdas at the racetrack."

"I hope you apologized for having come down hard on him," Raja said.

"I didn't have to. With tears in his eyes, he said he is ashamed of what he'd done. Surprisingly, he'd heard about the SS *Araima* taking passengers back to India. Now that you would be on it, he said he would be happy to return to the motherland with his old jahaji bhai."

"Beta, did you by chance tell him we could help with his passage?"

"There's no need, Uncle. He said that the British still owe him a return ticket because he'd never taken up land in the colony." Beta laughed before continuing, "That man does not miss a thing."

"He must have another reason for wanting to return."

"He said, he hadn't led a good life in this country—drinking, gambling, and abandoning his Indian family—so, in death he would make atonement and have his ashes thrown into the Ganges."

Raja reflected on those words from his old friend and was surprised that Ramdas, despite his carefree attitude, was at heart a true Hindu, who dreamt of attaining moksha.

Using the proceeds from the sale of a few head of cattle, Raja paid for his own passage and had money left over to take with him.

Sheela did not carry out her threat, and in the end, came to understand Raja's reasons for wanting to return to India. She even helped pack his bags for the trip.

A long foreign journey meant that his business affairs had to be put in order, especially for a man of seventy. To this end, he requested that his two grandsons accompany him to Georgetown to meet with L.R., the solicitor. In order to keep his property away from Nandi, he gave power-of-attorney to John, who would have total control of his lands, cattle, and remaining assets.

At Barclays Bank, Raja exchanged cash for bank drafts, and gold sovereigns to add to those he'd already saved. From the jeweller next door to the bank, he picked up a pair of gold bangles and two necklaces, one made from the three gold sovereigns he'd kept especially for Savitri. He was taking his gift as a token of his erstwhile affection for a once beautiful bride, even if she were dead.

Demerara Lithographic Co. Ltd. delivered to John his pre-ordered envelopes printed with the family's De Droom address. "With these,

Grandpa, you just have to enclose a note, lick a stamp and mail," John said. He picked up a third-class ticket to Calcutta for his grandpa on the 2,500 ton SS *Araima*, part of the Jones group of steamships. It was the first ship to take passengers back to India since the Great War.

On the day of Raja's departure, the women were all sobbing. Tears rolled down Sheela's cheeks and splashed onto the pitch pine floor. No words could comfort her. At Raja's age, there would have been little hope that they would see him again.

Beta, who'd remained single and was himself approaching old age, embraced Raja. "I'll miss you, Uncle. But don't worry, I'll take care of Ma."

"I will miss you, too, my son." Raja said. He made no attempt to mask his emotions. "From the early days, you helped me get established in De Droom. You remember those rice plants you nursed like babies?"

Beta smiled. "You were more like a father—"

"Time to go, Grandpa," John said, holding his grandfather around the shoulders.

Paul loaded three flour sacks into the vehicle. The one tied with a red ribbon, containing gifts, he placed in front. As soon as the brothers joined the old man in the rear seat, John shouted, "Chalo!" to the driver.

What a stir the polished black roadster, which everyone called the Tin Lizzy, created as it puttered down the De Droom Side Road. Mr. Pereira had sent his Model T Ford with chauffeur to take Raja to Georgetown. It was a magnanimous gesture from a former rival.

"Chauffeur in his matching black top hat and tuxedo at the wheel, man," an admirer shouted.

All along the De Droom road, village folk lined up shoulder to shoulder on both sides of the route. Cowboy waved his tattered Stetson and Kwame, in his usual gentle way, said, "Walk good, man. Walk good!"

Raja could not have expected a grander send-off. Indeed, many acted as though they were the ones making the trip.

The SS *Araima* lay docked at the wharf, its foundation a seemingly bottomless pit of ever-shifting mud. Georgetown, with its elegant wooden buildings, now looked so much bigger compared to what Raja remembered from that first day of his arrival on the SS *Arcot*. On this Sunday morning, much of the city was quiet, except for the horse-drawn carriages transporting white gentlemen and ladies in their haute couture dresses and matching bell-shaped cloche hats, topped with jaunty feathers, all heading off to church.

Bajan stevedores were loading the ship with Demerara sugar, rum, greenheart timber, hides, and balata gum. One of them teased, "Babu, it looks like you're going back to die in the mother country."

"Yes. To be cremated in Banaras on the Ganges," Raja answered, almost mockingly. He hardly expected that to happen since, in his heart, he still believed his visit to India would be short, for one purpose only—to satisfy an urge.

"Kiss-kiss-kiss-kiskadee." The yellow-bellied bird, perched on a tall sea-grape tree belted out a farewell song, so doleful compared to the bird that had welcomed Raja to the colony; it made him realize that a part of him would remain in a country where he'd spent a good part of his life.

A Portuguese vendor on a Pereira's Groceries carrier bicycle came around selling Massa Sovada and Cadbury chocolates. Raja bought one of each to take with him. The Portuguese sweet bread, and the chocolate—a novelty in the country—would boost his spirits during the long boat journey.

Along with the hundred passengers, he lined up waiting for permission to embark. He looked around for Ramdas but there was no trace of his friend. It bothered him not a whit, for he'd already prepared himself to make the voyage on his own.

Once the cabin passengers and their luggage were taken care of, the steerage passengers boarded. John and his brother carried the flour sacks right up to the ship. They broke away from their grandfather when a crewmember shouted, "Time to go, babuji."

As the sailors removed the gangplanks, Raja looked back and caught a glimpse of his grandsons waving frantically. The ship pushed away from the dock to one long and three short blasts of the horn.

Before climbing down the ladder to find his berth, he watched the eighteen-foot draft vessel manoeuvre the sandbar. The salty smell of the sea soon replaced the odour of fish and vegetables while the Stabroek Market clock tower and the lighthouse became just pea-sized images that faded into the mist. It was everything in reverse from the first time he'd set eyes on the Georgetown coast.

The stairs were steep and he soon was confronted with a pile of sawdust and a stale, musty smell. Fortunately, he had an upper berth. It was six feet by three, with an overhead room of around four feet.

Because of the cramped quarters, he asked for permission to spend most of his time on the upper deck. *Why should I complain? Compared to conditions on that coolie ship, this is luxury.*

Later that day, among the sea of passengers, a stooped man was hobbling around in a threadbare white drill suit that looked like it had been slept in. He was trying hard to keep his balance on the rolling ship. His hands trembled and his eyes seemed not to focus. In the middle of a grey moustache and beard, a familiar rogue's grin shone through.

Raja looked at the man closely and exclaimed half-questioningly, "Ramdas?"

"Yes, man. With you rubbing shoulders with big shot Kawall, I kept my distance." The hint of a musical voice belied this wreck of a man, so much had he deteriorated in the last six years. This was what time had spared of Ramdas—the final flickering of the flame of life before being snuffed out forever.

Raja forced a grin. "The Water Street merchant travels first-class, but like you I have no cabin."

"True. And fortune has allowed us to travel on the same boat again," Ramdas said.

"Life is like a cycle—it starts and ends at the same place."

"Hmm! So that's what brought us back together," Ramdas added. "Our old guru, Shankar, couldn't have said it better."

"I was his student right up to the end," Raja said, knowing that if anyone had the answer to the mystery of life it had to be Shankar. With this trip, Raja hoped to get closer to the answer. Curiosity now got the better of him. "Except for being a bit mashed up, you don't look too starved, Ramdas," Raja said, gesticulating. "How have you been?"

"Man, am I not there?" Ramdas had responded in the local lingo with a question of his own.

Now that they were both returning to the old country, it dawned on Raja that he and Ramdas now spoke differently. So much had changed.

"How did you make out with food?" Raja asked.

Ramdas shrugged. "After a few punters had collected their winnings, they didn't mind passing a small piece to a down-on-his-luck friend."

"It grieved me much when you left De Droom."

"I took a calf that didn't belong to me."

"We all make mistakes, and I'm no exception," Raja said, raising his hand to show that all is forgiven.

The first stop was Trinidad, where the ship picked up passengers and stocked up on coal for its two boilers, the two masts ready for backup.

As the steel-hulled steamer rounded the Cape of Good Hope, it ran into billowy waves as it had done on that first voyage eons ago, or so it seemed. While in Durban, the ship replenished its coal and exchanged cargo. Five weeks after leaving Georgetown, less than half the time the SS *Arcot* had taken for the same distance, the SS *Araima* arrived at Calcutta.

Gone were the mangrove shoreline and the thatched houses, replaced by country homes and Garden Reach Shipbuilding and Engineering Works. Gone were the seagulls hovering over fishing vessels, displaced by sandpipers scurrying on mud flats. If Georgetown had grown, Calcutta surely bowled Raja over.

He gathered up his bags but realized that they were quite a handful for a limping and aging man. "Help me with one of the bags," he called out to Ramdas.

As they wended their way from the dock site at Garden Reach, Ramdas stopped and waved his hand about. "That must be the site of our former coolie depot over there," he said, pointing at some high-walled, ramshackle warehouses.

Raja closed his eyes and shook his head. He did not want to remember the time when he was held captive in Calcutta. "They look very drab and depressing to me," he ventured.

They squatted on the bare ground in full view of the ship, two old men, within earshot of the crashing waves. Raja shared his remaining chocolate with Ramdas while he sized up his situation.

It was late afternoon and the slanting rays of the September sun sprinkled the air with slivers of light. Raja did not wish to spend a night at the wharf where he could be robbed. After all, he was not Sen, his sailor friend from the past, who, when not on a ship, slept on the dock to the lap-lap of the waves.

"How will you spend your last days in India?" Raja asked.

Ramdas, whose wobble of the head had long since disappeared, sang out, "I've come not to live but to die here."

"In that case, go to Banaras on the Ganges, bhai."

After he'd spoken, Raja realized that cremation required money and only relatives or friends could ensure its completion.

"That calls for paisa, which I don't have," Ramdas replied, "but the Hooghly is a tributary of the holy Ganges, so I will settle for Calcutta."

Raja now asked the question that had plagued him throughout the voyage. "Do you have any money, Ramdas?"

"Enough for a few weeks' ration till I find my resting place." Ramdas's expression said it all. "It will be a short wait, Raja." Just as quickly he was his usual self. "By the way, what have you got in the sack with the red ribbon?"

"Just a few knick-knacks for relatives, if any are alive." Raja was reluctant to say more. It was not that Ramdas would tip off dacoits who could rob him—his friend was never that sort. Still, he didn't wish to make Ramdas feel guilty for squandering his money on horses and rum. Further, he didn't wish to leave himself open to envy from one who, if he lived long enough, could very well starve in India.

He hailed a rickshaw man to take them to the Calcutta Railway Station. The fellow trotted barefoot over puddles and fresh cow dung to a currency exchange where he called a price in rupees that Raja suspected was for foreigners. To compensate, the rickshaw wallah gave them a conducted tour of the heart of the city.

At a brisk trot down the Diamond Harbour Road, he cleared a path through cows, cyclists, and ox-carts, then whizzed past Chowringhee Road and old Leslie House. He stopped at Dalhousie Square near the red brick Writers' Building where Raja ordered chaat and sabzi masala for two from a street vendor. Off they went past the Royal Exchange, the former residence of Robert Clive, the man who had secured India and its wealth for the British crown. Past the white-domed GPO building and across the floating pontoon Howrah Bridge over the Hooghly River to the Calcutta Railway Station, where people like rice grains stood or

280

stretched out. Beggars! If you give to one, there will be others. It was the same as when Raja was last there.

In India, a fate similar to Ramdas awaited Raja. His village might be beyond recognition and his relatives long dead. In order to make the break from his friend as smooth as possible, he must distance himself from him. That would be one of the hardest decisions of his life. More than a lifetime ago, they were shipmates, he and Ramdas—brothers who had pledged to be there for each other, and had succeeded, in the new land.

Raja examined a blackboard list of destinations, written in the Devanagari script. With help from an Anglo-Indian ticket seller, he paid the train fare to Siwan with a short delay in Patna, the capital of Bihar.

Now came the moment Raja had dreaded: a severing of ties with Ramdas, who looked like he could drop dead at any moment.

First, he gave his friend enough rupees to survive for months, perhaps a year, providing he didn't drink or gamble.

India was not like British Guiana with just three hundred thousand people, where everyone was like one big family. Here in India, in difficult times, which happened often, it was each man for himself.

"Raja," Ramdas said, "thank you." He remained silent for some time, then continued, "What is more important is your company. Won't you stay with me awhile and give me that last farewell as I float down the river to my resting place?" With teary eyes, he burst out in hysterical laughter. "You remember the good times we shared at the racetrack, how your lame-foot horse knocked the dust off the favourites? Right Raja!" Ramdas broke down and cried.

Raja lowered his head. "Yes! In that special way of yours, you showed me how to have a good time, how to enjoy life. You even made me some money. But now, in this big country, we must go our separate ways. Please understand!" Those words coming from Raja's own mouth pierced his heart like daggers.

"Why does it have to be so?" A single teardrop now rolled down Ramdas's cheek. "Are we not ship brothers?"

"Of course," Raja said. "However, I have a job to do—to find my village. The sugar planters took an entire life from me and changed it from what it could have been. Today I return a shell of what I used to be."

"But a rich man with a wonderful family!"

"Family, yes, but money can never replace the free choice, which they deprived me of during the early years of my life."

"Unlike me, you've made it in the colony. So there is no need to be bitter in old age."

Raja considered what Ramdas had just said and the separate paths they had taken to arrive at their place in this world. Perhaps Ramdas was the better man in the sight of God.

"In some ways," Raja said, "you were the successful one, the happy man who was not covetous or wild with ambition." Raja looked at his friend, clad in a ragged suit, its material so different from the finery he had worn on that sailing ship of yesteryear. He had to admit that Ramdas—the weaver, who had lost his traditional way of making a living was a total misfit in the colony.

Ramdas dropped to his knees. "A beggar without a home such as I am! Don't mock at me, Raja. Please don't leave me all alone in Calcutta, bhai." He used his sleeves to wipe away the tears. It touched Raja to see his friend that way. "Two or three weeks won't kill you, Raja. I won't last that long, bhai."

Ramdas had placed Raja in a situation where he must choose between loyalty to a friend and his own survival. Hardly a man for crying, Raja wiped a single tear from his cheek. Words failed him for quite some time until he said, "I'm sorry. You were the best jahaji bhai. But now we're back in the mother country. Like you, I'm old, and I have a long way to get to Belwasa. I don't know if I'll find my people." Raja's voice cracked as he helped Ramdas to his feet. Indeed, they were some of the toughest words he had ever spoken.

After a tight embrace, from which Ramdas would not let go, a waiting porter took charge of Raja's luggage, forcing him to break away and leave Ramdas standing like a foreigner among his own people.

"Slow down!" Raja shouted in a trembling voice. He gave Ramdas one final wave before negotiating several flights of stairs, all the while trying hard to keep his eye on the coolie balancing all three sacks on the red kerchief that cushioned his head. For a brief moment, Raja lost him in the crowd, but the coolie's red rumal finally led him to his designated carriage.

As he settled down in his seat, his mind went blank, and like the time when he had been lost in the jungle, he felt all alone in a foreign country.

CHAPTER TWENTY-SIX

Bihar, 1920

Vast stretches of farmlands interspersed with hills and valleys flashed past the train window. Fields of yellow mustard and endless rice paddies dotted the lush Bihar landscape. As in the old days, the stalks of wheat, sugarcane, and jute still danced in the wind.

Puffs of smoke rose from brick kilns and sugar and rice mills. At a bend in the tracks, Raja caught a glimpse of the tail end of the train as it moved through the countryside like a giant caterpillar.

Late at night, lonely and listless, he covered himself with a cotton sheet provided by the Anglo-Indian conductor. Ramdas's parting words came back to him and he had difficulty falling asleep, for the travel had begun to take its toll. His body hurt from the constant jarring and swaying of the train and the hard bed he had to lie on. Instead of this torture, he could have been lolling back on his Berbice chair in De Droom, puffing away at his pipe.

Upon arrival in Siwan, he found lodging at the Siwan International Inn, a one-storey unpainted concrete building.

Early the next morning, after a breakfast of spicy rice and lentils, he approached the hotel manager and asked, "Can you find me transportation to Belwasa?"

"My cousin will take you there," the manager said, calling up a man standing beside his ox-cart. "Just pay him ten rupees."

The driver, his cow horn moustache neatly twirled, loaded Raja's three sacks into the cart.

"Where to?" he asked after Raja had placed the sack with the red ribbon next to his feet. "First we must go through Hussainganj Block," the driver continued after he'd heard the name of the village.

"Yes, and our family's mud house, as I remembered it, stood on the bank of the Daha River."

"Mud house, you say. When did you last live there, babuji?"

"Some fifty years ago, 1869 to be exact."

The driver whistled. "That's when my father was born. You sound a bit cuckoo."

Raja uttered a loud sigh. "If you'd spent that many years in a place called Demerara, you'd sound like me." Raja said.

"Well, I guess so," the driver said, then broke out in laughter.

He lit up a hand-rolled bidi. The white smoke he exhaled floated away. He made a "tchk-tchk" noise with his tongue, followed by a whack of the whip.

The oxen, as though wary of another blow, broke into a fast trot, then kept a steady pace along a winding dirt road embedded with bricks. Raja's bones complained; he longed for the powdery, red brick roads of British Guiana.

Half an hour into the final phase of the ride, after a rest stop at Hussainganj Post Office, Raja shouted, "Stop!" A giant peepal tree with roots like the veins on the back of his hand came into view. "I know where I am," he said. "My house should be over there where the Daha River takes a bend."

The driver rubbed his eyes and blinked. "I see no house, babuji." He prodded the oxen right up to the river and parked. "Either your mud house existed in another life or you're imagining things."

Raja looked over the area. For quite some time, he peered into the horizon not wanting to believe that his house had vanished. "Park your cart under the peepal tree," he said.

He got off the cart and sat under the shade, cupping his hands over his eyes. The tears flowed freely, falling onto the roots of the tree. The journey to find his ancestral home seemed to have been in vain.

"My life is over! Ram! Ram!" he called out, invoking the sacred name of an avatar of the god Vishnu.

Wringing his hands, he got up, walked around in circles, then collapsed onto the ground. *Are the gods upset with me for abandoning my friend at the train station?*

The driver walked up and down the path looking at his passenger with suspicion.

"Bhagavan, help me!" he cried out. "I have to carry this old man to the mental hospital."

Jolted by that remark, Raja shouted at the driver, "Take me to the closest house! Someone there may know my family."

The driver drove the bullocks toward a thatched house where an elderly man stood outside.

Pointing at the bend in the river, Raja said to him, "Babuji, over there is where my mud house used to be."

"Yes! Yes! A mud house once stood there. Try the next hut. Maybe they knew the owners."

It was the same story a mile away, so Raja turned to the driver, "I am too old for this. Take me back to the river."

The driver shook his head, raised his bamboo cane, much like a fishing rod, and dropped it on the back of one of the bullocks. Before he could repeat the action, Raja was forced to use his foot to block one of his bags that threatened to jump out. With a slight gruffness in his voice, the driver said, "Listen old man, how many times must I tell you that your mind is deceiving you? There is no house by the river."

"Just do as I say. I'm paying you."

They returned to the place where they had been half an hour before. Raja got out of the cart and looked over the site once again.

How could he be imagining the once-familiar smell of jasmine? He examined the wild corn. It probably came from the very stock that grew in the vegetable garden he tended as a boy. The same with those arbi plants known as eddoes in British Guiana—they all struggled amidst acacia shrubs, and vines, and exposed roots of asan and neem trees. Remnants of a burned garbage heap, and a glazed, round marble, which he might have played with as a child, carried him back in time. So did the leg of his rope bed, from where he used to listen to the koel sing and watch the eagle soar in the sky. All the local names for the golden shower tree, the orchid plants, and lemongrass came flooding back. Thankfully, there were no razor grasses like those that had ripped his dhoti when he was lost in the British Guiana jungle.

He remembered the swallowtail, and the yellow-white butterflies that flitted from flower to flower and how he and Prem used to trap them with sticky gum. He found the burrows where green frogs and garden lizards lived. The once familiar chirpings of bulbuls and sparrows perched on mango limbs, the distinct smell of the trees, and the earthy garlic odour from the greyish Daha River at this time of year—they all came back to him.

Among black mulberry bushes, he came upon the foundation ruins of a house. Rotten bits of dark brown arjun timber that could have been used for posts and beams, and bamboo that had supported the thatched roof, lay strewn around. A rusted axe, its babul handle long decayed, could have been the very axe he had used to shape lumber and chop firewood. Past memories overwhelmed him. "I have found my home!" he cried out.

With elbows propped on knees, he buried his face in his hands. The uncontrollable sounds that rose from deep within his throat told a tale that the bullock driver could understand.

A few minutes later, the driver whispered, "So, are you going to stay here, babuji? Tell me, for I must return to Siwan before it gets dark and dacoits steal my oxen, cart, and clothes off my back."

Raja ignored the driver. A yellow-throated bird at the river's edge splashed water over its feathers. It caught his eye as it flew to a black mulberry shrub.

"Babuji!" the driver yelled. "Tell me what you want me to do."

Raja screamed back at the driver, "I don't care!" Raja had indeed found the site where his house once stood and he was prepared to camp and die on that very spot.

In an adjoining field, two men were harvesting pulses and stacking them. The older one stopped what he was doing. With his back still bent, he walked over to Raja.

"Why all this shouting?"

"My name is Raja Singh. I once lived in a mud house right over there."

The farmer looked Raja over. "As a boy, I knew a wrestling champion by that name, the one who went missing," he said. "His family's hut got washed away by the Big Monsoon, babuji."

Raja covered his face with both hands. His heart quickened. "Did the entire family perish?"

"Like most of the villagers, they might have made it to higher ground."

Raja took a deep breath, pacing back and forth, praying that his family was one of the lucky ones.

The driver turned to Raja. "Take your time, babuji."

Raja wanted to smile at the complete change in the driver's attitude. A soft breeze rustled the branches of trees and shrubs along the river. An emerald tailorbird alighted on the old peepal tree. It chirped, "cheeup-cheeup-cheeup," and Raja became hopeful. Even if he did not find his relatives, nature's creatures were there for him to enjoy.

Turning to the farmer, he said, "Someone here might know where my family moved to."

The farmer pointed. "Check that house over there. I'll send my peon to announce your arrival. If you can wait till I finish this row, I can take you there myself."

As the farmer walked alongside the cart, a bald man in his multi-coloured lunghi came down the middle of the road. A grey mutt yapped a few paces back. The man waved for the cart to stop.

The driver turned his head toward the farmer. "You know this man who is blocking my way?"

"Yes, he lives in that very house."

The driver shouted, "Ho!" and the bullocks came to a dead stop.

The bald man pointed at Raja. "I heard that you call yourself Raja Singh."

"Ye-es," Raja said in a soft voice.

"You're a liar!"

Raja bit his lip. The pain helped to calm him. He sniffed the hot noonday air, redolent with the scent of jasmine flowers. It lessened the sting of the insult. In the end, with great effort, he forced a smile. "This is as much my village as yours."

"Have you come to claim your share of our land, you old dog?"

Raja held on to the side of the cart to avoid falling. He sized up the man who was muscular but as wrinkled as he was. "You call me an old dog. I can still whip you, if you give me cause."

"Whoa! Hold it you two!" the farmer yelled.

The bald man placed his hands on his hips. "Let's not come to blows."

Raja rubbed his soft grey moustache and the stubble growing over the fold of his chin. "Who are you?"

The bald man said, "Never mind." He turned his back on Raja and stirred up dust as he trudged in his bare feet toward the house, the dog scampering behind.

At the clicking sound of the driver, the bullocks followed. The house appeared to have been constructed in a hurry though it was a lot sturdier than the old mud house Raja once called home.

The driver helped Raja place his belongings on the ground.

"Why are you unloading your bags?" the bald man asked in a raised voice. "You can't very well be Raja Singh. He died, disappeared . . . like that!" he said, snapping his fingers. "Over fifty years ago."

A youth dressed in Western clothes strolled up to Raja. He spoke perfect English. "You are an impostor. My Grandpa Prem always believed his friend perished on his way to the market to buy egg plums for his little brother."

Raja decided to play a waiting game. *He looks so much like Prem.*

From among the bushes came another voice. "Raja Singh has returned to haunt us. Hah! Hah!"

"Come show your face," Raja said. "Are you too afraid to face a ghost?"

"I will in time," the voice continued.

Raja's brow creased as he now faced the bald man. "Let me examine your back."

"Why?" the man asked. With reluctance, he turned around.

Raja rubbed a finger on the birthmark he knew so well when he used to give his little brother a bath. Then he inhaled a chestful of air and let it out. "Aren't you Baran?"

The man leaned back in surprise. "Yes, I am Baran Singh."

If Raja's life could have ended at that moment, he would have died happy, knowing that he had found his "little" brother. This was more than his heart could bear.

"Baran, I am your lost brother." Raja's voice broke into a myriad pieces; his legs trembled. The heat rose from the bare earth, through his laced-up boots onto the soles of his feet. He stepped forward. Tears poured out of his eyes like rainwater.

The brothers embraced.

"Only you would have known what to look for," Baran said. "You truly are my brother," he continued, gently pushing Raja away and drying his eyes.

"Let me not keep these men waiting. They helped me to get here," Raja said, fighting to control his emotion.

He now faced the driver. "Take this farmer and his helper back to their field," Raja said, throwing in a bonus and giving everyone a baksheesh.

"Forgive me for doubting your story, babuji," the driver said. He hugged Raja and patted him on the shoulder.

Raja clasped his hands together then faced the youth. "Your Grandpa Prem and I were best friends."

"He told me so. Please forgive me, Mr. Raja. And the coward who called you a ghost is Roy's grandson."

To meet with the grandsons of Prem and Roy, friends from his boyhood days, made Raja's journey to his ancestral home all the more meaningful. He could now close the book on that pilgrimage.

The smell of spiced tea grew stronger. It caused his saliva to flow. Surrounded by the familiar guava trees and arbi plants, he sniffed the air. Turtledoves cooed, mynas chattered, and house sparrows chirped. This was the Belwasa of old.

Baran led his brother to the house and invited him to sit. Panting with excitement, Baran called out, "Ashish, look who's here!"

A young man appeared and went to pick up the bags.

"Hold it, son! First meet my big brother."

The young man gave a small bow and Raja got up and placed his palm on the lad's head.

"This is my son Ashish," Baran said.

Raja greeted him. Ashish was shorter but broader than Raja had been at that age.

"I have heard a lot about you, Uncle Raja. I'm glad to know you're still alive and that you've come from far to see us." The lad took Raja's bags into the house and left.

Baran pulled at the red ribbon. With a wide grin on his face, he asked, "Are my egg plums inside this one?"

Surprised at the question, Raja grinned. "All those years and you still remember."

"Ma and Pa always teased me about egg plums."

A woman came in and stood beside Baran.

"This is my wife, Indra," Baran said.

Raja bowed and clasped his hands in greeting.

The woman touched Raja's feet. "I don't intend to be rude, but we never expected to see you alive again."

Her expression told Raja that she too believed he had returned to claim his share of the family's property.

"Sorry to disappoint you, Sister-in-law," he said, "I'm not after anyone's land for I have enough of that in De Droom."

"Indra, how about a cup of chai for Big Brother?" Baran asked.

Raja was glad that Baran had got him out of a difficult situation.

Soon after, the front door creaked open. A withered, grey-haired woman entered the house. Her stooped posture belied her average height. Holding a stick in one hand and hanging onto Ashish, she lowered herself and took a seat on the floor across from Raja.

He tensed at the sight of the woman's bumpy skin, its texture so much like bitter melon. His hands shook and when he placed one hand on top of the other to steady them, his skin looked almost as folded as the woman's.

Baran came forward and faced Raja. "Do you know who this is?"

"Someone I should know?"

"Yes!" After a lengthy pause, Baran said, "She's your wife, Savitri."

Raja almost fell over. He'd had slim hope of seeing Savitri again. As he looked at the woman, he shuddered. For relief, he closed his eyes and reached back to that last morning when she'd come out of the house to say goodbye. As he opened his eyes, the image of his beautiful wife had been transformed into someone he failed to recognize.

Savitri stared at him, seeming reluctant to relieve him of his discomfort.

Baran broke the silence. "Sister-in-law, aren't you going to greet your husband?"

Her eyes seemed to be reviewing her entire life, spreading it out like a vast panorama, each scene merging into the other, for that was what Raja himself was experiencing.

Everyone remained silent. The tension was more than Raja could bear. He wondered if he'd done the right thing by returning to a village he hardly remembered, and to an old woman who showed no trace of the beautiful Savitri.

Baran again came to the rescue. He addressed his sister-in-law, "Your husband, my big brother—the one we thought was dead—is back with us. Won't you welcome him?"

Her mouth formed words that failed to come out.

Raja tried to imagine the agony she must be enduring. He wished she had had more time to adjust to his sudden reappearance in her life.

Savitri shook her head and in doing so found her voice. "How can I accept a husband who left me, abandoned me?" She could not continue for some time. "The first two years . . . I stayed up almost every night waiting for your return." After she'd dried her eyes, she continued, her voice cracking and barely audible. "Now, you're just a memory."

Moments went by before Raja gained the courage to speak up. "I wish I could wipe away your tears." He placed his hands together. Acceptance by Savitri, he knew, would be difficult because of all those decades—almost a lifetime—of living without a husband.

Her lips trembled. She clutched the cane until her knuckles became white. "When you left, Raja, life was never the same for us. In any case, it is much too late to talk about the past."

Raja figured it was pointless to explain that he did not leave India of his own accord. What good would it do? Therefore, he said, "We're both old and our lives are almost over. However, I've come from far to tell you I'm sorry for being away so long." Raja's voice trailed off when he saw the look on Savitri's face.

She appeared to ponder what she'd just heard. "It would have been best for you not to have come. Why didn't you let me die in peace?"

"I would have left this world without completing my life's journey . . . ." Raja did not wish to carry on a conversation that made Savitri so unhappy. Her words also made him cringe. Now, more than anything else, he longed for her forgiveness.

He tried his best to hide his disappointment when Savitri asked Ashish to escort her back to the neighbour's home. Raja rose to see her off. *If only she had left on a happier note.*

Two days went by, and in the presence of the family Raja untied the bag with the red ribbon. He sifted through its contents and handed a gold sovereign and a bank note to Baran, who couldn't thank Big Brother enough. "Better than egg plums, Bhaiya," he said.

A gold necklace for Indra brought a smile to her face. For Savitri, he must wait for the right moment. With a bit of luck, he might win her affection.

And what better place for a reconciliation with Savitri than on the beautiful bank of the Daha River. Two weeks later, Raja's heart raced at the sight of Ashish taking Savitri out for a walk one afternoon. They headed for the river and Raja hobbled behind, wending his way through the narrow path. He was armed with his gifts.

They had just sat down on a fallen log when Raja joined them and sat next to Savitri. They engaged in small talk while they peered into the sunset. For Raja, the scenery was breathtaking and it brought back memories of a particular evening on a starry night when he had made love to her. With that setting, he turned to Savitri and said, "Here are a pair of bangles and a necklace of gold sovereigns for you."

She placed both against her wrists, which looked even more creased than before. After a pause, she said, "Thanks." She turned to Ashish. "I will save them for your bride."

Those words hit Raja like a punch to the stomach. He'd kept those sovereigns for almost a lifetime.

The necklace had outdone their usefulness. His hands trembled and he placed them on his knees to steady them.

For a moment, he pictured the days when they both were young, when they would sit on the riverbank, join in the song of the koel and watch the pink lotuses and the twigs go by. Raja willed himself to believe that Savitri was still as fair as she used to be. It was so difficult, he gave up. However, the mere idea that he had reunited with both Savitri and Baran was more than he could have expected. He had to be thankful.

The following week, he wrote to his De Droom family that he'd arrived safely and had found his folks in Belwasa. Of course, he omitted the difficulties he had faced. He didn't want to cause any more pain to his loved ones back in De Droom if he could avoid it.

As the weeks went by, he told Savitri pieces of his story. It was like pasting images of his life to make a collage on canvas without a coherent whole. Much of it he left out since those events were now history. He had to move on with his life.

"Why didn't you have a scribe scratch a few lines to tell us you were alive?" Savitri asked.

"I sent you two letters."

She shook her head. "I checked at the Siwan Post Office more than once, but received nothing."

He lowered his head covering his eyes with his hands. "A friend wrote that first letter for me. He told me that mail delivery to small villages in India was unreliable. The mail runner must have stolen and cashed the money order."

"I was not needy. If you had come years ago, the same way you have come now bearing gifts, we could have had a life ahead of us."

"You are right, Savitri. I wish I could undo the past."

Raja recalled the time when he had gone prospecting for precious stones up the Mazaruni River hoping to strike it rich and return to his village a wealthy young man. In the end, his new family plus greed to become the most prosperous rice and cattle farmer in the district had kept him away.

"The years have caught up with both of us," Savitri said. She waved a hand at him. "Ma and Pitaji suffered a lot. They died soon after you left, so I became a mother to Baran." Raja closed his eyes but said nothing. "At such a young age he had to help with the farm." She tugged at her shawl and covered her eyes. "He grew old before his time," she said, bursting into tears. "He won't tell you that."

The air around Raja became suffocating. In the Indian culture, it was the elder son's duty to take care of his old parents until their dying days. Baran had been saddled with that responsibility. However, Raja took consolation seeing that he had no control over the first ten years of his life. For it was during those years that his parents had died and Baran had lost his childhood. The government and the contracting company had failed to return him to his homeland, and at that time he did not have the resources to do so on his own. However, he would admit that the drive to prove himself, to rise above being a simple cane cutter had taken hold. In the end, it was a tragedy that could not be corrected.

Raja's legs buckled as he tried to rise from a squatting position. Finally, he gave up and just pressed his knuckles hard onto the floor as if bracing himself for another onslaught.

His thoughts took him to the Bhagavad Gita, which teaches that man creates his own destiny, his own karma, by his actions, whether in this life or another. The Bible, on the other hand, says that God would forgive whatever wrong he did if he repented his sins. From the scriptures, therefore, he would try to find solace.

At that moment Ashish arrived to find Raja on his knees, his hands clasped together. Ashish helped him to a sitting position. "I have some news for you, Uncle."

"I hope it is good."

Ashish nodded with a smile that endeared him even more to Raja. "Your return has spread throughout the village. Young and old would like to hear your story during the time you went missing."

At that gathering, Raja told the villagers that he was sorry for staying away so long. Only now he realized how much he loved Belwasa and his motherland. He would make it up with his Indian family and with them. After some discussion, in which the younger folk especially had to be swayed, they garlanded and welcomed him back into the village community. Prominent in the gathering was the village priest, whose father had encouraged Raja to go on his pilgrimage.

Some gave speeches. They had heard tales of the ex-champion, Raja Singh, and his disappearance. One ventured to say that Lakshmi, the goddess of good fortune had brought him back.

The way Raja told the story of his travels and adventures caused many to cry. They hugged each other and danced to the music of the sitar and harmonium and the melody and rhythm of the tabla drums.

"Why are you treating me so well when my family has suffered much in my absence?" he asked an elder.

"We thought you were dead and now you have come back to us," the old-timer said. "Belwasa has regained her son. Isn't that reason to celebrate?"

As the weeks went by, Raja pieced together Savitri's personal history as told to him by neighbours, Baran, and Savitri herself. Nothing could have prepared him for this most tragic episode as told by Savitri.

CHAPTER TWENTY-SEVEN

Belwasa, 1875

Pitaji died of a heart attack five years after you went missing. The villagers took charge and held a wake the first night for friends of the family. I served chai while neighbours passed out finger foods to nibble on. At sunrise, the village priest arrived to conduct the cremation ceremonies on the bank of the Daha River.

Overcast skies threatened the proceedings when the villagers gently placed the shrouded body on the ground next to the cremation site. Far away, came the plaintive call of a cuckoo. While sparrows fluttered from limb to limb, your pilgrim companions stacked additional dry wood and placed earthen pots filled with clarified butter beside the body.

"Where are you, Raja?" I cried out. "We need you now, more than ever. You should be here." I sank to the ground beside the body. "Oh, Pitaji, why did you leave us so soon?" I pleaded. "I wish you could have seen your son before you died."

"What are we to do, Sister-in-law?" Baran asked. "Our family is no more."

"Ma is still with us," I replied, "and you will be the head of the family."

Baran pushed out his chest and stood on his toes. "I will, Sister-in-law, I surely will."

Tears flooded my eyes. It broke my heart to see him trying to act so grown up.

Poor Baran! Did he understand what the old man's passing meant to the family? How could he at such a young age? For Baran's sake, I composed myself.

What a turnout the old man got for his funeral that autumn day! Someone from each Belwasa home was there. At last, the sun peeked through the dark clouds. A gust of wind freshened the air. The village men stacked the wood in layers. At a cue from the priest, the spectators chanted Sanskrit mantras as the pilgrims placed the marigold-decked corpse at the centre of the raised pyre.

"I'll light the fire," Baran said.

Prem and the other pilgrims jostled their way into the foreground. "You're too young," Prem said. "For our dearest friend Raja, let us do the honour."

"No. At least let me try." Baran broke out in sobs. "Sister-in-law said I will now be the head of the family, so it is my duty to start the fire."

"Go right ahead," Prem said with a dismissive yet encouraging wave of his hand.

Baran rubbed the sharp edge of quartz against a slab of steel set close to dry twigs. He worked nonstop for quite some time and though hard physical work had toughened him, in the end he needed help.

"I told you," Prem mumbled as he and Puran took charge.

A good half hour more elapsed before the tinder ignited and the flames, fed by the clarified butter, leapt high into the air.

As the fire began to consume the corpse, the heat caused it to shift, much to my amazement, forcing two men with bamboo poles to re-centre the corpse.

The priest added more clarified butter, all the while chanting verses from the Vedas. Fanned by the high wind, red and orange flames leapt high into the air.

During this part of the ceremony, Ma came to the front in her new, white sari. A red bindi adorned her forehead, and her eyes had a vacant look.

She stood there, transfixed, and as the flames engulfed her husband, the village women sang the devotional song, "Om Jai Jagadish Hare," thanking the Lord of the Universe for banishing their sorrows.

At that moment, when the flames were just a blur from the tears in my eyes, I said aloud, "Oh Raja, I wish that through some miracle you could find your way here to say goodbye to Pitaji and give him the last rites."

The pyre had been reduced to almost ground level when Ma poured the remaining clarified butter from a pot into the flames and stepped within inches of the pyre. At first glance, her faint smile seemed solemn and spiritual, tinged with a hint of mockery.

I lifted my shawl to wipe my eyes.

In that instant, Ma stepped forward and prostrated herself in the middle of the burning pile.

I stood dumbstruck, unable to move.

Baran uttered a high-pitched, deafening scream. "Ma! Oh Ma!"

Several villagers cried out, but no one tried to pull Ma from the fire. Everyone seemed hypnotized, as the flames danced around and consumed her.

I stared into space, transfixed by the sight. Not for one moment did I imagine that Ma would do such a thing. No widow from Belwasa in recent memory had committed sati. It seemed so cruel, so barbaric.

"Oh, Ma, we would have been all right. Why? Why?"

I wrung my hands. I could not understand how Ma could have looked upon her death as a sacred duty to her departed husband. Perhaps in choosing to die with him, she believed she would achieve great honour, and that she was fulfilling her dharma.

I wished Ma had taken Baran's youth into consideration. The poor lad remained speechless for a long time, a stoic expression on his face, for in one stroke at age twelve, he had lost both his parents. No longer a boy, he must be strong, for now he had no one, except me.

Baran turned to me and said, "You and I will carry on, Sister-in-law."

"We will, Baran," I said. "Life has its sad moments, but we must never give up. That's what your big brother always said."

The women moaned as Baran, with his eyes drenched in tears, took his turn and poured clarified butter onto the funeral pyre. "Om Jai Jagadish Hare," they sang as the flames mingled Ma's body with that of her husband, nothing spared.

The men added more wood to the fire. Eventually, both bodies turned to ashes. The tragic outcome was union of husband and wife even in death.

It started to drizzle, but no one took shelter from the tiny droplets. Everyone stayed till the last embers smouldered no more. Then the world grew silent.

Days later, in a private ceremony, with Baran standing beside me, I threw the combined ashes into the Daha River and prayed that they would find their way into the holy Ganges.

CHAPTER TWENTY-EIGHT

Belwasa, 1921

In the summer of 1921, Raja expanded and renovated the house, at the completion of which he held a puja.

That morning at 4:30 a.m., he sprinkled water into the doorway of the house and lit camphor at the altar, set up under a huge tent. He used an ember from this holy fire to light the mud stove in the kitchen where women would be preparing sweetened rice mixed with almonds and pistachio nuts, and the sacred food offering, prasad—a pudding made from flour, clarified butter, and syrup. Later, family and friends sat around in a semi-circle facing the priest, who conducted the service.

To release the village women from the time-consuming task of fetching water from the river, Raja hired men to dig two wells with hand-operated pumps in the family compound. At first, only muddy water came up.

"We cannot drink this ditch water," someone shouted.

"Raja, your engineer doesn't know what he's doing," another onlooker chimed in.

On and on it went until some boys shouted, "Look, it's clean." They sang and danced around the well to loud cheers and smiles all around.

Within a few short months, cold winds from the north descended on Belwasa. Savitri's thin coverlet could not stop her shivering, and so Raja bought her a cot and quilt. She accepted the gifts gracefully, giving him the courage to ask, "Won't you move back into the family home?"

"You have another wife back in De Droom," Savitri pointed out. "It wouldn't be right for us to live under the same roof. Besides, you've changed so much in the way you speak and act that you are now a foreigner."

Those words struck like arrows. "I had vowed to retain my Indianness in the new land," he said. Sighing, he continued, "I guess I have failed in that regard."

Savitri made a clicking noise with her tongue. "You waited too long to return. Meanwhile, we both have moved on and so has the world."

"Sadly, this is so," Raja said as he took a deep breath to steel himself to the hurt deep within. "From my conversations with a learned friend, I gathered that change is the law of the universe." After a brief pause, Raja continued, "He told me that you can never step into the same river twice for a river's water is always changing, always flowing, like man and life itself." Raja, from his own growth and education, went a step further. "Why should I have regrets about the past when the present is happening now? When it comes down to it, it's still the same old story."

"That's why we can never return to the old days," Savitri said, and Raja nodded his assent. "I have no ill feelings toward you; but to carry on from where we left off is impossible, Raja."

From among the mango trees at the back of the family home came the song of the golden oriole, a bird that had perhaps displaced the koel from its territory. Raja was entranced by its musical notes. As he listened, his heart became heavy, and he was overcome with emotion.

His troubles multiplied when word had gotten around that he'd attended a Christian church, indulged in alcohol, danced with women, and had eaten all kinds of meat. Nevertheless, he ignored the gossip and stood firm in his beliefs, for he considered himself a worldly man.

There was silence all around when Raja declared his intention to take Ashish and his wife back with him to his home in De Droom.

Ashish, not particularly enthused, looked at his father.

"If they leave, there will be no trace of our family in this country." Baran said. "Our family ties here are unshakeable."

"British Guiana's rivers and sea abound with fish," Raja added. "A rice and cattle farmer can become prosperous. With time to spare, its citizens relax in hammocks in their open-air bottom houses. So the future of our family would be guaranteed."

"That's another world," Indra added.

"In that case," Raja exclaimed, trying hard to lower his voice and hide his disappointment, "I shall return to De Droom alone."

Baran rocked his head back and forth. "You've decided to leave us this time for good, Bhaiya."

"I have completed my spiritual journey," Raja replied. "Now I must return to the country where I've spent most of my life."

Only now did Raja realize that the ties to his adopted country were stronger than to the land of his birth. He could hear the kiskadee's song, calling him back to British Guiana. How could he resist? Though he had early memories of his homeland where he'd spent his youthful days, he no longer fitted in. Besides, he had left his seed in De Droom, and he had started to miss his second wife, their only child, and grandchildren.

"Bhaiya, go if you must," Baran said with tears in his eyes. It was a bold statement.

With a heavy heart, Raja used one of the printed envelopes John had given him. He wrote:

Dear Rena,

All is well here in Belwasa.

Can you ask John and Paul to sell off some cattle and send me the funds for a passage back to British Guiana? Now that I have satisfied that desire to return to the motherland, there is nothing to keep me here.

Your loving father,

Pa

Several months later, Raja heard back from John: The enclosed bank draft is for a first-class passage. We eagerly await your return.

Raja settled for a steerage-class ticket and shared the money left over with his Belwasa family.

On the day of departure, he was up before dawn. Not a whiff of jasmine perfumed the air that autumn morning of 1927.

With a lone jute sack of sparse possessions slung over his shoulder, he took one last look at the Daha River and the thousand-year-old peepal tree, then at the neighbour's house where Savitri stayed. Few came to say goodbye—certainly not Savitri. Nor the birds. The golden oriole had already sung its farewell song, and the koel had long disappeared.

Baran gave his big brother a hug and, teary-eyed, said in a broken voice, "You must hurry if you wish to catch that train, Bhaiya."

Raja had time. At age seventy-seven, his shoulders almost touching his ears, his eyes moistened as he embraced Baran. He had little to say.

"Wish your sister-in-law good luck for me," Raja whispered in Baran's ear as he released his "little" brother. The look in Baran's eyes said it all.

With Ashish's help, Raja boarded the cart. The smell of burning wood and flatbread from the neighbour's kitchen wafted through the cool morning air. He took one last look at the house but still no one came out. A solitary teardrop glided softly down his cheek, then he turned away. The murmuring of his beloved Daha River from his youthful days and the gentle wind blowing through the trees lent a touch of sadness to the atmosphere; the time for parting with his dear Belwasa had arrived.

Ashish accompanied his uncle on the train bound for Calcutta.

"Paisa for food," an old beggar said as soon as they stepped off the train.

"We have no spare change," Ashish said.

"Just one paisa, Bhaiya," the old man said with a musical voice that sounded familiar. The beggar held out his only hand, all withered and sandpapery. He had asked for a single coin.

The resemblance seemed clear, unmistakable, but Raja reminded himself that this was Calcutta with its teeming millions. Still, he asked, "Whose son are you?"

"Ramdas."

Of all the beggars at the railway station, to run into Ramdas's son, himself now an old man, had to be God's work. Raja told the old man that he was Ramdas's friend. "Did you meet your father?"

"I did . . . alas, he didn't even live three weeks after you both parted at the station, babuji."

Raja closed his eyes and looked away. That was all Ramdas had asked for. Raja took a deep breath. *I am sorry, jahaji bhai.* "What did you do with his body?"

"I used some of the money you gave him for a full cremation and in the dead of night scattered my father's ashes in the Hooghly River, as he had wished."

Raja gave the man his remaining rupees. He and Ashish worked their way toward the docks. It dawned on him that he was no closer to the answer regarding the mystery of life. It had proved to be elusive. However, one thing he was sure about—he had become a wiser man.

CHAPTER TWENTY-NINE

British Guiana, 1927

Awaiting passengers at the Kiderpore wharf was the distinguished SS *Rajula,* a passenger/cargo ship. Rumour had it that this famous vessel, powered by a screw-type engine, had been contracted out to make this voyage to the Caribbean. Raja felt proud to be on it.

The time had come for him to board; he went for his cloth purse, wrapped his fingers around his last gold sovereign and placed it in Ashish's hand. "Keep this coin as a souvenir."

"I will miss you," Ashish said, "and will always cherish this gift."

In a daze, Raja pulled himself away and, with the aid of a bamboo cane, boarded the ship. Now he must conserve his energy for the voyage back to Georgetown.

The air over the water was brisk; it smelled fresh when Raja bade goodbye to Calcutta and the Bay of Bengal shoreline for the last time. The whistles of the spoon-billed sandpipers carried him back to that morning in 1869 when a seagull on deck had given him a few moments to take one last look at his homeland. He remembered it well; it had certainly beckoned him back to its shores again.

The boatswain helped Raja to the tween deck and his bunk.

Often, to escape the heat and noise of the engines below, he'd climb the stairs and lie on the deck soaking up the sun, allowing his mind to wander. Sometimes he was a boy swimming in the Daha River with friends, other times in the cut-and-load gang at Sugar Grove Estate in Demerara. Just as readily, he was in his house of coloured glass beside the Aciah River.

One morning, before he knew it, the Cape of Good Hope and its rocky range peeped out of the mist. He had slept through the stop at Durban. Giant petrels and cormorants flew above while dolphins swam playfully around the ship. As soon as it rounded the Cape, high winds and waves lashed against the hull; sea spray bathed his face and gave him goose pimples. After the seas had calmed, he picked up his cane and walked around the deck to exercise his legs.

On a subsequent morning, the northeast trades kicked hard against the upper deck and threatened the vessel with great force. The rolling ship pitched the old man against the bulkhead and almost tipped him over, causing him to hurt his back. Perhaps he should have travelled first-class. But it would have been against his principles. For the rest of the journey, he couldn't move about much.

After four weeks at sea, the vessel stopped briefly at Trinidad. Early one morning, two crew members placed Raja on a makeshift canvas stretcher and brought him up on deck. Below a rainbow, the Georgetown Lighthouse came into view followed by the familiar Stabroek Market clock tower.

The crew delivered Raja into the waiting arms of his two grandsons. "Just a sore back from being tossed around the ship," a seaman said.

"We imagined the worst when you did not appear among the regular passengers," Paul said. He helped place the old man flat on the rear seat of the carriage awaiting his arrival.

When the horse and buggy pulled up opposite the mansion, and Raja was brought out on a stretcher, Rena uttered a loud cry, which sent the neighbours rushing, only to end up blocking the pathway to the front door of the house.

A few men took over from the grandsons and placed Raja flat on the living room floor on a cotton sheet. Everyone stared wide-eyed and spoke in whispers about an old man who had accomplished the unthinkable.

Rena brought her father Creole soup steeped in coconut milk.

"My daughter, only now I know how much I missed your cooking," he said. "By the way, where is your Ma?"

"Oh, Pa! She died a month ago. We couldn't inform you because your ship would have already left."

Raja was quiet for quite some time. Poor Sheela! He wished she could have held on for even one month. Savitri had shunned him and now Sheela was gone.

Raja soon learned that Cowboy had built a retirement home in Buxton, his old village, and that Kwame had passed away in his sleep. *My friends are all leaving me. Is this my destiny, to spend my last days a lonely man?*

Several times, as Rena brought her father up on news, he dozed off.

One evening, as Rena massaged her father's feet, she asked, "Did you find your wife, Pa?"

Raja took a long time to answer.

"I did, my dear."

"It's all right, Pa. I won't press you for details."

As if to brace himself from further embarrassment, he retrieved his pipe, packed its bowl with the fresh tobacco Beta had bought specially for him, and lit up. The sweet aroma of tobacco smoke filled the room. Raja removed the pipe from his mouth and said, "Beta, tell me what happened to Nandi," suspecting the worst for his son-in-law.

"Uncle, John and Paul hid all the money so he had none to buy rum."
Raja made a face. "That wouldn't stop him."

"It didn't. One night, in the midst of a downpour, he woke the rum shop owner and asked for credit. When the owner refused, Nandi went to steal one of Aziz's hens to raise the money for a half-bottle. Aziz did not recognize him—"

Raja's outstretched hand was a signal to Beta that he didn't want to hear the rest. He put out his pipe and for a few moments lapsed into inaudible mumbling. There was only so much that he could handle at one time.

As soon as Raja was able to walk with the aid of a cane, he paid Aziz a visit at his home. He accompanied him to the mosque and even participated in the Muslim services.

Like old friends, they chatted as they walked along the public road. During the conversation, Aziz turned to Raja and said, "You did me a great honour today."

"That's because I hold no grudge against you for the death of my son-in-law."

Aziz bowed to Raja and made a strange sound. "Had I known it was Nandi in my chicken coop, I would not have hit his head with the shovel."

Raja told Aziz about the time he'd found Nandi asleep among the chickens. "If I had informed you about that incident, you would have suspected that it was Nandi." After a long pause, Raja continued, "But you tried to save him."

"He bled to death in my arms while my donkey cart was en route to the nearest doctor."

Not long after Raja had returned to De Droom, the Great Depression hit the country. Pereira's Stores went bankrupt. Every week the bailiff carted away householders' possessions for outstanding debts, even for amounts as low as twenty-five dollars. The Demerara Bauxite Company and Jones Brothers laid off workers in droves. Raja's family kept their heads above water by selling cattle, rice, and milk at reduced prices to pay for rationed kerosene and the few groceries they needed.

In 1930, Raja made a bold move. "Anything to bolster community spirit," he said. He arranged a meeting with Rev. Cropper and the senior church members. For the price of one dollar, he signed over enough land to the De Droom Canadian Mission for the construction of a new school, health centre, and church to take care of the mind, body, and spirit.

At the time, most businessmen had stopped spending money because of the depression. Yet Raja paid for the construction of those three buildings. Artisans from as far away as Georgetown found work and were able to feed their families.

"I don't understand, Grandpa," John grumbled. "First you wanted to be the richest man on the East Coast. Now you're so generous in these hard times, I'm afraid you may end up a pauper."

"Now I look upon life differently," he said. "When ordinary people do better, so do we."

Raja borrowed money against the value of West Henriette and used the funds generated to import a Diesel engine rice mill. His grandsons assembled the parts themselves. With the mill in operation, they were able to provide employment to many of the villagers.

In 1937, when Raja grew a second set of upper canines—eye teeth, it became a cause for concern. To the family's surprise, a radio journalist and a *Daily Chronicle* reporter burst onto the scene. They propped Raja's jaws open and took a flash picture that showed his new teeth. They also took one of him sitting on a chair outside his home in his signature white long shirt and leggings.

"You must be desperate for news," he said to the journalists, laughing at the way they fussed over him in their attempt to get the "right" shot.

Before long, the radio announcer cut in. "This is a live interview with Mr. Raja Singh from the East Coast village of De Droom. He is one of the colony's oldest citizens and a living link with the past. Mr. Singh, are you still angry with the plantocracy for their failed promises?"

"If you mean the sugar planters, I would say that age brings wisdom. So why should I take anger or grudge to my grave?"

"That is a worthwhile lesson for us all. Can you tell us your two most interesting life experiences?"

"Returning to my ancestral home in India after more than fifty years takes first place. The second is when I drank creek water and ate agouti labba while living among the Arawaks. Perhaps that's what brought me back to Demerara."

Everyone broke out in laughter.

One morning, a honk of horns caught Raja's ear.

"Shiny Rolls-Royce coming down the De Droom Side Road with Union Jack on the bonnet!" shouted John. Raja could not believe what he heard. The governor of the colony, Sir Wilfred Jackson, soon arrived.

"Raja Singh," he said, "my best wishes and congratulations on reaching your eighty-seventh birthday."

Exuberant that the governor had called him by his correct name, Raja said, "That does not require a visit from Your Excellency."

"I read that you'd served your indentureship at Plantation Sugar Grove where my grandfather was manager. He kept a journal and in it he mentioned the time when you went missing from the plantation."

"I would rather forget it."

"Some sixty-five years later, I've come to apologize. Though my grandfather did not wield the cat, he gave the order to do so."

"He did what he had to do to discourage Indians from escaping."

"Such punishment is no longer acceptable. When all is said and done, men like you and Driver Kwame made sugar both the king and subject of this colony. In some respects, you've changed the world, since more sugar is consumed in every home than ever before; Demerara sugar has sweetened the lives of many."

To Raja, this was more than a fitting tribute, not so much to himself but to Kwame, a man with deep African roots.

The excitement over, most of the relatives returned to their homes. That evening, Raja began to run a fever. He threw up and refused food. Indeed, his innings would soon be over. He looked back at his life and would let others be the judge as to who was its real hero. *Life's greatest gift is having a wonderful family.*

He asked to be placed on a mattress in the living room. "I want my daughter, grandchildren, and great-grandchildren to be around me," he said.

The early morning light reflected off the windows onto the walls. The old man watched the children darting in and out through the play of greens, blues, yellows, and reds cast by the coloured glass windows. Amidst their childish babble, he cried out, "Pani. I want pani."

Rena rushed into the room and spooned a few drops of water into her father's mouth. Most spilled onto the pillow. He asked her to sing the hymn, "Tell me the stories of Jesus I love to hear." With the lyrics of the hymn ringing in his ears, the old man took his last breath; there was a smile on his face.

ACKNOWLEDGMENTS

I have read excerpts from this story to members of the Brampton Memoirs Writing Group, the Brampton Writers' Workshop, and the Georgetown Reading Group. Over the years, they have offered me invaluable feedback; a special thank you goes out to them. Special mention goes out to Antanas Sileika, Director, and Tim Wynn-Jones, mentor, of the Humber School of Creative Writing. Also to Melanie Little of Anansi Press for her encouragement. A sincere appreciation goes out to those who have read early drafts of my book: Ross Smith, Scott Witham, Wilfred Mohabir, Mohabir Ramnarine, Joan Scannell, Trish Ball, Joseph and John Ajodhia, Claude Ho, Joy Thomas, and family members. Thank you Maureen O'Connor for copy editing an early draft of my work. I'm deeply indebted to my three sons, Edward, Ronald, and Richard for their professional support in seeing this project through. First and foremost, I would like to thank my wife, Pauline, for working with me throughout this journey and relieving me over the years of the many household duties that allowed me to write this novel.

Lightning Source UK Ltd.
Milton Keynes UK
UKOW02f0943200115

244744UK00001B/126/P